AN AFFAIR WI...

Cassie tugged at Zak's arm and he followed her to a dark corner of the balcony without protest. Silently, she maneuvered herself in front of him and bit her lower lip. He wagered he knew exactly what she wanted. "You are either desirous of me or my cigar."

He turned the mouthpiece of the stogie toward those luscious lips. "Which one is it?" Covering his hand with hers, she guided the tip into her mouth. He rolled his eyes upward. Good God. After several puffs, she lifted her gaze to meet his.

"You know about my smoking?"

He stared unapologetically at her mouth and tilted his chin. "I'm afraid my informant must remain a classified source—" Softly spoken words brushed against her lips as he pulled her close.

Heavy footsteps padded along the roof above. Zak opened an eye. Two dark figures jumped from the mansard to the top of another house nearby.

"Rude of them to leave without a farewell," he murmured, "and they've left a nasty bit of—"

A stream of dark liquid dripped onto the ground inches from where they stood. Quickly assessing the gruesome scenario, he backed Cassie away from the pooling blood.

This title is also available as an eBook

AN AFFAIR
with
MR. KENNEDY

JILLIAN STONE

Pocket Books

New York   London   Toronto   Sydney   New Delhi

The sale of this book without its cover is unauthorized. If you purchased this book without a cover, you should be aware that it was reported to the publisher as "unsold and destroyed." Neither the author nor the publisher has received payment for the sale of this "stripped book."

Pocket Books
A Division of Simon & Schuster, Inc.
1230 Avenue of the Americas
New York, NY 10020

This book is a work of fiction. Names, characters, places, and incidents either are products of the author's imagination or are used fictitiously. Any resemblance to actual events or locales or persons, living or dead, is entirely coincidental.

Copyright © 2012 by Jillian Stone

All rights reserved, including the right to reproduce this book or portions thereof in any form whatsoever. For information, address Pocket Books Subsidiary Rights Department, 1230 Avenue of the Americas, New York, NY 10020.

First Pocket Books paperback edition February 2012

POCKET and colophon are registered trademarks of Simon & Schuster, Inc.

For information about special discounts for bulk purchases, please contact Simon & Schuster Special Sales at 1-866-506-1949 or business@simonandschuster.com.

The Simon & Schuster Speakers Bureau can bring authors to your live event. For more information or to book an event, contact the Simon & Schuster Speakers Bureau at 1-866-248-3049 or visit our website at www.simonspeakers.com.

Manufactured in the United States of America

10 9 8 7 6 5 4 3 2 1

ISBN 978–1–4516–2900–2
ISBN 978–1–4516–2907–1 (ebook)

For Gloria Gillis Brehaut,
who had the romantic instincts and good sense to marry a
man in need of charm lessons.

Acknowledgments

To begin at the beginning, I'd like to thank a motley crew of online "critters" (Marianne, Mason, Lisa, Mindy, Stacy, Kira) whose brutally honest, insightful, and encouraging critiques gave me the confidence to contest and query the very manuscript that has become *An Affair with Mr. Kennedy*.

Next, a humble thanks to the Romance Writers of America and all the judges who scored *An Affair with Mr. Kennedy* (*The Yard Man*) high enough to make the finals, then win the Golden Heart.

A special thanks to my amazing agent, Richard Curtis, and the acquiring instincts of Danielle Poiesz and Abby Zidle. Abby's editorial insights and creative guidance have helped hone *An Affair with Mr. Kennedy* into a tale full of danger, adventure, and romance.

And lastly, a heartfelt thanks to my family, without whose sacrifice, love, and support I could not have dedicated every waking hour this last year to the Gentlemen of Scotland Yard.

∽ Chapter One

$\mathcal{D}$etective Inspector Zeno Kennedy unbuttoned his collar and pulled out a shirttail. "What have you got for me?"

Scarlet, aka Kitty Matthews, reclined on the mattress and struck a seductive pose. Propped on her elbows, the girl lowered and raised sultry green eyes in a brazen inspection of his person. "You blokes from Scotland Yard are a handsome lot."

She arched her back and thrust her breasts up and out at him. Quite a robust figure—ample bottom and curvy topside. Studying her, he decided she could not be more than seventeen or eighteen years of age. A shapely little thing with chestnut-colored hair, big green eyes, and a button nose. She could easily raise a man's temperature.

Zeno did his best to ignore the girl's bountiful charms as he took up a post at the end of the bed-frame. "Actually, I work for Special Irish Branch." He leaned over the brass rail.

Scarlet gaped at a bit of exposed chest. "Blue eyes and dark hair—Black Irish, are you?"

Zeno hastily pulled his shirt closed and admonished himself to be patient with his newest recruit. "Special *Irish* Branch is a division of Scotland Yard aimed at investigating anarchists. Fenians mostly. We're after the blokes who want Home Rule for the Irish at any price, by any means."

Her eyes grew wide. "The dynamiters?"

A low groan and squeaking bedsprings drifted through the wall. Zeno raised an index finger to his lips and gave a nod to the adjoining room.

The budding beauty in front of him typified the adolescent female offerings of this pleasure house. Mrs. Jeffries's, as it was referred to in hushed tones among gentlemen at their clubs, was a popular brothel marketing young women—very young. Some were girls who had not yet been spoiled, for a steeper price.

With venereal disease rampant, and the Contagious Diseases Act repealed, men of means found the idea of a virgin, even if less bawdy, certainly a healthier amusement. It seemed the baser instincts of gentlemen of privilege would continue to find ways to avoid the pox at any cost, both to their pockets and to the lives of the innocent juveniles conscripted for such harsh duty.

Scotland Yard's Criminal Investigations Department of the Metropolitan Police had moved on some of the worst offenders, but there had been tremendous pressure from the top echelons to keep the safer brothels open. As for the use of young girls, Zeno's position was well known. Turning a blind eye to their plight made them all dirty.

"You sent an urgent wire, Scarlet. Anything to report?"

"No, sir—I mean yes, sir." She rolled her eyes. "Evening last, I was on my way home from the bedside of me sick mum. Just past the steam vent on Bixford, I see four gentlemen leave Mrs. Jeffries's in search of their carriage, somewhere amongst the fancy rigs parked outside Drake's."

The girl referred to the gambling hell located close by. "Yes, I'm sure they were queued up around the block." He tried a wry grin of encouragement "Did you recognize anyone by name?"

"Not much to notice about them, except for Lord Delamere."

"Delamere?" Zeno's eyes narrowed. "Are you sure of this?"

She bobbed her head. "Hard to miss that handsome, cocksure puss. He's not one of my regulars; he fancies Roxanne or Jemma."

The elusive Lord Delamere had been a person of interest for some months now, along with his cadre of misfits—peers who styled themselves the Bloody Four. "Please continue, Scarlet."

"Lord Delamere, he points to the next coach in line. 'Where the bloody hell is our driver?'" A bit wild-eyed, she hesitated. "Next thing, he opens the carriage door and the nearby gas lamp lights up the inside—I swear, sir, I saw a pair of gents with their knickers down around their knees."

Zeno needed confirmation. "Committing sodomy?"

She nodded. "One of Delamere's boys raised a shout, 'I say, what goes there?' Then two of them reach inside and pull the buggers out, one after the other. Once they had them down in the street, they started kicking and pounding. Straight off, the younger molly wrenches away, pulls up his trousers and escapes down the lane."

"No one ran after him?"

Scarlet shook her head. "Those blokes were too bladdered to give chase—turned back to their punches and kicks. Lord Delamere and another man stood near the coach door watching the tussle."

Scarlet gulped. "His lordship leans in for a closer look. 'Well, well, Albert. I wouldn't have pegged you for a light-foot lad. Sorry about the thrashing.'

"The poor bashed-up gent, he spits blood and calls them a bunch of thickheaded cock-ups. Says they got the wrong coach, and now they're all going to die for a mug's game. Then he says, 'I know every one of you by name. Rest assured, you'll pay for this assault.'"

Scarlet chewed on her bottom lip. "Delamere's puss turns right sneery. 'I think not, Albert,' he says, ''Tis you, my lord, who is going to pay for our silence.'"

Zeno clapped his mouth shut, just to make sure it wasn't hanging open. "The younger man who got away. Did you get a look at him?"

"He knocked me onto my bum, sir." She rubbed the back of her hip. "Close-cropped dark hair and light-colored eyes—ice blue they were. Handsome as the devil he was."

"Lighter blue than mine?"

The girl wet her lips and flashed a sultry smile.

"Scarlet." He lowered his chin and eyed her impatiently.

She rolled her eyes and sighed. "Different, very pale, almost like they were moonbeams."

He placed an elbow on the brass rail and cupped his chin. "You are either in possession of an extraordinary memory or a wicked imagination."

"You think I'd imagine such a tale? I'm telling you the God's honest truth, sir."

"Then might you provide a description of the men with Delamere? Take your time—the smallest detail would help."

Her frown eased into a contemplative pout. "One of the young gents was light-haired, with a bit of a wave to it. Several locks fell down over his eyes. The other had dark chestnut hair. No beard or whiskers, like yourself. The third man was large, thick in the waist—ruddy cheeks on him. He stood beside the carriage door in a perspiration—"

Scarlet sat up straighter. "Lord Delamere eyed the nervous bloke. 'Seen enough, James?' Or he might have said—'Seen too much, James?' Plain enough words, but delivered in a harsh tone. More like . . .' Absently, the girl worked a bare foot up and down the bed sheet.

"A threat?"

She drew her brows together. "Perhaps a jeer—or a warning."

Zeno studied the young informant while he processed her story. "Good work, Scarlet." The clever chit had even managed to dredge up another name, likely one of the Bloody Four. "I have a mind this small event you happened on will prove useful." Even as Zeno praised the girl's natural talents, his eyes betrayed him.

The coquette ran her finger along the edge of her camisole, across plump breasts, which revealed a hint of light, rose-colored flesh at their tips. "You want a sample, sir? All the others do."

Caught in the act of ogling, he coughed. "Others?"

"Most inspectors want a taste. Everyone but you, Mr. Kennedy."

Everyone? His stomach roiled a bit.

"Is there something wrong with me, something you don't like?"

He tilted his head. "I think you are a very pretty girl." Skirting the bed, he sat down and spoke softly. He used her real name. "Kitty, you are not contracted to perform favors for detectives unless it is a part of an authorized operation. If you are ever uncomfortable with these requests for your services, I want you to feel free to boot them out. Is that understood?"

She tried to blink back any show of emotion before throwing her arms around his neck. He managed a hug and a few pats on the back. These girls did not experience much fair play or kindness in their line of work.

"You're a decent man, sir." A thin smile crept across her face.

Not altogether pleased about being thought decent by such a fetching girl, he let go of her and stood. Prostitute or no, he would take no chances with her safety. This liaison must go off as authentic.

"All right then, let's make this sound like we're having a jolly good tumble, shall we?" Zeno gave the bed a hard push with his foot and went on to create a series of rhythmic thuds and thumps. The game little harlot added sighs and moans to the jiggle and squeak of the bedsprings. A final staccato of rapid knocks against the wall made it perfectly evident to all those in the house that hardworking Scarlet was on the job.

CASSANDRA ST. CLOUD hurried up the steps of New Hospital for Women. A tingle of anticipation rushed through her body. On the second floor she turned toward the offices of the Women's Health Organization of Britain. A line of patients spilled out of the waiting room and snaked down the corridor. "Excuse me, ladies." She wove a path between high-bustle skirts, and turned down a narrow passageway marked *Deliveries*.

Cassandra gave the brass doorknob a turn, and poked her head in the door. "Dr. Erskine . . ." Her voice queried in a singsong fashion. "Mother?"

No answer. Just some low, mewling whimpers and a gasp of suppressed laughter.

What was Mama Olivia up to? She ventured inside the office and slipped past a few crates of medical supplies. A gas lamp hissed quietly above a stack of crates marked *London Rubber Company*. Cassandra grinned. No doubt a box full of Earl of Condom rubber goods.

A turn of the corner revealed a sparse but meticulously scrubbed examination room. Her mother held a cupped ear to the adjoining office wall.

"Cassie." Dr. Olivia had a look of devilry about her. "Come have a listen." She waved her closer. "Come. Come."

She pressed affectionately up against her mother and cocked her head. Soft whimpers escalated into the most lurid moans as the unseen woman behind the wall continued to gasp and groan. With a surge of shock, she recognized the euphoric sighs of sexual intercourse as they passed through the plaster wall between surgeries.

Cassie shot upright. "Stanley Hargety is having an affair?" She had met Dr. Hargety and his wife several times at her parents' home. There were rumors the man's medical practice failed to prosper, and now this turn of events. She tried to hold back an uncharitable grin. "He hardly seems the Lothario type."

Her mother snorted. "Did you have a look at the queue of women in the corridor? What a reversal of fortune! My colleague's services are now very much in demand." The moans grew louder and more frequent.

Cassie muffled a burst of laughter.

Olivia held a finger to her lips. "The paroxysm cometh."

And it came in a bursting shriek followed by a nearly inaudible sigh. "Well, at least the lady's hysteria is assuaged, thanks to Dr. Swift."

More than curious, she followed her mother from the examination room to a small office in the rear of the suite. "Dr. Swift, you say? What happened to Dr. Hargety? And who is this Dr. Swift? Is the man properly licensed, Mother?"

Olivia tossed her a backward grin. "Dr. Swift is not a who, it's a what, darling. A new electric vibration machine."

Once inside the rumpled, comfortable office, her mother removed the kettle from a spirit-fuelled burner and filled the teapot. "Not long after I acquired this Bunsen burner, what did Stanley Hargety do? At great expense, he purchased himself a set of Leclanché cell batteries."

Cassie clamped her lips together. She had read the scandalous advertisements in the back of women's journals. An amused chortle rippled close to the surface. "Dear lord, he's got himself a machine to relieve female hysteria."

"The electric vibrator is also an effective treatment for arthritis, muscle spasms, and insomnia." Olivia winked. "But a most profound cure for the over-excitable female. And what a boon to his practice. They'd come in twice a week if he could find the room to fit them in."

"I take it not every lady is quite so expressive as this last patient?" She swept a few books off the corner of the desk so her mother could set down the tea tray.

"Lord no, although I have my theories." Olivia shooed Baxter the cat off a well-worn wing chair. "Coincidental to his partnering with Dr. Swift, Stanley has suddenly shifted his practice to hospital half the week. I suspect an enthusiastic patient may have proved herself entirely too vocal for his posh Harley Street surgery."

Cassie could not hold back the news a second longer. Her stomach fluttered with excitement. "I must tell you my solicitor wired wonderful news this morning. At my behest, a small but well-appointed town house edging on Belgravia has been let in my name."

Olivia stopped short of biting into a lemon biscuit.

"Well, it's about time, dear. No one will take greater pleasure than I to see you cast off those widow's weeds and return to your painting. You have great talent. A gift from God—"

"Don't squander it," she recited along with her mother. "You'll be pleased to know I have plans to show in London and Paris this year." Cassie raised her chin. "I mean to concentrate on my art, and art alone."

As shocking and cruel as her husband's death had been, she had been given a reprieve of sorts, a chance to start life anew. "There will be no eager gentlemen callers complicating my ambitions this time."

This time, she would remain steadfast to her aspirations. This time the thing she desired most in the world would be hers—to be worthy of the sobriquet "impressionist." Mary Cassatt's *Child in a Straw Hat*, Claude Monet's *Woman with a Parasol*, Edgar Degas's *Dancers at the Bar*. And Cassandra St. Cloud's . . . ? Lost in a world of brilliant color and swirling brushstrokes, she was barely aware of her mother's ramblings.

". . . and when word gets out the young widow has taken a residence of her own?"

"Yes. The presumption is I will take a lover." Cassie shrugged. "Let them think what they wish."

"Well." Olivia grinned. "*Libertas*, Cassie! And when does this all take place?"

"I begin the move tomorrow. My dear companion, Aunt Esmie, leaves Rosslyn House for the countryside to care for an ailing sister." Cassie set her cup down and beamed. "The timing is perfection itself, I shall make my escape from the in-laws."

"After six months of marriage and two years of mourning, I would say so." Mother's eye roll was less than subtle, though her voice softened. "You have done your duty."

A brief silence graced the room as the reality of Cassie's break from her late husband's family sank in. Sipping tea, Olivia gazed at her over a tipped cup. "I was pleased to know you recognized the sounds of sexual gratification, dear. I do hope that when Thom was alive he managed to show you some pleasure?"

She pressed her lips together. How Mother dearly loved to be shocking.

There really was only one way to answer one of Dr. Olivia Erskine's social deportment salvos, as Father often referred to them. "Yes, Mama, he knew precisely the spot and what to do once he got there." Not that the man had seen her in a state of bliss, much. Heat radiated from her throat to her cheeks but Cassie took a great deal of satisfaction in what appeared to be her mother's generous approval.

Olivia smiled. "Ah, the magic power of a fine, gentle massage."

Now and again, Cassie wondered what it might be like to have a retiring, reserved mother. She set down her cup. "I cannot think of another subject I would rather converse on, but I must be off to see Mr. Dowdeswell. I dropped off a folio of drawings last week, which he kindly offered to critique."

"And how goes the gallery business? After that ridiculous show he gave Whistler." Olivia clucked her tongue. "When I think of how bold your work is in comparison to that meek little portrait of his mother. I do hope Dowdeswell comes to his senses and offers you space."

"All right, Mummy, shall we give him a go? Sit for me. Perhaps a reclining pose—*Olivia in the Nude*?"

Mother nearly choked on her biscuit. "I will say your father does admire my derriere."

Cassie pulled on gloves. "Should you decide to retire from medicine, promise me you will never attempt artist representation. You'd make short work of the gallery owners on Bond Street." She blew her mother a kiss as she left the room.

Chapter Two

Zeno exited the notorious bordello and decided to walk off his frustration. He hoofed it back to Piccadilly Circus, where it would be easy enough to find a hansom for hire.

After a few years with the Yard, a man developed instincts. Something about this small incident of Kitty's made his gut react as if he'd held a match to a stick of dynamite. At the intersection of Haymarket and Shaftesbury, he sucked in a breath of sooty air, and spied a cab emptying out passengers.

"Number Four Whitehall."

"Cost ye two bob."

Zeno frowned at the driver. "That's double the fare."

"Time a day, sir. Cab's in demand."

Robbery, plain and simple. Since construction began on the Underground expansion, cabbies had become money-grubbing highwaymen.

Disgruntled, he settled against the hard leather seat of the cab. The last batch of dynamiters had taken him eighteen months to find and bring to trial—another six to reach verdicts and sentencing. Several of his cases against known conspirators had been dropped for want of evidence to bring before the chief Crown prosecutor. The files had long since been stored away. He couldn't wait to get back into the office and dust them off.

Zeno stepped out of the cab and tossed the driver two shillings. He nodded to the security police at the entrance and took the stairs two at a time.

The elderly janitor stopped sweeping and tipped his cap. "Onto something big, Inspector Kennedy?"

"One never knows, Bert." Mumbling to himself, Zeno turned down the corridor toward Records. He collected several folders and returned to his desk. Leafing through the first file, he came across an old list titled "The Bloody Four." A hotchpotch of names had been added and crossed out over the years.

Andrew Hingham, Lord Delamere.

Zeno angled the notepaper to read a hurried scrawl in the margin. *Possible financier of dynamiters?* And another line: *Appears to work in support of Irish Home Rule, but . . . ?*

"Evening, mate."

Zeno recognized the detective's voice. "Mr. Lewis, you worked this case with me. Do you recall anything of interest regarding Lord Delamere?"

"Irish peer, there's also a title held in the peerage of England. Earl of Longford, I believe—but check that." Rafe leaned against the doorframe. "I seem to remember suspected linkages to a group of American Irish anarchists. *Clan na Gael*, possibly."

Zeno studied his scribbled notes peppered with question marks. "What if—say—Delamere wanted a bloody Irish revolution? A complete break from England? Might he plot to keep all of London in a state of terror, including the Lords and members of Parliament?"

"Keep the natives stirred up—Home Rule might never pass." The young detective tilted his chin. "Interesting, Zak." He pushed off the doorjamb. "I'm off to meet Flynn."

"The Rising Sun?"

"Dog and Duck." Rafe shrugged. "Flynn's after a nice bit o' tail. I'll settle for a pint. Pop by if you're thirsty."

Zeno returned to the list and searched for the second name, James. Kitty's cowering man of round girth and ruddy cheek. Among the jumble of names and titles he could find only one man who fit the description.

James Reginald Hicks-Beach.

Good God. The man worked in the Home Office. Word was Hicks-Beach was being groomed for greater things. How the anarchists would love to have a man on the inside. Zeno took up his pen and circled four likely candidates. After Delamere and Hicks-Beach, he scratched a loop around George Upton, a known confederate of Delamere, and another close chum, Gerald St. Cloud, Earl of Rosslyn.

Could these peers be the Bloody Four?

He lingered on the last name circled. If he was not mistaken, the young widow about to become his latest tenant was a St. Cloud. Rubbing his eyes, he sat back in his chair and blew a low whistle through his teeth.

Rather odd his new neighbor was related to a person of interest implicated in his case. By coincidence or design?

Hang it all, it was about time a bit of luck fell in his lap. Zeno wrote down a code name for Delamere. *Rat-Rí*. King rat in ancient Irish speak. Then he filled out a personnel request authorization to move two agents, Flynn Rhys and Rafe Lewis, onto his case.

Ah yes, one more thing.

Before reaching for his coat, he got out a blank telegraph form and jotted the name of his solicitor and the words *Saint Cloud* on separate lines. After scribbling the word *saint*, he found the honorific entirely too . . . saintly. He crumpled up the sheet, opened a top drawer, and pulled out a pad of wire forms. This time he abbreviated her surname and scrawled along absently. *Make sure keys deliver to new tenant by . . .*

The pencil lead snapped.

"Bollocks." He removed a penknife from his pocket and sharpened the writing instrument. Now, where was he? Zeno scratched the stubble on his jaw. Ah yes. The idea of a young woman with possible connections to his case intrigued him. His solicitor, a clever fellow who didn't miss much, had mentioned she was rather attractive. His new lessee would take possession of Number 10 Lyall Street at dawn on the morrow. Something about this rather ordinary event hinted at a kind of positive shift in the atmosphere, a tingle of excitement. He experienced a fleeting, prescient sense of expectation. Of what, he had no idea—but he itched to find out.

*   *   *

CASSIE CRANED HER neck to admire the Prussian blue sailcloth. A rather chic new awning was being constructed over the door of Dowdeswell and Dowdeswell Gallery. One side of the exhibit space remained open, while workmen readied the other half for a new installation. Enamel paint and sawdust permeated the air as she ducked past busy workmen and made her way toward the rear of the display room.

The office door was open. Dowdeswell stood with his back to the door and examined a painting. She rapped on the entry molding before entering the untidy space strewn with framed and unframed canvases.

The gentleman pivoted slowly and she froze. "The talented Mrs. St. Cloud! A beautiful woman who is also on time, how delightful."

The strikingly handsome man standing before her was decidedly *not* Oscar Dowdeswell. Rather, he was a persistent scourge. A nightmare. A man she went to great lengths to avoid, whether at private social events or in public.

"Lord Delamere. What are you—?"

His cool, green-eyed gaze raked up and down her frame. "How are you, my dear?"

She dipped a curtsy. "Very well, my lord."

"Gerald tells me you mean to strike out on your own. Something about a flat in Belgrave Square?"

"Knightsbridge." Cassie squared her shoulders and met his gaze. Still, the tingle down her spine caused a kind of breathless stammer. "Perhaps it does edge onto Belgravia."

She turned to leave and he swept past her. Taller than she remembered, Delamere moved like a panther. Not surprising, the man was a predator. His frock coat swung open to reveal a deep Alizarin crimson silk waistcoat. Black cravat. Ruby tiepin. His Savile Row tailor would be proud.

"You will hear me out, Cassandra." Arrogantly nonchalant, he leaned against the door, barring her exit.

She ignored her rise in heart rate and the slight tic in her left eye. There was something raw and surly about Delamere today. He needed a shave, which was impossible. Not this immaculate, elegant man who dressed to perfection. He must be growing a beard.

She lifted her chin. "I have an appointment with Mr. Dowdeswell, where is he?"

"Down with a terrible malady, I'm afraid—some kind of spring fever. And since I have recently become a silent partner of Dowdeswell and Dowdeswell, I volunteered for this meeting."

"I was to receive Mr. Dowdeswell's comments on a folio of drawings."

"Ah yes, the sketches of the lady in toilet. Powerful, sensual work, almost scandalous for a female artist."

He moved away from the door. "Since you are far from the blushing ingénue, tell me, Cassandra, did you disrobe for your husband in such a provocative manner?"

Cassie bit her lip. "I'll just retrieve them and be on my way." Unable to return his gaze, she scanned the room for her portfolio. There it was, on a side table, behind the desk.

He leaned forward to scold her. "I'm not sure I will ever forgive you for marrying Thomas."

Blood and panic pulsed through her body. "Lord Dela-mere, you have contrived to lure me here to insult and threaten me." Her brows knit together when she frowned. "Why must you persist with these unwanted advances?"

The man had a reputation as an accomplished rake who enjoyed the chase as much as the conquest. Rapacious, wolf-ish. She could not bear to look into the flinty spark of his emerald gaze. Whenever he contrived to venture near, she was always made to feel as if she stood naked before him.

Already he was too close. She took several steps back. "There are many women far more attractive than I who would adore your attentions, my lord."

"But they are not you." He yanked her into his arms and dipped his head as though to force a kiss. But his mouth did not touch hers. Instead, he stared intently as his hand pressed into the fabric of her dress.

"Do you miss the lovemaking, Cassandra?" One hand held her firmly within his grasp while the other traveled lower. Heat rose up her neck to her cheeks. Damn the man. She placed both hands on his chest and pushed him aside. "Touch me again and I will—"

Undaunted, the man boldly advanced. He held an arm out in invitation. Presumably, if she didn't obey, he would grab her again. Cassie backed farther away.

"Oscar?" A strong rapping caused the door to rattle.

"Please come in," Cassie called hastily. Startled by the knock as well as the strength of her reply, Delamere hesi-tated. The door opened. She recognized the disembodied head of Jeremy William Powell, one of the gallery's artists.

"Cassie, is that you?"

She uttered a nervous ripple of laughter. "So good to see you, Jeremy."

His lordship glowered.

She breathed a sigh of relief. She and Jeremy Powell had studied in Paris together, a summer arts program at the Sorbonne. Always stylish, though a bit unkempt, the artist entered the office and straightened a paisley cravat. A lock of fawn-colored hair fell over his forehead. Jeremy swept it back with a nervous grin. She knew instantly he sensed the raw energy in the room. "Have I interrupted something?"

"Not at all, Jeremy. Lord Delamere informs me he is now a partner in the gallery. Have you been introduced?" Barely holding herself together, she managed a tight-lipped smile. "Jeremy William Powell is one of your gallery's contracted artists, my lord."

"Lord Delamere." Jeremy made a courteous bow. "I was in the neighborhood. Thought to pop in for a chat. Oscar still under the weather?"

"Mr. Powell." His lordship deigned a nod. "I'm afraid he continues to suffer the occasional fever." Nothing had changed about Delamere. His polite civility always seemed strained, on edge. "I understand he is improving."

"Well, that is good news." Jeremy shifted his smile. "So, Cassie, what brings you here?"

"Mr. Dowdeswell offered a critique. Another day, perhaps?" She crossed the room, picked up the folio and tucked it under her arm.

Was that a wistful look from the wretched man? If she didn't know better, Lord Delamere appeared almost contrite. "Oscar quite lavishly admired your sketches, Cassandra. He planned to discuss show dates in the fall."

"Yes . . . well." Her gaze faltered. "If you would pass along my best wishes for Mr. Dowdeswell's restored health?"

"Please do relay mine as well." Jeremy nodded a dignified bow. "Honored to have made your acquaintance, Lord Delamere."

His lordship barely acknowledged the artist, steadying his gaze on Cassandra. "The pleasure was mine."

Cassie stepped into a blur of bustling pedestrians on Bond Street. As soon as they were safely away from the gallery, Jeremy turned to her. "Cassie, you are as pale as a ghost. What was going on back there?"

She took hold of his offered arm. "Your knock on the door could not have been more timely."

Youthfully handsome, both in body and spirit, Jeremy's bright eyes filled with mischief. "I do hope you have a sordid and shocking tale to tell."

He was exactly the right tonic for her. "Positively scandalous."

"I must hear everything." Her dear colleague checked the cross traffic and escorted her across the street. "Gunter's is still open. I could use a lemon ice or cup of hot chocolate."

She flashed a thin smile. "You're going to need one of each."

The ground trembled underfoot, followed by a low rumble of thunder in the distance. "Did you feel that?" Jeremy asked. They both pivoted in the direction of the river.

*   *   *

ZENO DODGED HIS way through a snarl of cabs and carriages. At the curb, he purchased a *Gazette* and a *Daily Telegraph*. He tucked both papers under his arm and made for the Underground entrance on the Embankment. A low-pitched rumble rattled every shop window on the corner. The vibration instantly escalated into a violent shaking as sidewalk pavers shifted underfoot.

A flash of brilliant light pained his eyes. An eerie squall of orange-red fire blasted out of the station. The shock wave blew him off the curb and into the street. Flat on his back he tried to catch his breath, gasping for what little oxygen there was in the air. Somehow, through a sensory fog, he was aware of carriage wheels and striking hooves. Rolling out of the vehicle's way, he staggered to his feet. A newsboy lay motionless nearby. He reached out and lifted the young hawker into his arms.

Vaguely, he was aware he was hatless.

Zeno's auditory faculties cut out. Silence. His perception of events became a jumble of disjointed visual impressions. Ghostly figures circled around him, all in a panic. Buffeted by a second ferocious blast, a huge cloud of smoldering wreckage rocketed out of the Underground entrance.

He checked behind him and then, on a hunch, checked again. As if in a dream, a silent, driverless team and coach emerged from a cloud of smoke and debris. Zeno held the child tight to his body and took refuge behind a capsized wagon.

His eardrums popped. Cries of panic came from every corner of the busy intersection. The shrieks of frightened horses and the clatter of the runaway carriages echoed through the streets.

Debris darkened the sky and spread outward. Black smoke rumbled over the concourse, smothering every person and object in its path. A blanket of vaporous, noxious particles enveloped him. Zeno tucked the newsboy into the shelter of the cart. He could barely see a foot in front of his face. From his waistcoat pocket he removed a handkerchief and held the fabric over his nose and mouth. Eyes burning, disoriented, he crossed the small square.

It was happening again.

Nearly three years had passed since the last bombing stunned all of London. Zeno's squint shut out everything but the memory of one explosion. The one he could never forget.

Covered in a fine layer of ash, he made his way toward the tube entrance. Somewhere on the stairs a child screamed in fear. He descended no more than a dozen steps and tripped over a pile of bodies. The stink of smoldering woolen coats and singed hair hovered over the dazed commuters. These people were near to suffocation. He shook each one and hastened them on up the stairs.

Lungs choked with thick gray dust, he could barely breathe. Couldn't see a thing. Out of the murky stillness came a weak, frightened voice. "Is there anyone here? Can someone please take my hand?" He reached through a fog of ash and grasped outstretched trembling fingers.

"Don't let go."

"No." Zeno lifted the woman onto her feet.

"My child!"

Blindly, he searched the ground and grasped a woven shawl. No cry of life came from the bundled infant. With the babe under one arm, he held the woman upright and made his way aboveground. A hint of sky appeared to each side of a spiraling plume of charcoal vapor. Then, a godsend, a gust of wind and a patch of fresh air. Zeno sucked in a deep breath.

A group of dazed citizens approached to help settle the woman and child on a stone bench. Tiny daggers of smoke particles burned and blurred Zeno's vision. Meanwhile, people were dying.

The infant's wail permeated a cloak of haze and shadow. Hope.

"Someone alert the fire brigade. Scotland Yard is blocks away, the Metropolitan Police should be on scene any moment now." His eyes watered profusely as he blinked away soot. "I could use a few able-bodied men." He turned into a thick blanket of fumes and didn't look back to see if anyone followed.

With each trip to the surface, as the threat of additional bombs eased, Zeno picked up a makeshift auxiliary of volunteers. Day had turned to night. The cool chill of evening air washed over him. The fire brigade, now on the scene, went straight after burning pockets of flame, while trained men helped to excavate the injured and dead from under the rubble.

"Sit yourself down and have a swig." Someone shoved a ladle of cold water into his hand. He guzzled with a thirst he wasn't aware of until now. After several deep swallows he returned the dipper for more. "Thank you."

"No dear, thank you." The woman's kind face matched the tone of her voice.

Zeno shook his head. "There are so many." At least eleven dead thus far. Or was it twelve? He had lost count of the injured.

Every muscle in his body ached. He rubbed a scrape on his chin and reopened the wound. Blood mingled with dust on his fingertips. A deep inhalation triggered a spasm of coughs. Slumped onto a bench, he gave himself a minute or two and no more. He took another gulp of water, and poured the remains over his head. The cool liquid shocked and revived him. He kneaded his neck and let his head roll back onto sore shoulders.

His mind chased a tumbling crimson maple leaf along memory lane. Fall had come early that year. Zeno shook his head in a futile attempt to avoid a parade of painful memories and lurid headlines, articles filled with detailed descriptions of the carnage. And eclipsing all of it, a tragic love story.

YARD MAN LINKED TO BOMB VICTIM ACTRESS JAYNE WELLS

Plenty of newspapers sold that day and for weeks afterward. A nasty shot of anger pulsed through his body as he recalled the intrusive press reports. Like a persistent recurring nightmare, the memory of his dead mistress ravaged his thoughts. Three years had passed and yet her murder was as fresh as the blast of—how many hours had passed?

Someone clapped him on the back. His body jerked upright.

A small cadre of volunteers stood waiting, faces blackened with ash and grime. They had stuck fast with him since the explosion. A few were gentry. Frock coats and hats long since discarded, these gentlemen of quality had rolled up their shirtsleeves and worked tirelessly alongside working-class chaps with stronger backs—young men who could shoulder dead weight up two flights of stairs and turn right around for more.

One of the men spoke up. "That bloke over there took our names, sir. Sez your name's Kennedy of Scotland Yard. Sez yer famous."

Zeno's gaze traveled across the chaotic thoroughfare and narrowed on the man standing beside Fire Brigade Captain Fraser, pad and pencil in hand. He exhaled a sigh and surveyed his motley crew of volunteers, every one of them weary to the bone.

He approached the reporter interviewing the fire chief, and gestured to the men beside him. "Make sure you spell their names correctly and leave mine off the story."

The impertinent newspaper hack snorted. "Leave you off, Kennedy? Why, you *are* the story."

Zeno grabbed the man's jacket lapels. "Do your utmost to get this straight. Innocent people are down there, dead or dying. *They* are your story. Along with these men behind me, regular citizenry, who have risked their lives to rescue the victims of this violence."

He shoved off the bug-eyed newsman and walked back into hell.

⟨ Chapter Three

Revived by a hot bath and change of clothes, Zeno paused at the window of his second-floor library. He had left the smoldering remains of the Underground station at daybreak and stumbled home. Too keyed up for bed, he wondered how long he would remain upright. He made a private wager with himself and kept the stakes small.

For the time being, the early morning arrival of furniture to Number 10 Lyall Street would serve to amuse. As he observed the removal of a large packing crate from the van, a section of windowpane reflected the distracting movements of his housekeeper. She guided a busy feather duster across the library table and hesitated. With a furtive glance in his direction she brushed over a stack of books and reports piled in a haphazard fashion.

For years, Zeno had studied Alma Woolsley's household misadventures and found he could, at times, anticipate her behavior. Tentatively, she reached for several of the heaviest volumes on the top of the heap.

"I'd rather you wouldn't, Mrs. Woolsley."

With an audible tsk and exaggerated sigh, Alma shifted her duster's attentions to the side table of his favorite reading chair. "You've got eyes in the back of your head, sir."

"Rather useful in my line of work."

The woman did not know her place. Besides being impertinent and bossy, she moved things. This habit figured by far to be her most exasperating quality. He had spoken to her at length and on many occasions about this systematic invasion of his privacy.

Of late, she had redoubled her efforts to antagonize him with an assault on his dressing room. Without so much as asking, she made it her business to reorganize both his wardrobe and dresser drawers. Just this morning he was obliged to call her upstairs to show him where his tattersall waistcoat might be found.

From the corner of his eye, he caught a *swoosh* of feathers along the window mullions. "I do hope the new tenant will be amiable, Mr. Kennedy. Do you know anything more about her, sir? You did mention she is a single lady, a widow, I believe?"

"I am in receipt of a full year's rent paid in advance. What better to know about a new tenant, Mrs. Woolsley?"

With a sniff, she rattled off a barrage of questions in short order. "I believe it would be nice to know all sorts of things about her. Perhaps an idea of the lady's age? Does she bring any relations with her? How many servants might she need? What are her family connections? Many details, sir, would be profoundly interesting."

"Profoundly interesting?" Zeno arched a brow. "You lead an exceedingly dull life, ma'am."

"Well, you would best know about that, Mr. Kennedy," Alma pushed up next to him and peered around the window drapery. Like it or not, her insistent nudging caused the bare semblance of a smile. Anything more would have cracked open wounds sustained in the blast.

"I do worry you'll be off after those dynamiters without the proper rest." She sniffed. "And I'd be happier if those bruises and cuts looked a sight better."

"To ease your mind, I shall endeavor to heal as quickly as possible."

"Sleep would go a long way, sir."

"For your edification, take a moment to observe the furnishings carried into Number Ten by the drayage laborers." He checked his pocket watch. "Perhaps you might find an object of interest? An unusual item or two that could tell us something about our new neighbor?"

He kept one eye on the furrowed brow of his housekeeper as she concentrated on the comings and goings below. "Come now, Mrs. Woolsley. Do you not apprise me on a near-constant basis regarding your inborn talent for sleuthing?"

Alma hesitated. "Might our new neighbor have an interest in the arts?"

"An interest or an avocation? You must elaborate."

"I've counted several easels as well a large roll of sailcloth. And a number of instrument cases. Might they hold brushes, oils, charcoals, turpentine, and the like? I believe she could be a painter if I am not mistaken." Alma's eyes widened as she awaited his reply.

"A very good start, Mrs. Woolsley."

She snorted. "Not a difficult deduction, beggin' your pardon, sir."

He pressed his lips together. "I suppose it is an observation that, no doubt, a simpleton could discern. Might the lady in question be a serious artist or would you call her a dabbler, perhaps as a hobby?"

Alma tilted her head. "Why, I believe the former, sir. Why else all the equipment?"

"Excellent perception. And what style of painting, what school of artists might she be identified with?"

"Mr. Kennedy, how might I know what the lady paints without an opportunity to see the paintings themselves?"

His focus shifted to the arrival of a town coach as it pulled ahead of the furniture van. Zeno ticked off numerous observations, including an elaborate coat of arms. The Rosslyn crest, no doubt. Zeno reminded himself of his new tenant's connection to the Earl of Rosslyn, Gerald St. Cloud.

A woman of an age near middle twenties emerged from the carriage. Stringing behind her on long leads were two tail-waggers—tricolor foxhounds. The young lady waited patiently for the dogs to assess the distance from the coach floor to the ground before they made a scrambled leap to the street.

She wore a slim skirt with a modest bustle. A crisp white shirt under a formfitting jacket denoted a shapely figure. Comically, a hound's leash caught in her skirt. She quickly raised the hem, exposing a trim length of leg as she untangled the frolicking animal. Zeno politely redirected his attention to the sunlight rimming her hair, which glowed a honeyed brown color under a smart straw boater.

"My word, she appears to be a handsome, athletic sort of young lady."

The near thrill in his housekeeper's voice caused him to raise a brow. "Kindly explain how you might come to the conclusion that Mrs. St. Cloud is athletic?"

"Is that her name?" Alma sighed. "Very pleasing and romantic, wouldn't you say, sir?"

"Answer the question, please."

"Well," she hesitated, "there are the hounds, which indicate—"

"Nothing." He frowned. "They could be leftover runts from a large litter of sporting dogs the lady decided to rescue and make into house pets. You'll have to do better than that, Mrs. Woolsley."

"There is the matter of a very fine new horse in the stables. Arrived just yesterday, late in the afternoon. I happened to overhear instructions to the groom."

Zeno tore his gaze away from the street. "Which were?"

"The new tenant," Alma stammered, "Mrs. St. Cloud, that is, enjoys an early ride most every morning. Weather permitting, sir."

He quirked up the ends of his mouth. "Mrs. Woolsley, I believe you are soon to be graduated to an occasional research contract with the firm."

"Does that mean I get to spy, sir?"

"Indeed it does."

*   *   *

IT TOOK EXACTLY three days for Mrs. St. Cloud to send word to the stables to ready her horse for riding. Zeno knew this for a fact, for he had skulked around the mews each and every morning hoping for a chance encounter with the young woman.

Of course, he might have just knocked on her front door. "Greetings, madam. Welcome to the neighborhood." But that sort of formality, while neighborly, was hardly conducive to poking into her brother-in-law's involvement with the Bloody Four. No, he had in mind a more serendipitous meeting.

Checking his saddle, he watched the lady's well-bred hunter circle the stable groom at the end of a long leading ribbon. "Natural collection, nicely gaited."

Rory tossed a shock of red hair over a nose sprinkled with freckles. "A right pretty mover she is, sir."

"Good morning, gentlemen."

Zeno pivoted toward the pleasant female voice. His jaw dropped and his mouth went dry. Days ago, he had observed a handsome, intriguing young lady take possession of Number 10. This morning, up close?

She was stunning.

Captured by her gaze, he noted crystal gray eyes framed by dark lashes. She studied him rather intently. Her features, though symmetrical, were quite overpowered by a rather predominant mouth, which at the moment tilted up at the ends. In fact, he could not be sure she wasn't laughing at him. He stared a bit too long at those well-defined lips.

She wore a riding habit in a shade that might be described as a medium blue—what would a lady call that hue? Beneath her jacket, a paisley waistcoat peeked out from under black velvet lapels. A top hat adorned with a netted veil completed the picture.

He attempted to speak as his heart pounded too much blood from his brain. *My word, this is going to be stimulating.* An intriguing new neighbor related to a person of interest in his case against the dynamiters. A tantalizing mix of business and pleasure, indeed. "Pardon me, but I thought to bring around . . . ?" Zeno gestured toward the circling equine.

"Daisy."

He choked on the silly name for such a refined mount. "I was about to bring—Daisy—to your door, as I myself am riding this morning."

Her gaze moved up and down. "I assure you, sir, I am quite capable of getting to the Lyall Mews on my own, but I do appreciate the kind gesture, Mister—?"

"Please forgive my indecorous manners, Mrs. St. Cloud." He tipped his hat. "Zeno Augustus Kennedy, at your service."

"You know my name, sir?"

"I do, madam. As it happens I am the owner of several row houses on Lyall Street. I admit to a cursory review of the applications I receive from my solicitor, but I am mindful enough to remember the name of a new tenant."

The groom positioned her horse at the mounting block. Before either male could offer a hand, she stepped into a stirrup, hoisted herself onto the saddle, and arranged her skirts.

He noted the soft, supple leather of her riding boots

before pivoting in the direction of the young stable hand. "Mrs. St. Cloud, may I introduce you to your groom?"

"Rory O'Connor, ma'am." The boy doffed his cap and nodded a bow.

"Named after the King of Ireland, I presume?" Her smile was radiant. Of course she would have to have one of those.

"Yes, ma'am." The lad's fair skin turned a vivid shade of pink, a striking mismatch against his fiery orange hair.

"Very pleased to meet you, Rory."

"Likewise, ma'am."

She narrowed mercury eyes over the head of her shy groom. "So you are my landlord, then?"

Zeno nodded a discreet bow. "We need not converse as lessor to lessee, but rather, my intention is to welcome you to the neighborhood. Perhaps I can answer questions or direct you to services around the vicinity of our small community?"

"Shall we ride together, then? Show me points of interest. A short route to the track, once we're in the park."

"Exactly, madam." From the corner of his eye, as he lifted himself onto his saddle, he caught her inspecting his backside. Hard in an instant, he sat cautiously so as not to cause himself injury.

"You live on Lyall Street, Mr. Kennedy?"

Adjusting his reins, he met her gaze. "I am your next-door neighbor, Mrs. St. Cloud."

"MY GIVEN NAME is Cassandra, but you may call me Cassie." She reined Daisy off a narrow horse trail and onto the wide dirt track of Rotten Row.

She caught a raised brow from her neighbor. "Are you always so informal, Mrs. St. Cloud?" What a cold, taciturn impression he made, speaking in clipped tones with a frown on his face. She concluded he must not recognize this disagreeable behavior in himself.

"Perhaps you should call me by my title, then. The dowager Lady Rosslyn. Much more starchy and impersonal. Are you always so stiff, Mr. Kennedy?"

The curl at the ends of his mouth seemed to indicate he was amused. "According to a colleague of mine, I need to foster a more congenial side to my acerbic nature. All work and no play, I'm afraid. Perhaps you can help me improve on my charm . . . a bit of advice?"

An honest evaluation, delivered with a large dose of sarcasm. Still, she smiled. "I don't believe there are charm schools for gentlemen who lack . . . *charm*, Mr. Kennedy."

Stealing a glance at the man riding beside her, she noted an imperfectly perfect nose positioned above a delicious wide-set mouth, his most expressive facial feature. In the short distance from mews to park, he had demonstrated a few subtle variations of a masterful frown. A smile from this gent, should she ever see one, might cause her complete discomposure.

"Then I will require private lessons. You have my permission to school me in the finer points of the winsome personality." The tensing of his mouth and the quirk of a brow intimated curiosity and something else. He enjoyed taunting her.

"Generally, people who cultivate charm enjoy using

the familiar. The use of a person's first name, for example, is an engaging gesture. And I still prefer Cassie, even if you do not."

He continued to appear nonplussed. "Ah yes, an agreeable personality is certain to win one friends."

She could not restrain a flicker of eye roll. "If you *were* to use my first name, how might I then be allowed to refer to you, Mr. Kennedy? Theoretically?"

His gaze darted across park scenery to meet hers. "There are a few colleagues or acquaintances," he ventured, his voice laden with irony, "who call me Zak—an acronym, of my initials."

"Zeno . . ." She bit her lip. "*Angus* Kennedy?"

He narrowed his eyes. "*Augustus* Kennedy."

"My, my, you do have clever friends, even if there are so few of them."

Was that a growl or a harrumph from the man? She grinned. "That sort of grousing is only endearing from a great-uncle in need of an afternoon nap." Cassie guided her horse onto a narrow path and glanced back. "A charm pointer, Mr. Kennedy."

They rode quietly past the Albert Memorial, Victoria's impressive epitaph to her most beloved husband.

"I always feel obliged to recite some sort of eulogy whenever I pass by here." Her landlord tilted his head. "Ah, here's one.

> *"Near this spot*
> *are deposited the remains of one*
> *who possessed beauty without vanity,*

Strength without insolence,
Courage without ferocity,
and all the virtues of man without his vices."

She recognized the poem. "You quote Byron's 'Epitaph to a Dog.'"

"I'm afraid our departed prince consort will have to make do with the only epitaph I have set to memory. A poet's tribute to his beloved pet." He nudged his mount up alongside hers and flashed a hint of a smile. It nearly took her breath away. "My uncle gave me a Newfoundland as a lad."

She couldn't resist a tease. "And I suppose you named your dog Boatswain after Byron, as well?"

"Not terribly original, I admit." His scoff added a nice touch of humility. "Boat died years ago. I was away at school."

She experienced a sudden awareness that Mr. Kennedy had shifted from curious enigma to someone she might wish to know better. A subtle reckoning, to be sure, and it began before she even realized it.

Gradually, he disclosed something of his background. Graduated Cambridge with letters, and a former rugby player—a blue shirt of all things! He had suffered a knee injury the start of his third year.

She found the story of his perfunctory cut from the team endearing. And he did have a strong physique. In fact, she noticed his tall, muscular body entirely too much. Regular attendance to an athletic club likely kept him in such fit condition for a man of his age. Pugilism or fencing? she wondered.

She guessed him at five-and-thirty, or thereabouts. The

decade's separation in their ages appealed to her. Her dear, departed Thom's boyish, impetuous nature had belied his six years of seniority. A foolhardy man, if she looked back with scrutiny. Perhaps that explained Mr. Kennedy's stoic appeal.

He made her a little nervous. And devil take it if he wasn't a handsome man. Earlier, he had parked his hat with an obliging groom before having a gallop down Rotten Row. She thought about the thick head of sable hair with a hint of gray at the temples. Wind-tossed from their run, a lock fell forward across his forehead and gave him a youthful, carefree appearance.

She ogled long legs in breeches and top boots as he posted the fast trot. A shocking, voyeuristic moment, which included glances at flexing thigh muscles, the shape of his buttocks when his coattails parted. A flush rose to her cheeks. Never in her life had she looked at a gentleman, other than her late husband, with such a prurient eye.

And he possessed the longest eyelashes, which framed cerulean blue eyes that seemed to penetrate a person's private thoughts. Rather unusual for blue eyes to be so wickedly piercing. Mysterious undercurrents stirred within, urging a closer evaluation of this magnetic, inscrutable fellow. Could there be a warmer, more passionate man under that high-pointed starched collar?

Cassie squared her shoulders. Using the back of her hand, she felt heat radiate from her neck to cheek. She shouldn't be having such thoughts about any man. She should be thinking about her new suite of paintings. *Scenes from the Boudoir*. The subject was simple and sensuous. A young woman in her dressing room. Light would rim the model's body and she would use rich strokes of color to add depth to the shadows.

Cassie inhaled a deep breath and glanced at Mr. Kennedy. It struck her as somewhat suspicious that her supposedly unsociable landlord was being so . . . neighborly. He was apparently a man with few friends, by design.

She broke the long silence between them. "I suppose, even if one cultivated the social arts, a handful of stouthearted chums is all one can ask for. I find it most diligent of you to have cast your lantern about the streets of London long enough to find a few honest souls."

Even though his countenance remained stern, a spark of interest lit in his eyes. "Ah, you reference Diogenes of Sinope, the Greek philosopher, perhaps the most noted of all the cynics. A profound influence, Mrs. St. Cloud, on my namesake, Zeno of Citium—a man likewise occupied with the tragedies of the human predicament."

"Speaking of which, Mr. Kennedy, I conduct art education at Foundling Hospital today. Might we head back for the mews, sir?"

"Would you like me to ready my carriage, Mrs. St. Cloud? I am in the office most of the day. It would be my pleasure—"

"Last evening I ate nearly half a roast chicken and a pile of roasted vegetables and polished off the remains of a lemon tart at supper. I shall walk—at a brisk pace."

His mouth dipped at the corners and his eyes took on a liquid, vulnerable expression. She found it disconcertingly adorable.

"I believe we are due for rain this afternoon. Class is dismissed at four o'clock. If your work is near its end—?"

"I will come fetch you at four."

At the mews entrance, Zeno swung a long leg over his saddle and jumped to the ground. He handed off his reins to Rory and moved over to help steady her dismount.

Indeed, the man made her so nervous she fell forward in a brief loss of balance. He braced her against his body.

Hard chest, hard stomach, and my word! Cassie froze at the recognition of something else hard and very male.

"So," he murmured, "Cassie wears Aimée."

"I beg your pardon?" She did not push away.

"Mrs. St. Cloud, you smell like lavender and rosemary with subtle notes of vanilla and bergamot. More specifically, you wear Aimée, created by Gervais Laurent."

She smiled. "Inspired by a French maiden he fell in love with while traveling in Provence."

"A clever marketing ploy, I'm afraid. The scent was actually named after a sister. Something of an adorable minx is my guess." At times, his discourse became an odd flurry of facts, small details, and conjecture.

"Sir. I take it you are familiar with the scent by intimate association?"

He returned her pique with a twinkle in his eyes. "Alas, merely from my research."

The gentleman was more than odd; he was *eccentric*. And devilish handsome. The startling combination caused a fleeting surge of warmth to course through her body. She tilted her chin, a curl at the ends of her mouth.

"Rather informal of you, to use both my nickname and the name of my *parfumeur*."

"Ah, but was I *charming*, Mrs. St. Cloud?" He bowed stiffly and led her horse off the cobbled backstreet and into the stables.

First cool and reserved, then trifling. She might believe Mr. Kennedy toyed with her, but did not think him a rakish sort of man. This was just a simple flirtation. Wasn't it?

CASSIE CURSED *THE Daily Telegraph*. Wrong again.

The forecast for afternoon precipitation arrived early and descended upon the city in more of a deluge than a shower. The storm hit as she neared the halfway point of her trudge to hospital. It took only a few short minutes of such inclement weather for her to rue the decision to walk off an extra slice of lemon tart.

On days like today, the underground trains were swamped with passengers and every hansom cab in London occupied and in service. Her coat would soon be soggy and damp. Well, there was nothing left to do but soldier on. She angled her umbrella against the slanted pelting drops and slogged ahead.

At the corner of Piccadilly and St. James, awash in rain and self-pity, she heard someone in the crowd call her name.

"Cassie!"

She pivoted toward the voice in the storm, and came face-to-face with Mr. Kennedy. He tipped his hat. Before she could register surprise, he grabbed hold of her and whisked her into his carriage.

Dazed and dripping, she took a moment to compose herself. A musty whiff of damp upholstery and soggy woolen coats pervaded the air. He sat opposite, wearing an amused, condescending expression, which she found to be entirely vexing. He leaned forward and coaxed the umbrella out of her hand. She watched in silence as he gave the handle a good shake.

"You are soaking wet, Mrs. St. Cloud, and I am late for a briefing. You should consider a return trip to Lyall Street for a change of clothes."

"Nonsense, Mr. Kennedy. I'll be dry in no time, once I get into my classroom." Cassie remembered her manners. "I must thank you for—" She halted, overcome with curiosity. "How on earth did you find me?"

"I chose a route you would in all probability take on foot." That piercing blue gaze of his shifted from the passing street scene to her. "To spy you amongst a rain-sodden crowd, easier still." He hesitated. "You are both tall and attractive, and I would have to say luminous, even in a rainstorm, Mrs. St. Cloud."

Heat rose from her collar, melting away her earlier vexation. Still, she resisted much expression, waiting to see if the corners of his mouth would ever turn up.

There, he cracked enough of a grin to make a dimple with a deep crease.

Very nice.

She returned a brief smile, dipping her head to peer out the fogged coach window. A glimpse of Trafalgar Square, gave way to a jumble of government buildings. As the carriage slowed, she wiped a medium-sized spot clear, just enough to see the entrance to Number 4 Whitehall Place.

"Scotland Yard."

"This is where we must part company, madam."

She sat up straight. "You work for Scotland Yard?"

"I do." He turned up his raincoat collar and gathered his umbrella. "I will instruct my driver to take you on to Foundling Hospital."

"You called me Cassie again, even though you'd rather not."

"Did I?"

She nodded. "Just now, when you fished me out of the rain."

He opened his mouth to respond and then paused. He wore a curious, contemplative expression, as if after considering her remarks he still could not account for such a familiarity. "I shall come collect you this afternoon, Mrs. St. Cloud."

Her gaze tracked the bob of his umbrella as he jumped a rain puddle and entered the grounds. After a bombing incident some years past, they'd fenced off the famous government agency. There was scarce foot traffic to be seen, as pedestrians were now directed down a narrow pathway that ran alongside the administrative offices. From what little she could make out, he passed by Horse Guards at the gate and disappeared inside the building.

Pressed to her seat as the carriage lurched off, her lips slowly curled upward.

"So Mr. Kennedy is a Yard man."

Chapter Four

The dossier he penned became known as the "Home Rule Conspiracy" and got Zeno called into Melville's office for a private debriefing.

From under eyebrows as bushy as his muttonchop sideburns, Director of Special Irish Branch, William Melville, shot a piercing glare over the top of a file folder. "Before we begin I want you to explain to me why I had to find out from Rafe Lewis that a bounty has been placed on your head."

"None of that is confirmed." Zeno settled into a chair opposite the mahogany desk. "Though I suppose any number of anarchists would like to have me out of the way."

"I have to ask, Kennedy. Do you believe the bombs set off in the Underground were targeted for you?"

Zeno's jaw clenched. "If I believed that I'd take myself off the case."

Silence never bothered Melville. Many an agent had listened to the wall clock tick off the seconds as those fierce eyes made a careful examination. "All right then, explain this theory of yours."

"The memo was written as hypothesis. Pure conjecture. An exploration of possible terrorist links to government officials." Couching his words as deferentially as possible, Zeno explained further. "If we root around a bit, we may find a few high-ranked peers as well as government officials linked to a clandestine insurgent group, with links to both the Irish Republican Brotherhood and the *Clan na Gael* in America."

His boss removed his spectacles and pinched the bridge of his nose. "Conjecture or not, something tells me this isn't everything. What more have you to add to this insidious little scenario?"

Zeno shifted his chair to see over a desk piled high with files and reports. He cleared his throat. "Treason is a serious accusation."

The director's leather chair squeaked as he rocked forward. "Indeed it is. Well, out with it, Kennedy."

"It is possible this could go above a few peers, perhaps as high as the prime minister."

Melville's gaze turned black.

Zeno quickly offered reassurance. "Before considering the prime minister, I first intend to find out what's hatching over at Home Office. I suggest we have a little talk with Castlemaine. He has a man under him—Hicks-Beach. I suspect he's a member of an informal cadre headed up by Lord Delamere."

He raked a hand through his hair. "There's another layer here, much more insidious. Zealots like Delamere might be funding the dynamiters to stir up a disastrous Irish revolt. The man has amassed an impressive fortune from railroad investments and, according to my sources, cheating at cards. He has two great estates in Northern Ireland and Surrey. More than enough wealth to fund a revolution."

"You're saying Delamere wants Irish Home Rule to *fail?*"

Zeno nodded. "The House of Lords voted it down twice. If we go back and trace Delamere's involvement—"

"Good God—you may be onto something. He always does find some niggling reason to lobby against passage." Intrigued, Melville tugged on his whiskers. "And how better to make the Irish cause unsympathetic than to abet seditionists with bombs?"

Gears turned in the inky glimmer of the director's eyes. As a matter of course, the man enjoyed toying with outlandish theories. "What station do you suppose Lord Delamere covets? King of Ireland?"

"The Irish have no love for crowns." Zeno grinned. "More likely prime minister."

Melville leaned over his desk. "You do realize you point the finger at the most influential men in government? Christ Almighty, Kennedy, these are men at the very top. And if what you surmise is true, we are talking about the possible disruption, if not dismantling, of an entire branch of government."

Zeno remained calm and implacable, the only way to survive Melville's unsparing scrutiny. "Not if we work behind the scenes to eliminate the problem."

Melville flipped open his pocket watch. "Well, that kills my luncheon appointment." He looked vexed. "I am convinced you are both a troublemaker and a genius, but nonetheless, good work, Kennedy. Now let's call in some of our best lads and get to work."

Zeno brightened at the man's praise. "Thank you, sir. I would like to ask Rafe Lewis to join, and perhaps Flynn Rhys?"

The director rang in his secretary. "I'm feeling uncivilized. Let's have lunch brought in, Mr. Quincy. I believe Lewis and Rhys are in the field. Have them find their way into this office within the hour. I don't care what gin joint or whorehouse they're loitering in, just get them here."

Quincy nodded. "Very good, sir."

Melville returned to Zeno. "My instincts tell me there is yet another related incident. The discovery of two homosexuals, in flagrante delicto, and the subsequent battery of a man identified only as Albert."

Zeno's tight-lipped grin faded. He flipped open a file and handed over a list of names. "The Bloody Four. A *nom de guerre* for a cadre of useless peerage. They may well be our victim's assailants." Zeno sat back in his chair. "Not at all sure they're involved with anarchists, but I wager there's a political play in it for Lord Delamere."

"Delamere, again." Melville mused aloud. "His name pops up all too frequently of late." In a kind of contemplative pose, with his elbows on the desk, his boss concentrated on the fingertips he pressed together. "This informant, Kitty Matthews, is one of the new girls recently hired, is she not?"

Zeno closed the folder. "I believe she is new."

"Good girl for a prostitute, no doubt?" Melville was fishing for something.

"Yes sir, she seems to have the right instincts. She could have just as well ignored the knocking about of an old—"

"Hm-mm, yes. The battered man's name, Albert, you say?"

"Yes sir."

"You are aware of the home secretary's birth name?"

He flipped through his file. "Here we are, Earl of Castlemaine . . . Charles *Albert* Hancock." Zeno met the steely eyes of his boss across the large expanse of desktop.

Melville's only expression was a slight twitch at the side of his mouth. "Closer friends and colleagues use his middle name. I don't believe he's a bad egg. He might even turn out to be an important ally. But if he's our victim, England's home secretary has been badly compromised.

"Arrange for a private meeting with Castlemaine as soon as possible, no later than tomorrow. From here on out, my schedule will remain flexible to the needs of this operation. Keep Mr. Quincy informed. When you get an appointment, I'll try to join."

The director stood and stretched. "You've stumbled onto a big one this time, Kennedy."

"It appears so, sir." Zeno rose to leave. "While we wait for Rafe and Flynn, I believe I'll poke my head in the lab, see if they've identified any of the bomb materials."

Melville trailed after him to the door. "I'd be interested to know your opinion regarding the hiring of prostitutes as informants. I am told some of my agents enjoy recreational benefits unauthorized in their employment contracts."

He returned the steady gaze of his boss. "I advised Miss Matthews she is in no way obligated to perform . . . extra duties with our agents, and if she is pressed or threatened, to contact me."

Never one to relax his scrutiny or temper for long, Melville nevertheless remained calm. "Please keep me informed as to how that works out, Kennedy. If this tomfoolery continues to be a problem, I'm going to have to get angry about it."

∾ Chapter Five

Orphanage or labyrinth?

"Bollocks." Zeno squinted through the drizzle as he prowled among the jumble of buildings, play yards and endless institutional hallways of Foundling Hospital. Forced to ask for directions twice before locating the orphanage school, he eventually stumbled upon art education in a basement classroom.

After making his descent to the lower floor, he approached an open door in the hallway. To his surprise, he beheld a pleasantly warm room, well lit by a number of high-placed windows. Mrs. St. Cloud moved between the children, collecting sticks of charcoal. "Think about the emotional context of your art. Do you wish to convey serenity or excitement? The difference between a sturdy elm on a bright, clear morning and the same tree in a windstorm. Same subject, very different feelings."

She glanced past the head of a girl clothed in drab gray uniform and white apron. "Mr. Kennedy, please come in and meet several of England's young artists of promise."

While she locked cabinets and collected rain equipage, he settled on a short stool and appraised the students' efforts. He studied the basket of fruit placed in the middle of the large table and then carefully examined their sketches.

"Apples and pears—nicely done."

Cassie smiled. "As I have kept them past the bell, I am obliged to see my pupils safely back to their dormitories. Care to join?"

He strolled comfortably beside teacher and pupils through the stately, imposing Georgian building, which featured a gallery of portraits, some by Hogarth and Gainsborough. Once her students were returned to their respective domiciles, he encouraged her to lead the way to the nearest exit. No reason to look like a fool.

"Miserable incessant rain," Cassie huffed.

"Indeed," he offered. "Prepare yourself for a mangle of traffic."

Inexplicably pleased at the everyday familiarity of their interactions, Zeno held her arm to guide her past a few wooden boxes stacked in a narrow stairwell. As she brushed up against him he thought about the carriage ride home with her. Alone.

They were in the foyer, nearly out the front door, when they bumped into a somewhat slapdash, disheveled young man.

Cassie made introductions. "Gerald St. Cloud, Earl of Rosslyn, please meet Mr. Zeno Kennedy."

"Mr. Kennedy."

"Lord Rosslyn." Zeno made a perfunctory bow and began a silent evaluation of Cassie's brother-in-law.

"I say, Cassie, it is interesting to find you cavorting with the famous Yard man. I remember a time when one could not pick up the *Pall Mall Gazette* without his mention."

Zeno took some offense to idea of Cassie "*cavorting*" with him, but the man's references to the more sensational aspects of his job were impertinent. He decided to amend the most blatant and misleading of the remarks. "I find, with great relief, it has been some time since the yellow press has sensationalized any of my efforts. As a matter of course, Lord Rosslyn, I go to a great deal of trouble to make sure the operations I am involved in go unnoticed."

After a brief but awkward silence, Cassie changed the subject. "What finds you here at hospital today, Gerald?"

The little worm squirmed under Zeno's purposeful glare and shifted his attention to Cassie. Gerald embodied the dissipated essence of aristocratic bachelorhood. Membership requisites to this subset of peers would include plenty of late hours spent drinking, gambling, and carousing with fallen women.

"Lady Evelyn asked me if I would drop off the donations already collected from the upcoming charity ball—cheques from those not in town, but still kind enough to send alms. Guilt money flowing in from the hinterlands."

The young earl held up a thick envelope tied with ribbon. "Speaking of which, Cassie, you do still plan on attending? The ball is set to be quite the gala event, an absolute crush. Pity Martin can't make it, what with that disastrous fall at the hunt."

Her eyes widened in concern. "Is the injury that bad?"

"I'm told he'll be limping about for quite some time.

Lucky blood, he's taken himself out of the ballroom for the rest of the season." A devilish grin animated his face. "All the swells will be there: Hingham, Hicks-Beach, Upton—do tell me you'll attend, Cassie."

A blast of chill air swept through the foyer. Zeno mulled the familiar names over. Andrew Hingham, otherwise known as Lord Delamere. Hicks-Beach, Upton, and the man standing directly in front of them, Gerald St. Cloud.

Well, well. The Bloody Four, indeed.

"I escort Miss Adriana Templeton and her aunt to the ball, but I know they would be delighted to have you join. Plenty of room in the carriage." Gerald's gaze shifted to Zeno. "I have a new town coach and four—like to show them off as much as possible."

Quite out of his control, Zeno's jaw clenched. A picture of Gerald, eye blackened and cheek bruised, came to mind. A disturbing overreaction when one considered he and Mrs. St. Cloud were so recently acquainted.

He took in a slow, deep breath as the two St. Clouds neared the end of pleasantries.

"I will keep your offer in mind, Gerald. I do expect word from Rob shortly. If he can't make it up from Muirfield I will send a message on to Rosslyn House."

"I very much hope to hear from you." The raised brows and lowered chin gave the young earl a wistful look. Zeno thought about a new look for his lip. Split and bloody.

"Well then, good to see you, Cassie. You will forever remain my dear sister-in-law."

"You are very kind, Gerald. You must know that I, likewise, set great store in our friendship."

"Mr. Kennedy." His voice curt, the earl added a dismissive nod.

Zeno returned the sentiment. "Lord Rosslyn."

The heavy rain and underground rail construction conspired to make their simple commute home a miserable slog across town. London streets were in a constant state of flux, what with the Underground expansion and electrical cables laid out in street gutters. On days like today, it could easily take the better part of an hour to transect the city.

The *rat-a-tat* of rain, though calmative, did not dispel a chill in the air. From their brief encounter at the orphanage, he gleaned enough to surmise Cassie knew the Bloody Four as social acquaintances. He wondered if now would be a good time to broach the subject of Gerald St. Cloud with her. During their ride in the park, all that charm school business had knocked him off his game. Zeno settled into his seat, unable to stop staring at her. Not unhappily, she appeared to return his interest.

"Do you dance, Mr. Kennedy?"

"I try to avoid it whenever possible, Mrs. St. Cloud."

She studied him with a beguiling half smile, just the barest ends of a superbly sensuous mouth turned up in quizzical amusement. "I take that to mean you do dance, but perhaps only in the course of duty. When it is forced upon you?"

She made him feel as silly as that exhaustive, tedious brother-in-law of hers. Zeno no longer tried to feign indifference toward the attractive widow, particularly since he could not seem to tear his gaze away.

He exhaled a loud sigh. "Women take pleasure dressing in evening gowns, being waltzed about a ballroom and whispering tittle-tattle." He loosened his cravat. "Men, on the other hand, must endure high-pointed collars, feet crushed by dainty toes—and tittle-tattle."

She pressed her lips together and formed a dimple. "The only reason I ask is I am quite sure my brother will wire back and beg off at the eleventh hour. And frankly, I've not much time. The ball is tomorrow evening, you see . . ."

Her conversation faded, accompanied by a wistful, resigned shrug. "I suppose I could always tag along with Gerald and Miss Templeton."

He contemplated the idea of escorting her to the ball. On the yea side, she provided perfect cover. He could observe the Bloody Four unawares in their milieu, take note of their friends and associates. As for the nay?

Zeno listened absently to the pattering of rain on the carriage roof. The woman frazzled him at times. Especially when she bit her lower lip and let it slip out from under pearl white teeth. Like now.

"Mrs. St. Cloud. Do you wish for me to escort you to the *crush* of the season?"

Her gaze slipped away, then back again. She added a nod.

"Please accept my offer of escort, as long as my company brings you greater happiness than the attentions of Lord Rosslyn."

"It brings me a great deal more happiness, Mr. Kennedy." The sparkle in her eyes so beguiled him, he allowed his smile to widen.

"I believe we have an engagement, madam."

*   *   *

HIS BOSS CAUGHT up with Zeno in the corridor, moments before their appointment with the home secretary.

"Here, read this, damn you." Melville passed the wire message over. "Explain how this message, sent from the *Clan na Gael*, gets into the hands of one of your suspected subversives, namely Hicks-Beach." Melville couldn't suppress a grin.

Zeno read the deciphered message dated a week prior.

> BE ADVISED EAGLE HAS LANDED STOP
> AWAIT DELIVERY INSTRUCTIONS STOP
> LE CARON

Zeno sucked in a breath through clenched teeth. Concrete confirmation of his hypothesis. The eagle reference had to refer to a shipment of dynamite sent by Irish Americans. He doused a momentary surge of excitement with a heap of skepticism. "A coded message meant for anarchists ends up in the hands of a Home Office appointee. How exactly did we come by this?"

Melville lowered his voice. "Shall we say it was misappropriated off Hicks-Beach's desk by a most diligent interoffice mole?"

Zeno reread the wire. The shipment could arrive in London any day now. "Careless of him. I say we place a permanent tail on James Hicks-Beach."

"Ahead of you for once, Kennedy. He may well have changed sides. In league with a radical Irish contingent."

"Let me guess . . ." Zeno returned the scrap of paper. "Funded or even led by Delamere."

His boss wore a gleam in his eye as he opened the door. "After you."

Zeno and Melville entered the home secretary's stately office and traveled a length of polished wood floor. A staunch figure peered out a set of mullioned windows. Charles Albert Hancock, Earl of Castlemaine, stood with hands clasped behind his back. Everything about the picture might have impressed on some other occasion. But not this night.

A white-hot vein of lightning flashed in the distance an gray clouds tumbled low over the building tops of the city. "Another storm front coming in." Castlemaine barely turned his head to acknowledge them. "Would you be so kind as to close the door, Mister—?"

"Kennedy," Zeno offered.

"Ah yes, Mr. Kennedy. The door, please."

While Zeno dutifully secured the home secretary's office, Melville got straight to the point. "Plainly put, Castlemaine, you're compromised. Don't bother to ask how we know or deny the events of Tuesday last. No doubt Delamere has already asked for your help with the latest Home Rule Bill."

Melville's pause in speech was punctuated by a low rumble of thunder. The home secretary continued to stare out into the evening cityscape. Lamplighters were about. Even from where Zeno stood he could see a number of flickering streetlamps.

"Delay the bill and five thousand each." The stone-faced Castlemaine blinked.

Zeno stepped forward. "We need you to confirm the names of your assailants."

Castlemaine exhaled a raspy sigh. "George Upton and Gerald St. Cloud roughed me up. Delamere stood nearby. There was a fourth man in the shadows."

"We believe the fourth man to be James Hicks-Beach." Zeno added.

"A hopeless, indolent lot of peerage. But I am quite sure they are prepared to vigorously bear witness against me, should I ignore their demands." Castlemaine wrinkled his brow. "Hicks-Beach, you say?"

"And their terms?" Melville asked.

"The money, in their hands, by the end of the week, or the story gets leaked to every newspaper and gossip sheet in the city. As a member of the House of Lords, Delamere will press for a formal inquiry."

Zeno jumped in. "Do you have anything in writing? Amounts, bank account numbers?"

Castlemaine faced them, the evidence of his recent debacle written across his face. Dark bruising, healed-over cuts, scrapes to the chin, cheek, and under eye. The home secretary pointed to a folded paper on the expansive, ebony-lacquered desk.

Zeno scooped up the proof of extortion. A single account number and a fabricated name. He passed the note over to his boss.

Castlemaine looked beaten, but not necessarily down for the count. Much sought after for his governance and his abilities as a lawmaker, it would be a shame to see his appointment as home secretary withdrawn. "We'd prefer Hicks-Beach carry on here at the Home Office."

Castlemaine raised a brow. "You mean to use him? Always been a nervous sort of chap. Hard to believe he has the pluck to be a traitor."

Melville folded up the note. "We're going to let this play out. See where your timid little mouse may lead us."

A steely glint flashed in the home secretary's eyes. "All right then, business as usual. What do you need me to do?"

A strong rhythm thumped inside Zeno's chest. They were about to make Castlemaine a straightforward offer. Cooperate with Scotland Yard, help them draw the net around Delamere and his anarchist factions, and Melville was prepared to do everything in his power to see Castlemaine continue on as head. Turn them down and he'd have to take his chances with that grubby lot of peerage.

It was a proposition fraught with pitfalls. For one thing, Castlemaine was their boss. The Home Office was in charge of domestic security for all of England. The man himself allocated their budget. Christ, he'd hired Melville to head up Special Branch.

The home secretary scrutinized Zeno, then Melville. "So, William, whose side are your men on?"

Melville pushed his chin forward. "Yours, Albert."

STANDING BESIDE THE fireplace in his study, Zeno sipped on a dram of whiskey and crumpled the wire message. The royal family would be summering on the Isle of

Wight. A coded communiqué from the Home Office. The handwritten scrawl from Melville at the bottom clinched it.

The game is on

He tossed the missive onto glowing red hearth coals and watched the ball of paper turn to ash. So, Castlemaine had made his decision. He would trust in Scotland Yard for the time being. With the man's help, they would surely net Delamere and his co-conspirators. If all went well, Melville had assured the home secretary his embarrassment would be forgotten.

Zeno shifted his musings to a new preoccupation: the upcoming charity ball and Cassandra St. Cloud. As it turned out she was the perfect cover, but he wondered, frankly, how much sleuthing he would get done as the announced escort to the distracting young widow.

He had done his best to keep his name out of the yellow press these past few years, but like it or not, his legacy had grown. Even if a person did not recognize the face, they often remembered his name. On the plus side, the fact that he was known to Delamere and the others put the press on. The dynamite had arrived in country and was most likely in transport to London. The explosives would quickly be readied for their next act of mayhem. Mistakes were often made when the heat was turned up.

This was a dangerous game he flirted with—and it included the unsuspecting lady. He inhaled a deep breath and exhaled slowly. Perhaps he might make time for a waltz.

"Oh, Mr. Kennedy, you must come quickly!"

Wrenched from his musings, Zeno pivoted toward the frenzied ramblings of his intrusive housekeeper.

"My word, Mr. Kennedy, but I do believe that our Mrs. St. Cloud smokes cigars!" Mrs. Woolsley herded him to the rear window of the study so he might witness his neighbor *in actu*.

Alma seemed inordinately pleased by the sight. "Oh, I must confess, sir, I rather envy her."

"Envy, Mrs. Woolsley? Try your best to liberate the constant, unadventurous male in me by elucidating further."

"The lady lives a life the likes of which we married women can only dream about. No one to answer to. Come and go as you please." Alma paused for a sigh. "I think the cheroot, sir, is a harmless indulgence, and a symbol, is it not, of her independence?"

Zeno tore his gaze away from Cassandra long enough to witness his housekeeper's eyes glisten with admiration.

"Do you have these kinds of frank discussions with Mr. Woolsley?" Alma's husband ran the mews stables for a duke who lived in Belgrave Square. Their children were all grown, and the middle-aged couple occupied the comfortable flat above the carriage housing.

"Oh, Mr. Woolsley doesn't pay any attention to what I say, Mr. Kennedy. For the last year, he's occupied himself with his corns and bunions . . . mostly." Alma adjusted her apron and patted down the wilder wisps of gray hair. "I do believe it is rather painful for him, sir."

Zeno grunted his reply. People often provided him with the most startling confessions and enigmatic facts. There were times, frankly, when he wished they would not.

∞ Chapter Six

After several puffs, Cassie snuffed out the cigar. She had a bath waiting. "Oscar, Psyche." The dogs followed her into the house and up the stairs. She undressed with the help of her maid and stepped out of her petticoats.

"Could you bring me my wrapper?" She sat down at the dressing table.

Cécile slipped the robe onto Cassie's shoulders and unpinned her hair. Separating tangled locks, her young servant brushed with long strokes to encourage shine. "Will you be riding tomorrow, madame?"

"I believe so. The storm seems well past."

Her young maid lifted a pretty brow. "Monsieur Kennedy, he is quite virile, no?" Cécile's English was improving by the day.

Cassie met her eyes through the vanity mirror. "Do you think so?"

"I saw him briefly—just a peek, but he is very—" The little maid shrugged her shoulders. *"Très beau, oui?"*

Cassie grinned. *"Mais oui."* Cécile twisted her hair into

a loose knot and tied it with a ribbon. "There, madame, you are ready for your bath."

Her favorite room in the house was her studio, with its tall windows and ethereal light. But the next, most wonderful room had to be the tiled bath adjacent to her bedroom.

Vapors of steam rose from the claw-footed tub, partially fogging the mirror above the pedestal sink. Cassie stepped into the bath and caught a misty reflection of her nude body. She paused to make a brief appraisal of her figure. Plump breasts, pleasing enough in shape. Turning sideways she noted their upward curve and rosy-beige tips. She cupped their roundness with her hands.

Sinking into the bath up to her chin, she lay back against the smooth slope of the tub. She closed her eyes and inhaled the spicy, restorative scents skimming the water's surface. Carnation oil and Epsom salts. Cassie smiled at her pretty French maid, who took more of an interest in styling hair or perfuming baths than dusting.

She changed the subject of her thoughts to a newly stretched blank canvas that rested on an easel downstairs. An image had begun to form in her mind, one which called rather persistently for the touch of her brush. She envisaged the tableau with a woman she thought . . . or perhaps a male model?

Her reverie drifted to the enigmatic gentleman next door. Could he be at home? There were times when she experienced a squeaking of floorboards and the slightest tremble beneath her feet. Was he pacing in his study? The idea of him striding up and down seemed to fit, for he struck her as a brooding, contemplative fellow.

And that fascinating locked door on the second floor. It must adjoin Mr. Kennedy's residence, where else could it go?

She plunged a sea sponge underwater and conjured an image of a naked Yard man. Would he have much body hair? Yes, she would give him some. The artist in her sprinkled a light dusting across his chest and a narrow trail of fuzz down a muscled torso.

Cassie squeezed the sponge. She had made a promise to herself. No involvements with men. None. Least of all with one's neighbor.

What would happen if she decided she didn't like Mr. Kennedy in the least—loathed him in fact? He would still live next door. Worse yet, he was her landlord.

She sighed. This afternoon in the carriage, she'd practically thrown herself at him, asking him quite directly to escort her to a charity ball. No doubt he thought her a wanton and would try to take advantage.

Come to think of it, he had asked a number of rather personal questions about Gerald. Questions she found to be somewhat intrusive. She wondered if this was Yard man behavior—meddling and rather brash about it.

Cassie bit her lower lip.

She recalled the much more pleasant gallop with Mr. Kennedy down Rotten Row and her awkward dismount from Daisy. Falling against his body, she had brushed up against a hard bulge.

Cassie moistened her lips. She had to admit, she was

curious. One button at a time, she freed the beast inside those breeches. After all, she was no blushing virgin, she knew how to handle a large, twitching—

Or did she? Nearly two years had passed since she had lain with her husband. Good God. Sitting up straight, she picked up the waterlogged sponge and scrubbed.

She remembered her ride with Mr. Kennedy in the morning. Would it be possible to look him in the eye without blushing?

ZENO CONTEMPLATED HIS most recent observation of Mrs. St. Cloud's alarming secret behavior as he urged his mount into an easy canter alongside the provocative young widow. He had clearly seen her from the rear window of his study. She sat on a painted iron bench in the garden puffing away on a good-sized cheroot. Might she prove to be one of those shameless modern women of independent means who thought the rules did not apply to them? Oddly enough, he found the idea enormously attractive.

Certainly, her flagrant disregard for social norms could lead to odd affiliations and causes. A liberated woman might easily fall in with a radical group of anarchist sympathizers. But thus far he could find no evidence to connect her to the Bloody Four, other than she happened to be an unfortunate relation to Gerald St. Cloud.

Besides, he found her . . . tempting.

He adjusted his reins and exhaled. Oh yes, Mrs. St. Cloud was quite emphatically the cause of his recent carnal unrest. Last night he had entertained the idea of playing rock-a-bed with his enchanting new neighbor. In his fantasy, she wore nothing but a seductive smile.

Now, the morning after such lurid imaginings, he stole glances at her like a besotted schoolboy.

She rode pleasantly alongside him all morning without the exchange of many words. He very much liked that about her. She could be pensive and did not feel the need to fill up the silence with frivolous chitchat.

Not until they turned the horses for home and the mews did Zeno ask for details regarding their evening's engagement. Once he noted the Stanfields' address, and they agreed upon a time, the conversation turned to an innocent enough discussion on the joys and pitfalls of jumping hedgerows in the country.

"When I am at home, I prefer to ride astride, in breeches and top boots."

"Why does that not surprise me in the least?" Zeno thought he could easily fall into reckless mischief with his pretty neighbor. "I am quite sure it won't be long before women will be sporting breeches as regalia on their way to cast their votes at the poll."

"We live in challenging times, Mr. Kennedy. There is a small window open for women to gain some long sought-after liberties. To start with, better legal recognition in the shape of more equitable property rights and divorce legislation."

She turned her head from the long stretch of track ahead, eager, it seemed to him, to appraise his reaction to her statement.

"You will be pleased to know, Mrs. St. Cloud, that I am sympathetic to many of the issues attached to women's suffrage."

"Be sure to mention that to my mother, should you ever meet and wish to impress."

"Two suffragettes in one family. My additional sympathies to your father, madam."

He found her outburst of laughter immensely gratifying.

"Mother does wield considerable influence over both my father and brothers." She assessed him with a look of resignation. "And there are a few alarming facts about my family I suppose you should be warned about."

"Yes, pray tell, Mrs. St. Cloud. How are you prepared to shock me?"

"To begin with, both my parents are physicians, and what a pair they are, Mr. Kennedy. Father is chief of medicine at St. James Hospital, and my mother has forged a specialty for herself in the area of women's health. Primarily, she doctors to wealthy women and prostitutes."

When he raised a brow, she paused. "On the less controversial side, several years ago, Father got himself appointed royal physician. He is often at Windsor and will soon be called to either Balmoral or Osborne House. Nowadays, we rarely see him in the summer months." She nodded his way. "You most certainly know better than I where Victoria plans to summer this year?"

"Top secret, I'm afraid, until she is safely ensconced in one of the royal family's resort cottages."

She smiled at the understatement. "Under normal

circumstances, I suppose we would be largely ignored as part of the new emerging professional class of England. But this royal physician business and Mother's regular testimony to special committees of Parliament regarding women's legal rights makes us a rather unusual clan." She swept a teasing, devilish gaze his way. "I'm afraid I come from a shockingly progressive family, sir."

Zeno's brain ticked off the security files of personnel serving the royal family. "That would mean your maiden name is Erskine."

Her wide-eyed reaction prompted a grin.

"Your father is Dr. Henry Jocelyn Erskine, head of surgical medicine at St. James. Landed gentry. I believe there is a manor in Surrey. Married to Dr. Katherine Olivia Erskine, New Hospital for Women. As I recall, your mother took her degree in America, a female medical college in Boston?"

"You do very detailed work at Scotland Yard, Mr. Kennedy."

Cassie halted her horse. She appeared to view him with a modicum of admiration, and more than a touch of suspicion. Until today, he had sensed some reticence on her part with regards to disclosing much about her personal affairs. Now he feared he may have divulged too much—she might shut him out again.

How could he ease her mind? Perhaps he might explain—let the cat out of the bag. Frankly, it was textbook—there was no better way to gain a person's trust than to share sensitive information. "Can you keep a secret, Cassie?"

She squared her shoulders. "Actually, I am rather excellent with secrets, having been raised the only female child amongst four brothers. They constantly swore me to silence over their exploits and misadventures. I am no snitch baby."

He leaned forward in his saddle and adjusted the reins. "If I am not mistaken, your father is soon to be knighted. An appointment to the Order of the Grand Cross."

When her mouth dropped open he could not restrain a chuckle. "The only reason I manage to remember any of it is—" Zeno lifted his hat, enough to scratch his head. "I must have recently updated his vetting report, most certainly brought on by the proposed knighthood." He shot her a stern look. "This is very much a test of our friendship. You may not breathe a word of the recognition to your family."

A smile curled the ends of her mouth. "You called me Cassie."

She amused him. So few women did. Irksome as it was, the combination of progressive suffragette and bohemian artist turned out to be surprisingly attractive. "I shall take that to mean my charm quotient is improving."

She tilted her head in mock contemplation. "Exponentially, Zak."

HER LIMBS FELT a bit like rubber. After a sweat in the steam room of the Water Palace, a dip in the cool vapor plunge, and a Turkish massage, she was happy to let Mother set the pace for the first leg of their walk down Regent Street.

"Your father and I are dining with the Burnsides to-night. Henrietta will offer up the usual tasteless leg of beef and fillets of cod. I intend to shovel in tarts and tea sandwiches like a dockworker so I might appear the daintiest of eaters this evening."

"I thought you'd given up on the Burnsides after he withdrew his hospital donation?"

"My hero twisted his arm a bit and the man doubled his contribution, as well as a donation for the Women's Franchise League."

"I take it you and Emmeline still scheme to form some kind of women's union?"

"Soon, darling. And we have both agreed to name our daughters as charter members."

Cassie grinned. "I shall wield my placard proudly."

At the corner of St. James Square, they turned down a small lane of eateries and entered Patisserie Madeline.

"Of course, if we ever get the movement launched, it will be thanks to men like Mr. Pankhurst and Dr. Erskine. Did I ever express to my children how attractive that makes your father?"

"I can't fathom how any of us missed the fact. You bore him four sons and a daughter."

Olivia plopped herself down at a small table in the courtyard garden and sighed. "Every time I consider washing my hands of the man he reels me back in with some act of chivalry or romantic devilment."

Cassie perused the elegant bill of fare. "Shall we order the full tea?"

"Perfect." Mother set her menu aside.

After several steaming cups of Earl Grey, a number of petite sandwiches, a lemon-iced scone and a chocolate cream tart, discussion moved to one of Olivia Erskine's favorite topics.

"Tell me what form of contraception you plan to use, dear." She poured a last half cup for each of them. "Now that you're away from that Mayfair crowd and living in a stylish new row house."

Cassie dabbed a napkin at the corners of her mouth. "None of my friends are as fortunate as I am to have a mother who promotes promiscuity as well as pregnancy prevention."

"Should you ever decide to live as boldly as you paint—" Olivia winked. "I suspect life will become quite an adventure for you."

She fought the urge to grin like a Cheshire cat. "Since you assume I will take a lover, what does the doctor advise in the way of condoms?"

A tingle of anticipation rushed through her body as she experienced a perfectly delicious, wicked thought. Now that she was living on her own, an amorous intrigue might be just the thing. Something discreet but rather daring. She had made a promise to herself, no gentlemen callers—but what of a lover? Cassie caught her breath. A liaison without the usual social obligations and entanglements. Something primal and passionate. The very idea caused her toes to curl.

And she had the perfect man in mind.

*   *   *

ZENO FOUND A spot behind a long, floppy ear and scratched. The lumbering hound's tail whipped a slow beat against this pant leg.

"Say hello to Alfred. Scotland Yard's first and only canine operative." Archibald Bruce exhaled a warm fog of air onto wireframe spectacles and wiped the lenses with a pocket square. "Watch your shoes, he's a drooler."

Zeno very much liked Archie Bruce, the Yard's new director of the crime laboratory. Young Mr. Bruce was a certifiable genius when it came to all forms of chemistry, which included a special knowledge of explosive materials. But the most extraordinary thing about Arch, without a doubt, was how dangerous he was. He quite liked to blow things up.

Archie was on loan to Special Branch from his teaching position at Oxford, and his hire had taken the approval of a hefty budget variance. As a condition of contract, the young scientist had expanded his footage requirement for lab space from their proposed unused corner of Number 4 Whitehall to nearly an entire floor. In addition to real estate, an exhaustive list of expensive equipment and trained technicians had been forwarded on from Melville to Castlemaine, and the headman for Britain's security had given Mr. Bruce little argument.

Having suffered under budget restraints for years, Zeno rejoiced when word came down from the Home Office that funding had been approved for the new forensics laboratory. This morning, he and Rafe Lewis enjoyed a tour of yet another adjunct to the Yard's science facility in Whitehall. An old dry dock, located east of town, had been reconfigured into a remote bomb-testing site. With the Thames Ironworks as their closest neighbor, the occasional dynamite blast would hardly be noticed.

He and Rafe had spent most of the morning with Arch, viewing his latest invention, a lead lockbox so heavy it took a block and tackle to lift. The simple invention was designed to be a kind of bomb safe for the detonation of dynamite. The "black box," as Archie called it, was just weeks away from final testing.

And to detect trace amounts of nitroglycerin, there was Alfred.

"We've trained him to alert to the scent of diatomaceous earth and sodium carbonate as well as nitro."

Since dynamite was often packed and shipped in a combination of wood shavings and wood straw, Arch had suggested the agents scour the floors of warehouses under surveillance and collect samples of packing crate materials.

In the dead of night, he and Rafe had gathered more than thirty samples. Now it was up to Alfred to sniff out any chemical residue.

"Set them up along the tables and let's see if Alfred can snuffle out a clue for us," Arch instructed his technicians, who placed the bags in a neat lineup along both sides of two long tables. He nodded to Zeno. "Remove the leash."

The long-eared hound ambled over and ran his nose along the edge and around the back of the first table. Nothing.

They held their breath as the old boy moved to the second table. Upon reaching the fourth bag from the end, the dog instantly parked himself on the spot. "*Wr-r-ughh-ruff.*"

Rafe whooped. "Plain sailing, aye, Alfred?"

Zeno grinned. Rafe's exuberance echoed his gregarious, cheerful nature. The man was also loyal to a fault—to Zeno and Scotland Yard. Rafe was a fierce fighter, and a good man to have by your side when cornered by anarchists. One would never suspect he hailed from the ancient earldom of St. Aldwyn.

"What's the tag read?" Zeno edged forward.

Arch picked up the bag. "Number Thirty-three Hartley Warehouse, Salthouse Dock."

Zeno gave the Yard dog a pat on the head. "We may have caught a break."

Up on all fours, Alfred plodded around the table and sat beside another bag.

Rafe shot Archie a look of concern. "What's he after now?"

The forensics man grinned. "He's alerting to the presence of secondary chemicals. Check the tags on the samples. You will find they are from different areas of the same warehouse. His nose is unbelievably sensitive."

Zeno raised a brow. "Indeed."

So far, the few suspected drop sites they had placed under surveillance had proved disappointing. All their leads were run down or dry. But if they could identify the warehouse the dynamite had been stored in, there might be a chance to track the explosives to the dynamiters themselves.

This entire smuggling operation had begun as a kind of

beating of the brush by Zeno and the small staff of agents assigned to Special Irish Branch. The wire confiscated from the desk of Hicks-Beach had used the code word *eagle*. Which meant a large shipment of American-made dynamite had found its way in country.

Alfred's nose went a long way to confirm it.

"Tests aren't complete as yet, but you'll be glad to know we are close to confirmation on the Underground bombing. The blast was not caused by your Irish American dynamite." Zeno guessed Archie's grin had something to do with the look of relief on his face. "The chemical analysis confirms the diatomite is from Northern Germany, likely made into anarchist bombs in France. Several bombs failed to explode, leaving us to believe there was an installation error. The dynamite may have been inadvertently set off before the explosive was rigged properly, one of the anarchists strikes a match and—"

"*Ka-boom.*" Rafe's usual exuberant grin was grim. Whether they were militant Irish Nationalists or a rogue bunch of continental anarchists, dynamiters prowled the city, particularly the Underground. Cloaked figures concealed orb-shaped bombs with sizzling fuses, faceless shadow players in every Special Branch agent's nightmares.

Zeno exhaled a deep breath and with it all the tension he had carried since the Underground explosion. Months ago, he had proposed an offensive operation to Melville. The gambit carried with it huge risks, but an even greater payoff, since the ruse would likely flush out the dynamiters.

Scotland Yard would arrange to have a large quantity of dynamite made available in America. A proposed "stolen shipment" of something in the nature of seven hundred and fifty pounds of explosives, up for sale by international mercenaries. In actuality, these arms dealers would be agents who worked for Special Branch. Their men would offer it up and see if the bastards took the bait.

Melville would be kept informed—*ears only*, no paper trail. If anything went wrong—God forbid the bombers *used* the dynamite Scotland Yard supplied—he would have total deniability. They called the plan "Operation Snuffbox" to remind themselves the risky undertaking could never be allowed to blow up in their faces.

Even as one nagging concern eased, his caseload remained threefold. Reel in Delamere and his Bloody Four; trace the shipment of explosives; and attend the Stanfield Charity ball.

He mulled over his case and found Mrs. St. Cloud to be the most combustible of all.

∞ Chapter Seven

Zeno hadn't dressed for a formal affair in years. Tails, white tie, white gloves. Starched collars were higher and more uncomfortable than ever. Good God, he felt as stiff as a board already. On first attempt, he wrinkled his tie irreparably.

Luckily, he had additional crisply pressed white cravats in the drawer and his housekeeper stationed outside his dressing room. "I need you in here this minute, Mrs. Woolsley."

Alma proved to be wonderfully accomplished at the job, when in just a few moments a smart bow materialized at his neck.

"There. Very handsome indeed, sir." She beamed.

He lowered his chin. "Any observations of interest regarding our new resident, Mrs. Woolsley?"

"Not much activity today, other than a florist delivery this afternoon."

There it went again, a flip-flop in his chest and an uncontrollable desire to know who sent Mrs. St. Cloud flowers. This, categorically, was none of his business. But would it be of interest to Scotland Yard? Possibly. He gathered his opera hat and several pairs of white gloves and walked from Number 11 to Number 10.

Zeno counted every chime of the clock as he waited at the bottom of the narrow, curved stairway in the foyer. He bounced a bit on his toes and took in the surroundings. A gleaming pedestal table stood unadorned, tucked into the turn of the stairwell. He inhaled the faint scent of beeswax. A large bouquet of flowers would do nicely there. So where were the posies that had been delivered today?

The rustle of her skirts snapped him to attention. His gaze lingered over the very picture of elegance as she made her descent. It came to him as a kind of revelation. It was the noticeable lack of frills and lace in Mrs. St. Cloud's wardrobe that made her style so becoming.

Zeno swallowed. The skirt of her gown was an iridescent neutral gray that shifted in subtle ways as she moved, from pale violet to green and crimson.

Delicate black velvet sleeves rested off bare shoulders. The pristine white bodice appeared to be as stiff as a tuxedo shirt, and featured a row of elegant cut-crystal buttons running from the waist to bosom. The plunging décolleté accentuated high, rounded breasts, braced enticingly within the tight-fitted bodice. Zeno's gaze lingered for a moment.

"Good evening, Mr. Kennedy."

Rather than stammer a greeting, he nodded a polite bow. She picked up a boutonniere from the console table in the entryway. A white rosebud wrapped partially in a silver leaf. It was exquisite, just like her. A swath of black velvet swept around her waist and hips, finishing in a butterfly bow above the bustle at her back.

"This dress is not from a London modiste."

She turned. "No, it's from a couturier in Paris."

"It changes color." Zeno pointed to the narrow shirred skirt.

Cassie seemed pleased and amused at his interest. "The fabric is silvered moiré taffeta." Moving closer, she touched his chest. She could have no idea how her proximity affected him. Her scents permeated his senses— violets from her bath soap and that wonderful French perfume. She removed the pin from the boutonniere and took hold of his lapel.

Good God, he had forgotten flowers. How had this happened? "In keeping with my woeful lack of charm, I seem to have forgotten a corsage of some kind."

She stood inches away, her mouth in a bow and brow wrinkled in concentration. "I am always at a loss as to where to put a corsage, Mr. Kennedy. They often ruin the effect of the dress and droop sadly before evening's end. It occurred to me, though, that you might need one of these." She tilted her head to check the effect of her work. "A tuxedo suits you. And now that you have a flower on your lapel, I believe you are ready for a ball."

She looked into his eyes and smiled. A moment savored before he held out an arm. "Shall we betake ourselves to Grosvenor Square?"

Outside in the brisk night air, Zeno drew in a deep a breath and collected his wits about him. Small cut crystals fastened throughout the back of her hair sparkled in the flickering light of the streetlamps. She gathered her skirts to board the carriage. "You will save me a waltz tonight, as compensation for several tedious hours of Evelyn Stanfield's ball," he said.

Her feigned glare and arched brow might have worked with other men. "Goodness. For a moment I imagined a demand from my late husband."

"You heard correctly, Cassandra. I insist on a waltz as payment for an entire evening spent with the *haut noblesse*."

"I believe you warned me quite emphatically you fight shy of dancing, did you not?"

His eyes wrinkled. "Possibly. But not with you." He caught a flicker of light in her eye. Zeno drew in a long breath before he stepped into the coach. Cassandra St. Cloud could not be a more invigorating partner.

LORD AND LADY Stanfield were more than pleased to greet them both; in fact, they were effusive. Zeno made a concerted effort not to smirk when Lady Evelyn gushed over his unexpected attendance. His appearance, she claimed with great enthusiasm, made it a certainty the Stanfield ball would be the talk of the season.

Zeno bobbed a bow and humbly demurred. As expected, his sensationalized crime solving exploits continued to haunt him. He was a diversion, in the same way they were titillated over the Duke of Ancaster and his very public affair with actress-courtesan Perdita Savile.

With a smile plastered on his face, he endured the rest of the reception line as the beautiful Cassandra St. Cloud's most unusual escort.

She tucked her arm in his. He took a long, appreciative glance at the lovely woman by his side. Indeed, she was stunning. This was the second time in so many days he wondered what she might look like in nothing at all. "You are entirely too distracting."

"What was that, Zak?"

He exhaled. "I'm having wicked thoughts about you."

She pressed sensuous lips together and a dimple emerged.

Halfway down the grand staircase he halted their descent. "Was that charming?"

A wonderful, slinky eye roll swept over him. "In a wolfish sort of way."

Zeno brightened. "Excellent."

Entering the ballroom, he could not help but notice the raised brows and curious stares. He leaned closer. "One can almost feel the whispers in the air."

A thickset, middle-aged gentleman of jovial expression was the first to emerge from a small group nearby and catch their attention. "Lovely to see you out and about, Cassie."

"Likewise, Lord Cranbrook. Are you acquainted with Mr. Zeno Kennedy?"

Zeno nodded a bow. "My lord."

The gentleman's eyebrow raised enough to loosen his monocle. "I say, this is a rare occasion, Mr. Kennedy. I'll wager you're on a case, no doubt?"

"Nothing of much importance, Lord Cranbrook. For the moment, I am pleasantly captivated by Mrs. St. Cloud."

His lordship pivoted a bulky frame. "And is this your first soiree of the season, Cassie?"

"Yes, it does feel good to reacquaint oneself with old friends."

Across a blur of whirling dancers, Zeno focused on a youthful chap of burgeoning girth. James Hicks-Beach, if he was not mistaken. With an ear on tittle-tattle, he let his gaze follow the large man into the card room. He swept a hand through his freshly cropped hair. "Please excuse us for a moment, Lord Cranbrook. I promise to be brief." He offered Cassandra his arm, and took her for a turn around the end of the room.

"Might I have a clue as to where my name appears on your dance card?"

"I have reserved a waltz just before late supper buffet, Mr. Kennedy. Since you were gracious enough to be my escort, I believe we are expected to take refreshments together. I hope this meets with your approval."

"I shall make it my business to find you as we near the midnight hour."

"Off on a sleuth about the ball?"

"Thought I might retire to the card room—lighten a few gentlemen's pockets." He winked.

Zeno returned Cassie to Lord Cranbrook's circle of intimates. He placed her purposefully between two pleasant, mature ladies and excused himself. In the card room he made his way past several tables of whist to the larger baccarat table. Invited to join by Lord Stanfield himself, he sat down to play with a number of titled chaps, including a less-than-amicable Hicks-Beach, who was taking a turn as banker. He squared off across the table from the large gent, who made a pointed comment about Scotland Yard detectives in attendance at a ball.

Zeno did a quick shuffle and recount of his gaming chips. Hicks-Beach raised a supercilious brow. "Suspicious by trade, Mr. Kennedy?"

"The bane of my profession. Of late, I am particularly wary of seditionists." Finished stacking his counters, Zeno sat back and grinned. "Fear not, gentlemen, only bankers who finance dynamiters hang." He picked up a chip from the top of a stack. "Aid and abetment, on the other hand, will get you thirty years in Newgate gaol." He slid the gaming chip across the table. "I believe you counted wrongly, this is your money."

During periodic breaks throughout the evening, Zeno ventured forth into the ballroom just long enough to stretch his legs and check on Mrs. St. Cloud. The tiresome spectacle of insipid young girls offered up for marriage hadn't changed this season, or any season for that matter. And while he found the new chits pretty but witless, his observations regarding Mrs. St. Cloud proved unsettling.

On this particular stroll into the ballroom, he noted a rather large circle of men surrounding the attractive young widow and decided to make an appearance, stake out a bit of territorial domain for himself.

Zeno appraised his competition and determined he did not wish to politely acknowledge any of the interested men circling the pretty widow. Not yet, anyway. For now, he wanted very much to make her laugh and see her eyes sparkle. He entertained a sudden urge to stand whisper close.

She turned to him. "You wear a very distinctive cologne, or is it your shaving soap, Mr. Kennedy?"

"Blended by a chemist the name of Taylor on Bond Street—Number Seventy-four. Lime. I do hope you enjoy the scent."

"I am intrigued."

He made sure his frown was more of a tease. "Not excited or stimulated?"

Her gentle laugh and those lips so close to his cheek. Desire strummed pleasantly through his body as arousal surged lower.

"Come now, Cassie, please share the amusement with us."

SHE TIGHTENED HER lips into a rigid half smile. The familiar whine of Gerald's voice grated more than usual this evening. His reputation as a rake and his need for attention appeared undiminished. He had always flirted outrageously, even dangerously with her. On one occasion not long after her marriage, he had entered her bedchamber one evening to make an unseemly advance and a shattering confession. The earl, Gerald had informed her, was with his mistress, but as second in line, he would be more than happy to provide the Rosslyn cock *in absentia*. She had shrieked loud enough to prick up the ears of every purebred hound in Mayfair.

Her marriage to the Earl of Rosslyn had been a terrible mistake. Considered a very advantageous match, she had allowed herself to be seduced by a man who, just months after the wedding, lay in another woman's bed across town. *In absentia*. Oddly enough, that wasn't worst of it. Her ambitions to become a serious painter were also *in absentia.*

Cassie studied Gerald as he stood before her in the ballroom. The newly named Earl of Rosslyn continued to be the type of man whose attraction to a lady increased the less available she became. Cassie suspected the very presence of Zeno Kennedy, both at the orphanage and again this evening, had reinvigorated Gerald's interest.

"Thou dost love her, because thou know'st I love her." Zak whispered in her ear.

Even though she readily grasped his meaning, the intimacy of affection in the prose made her cheeks flush with heat. "Only the bard is clever enough to draw such insight from passion's folly."

He leaned closer. "In the future, please remind me to recite 'Sonnet Eighteen' for you, Cassandra."

She offered a shy smile. "One of my favorites."

He chuckled. "It's the only one I've put to memory."

She marveled at how young he looked when he allowed himself a happy, unguarded expression. "And how goes your luck at cards?"

Zeno straightened. "Middling. Up four hundred quid at the moment."

"Up is always good, is it not?"

He snorted. "Not when Lancaster is up a thousand."

She followed his gaze to a portly gentleman entering the card room. "Best be getting back."

"Don't forget our dance, *Zak*."

Several strides away, he swung around. "Quite impossible to forget you, *Cassie*."

She smiled. When he deigned to make an effort, Zeno Kennedy did not want for charm. Intuitively, she experienced a sweeping hot wind of whispered words as a second wave of gossip spread like fire through the ballroom. Well aware of how fast and loose hearsay traveled among the *très bonne société*, she braced herself for the onset of questions about and interest in her escort.

A number of well-meaning friends sidled by to inform on the celebrated intelligencer. Apparently Detective Kennedy had once been romantically tied to a woman murdered by Fenian dynamiters. An *actress*. As brows raised, Cassie did her best to take in the tattle with equal amounts of curiosity and aplomb.

Eventually, the ladies excused themselves and circled the perimeter of the dance floor. The tongue-waggers shamelessly crowded the doorway to the card room to catch a glimpse of the intriguing Mr. Kennedy, leaving Cassie to fend off the hungry wolves better known as interested gentlemen.

The most shocking part of attending a ball as a widow newly returned to society was the amorous attention of all the most eligible men of the aristocracy. These unattached gentlemen spent a great deal of time and energy chasing after married or widowed women. A favorite sport among the bachelors and ladies alike.

As the midnight hour neared, Cassie caught sight of her escort. Zeno deftly sidestepped a group of giggling ingénues and made a mad dash across the ballroom.

In a rather brilliant gesture, he reached across the circle of men and drew her, with murmured apologies, into the safety of his arms. They were on the dance floor moments after the waltz began. And he turned out to be a relaxed, skillful partner, which made it so much easier to enjoy the dance.

Cassie leaned closer. "I say we stay just long enough for a bite of dinner, then we make our excuses."

He smiled. "I cannot tell you how relieved I am to hear you say the words. What pretext might we make to Lady Stanfield?"

"Toothache?"

Sucking air through his teeth, he grimaced.

"A headache, then?"

Zeno's brow furrowed. "Yours or mine?"

"Mine."

"Front or back?"

"Well." She played along. "It started in the back and I'm afraid the little devil has worked its way forward." Cassie moved her hand from his shoulder to the side of her head. "My temples are throbbing."

A grin formed at the edges of his firm, square mouth. He paused in a turn just to smile at her. "Married with children, now *there's* a ready excuse to leave early. Check on little Rupert's case of the sniffles?"

The thought of children with this man forced a change in subject. "You dance very well, for someone who avoids it."

He drew her in close, his voice huskier. "Perhaps—" Zeno picked her up and whirled her away from a couple spiraling out of control, neatly avoiding a collision.

When she regained her footing, she grinned. "Perhaps . . . ?"

"Perhaps it is because I have you in my arms." He lengthened his stride and led her around the floor in a series of graceful turns.

She could hardly believe her ears. She tried to think back to the days before her marriage. She did not remember men being quite this . . . well, romantic. Or was it just this man?

Cassie followed every movement of his body, the power of his legs, the way he so effortlessly led her around the ballroom floor. Varying the length of his steps and the speed of his turns, he made it impossible to not appreciate the way they moved together. She no longer wanted to talk, she wanted to brush up against him and to feel the heat of his body.

She arched away to hide a shiver as she imagined them skin-to-skin. What on earth had come over her? The obvious answer to that question held her in his arms. Zeno twirled her into the center of the dance floor, where he could practice those mysterious, unpredictable charms of his.

He turned her in small circles and no longer waltzed at a respectable distance. Candlelight from the ballroom chandeliers whirled around his face. Blue eyes deepened to violet as his gaze fell to her mouth.

Cassie tilted her head and parted her lips.

Chapter Eight

From the moment they entered the supper room all eyes were upon them. Cassie paused to reacquaint herself with their instant celebrity.

Her escort steered her toward the buffet tables. "Hungry?"

"Not very. Perhaps a few small bites of something."

"I suggest we share a plate."

"Perfect." Cassie leaned in close to whisper. "Why do I feel like I'm in a display window at Harrod's?"

He picked up a delicate china plate. "If you weren't so beautiful we'd go unnoticed."

Cassie thwacked him on the arm with her fan. "Hush, you embarrass me." He snorted a chuckle as he selected hors d'oeuvres. "Besides," she huffed, "I believe most of this attention is directed at you, sir."

Their newly bestowed éclat prompted them to seek out a more private area in which to refresh themselves. Zeno found a small table to serve their purpose, situated in an alcove in the back of the room.

Between bites of this and that, she studied him with a single question in mind. "I have never kissed a man while dancing. During the last strains of our waltz together, you were about to—"

"Did you want me to kiss you, Cassie?"

"Yes."

Rather than wipe the smug little grin off his face, which she rather liked, Cassie stuffed a forkful of cucumber salad into her mouth. When she finished chewing, he leaned close, opened his mouth slightly, and brushed his lips lightly over hers. Cassie shook off a tingle. As stolen kisses go, she would have to rank it a scorcher. "I suppose now that we have kissed, we can both relax and finish our supper." Except she didn't feel relaxed. In fact, she was rather stirred up.

He snorted. "That wasn't a kiss, it was a peck."

To take her mind off his mouth and what he might do with it, Cassie picked up a small buttered sandwich. "Don't look now, but I'm afraid old friends of my parents appear to be making their way over to inspect you."

Zeno reluctantly lowered his fork.

Lord and Lady Walmer arrived at their table with effusive greetings. Respectfully, Zeno relinquished his seat to Amanda Walmer, and they all endured his lordship's desultory remarks about the pressing heat of the ballroom, and the poor quality of the food from the buffet.

"Your mother informs me that you teach watercolors to the young ladies at Miss Martin's and volunteer as an art instructor at Foundling Hospital. That's quite a schedule, my dear." Lady Walmer spoke loud enough to include any and all within shouting distance of their conversation.

"I prefer to be active, engaged in service I enjoy. It does not seem much like work, Lady Walmer."

"I should think we would be instructing orphans in more practical vocations. Trades of some kind," Lord Walmer sputtered.

Cassie raised a brow in protest. "Several of my students have already been apprenticed to artisan trades."

Zeno spoke up. "I did not realize—"

His lordship cut in. "What possible kind of trades, Cassandra?"

Cassie sighed. The man could be contentious and dubious about . . . everything. "I suggest the next time you find yourself admiring a piece of Royal Doulton, my lord, you might think of my students. For it is likely at least one or two of them hand painted the china you even now find yourself eating from."

The ill-humored man grunted. "I suppose it is a good deal better than tossing them out on the streets to become pickpockets or beggars."

"So it is, Cassie." Lady Walmer patted her hand and lowered her voice. "Do not pay any attention to Lord Walmer this evening. His lumbago causes his temperament to worsen."

From behind their small group came a voice that sent a chill down Cassie's spine. "Well, well, Mr. Kennedy, I see it took the most beautiful widow in all of London to get you back out in society."

Zeno turned at the mention of his name. "Lord Delamere."

The handsome, arrogant man spent all of three seconds with Zeno before his eyes shifted to her. "And Cassandra, was it just last week we were together?"

She hated the insinuation. As if they had been trysting. "I recall a brief meeting at the gallery, Lord Delamere." She shifted her gaze to her escort.

Zeno stepped forward. "You are acquainted with Lady Rosslyn?"

"I proposed, years ago. She refused me, I'm afraid. Took me ages to get over it." He shot Cassie one of those charming wounded looks used by flirtatious gentlemen of the beau monde. "A rather bruising rebuff, as I recall."

"Please forgive me if I'm not terribly sorry to hear it." Zeno grinned. Delamere's glare caused a further chuckle.

Impressed with Zeno's biting levity, Cassie made a point to smile at him.

Lord Delamere wisely pressed on to other matters. "Lady Walmer." He nodded a bow and turned to acknowledge Lord Walmer. "Charles, how fortunate to bump into you. I mean to engage you for a very brief conversation, if I may?"

"No more about Home Rule, Delamere. Not a lord in the House will vote for passage."

"Come, come, Charles, this won't take but a moment."

"I warn you, Lord Delamere, he's in a mood tonight," Lady Walmer toyed with a large ruby at the end of an impressive necklace of diamonds. The brilliant red gem rested just above her equally impressive cleavage.

Delamere flashed a most breathtaking smile at Lady Walmer. "I promise to return him to you unabused, madam." It seemed the man could not resist being irksome, for he returned his attentions to Cassie. "May I call on you one afternoon, Lady Rosslyn?"

Her spine stiffened. "I think not, Lord Delamere. How does one in your important political milieu ever find the time to make such inconsequential social visits?"

Delamere's gaze lingered longer than was necessary or comfortable. "I have always found you most consequential, Cassandra."

ZENO DIRECTED HIS attention after Delamere, who steered a number of high-ranking peers in the direction of the smoking terrace. Abruptly, he pivoted back toward Cassie and Lady Walmer. "Would either of you ladies enjoy a piece of cake, or perhaps more liquid refreshment?"

"Share a piece of that vanilla fluff with me, dear. And more lemonade, Mr. Kennedy."

"Lemonade for Lady Walmer, and I believe I will have—"

"I recommend the punch, not overly sweet with an excellent kick to it." Zeno winked.

Amanda snickered and Cassie smiled. "Very good, Zak."

Peering through a tiered cascade of confections on the dessert table, Zeno made a note of the young man drinking champagne. If he was not mistaken, this was the very same man described by Kitty. The fleeing victim who had knocked her down in the alley. Exquisitely handsome, with pale blue eyes—*how had she described them?*—like moonbeams?

Could this mysterious young man be an invited guest, or was he perhaps a *homme-femme*, an exclusive male prostitute? Zeno suspected an even darker entanglement.

The pretty chap could very well be an agent contracted by Lord Delamere in order to compromise government officials. Castlemaine, for one.

Zeno found Delamere more irksome than ever, especially after witnessing his flagrant attentions to Cassie. Frankly, he couldn't wait to bring charges of sedition against the Irish lord. All he needed was enough proof. He stewed momentarily over the realization that Delamere and Cassie shared a previous history together. And the man appeared to trouble her, for she had declined him permission to call on her. Zeno made a mental note to learn the details of their past involvement.

A footman approached holding a silver salver resplendent with bubbling champagne flutes. "The gentleman across the room asked me to deliver this, sir." The server nodded to a folded sheet of paper under a long-stemmed glass. Zeno pivoted to catch a glimpse of the message sender. Nothing, other than a potted palm in the corner of the supper room.

> *Third floor. Second door on the right.*
> *At the close of the dinner hour.*
> *—H-B*

Zeno slipped the note into a coat pocket and checked the time. Hicks-Beach would be waiting upstairs in twenty minutes.

He picked up a slice of cake and delivered the ladies' requests. After a number of insipid chitchats with sundry acquaintances he managed to spirit his dance partner out the French doors of the ballroom into the cool enchantment of the terrace garden.

Out in the brisk evening air, he drew in a deep a breath and removed a silver cigar case from his inside breast pocket. The safety match sparked to life, accompanied by the familiar smell of sulfur. He rotated the cheroot and took a few welcome puffs until the smoke drew easily. The tobacco soothed nerves frayed more from the tedium of socializing than the sleuthing. Pale gray tendrils drifted into the atmosphere.

Cassie tugged at his arm and he followed her to a dark corner of the balcony without protest. Silently, she maneuvered herself in front of him and bit her lower lip. He wagered he knew exactly what she wanted. "You are either desirous of me or my cigar."

He turned the mouthpiece of the stogie toward those luscious lips. "Which one is it?" Covering his hand with hers, she guided the tip into her mouth. He rolled his eyes upward. Good God. After several puffs, she lifted her gaze to meet his.

"You know about my smoking?"

His gaze met silver-gray eyes, then lowered to sensuous lips. He ached to kiss her. Soft and slow, then deeper using his tongue. And perhaps a good deal of fondling—that sweet derriere and those peachy mounds of flesh, near bursting from their bodice. Was this the moment? He stared unapologetically at her mouth and tilted his chin. "I'm afraid my informant must remain a classified source—" Softly spoken words brushed against her lips as he pulled her close.

Heavy footsteps padded along the roof above. Zeno

opened an eye. Two dark figures jumped from the mansard to the top of another house nearby.

"Rude of them to leave without a farewell," he murmured, "and they've left a nasty bit of—" A stream of dark liquid dripped onto the ground inches from where they stood. He backed Cassie away from the pooling blood, quickly piecing together the gruesome scenario.

A lifeless shape slid to a stop directly above them. The bulky object caught, by chance, on the shallow drainpipe that ran along the slate-covered overhang. In the blackness, with scant illumination at the elevation of the roofline, he barely made out the twisted silhouette of a body. He pushed Cassie farther behind him.

A lifeless arm worked its way loose and swung out over the roof ledge. Cassie's frightened gasp came from behind his shoulder. "I want you inside, this minute."

Too late. The rain catch groaned under the press of weight and collapsed. The body fell with a *whoosh* and struck the ground. Several screams were uttered from startled guests as the lifeless figure slid from the roof to the terrace floor.

He turned to Cassie and barked orders. "Find Stanfield and have him send word to Scotland Yard." He caught her hand as she turned to leave. "Tell him to send for the Criminal Investigations Department. No Peelers yet, maybe later." He did not relish a swarm of Westminster police stomping around the crime scene.

Cassie's eyes were as big as saucers, and he felt a slight tremble under his grip. "Are you all right?"

"Of course I am." She lifted her chin and gamely set off on her assignment.

Zeno recruited several gentlemen nearby to help clear the terrace. He posted them along the bank of French doors that ran along the west end of the ballroom. No need to unduly frighten the guests in attendance. An inkling of mayhem could cause mass hysteria and an exit stampede.

He opened a narrow-paned door and commandeered a young officer dressed in Cavalry regimentals to stand watch while he knelt down to do a cursory examination of the body. A gentleman of portly stature dressed in formal attire. Zeno tipped a shoulder back. "Christ." Dead eyes stared out over his shoulder into the night sky. Hicks-Beach. Blood gurgled from a deep slash across the throat, drenching the tuxedo shirt and waistcoat in a swath of crimson.

Zeno peeled back the left side of the dead man's coat and checked the inside pocket. A sterling cigarette case, with the initials *H-B*. He rocked back on his heels. The men who dropped the body were likely not the killers, but Dockland thugs paid to lift the man out of Grosvenor Square via rooftops. No, he reckoned the killer was still inside tippling a glass of bubbly before slipping away.

With this amount of blood there was bound to be at least some evidence left to find upstairs. Zeno scanned the gabled windows above. Rising from his haunches, he patted the folded note in his coat pocket. Hicks-Beach had ventured upstairs early. But why? Had there been an earlier appointment? Was he to have walked into a trap of some sort? Or had the killer seen his opportunity and made his move?

His jaw twitched. He knew exactly where to look. *Third floor. Second door on the right.*

*   *   *

CASSIE TAPPED ON the library door before peeking inside. Stanfield was last seen headed in the direction of his study, along with several of his cronies. "Past the gallery and through the library, dear."

She ventured farther inside the austere reading room. "Lord Stanfield?" Coals burned low inside a heavily screened hearth. She let her eyes adjust to the darkness before making her way quietly through the cavernous library. A spiral staircase wound its way up to the leather-bound volumes lining the upper tier. Straight ahead, dim light spilled from a partially open door, likely the way into his lordship's private den.

The mumbled speech of at least two gentlemen could be heard in the study. She raised a hand to knock but stopped herself at the last moment. "Nasty business. Nothing can be done—over with in any case." Cassie recognized Lord Delamere's voice. She peeked past the crack in the door and spied a young man she didn't recognize. He spoke softly, in low tones with an accent in French, she thought. "There will be others, as well."

"Indeed." Delamere again. She couldn't see him through the narrow opening. "Now, back out in the ballroom and make a point of enjoying yourself. Approach one of those lovely young chits in the room and have a memorable flirtation." There was a slap on the back and a rustle of movement. The two men were likely headed for the library.

She leaned a bit too close to the door and it moved

with a creak. There was nothing to do but knock. Loudly. Delamere opened the door.

"Cassandra." He quickly assessed the room behind her.

Feigning surprise, she curtsied. "Sorry to interrupt. Is Lord Stanfield with you? I have an urgent message for him."

His gaze scanned the room and returned to her. Delamere stepped closer. "What kind of message?"

He reached out to pull her into the room, but this time she was ready for him and jumped back. "I'm afraid the message is for Lord Stanfield." A rumble of men's laughter came from behind a side door, unseen until it opened. "The cognac is in here, gentlemen."

"Come now, Cassie—" Delamere urged, as they both turned toward the disturbance.

From a narrow passageway Lord Stanfield entered the library, followed by two rather inebriated acquaintances. A young doxy stood between them. The girl was wearing . . . pantaloons and a corset.

Stanfield went rigid. "Lady Rosslyn?"

Cassie listed to one side, curious. She wanted another look at the two men hiding behind Stanfield. Yes, she knew both by name, and knew their wives even better. "Lord Bridgerton." Her gaze moved from one to the other. "Sir Halladay." The young woman was more likely an upstairs maid than a paid professional.

The light-haired Halladay yanked at his cravat. "I say, this is awkward." She made a quick curtsy and turned to her host. "Lord Stanfield. Mr. Kennedy has asked me to tell you—" She hesitated.

"Yes, yes, dear, what is it?" Flush from too much wine

and—one could only assume—woman, Lord Stanfield wrinkled both brows and dipped closer. "Has there been trouble?"

She nodded. "I'm afraid there is no delicate way to put it. A dead body has been found."

The stately lord jerked upright in horror. And there were gasps from his gentlemen friends.

Stanfield pivoted. Without a single word of verbal exchange his associates removed themselves from the library along with the female companion.

From the corner of her eye, Cassie slyly observed Delamere's reaction. She noted a shift in his eyes. Nothing new there. She caught a partial glimpse of the study over his shoulder. Where was the chap she had overheard him conversing with? Firelight flickered into the corners of the room, but not a shadow of movement otherwise. No doubt the younger man was already out the window and down the lane.

Cassie returned to Stanfield. "Two men attempted to carry a man across your roof this evening. Mr. Kennedy and I witnessed the body fall out of their grasp and slide down the mansard onto the terrace. Mr. Kennedy is with the dead man now and wishes for you to send for the Criminal Investigations Department—without alarming your guests, of course."

"Yes . . . of course." First startled, then dazed, Stanfield yanked the closest bell pull. "Good God. What's the world coming to?"

Cassie stifled a powerful urge to roll her eyes. "Indeed, your lordship."

Chapter Nine

Zeno led the inspectors upstairs. As with many of the homes in Grosvenor Square, the third floor of Stanfield House accommodated a number of bedchambers. They passed through a formal sitting room in the alcove of the corridor and on to a series of guest apartments. He did not share the note he had received earlier this evening from the victim. He wanted time to study it—let the laboratory run tests. He wasn't convinced Hicks-Beach had sent the message.

The second suite on the right soon became the focus of the investigation, for it proved to be the crime scene. The room was both expansive and expensively furnished. A bold spray of crimson splashed across a gabled wall, with more evidence of murder smeared over the carpet and flooring. A single dormered window remained open, its shutters clapped from a gust of early morning air.

The investigation department's initial response was stated plain enough by Inspector Pate, a bald-headed man with a great ruff of whisker. "The most obvious scenario is the victim made his way up here for an assignation. Either with another guest or for a quick tumble with one of the maids."

Zeno waited for the inspector to wink. Ah, there it was, right on cue. While Pate voiced an inventory of the crime scene, Zeno quietly explored the adjoining dressing room and discovered a servant girl cringing in the corner. He coaxed the wild-eyed, trembling maid out of the closet, but she remained too hysterical to offer any coherent information.

There was nothing left to do but wait until she calmed herself. Eventually, they were able to wheedle something resembling a lucid story from her.

She had been sent upstairs to turn down the beds. "I heard two people enter the room." The girl stuttered. "Gentlemen, by their voices. I was about to excuse myself when I heard a bit of a tussle. Several punches were thrown, then a gasp and a gurgling noise. Gave me a chill it did, so I peeked around the dressing room door. A man stood with his back to me. His hand gripped a silver blade—dripping red. The other gent was on his knees . . ." The girl shivered, but her misty gaze never wavered. "Covered in blood he was, his throat cut, ear to ear. The poor bloke tipped to one side and over he went onto the rug." A tear dribbled down her cheek. "For the life of me all I could think was . . . we'll have to pitch the beautiful carpet." She finally broke down and sobbed. "Was it evil of me to think such a wicked, silly thought?"

The weeping maid sat on a bench at the foot of the four-poster. "People often think nonsensical things when frightened." Zeno bent down to reach her eye level. "Did you happen to get a look at the man with the knife?"

"He took out a pocket square and wrapped up the dagger." She paused for moment then shook her head. "Never got a good look, sir. I was scared—crept back into the corner you found me in."

Zeno straightened with a sigh. "Did you hear anything else?"

"The door opened and closed—at least twice. There were heavy footsteps. Men speaking in low voices." The girl looked up at him. Liquid eyes searched his face. "I'm sorry, sir."

"Don't be sorry. What's your name?"

"Maggie Rose."

"Hiding in the dressing room likely saved your life, Miss Rose." Zeno mulled over the threads of information gleaned from the servant girl and made several mental notes. After a second perusal of the bedchamber, he excused himself and returned to the ballroom with Inspector Pate.

Things appeared well in hand as guests were systematically interrogated and released by the officers on site. The names of everyone in attendance were taken, just in case the Yard had further questions later on. Little did the Stanfields realize how fortunate they were to have William Pate on the scene.

Pate turned to Zeno with a look of sympathy. "Christ, Zak. You can't get a night out without being put to work." He slapped him on the back affectionately.

"Have you called a photographer?"

The inspector grunted. "It will take a while. Can't use any of the newsboys."

"Before I debrief your men, I must first escort Lady Rosslyn home." Zeno nodded to Cassie, who stood beside Lady Stanfield.

"You're with her?" Pate raised an appreciative eyebrow. "How is it Special Branch men get all the pretty women?"

Zeno tugged a side of his mouth upward. "I think your wife and three lovely daughters would take issue with that statement."

Cassie excused herself and crossed the grand foyer. He particularly enjoyed the subtle swing of her hips, and the way her bosom quivered ever so slightly with each step. He cuffed himself mentally for such prurient thoughts. "Cassandra St. Cloud, Lady Rosslyn, may I present Inspector Pate, from the Criminal Investigation Department?"

Cassie acknowledged the detective's bow with a gracious smile, mixed with a kind of electrified nervousness. The effect was distracting, to put it mildly.

"Inspector." She nodded to Zeno and back again. "Are there any suspects as yet?

"Little hope on the horizon, Lady Rosslyn, but it is early in the game."

"Indeed," Cassie replied. "I'd say it is very early—past three in the morning."

Zeno stepped closer. "I am to make a break shortly and will see you home."

"Oh, Mr. Kennedy!" A frightful, high-pitched cry emanated from the stairwell behind them. Zeno cringed at the sight of the matronly woman and her two young charges. Overwrought and frightened by the lurid, dangerous events of the evening, the woman appeared determined to push both young ladies in front of him.

"I do hope you remember our previous acquaintance, Mr. Kennedy? Two summers ago—Lord and Lady Fitz-Maurice? We met at Culzean."

"How may I be of service, Lady Fitz-Maurice?"

The histrionic woman clasped his arm and snapped out her fan. "I can hardly express what a comfort it is to have you here, Mr. Kennedy." The fan fluttered over a plump face flushed with nervous perspiration. "I find it affects my nerves nonetheless. Imagine such terrible goings-on during a ball. Have you ever heard of such a thing?" The woman actually created a breeze with her flapping. "I don't believe you have met my nieces? Clara and Violet de Blois, may I present Zeno Augustus Kennedy?"

He turned to the young ladies, a debutante version of Tweedledum and Tweedledee, though not quite as round. "Very pleased to meet you both. Miss de Blois." He kissed the offered hand of each young lady. "And yet another lovely Miss de Blois."

"Mr. Kennedy is related to of one Scotland's finest, the Earl of Cassilis, Sir Thomas Angus Kennedy." Lady Fitz-Maurice winked at her charges.

Zeno demurred. "A poor relation, I'm afraid."

Cassie stepped close and murmured in his ear. "One certainly can be charming when one makes an effort." She took his arm and nodded to the ladies. "It's been a frightfully long night, has it not? And Mr. Kennedy has been kind enough to insist on seeing me home."

Without further delay, Zeno and Cassie slipped out of the ballroom and into his brougham. Once the carriage turned out of the square, they both exhaled a sigh of relief.

"I don't know which is worse—murder in an upstairs bedchamber, or Lady Fitz-Maurice." Zeno tugged on his tie and loosed his collar.

Across the cabin, mysterious silver eyes sparkled. "Oh, I don't know—how about Lord Delamere in the study having a slap on the back and a toast with a foreign young man? 'Nasty business. Cheers anyway. Lay low—there's work yet to be done.'"

Zeno settled his gaze on her sly, devilish grin. "Sleuthing, Cassandra?"

She straightened her gown and returned his stare. "I thought to find Stanfield in the library, not Lord Delamere."

"Begin—" Zeno leaned forward. "At the beginning."

"After I left you on the terrace, I asked after Lord Stanfield and was directed to the library, which I found to be dark and empty. Stanfield's study, however, was quite occupied and the door ajar—a crack. Enough so I could overhear the conversation between two gentlemen. As I approached the study I recognized Lord Delamere's voice. He congratulated—or rather, commiserated with—another man who answered in a rather pronounced accent."

"Irish or French?"

Cassie tilted her head. "Why, it was French."

"I interrupted. Please continue." She appeared delightfully alive, though nervous. "The foreign gentleman indicated there was yet more work to be done, and Delamere advised him to go out and trifle with a few young ladies."

"Is that all?"

She shook her head. "I believe they were preparing to leave the study when the door creaked and opened farther."

Zeno's jaw tightened. "They saw you?"

"I knocked the instant the door moved. Delamere had scant time for suspicion." She brushed aside his concern and quickly added another layer. "Lord Stanfield appeared shortly thereafter." She cleared her throat. "With his gentlemen friends . . . and a . . ."

"And a?"

"A young lady, a maid perhaps. It appeared as though the men had been . . ."

"Enjoying her?" Cassie nodded. Zeno fell back onto the plush squabs of the seat bench. "So Delamere knows about the body?"

She grimaced. "And his friend—wherever the man disappeared to. Out the study window is my guess."

Zeno snorted. "Sorry to put a damper on the Frenchman's social life."

"You believe he and Delamere had something to do with the murder?"

He shouldn't encourage her but grinned anyway. "And what do you believe, Cassandra?"

Her eyes glowed with excitement. "I watched Delamere's face closely when relaying your message to Lord Stanfield." She leaned forward. "Shifty eyed."

He did not wish to unduly alarm Cassie, but she

underestimated Delamere and his kind. These men would take no chances. If they were in the slightest way suspicious, they would assume the worst. She was in danger.

She tilted her head, curious. "And what did your investigation turn up?"

Zeno sighed. "The murder took place in an upstairs bedchamber. There was a struggle and a stabbing before the victim's throat was cut. I was able to identify the dead man. Seems he was a member of a cadre of blackmailers." Zeno hesitated. "This may be a bit awkward, but your former brother-in-law is one of them."

"Gerald?"

"He is under surveillance . . . amongst other peers."

Storm clouds formed behind her luminous gray eyes, and a sudden chill. She studied him for a moment before looking past his shoulder and out the carriage window. "So . . . your offer of escort to the Stanfield ball?"

"By your invitation."

Her gaze darted back. "I take it back."

"Too late."

The carriage traversed Belgrave Square and a flicker of gaslight illuminated the inside of the coach. There was no denying the flash of anger and hurt in her eyes. "You used me."

"Yes." Zeno set his chin. "And I might have caught the murderer had I not been so distracted by you."

She frowned. "Or you could have been killed."

"Possibly, but not likely."

Her eyes bulged wider. "You're blaming me for the murder of this young man?"

"No, of course not. I blame myself—"

Cassie crossed her arms in a huff. "From now on you can attend social events on your own, Mr. Kennedy."

"I suppose I might have prowled about the ball on my own." He reached across the aisle and untied her evening wrap. The shawl slipped off her shoulders. "But I wanted to go with you, Cassie."

"How perfect to use me as—" She frowned and tugged her wrap together. "What do you detectives call it?"

"Cover." He stared into liquid mercury eyes, full of the devil. "Sadly, we live in close proximity to Mayfair." He flicked the lever of the carriage door and helped her out of the carriage.

Zeno trailed behind a bouncing sweep of black velvet bow and bustle until they reached her doorstep. She removed a key from her reticule, pressed the latch, and turned the knob.

"Good night, Cassie."

"Good night, Mr. Kennedy."

He reached out and stopped the door from closing. "That is twice now you've called me Mr. Kennedy." Pressing closer, his words fell against plump lips that parted ever so slightly. "I don't like it anymore."

Chapter Ten

He had wanted to kiss her. Badly. Zeno cracked an eye open. Sleep had proved impossible, and the lovely Cassandra St. Cloud was entirely to blame. The lush greenery of Kent rushed by his compartment window barely noticed. As it was, he would use the next couple of hours on the train to muddle through the established facts—and possible scenarios. The Viscount of Chelwood's son, James Reginald Hicks-Beach, was dead, murdered for unknown reasons.

One less Bloody Four member to be concerned with. Yet he felt sympathy for the family, even a modicum of pity for the young man, who did not deserve to die in such a vulgar manner. Then again, Hicks-Beach may not have been the actual liquidation target. At least one other guest had been invited upstairs to the crime scene. Zeno removed the note from his pocket and reread the brief, cryptic message. He would collect a few samples of the dead man's handwriting for analysis.

It was also possible Castlemaine was working his own plot using hired killers to eliminate the men who threatened to blacken his name. How simple it would be to set up Delamere to take the fall. It wouldn't be the first time a high-ranking official made a deal and then attempted to run a scheme around Scotland Yard.

The conversation Cassie overheard in the library could very well be related to the murder. As valuable as a man in the Home Office might be, Hicks-Beach had likely become a liability to the cause. The young man might have seen or heard something he shouldn't have. Something like a large shipment of explosives.

He would debark at Tunbridge Wells and make his way from there to the family estate. He had no appointment with the viscount and did not expect his visit to be a welcome one. The telegram notification of James's untimely demise had likely reached the Chelwood estate just hours ahead of him. The family would be in shock. Zeno hoped some would be able to gather their wits about them long enough for an interview.

He closed his eyes and envisioned his enticing new neighbor. He was edgy, more so than usual. The woman was a torture to him. And if he continued to have such indecent thoughts about her, he might have to chuck in the assignment and board the next train back to town.

He had used Cassandra St. Cloud as convenient cover, but he very much enjoyed her company. Mixing business with pleasure was always a bit of a sticky dog. He needed an apology. Something effusively charming to make up for his lack of same.

* * *

CALLED AWAY ON FIELDWORK STOP
RETURN WEEK'S END STOP
DO NO FURTHER SLEUTHING ON YOUR
OWN STOP Z KENNEDY

Cassie tore the wire into tiny pieces and let the bits scatter onto the polished marble floor.

Deadly dull and impersonal of him. The perfunctory tone of his wire put her in a temper. And just like a man to be so overprotective and domineering. Groggy and out of sorts from a fitful sleep, she had lolled about in bed the morning long.

How could one sleep after being so perversely treated? Oh yes, she was attracted to Zak, but she wasn't entirely sure about him. He was rather an odd duck, crisply cold at times, though he had made quite an effort to be charming at the ball. Perhaps too charming. She should have suspected something.

The question remained whether this was all an act on his part, a detective's ploy to get close to a suspect. She recalled their almost-kiss on the dance floor, the terrace, and finally the one that nearly brought her to her knees in the foyer. She shook off a quiver that ran from belly to shoulders. The strong tremor of pleasure belied every ounce of indignation she supposed she ought to feel. But she did not. Just thinking about her desire last evening—yes, well, that was it, wasn't it? She really must stop this nonsensical mooning about.

Cassie took a stroll in the garden and tried not to think about Detective Zeno Kennedy. But it seemed there was no avoiding him. She had pulled but a few pesky weeds when Mr. Kennedy's housekeeper shouted a cheery hello.

An hour later, Cassie was still shamelessly pumping the congenial woman for information on her employer.

"Oh dear me, it's been near to three long years now since the horrific blast took the life of Mr. Kennedy's mistress." The pleasant, round-faced housekeeper pressed against the low, ivy-covered wall that separated the two yards. She quickly corrected herself. "I mean to say Mr. Kennedy's actress acquaintance."

"That is quite all right, Mrs. Woolsley, well-meaning gossip hounds have already informed me of the affair." Cassie smiled reassuringly. "Frankly, I don't know how I missed such a debacle. I was married at the time, recently returned from a honeymoon trip on the continent."

His housekeeper tsked. "Poor dear. Your husband's demise—you don't mind my asking—an unfortunate mishap, was it?"

"Racing his cabriolet." Cassie grimaced. "A ghastly sudden shock, but then I suppose accidents are that way." In no mood to recall the event, she redirected Zeno's housekeeper. "You were saying the press was up to their usual scandal mongering?"

"Oh yes, ma'am, sold stacks of papers, I'm afraid. Topped Mr. Kennedy's pursuit and capture of the dynamiters for a time. To be right honest, your ladyship—"

"Mrs. St. Cloud, please."

"Missus." She nodded. "I did not know the poor woman's name until Mr. Woolsley read it in the *Daily Telegraph*—Jayne Wells, an actress of some notoriety, I gather."

The woman's lively expression grew serious. "And poor

Mr. Kennedy the morning of the burial services. Alone in the breakfast room all silent-like, looking for all the world like he needed a friend." His housekeeper sniffled. "I asked if I might attend the funeral. I swear to you, ma'am, I'll never forget the anguish on his face, eyes filled to the brim with tears. He took my hand and nodded yes, Lord bless him."

So the stoic and taciturn Zeno Kennedy possessed a heart. Cassie's earlier exasperation faded as she listened to Mrs. Woolsley recollect his grief and loneliness. Drat the man, she cursed silently. She had just spent the afternoon preparing to dislike him greatly.

"Such a bleak day it was, the sky opened up and poured a cold, hard rain. And him not moving an inch from the poor lady's resting place for hours after the service. It took a good deal of prodding to pull him away from the gravesite.

"Mr. Kennedy lay in bed a week after with a fierce head cold caused by the damp and chill of that churchyard."

From the laundry basket at her hip, Mrs. Woolsley lifted a corner of a bath towel and dabbed her eyes. "Ah well, then he throws himself into his work in search of her murderers."

"And did that help with his grief?" For some urgent but unexamined reason she needed to know.

"I believe so, ma'am, though he's suffered a few bouts of melancholy on and off." The housekeeper brightened. "Mr. Kennedy does seem to be in better spirits these days."

Mulling over the woman's answer, Cassie nodded. "Thank you, Mrs. Woolsley. Sorry to take up so much of your time."

"Oh, don't you worry about that, ma'am, though I best be getting back to my chores."

Cassie resumed her walk down the garden path and

onto the terrace. Her head whirled with a new understanding of the man.

For the hundredth time today, she was back at her front door with him. Never in her life had she experienced such arousal from something so trifling. But to stimulate a woman in such a deliberate way. He had left her flushed with desire, harboring an urgent need . . . to be kissed.

It must be the very kind of behavior accomplished libertines used to break down a woman's resolve. Still, she did not believe the man could be so cruel. Except for the actress killed in the bombing, he had no reputation for his *amourettes*. And his grief for Miss Jayne Wells touched her, a bond of like suffering perhaps, but her heart felt a kinship with him, nonetheless.

Then the flowers arrived.

She ushered the delivery boy to the pedestal table in the foyer. The bouquet of blooms featured parrot tulips, lilies, daffodils, and deep purple irises. The talented florist had even wound sugared morning glories throughout the romantic, whimsical arrangement. Among the greenery she found a wire message.

> FORGIVE ME STOP I AM A BEAST STOP
> RETURN BY AFTERNOON TRAIN
> SATURDAY TO KISS YOU STOP
> ZAK

Her heart skipped a beat.

Circling the bouquet, she thought the foyer a fitting spot for such a veritable celebration of spring. And from such a charming beast, at that. Cassie grinned. She had complained of dullness in her life, and *now* look at her. A man was murdered last night and another had almost kissed her. Mother would be so pleased.

The hall clock chimed four o'clock, a reminder to dress for an evening out with old friends. She and Lydia and Jeremy were to attend a production of the new Gilbert and Sullivan comic opera, *Ruddygore*, at the Savoy. Afterward, they would enjoy a late supper and for once, she would have some jaw-dropping to gossip to share.

CASSIE STROLLED ARM in arm with Lydia while Jeremy paced ahead, weaving his way through a tangle of vehicles parked hodgepodge along the Strand. Lydia was in a funny sort of snit. "Lacked something of the sustained brilliance of *The Mikado*, but the opera has abundant charm among its more forbidding qualities."

Cassie snorted a laugh more to herself than her friends. She knew a certain detective with abundant charm, among his more forbidding qualities.

"Oh, come now, Lydia, my dear Rose Maybud, there were some wonderful librettos. *'When a man has been a naughty baronet.'*" Jeremy leaped into a pirouette and landed in between them, singing snatches of tune from memory. *"'Oh why am I moody and sad?'"* He waltzed Lydia then Cassie in circles.

Cassie twirled around laughing. "Jeremy, you know Lydia doesn't admire comic songs the way you and I do."

"It wasn't my opinion. I read it in the *Manchester*

Guardian." Lydia snorted. "And I quite enjoyed *The Mikado*, if you recall."

"Ah, here we are, ladies." Jeremy opened his carriage door. "Shall we catch a late night sup at The Star and Garter?"

Lydia dipped her head as she entered the coach. "Verry's, please."

Cassie nodded. "Let's have some of their bouillabaisse to order."

Once they cleared a mangle of traffic on the Strand, their trip across town was brief. At Verry's, they supped on a wonderful shellfish soup. Jeremy and Lydia had a slice of butterscotch tart for dessert and Cassie ordered ice cream. Dessert was interrupted by John Collier, a prominent London figure artist who stopped by their table and started a heated imbroglio over a controversial article in the *Magazine of Art*. By the time they paid the check and left the restaurant, Lydia, who had a wonderful flair for the dramatic, had puffed herself up in a huff. "The article goes beyond candid. The ridiculous writer suggests male and female students work from the draped figure in segregated classes."

Jeremy scoffed. "Life School is such moral poison, wot?" Cassie waited on the sidewalk listening to Jeremy and Lydia's lively discussion. As Jeremy handed Lydia into the coach, he glanced down the street and turned pale.

The distinctive clatter of galloping hooves came from the sidewalk, not the street. She turned in the direction of Jeremy's openmouthed gaze. A rampaging steed charged directly toward her. The rider, dressed entirely in black, wore a wide-brimmed hat pulled low, and a scarf covered everything but his eyes.

She took a step back as the moment turned into a night terror, the kind of dream where her legs seemed mired in a bog. The clang of shod hooves striking pavers matched the throbbing of blood through her veins. Petrified screams filled her senses. Several blurred figures dashed out of the path of the dark rider as he leaned out of the saddle with his arm extended.

Her name, she thought she heard her name.

"Cassie!" Jeremy leaped across the path of the charging horse and pulled her out of the way. From ground level she watched horse and rider gallop past, the equine's head strained against the bit, nostrils blowing. The stampeding charger tore down the street and vanished into darkness.

The pulse of waves crashing in her ears faded. Cries from onlookers turned into sighs of relief. The terrifying event passed as quickly as it had begun. The hysteria would soon turn into a different kind of buzz—one of speculation. What on earth had just happened? Several gentlemen, including a restaurant employee, ran after the strange rider.

Jeremy's driver, Clarence, leaned over them. "Everyone all right?" He reached out and gave them each a hand up.

Lydia rushed to her side. "Thank God you are safe. You could have been run down. People have gone absolutely mad in this city."

Jeremy ducked his head to look her in the eye. "Nothing broken, I hope?"

Cassie patted down her skirt. "Perhaps a bruise or two. Nothing to fret over. Thank you, Jeremy. You likely saved me from grave injury." The valet brought out several warmed bricks to heat the carriage, and they discussed the sobering, most peculiar incident until the carriage stopped in front of Lydia's residence. Having exhausted every lurid detail, they ended the discussion with a ghoulish laugh over the affair.

"Do take a calmative this evening. Something with a bit of laudanum." Lydia pressed close and they each turned a cheek for a kiss.

"I will be fine, Lydia. Please don't worry."

Jeremy saw Lydia to her door and popped back inside the carriage. When they made a turn out of Russell Square, Cassie pressed her nose to the window and made a spot of condensation. She turned to Jeremy. "We're being followed."

"Clarence mentioned the possibility." He settled back into his seat. "What's going on, Cassie?"

She met his gaze, and looked away. "You read about the murder at the Stanfield ball?"

"Of course. It made all the papers." Jeremy rocked forward with the sway of the conveyance. "I thought your date suffered a fall—broken leg, was it?"

"But I did attend the ball, escorted by Zeno Kennedy." Jeremy perked up. "Your new neighbor—the Yard man?"

She nodded. "Quite a good dancer, as it turns out."

Her friend's eyes sparked with light even as he shook his head. "So . . . you're intimating what happened at the ball may have something to do with the vehicle behind us?"

"Scotland Yard may have me under surveillance or protection, possibly both." She pressed her lips together and nervously worked them back and forth. "Detective Kennedy and I discovered the murdered man last night. Actually, the body fell out of the sky."

Jeremy leaned forward and took her hands. "Your fingers are ice." He chafed her hands between his. "Slow down. Start at the beginning."

Parked in front of Number 10, she and Jeremy sat in his carriage and talked. She told him everything, with the exception of names and the most sensitive details. He was one of her dearest friends. She did not wish to endanger him. They each took turns peering out of the window in the direction of a dark vehicle stationed well down the lane, near the mews entrance.

"I'm guessing they're friendly. They haven't tried to abduct you, as yet."

"Jeremy!" Cassie erupted into nervous laughter. "Why ever would you say such a thing?"

He turned away from the window to stare at her. "About that dark rider this evening. I did not wish to say anything in front of Lydia, but I left out an important particular. The man nearly swept you up and carried you off."

Cassie checked the street again. "Promise me you will keep this a secret between us, should you ever meet Detective Kennedy."

"Why ever for—?"

She sighed. "It's just that he's—Mr. Kennedy, that is— well, he's overly shielding and rather solicitous."

Jeremy grinned. "Sounds chivalrous."

She glared at him. "Promise."

Her old school chum folded his arms across his chest and studied her. She raised a brow.

"Oh, all right, I promise."

∞ Chapter Eleven

"'*A garden is a lovesome thing, God wot?*'" Zeno Kennedy without his coat caused a rush of heat to her cheeks.

Cassie answered with the last line of the sweet poem, a perennial itself, from the *Oxford Book of English Verse*. "'*'Tis very sure God walks in mine.*'"

She hadn't taken a single puff on the cigar before he caught her, bang to rights. "Join me, Zak. We'll have a smoke together."

"As you can see, I am not wearing a jacket." He placed both forearms on the top of the garden gate and hooked an index finger around the tight roll of his cheroot.

"I will strike a bargain with you. I won't tell a soul about your laxity of wardrobe if you, in turn, promise to keep my occasional use of tobacco a state secret."

"I resolved some time ago not to breathe a word about the smoking. Your secret is safe with me." He unlatched and pushed open the painted gate. Ancient, rarely used hinges groaned in protest. Both dogs got up to greet him, tails whipping merrily against his bootleg. "Oscar, Psyche, do not pester the landlord."

He wore breeches and top boots with his shirt collar open and the sleeves rolled up. His attire could not have been more thoroughly improper and yet, he left her breathless. A fleeting memory washed over her. Her husband half-dressed in just this way. She had even sketched Thom in erotic dishabille.

Zak seemed to have an equally disturbing effect on her. She had not seen him in two days. Two days of making unnecessary trips downstairs to wander past that glorious bouquet trying to forget that handsome smile of his.

He took a position at one end of the cast-iron bench. "It is good to see you, Cassie." He lowered and raised his eyes in appraisal.

A simple tray table painted with an Oriental motif sat beside the garden seat. She nodded toward a crystal decanter filled with amber spirit. "Shall I pour you a brandy?"

"I believe I will need a drink if I am to watch you draw down on a cigar."

Cassie pressed her lips into a thin line to quell her amusement. What delicious fun it might be to provoke him this evening.

When they each held a brandy in one hand and a cheroot in the other, she moistened her lips and pouted, placing them well over the end of the cigar and sliding them slowly off its end. She sent a pink tongue out over the moistened tip again, for good measure.

He chuckled and shook his head as the color of his eyes

changed to a deeper, Prussian blue. After a large swallow of brandy, he tilted his head and studied her intently. She rolled her Hoyo de Monterrey languidly back and forth between her fingers. "So, you've known about this dreadful sneaky habit of mine for some time?"

He placed his cigar on the tray. "I have an excellent view of both our gardens from my study."

Her attention swept over the garden wall to the elegant set of palladium windows on the second floor of his town house. "Remind me not to go for a naked, free-spirited dance in the moonlight, since you enjoy spying on people in their most private moments."

He pointed to his ear. "Did I tell you that I have trouble with my hearing from time to time?"

"No doubt you wish for us to sit nearer together?" She scooted over.

"An old service injury—can't be helped. Nitro explosion." He gathered a handful of her skirt in his hands and tugged gently.

She shifted half an inch. "Any closer and I'm in your lap." She could feel the warmth of his breath on her cheek.

With her lips inches away from his mouth, she could hardly focus on anything else. She lifted her cigar. "Fire me up, sir?"

"Very well, Cassie." He covered her hand with his, and peeled away one fingertip at a time. Next, he quite purposefully removed the stogie from her hand and placed it beside his unlit cheroot.

"I presume you have attended a scientific exhibition of the electric arc light? I myself have witnessed Mr. Tesla run a rainbow of phosphorescence through his body." She inched closer and whispered, "Do you think we might be able to illuminate Lyall Street?"

His gaze dropped to her mouth. "I have a theory that on our first attempt, we could light up all of Belgravia."

She licked her lower lip. "I require a demonstration, sir."

He used his thumb to tease her lips apart and began with soft, playful bites. With each kiss, shivers and sparks rose up from deep inside her. His tongue slipped along the edges of her lips and he angled his mouth over hers, urging her to open.

Tentatively, her tongue met his. Her entire body responded to his kiss, which grew stronger, more urgent. His teeth scraped across her lips. Carried away, she bit him back, sharply. "Sorry." She touched the raw mark she made with her finger.

"And you shall be punished." Sweeping her up onto his lap, he cradled her in his arms. "I must ask your opinion . . ." His words brushed softly over her lips. "Do you prefer this?" He kissed her mouth, and used his teeth to hold, then slowly release her bottom lip.

His voice changed to a gruff whisper. "Or do you enjoy something deeper?" He licked the inner edge of her lip before delving in.

"Perhaps the answer is both?" He kissed a small mole at the side of her cheek, the bridge of her nose, the tip of her chin before he found an earlobe and nestled his head for a moment.

"Mm-mm," she murmured. "I could hardly have one without the other."

He toyed with a few loose waves of hair before he pulled back to sweetly nuzzle the tip of her nose. "My powers of concentration on the job have recently become impaired, Cassandra." Blue eyes flashed with dark, fiery sparks. "And I am sure you are the cause of it."

"The flowers you sent are beautiful."

"I take it I am forgiven?"

"A reprieve might be in order." Cassie fingered a bit of trim on his shirt. "I must admit to a rather disturbing adventure in your absence."

"Ah, the incident in front of Verry's." His wide-set, sensuous mouth thinned. "I'm afraid my men weren't able to chase down the rider. Their orders were to stay with you."

Keeping secrets from this man was going to be difficult. She pushed out a lower lip. She disliked this intrusion into her personal life. "Is this protection, Zak, or are you spying on me?"

He answered without much hesitation. "There are persons in your circle of acquaintances we are interested in."

"And how long will it go on?"

"Until I am sure you are safe."

Cassie sighed. Her body glowed from his kisses. No doubt the strange event at Verry's worked against any argument she might make for privacy. No matter how many men Zeno posted about the house, she'd never be entirely secure. Overset by conflicted feelings, she wondered exactly what his men had observed, or how much she might reveal to him.

He dipped his head to look her in the eyes. "I must

insist that you curtail future outings. At the very least, pare them down to as few as possible. I do not wish to make you a prisoner in your home, but—"

Cassie slipped off his lap. "But you are, Zak."

Her irritation, at the moment, could not be greater and yet there was a deep need, a fire in her belly, for this man beside her. Either because of, or in spite of her desire, a flush of anger washed through her. "I have a social engagement this evening that I must begin to prepare for."

Zeno stared at her. With his hair tossed about and his shirt open, the resemblance to a pirate was unmistakable. "You remember Arthur and Amanda, Lord and Lady Walmer, from the ball?" He seemed shaken, nonplussed, vulnerable. Never had he looked more adorable to her than in this moment. She resisted the urge to throw her arms around him and never let go.

She swept a few errant wisps of hair back in place. "My brother-in-law tells me Amanda went to a great deal of trouble to wangle this invitation. Margaret Fayette—I should say, Lady Fitz-Walter—is having a soiree this evening. Gerald is coming for me."

"Have a pleasant evening, Cassie." In an instant, Zak the potential lover disappeared, and like an unexpected, chilly spring breeze, Detective Zeno Kennedy returned with his clipped, dispassionate voice and grim countenance. "I'd best take my leave. Since you refuse to cooperate with Scotland Yard, I must organize additional protection at the eleventh hour."

He rose from the bench and nodded to her. The dogs trailed obsequiously alongside him, already sympathetic to his cause—the traitors. At the garden wall he patted them both on the head, descending to his haunches to give them a proper scratch and allow each pup a sloppy kiss along his cheek.

All at once, she felt perturbed by his sudden exit. But what nonsense! What did he expect from her? How dare he try to make her feel as if she must obey every request, every rule he set down? She forced herself to get up and walk toward the house.

"Call out the bloody Horse Guards, then."

Zeno closed the gate. "At the very least, I made good on my promise to kiss you, Cassandra."

CASSIE TURNED HER head side to side for kisses.

She had never cared for the way Margaret Fayette, Lady Fitz-Walter, effused over her. There was something disingenuous about the woman's fawning, as if she was hiding a deep-seated envy so disturbing it had to be iced over with plenty of sweet frosting.

"Delighted to be here, Margaret. What beautiful flowers you have arranged for the evening—you must give me the name of your florist—just exquisite."

Cassie turned away from the reception line to face a room full of obligatory socializing. After a number of "so-glad-to-see-yous" and "my-word-has-it-been-that-longs" she managed to regroup with her escort.

Ensconced in his circle of intimates, her brother-in-law gave a wave. "Cassie, over here." Gerald turned to the only new man in the bunch. "St. Aldwyn, allow me to introduce my sister-in-law." She offered her hand to the striking chestnut-haired man.

"Raphael Lewis. And you are Cassandra St. Cloud, the lovely young widow we bachelors are so excited about." The man cocked his head at Gerald. "Don't bother dissembling, Rosslyn."

Gerald's brotherly grin wasn't the least bit comforting.

"You are new to town, Mr. Lewis?"

He nodded. "My family hails from the north. Queensferry, on the outskirts of Edinburgh."

Cassie evaluated the handsome Mr. Lewis. Cheerful manner aside there was something capable, reassuring about him. "Well then, we are both newly returned to the social scene here in London. I confess I am quite out of practice with my chitchat."

"A bit like riding a horse after one has taken a bad fall." Mr. Lewis smiled. "A musicale, a soiree or two, and you'll have your seat back."

Her eyes flashed upward. "And without the sore bum, what luck." The laugh from Mr. Lewis was genuine and she returned a smile.

"As usual, you underestimate your charm, Cassandra. Nary a soul here who isn't enthralled to see you again." A shiver rolled down her spine as Lord Delamere moved in beside her. A quartet of musicians struck up a waltz. "Before you are deluged with requests, shall we?" With his hand on her elbow he turned her about.

"I'd prefer not."

He leaned in close. "And if I promise to behave myself?"

They were in a section of hall that had been cleared for

dancing. If she cut him now, in front of everyone, there would be talk. If she agreed to a dance there would be still be talk, but if she followed their waltz by dancing with several other eligible men, including the rather dashing Mr. Lewis, her turn about the room with Lord Delamere would soon be forgotten.

She bit her lip. "Very well, one dance, then."

His arm slid around her waist as he led her off into smooth turns. Carefully following his lead, she hoped to stare over his shoulder for the duration.

"Relax in my arms."

"Rather difficult to do, my lord."

More silence and circling. "Will you ever forgive me, Cassandra?"

A blur of painful memories surfaced and she lost her footing. He caught her up and turned her so deftly, no one saw the clumsy stumble.

She dared to look at him. "Thank you."

He smiled at her. Dear lord, he was a strikingly attractive man. Those green eyes with dazzling copper specks seemed kinder than usual tonight. Symmetrical facial features and a lovely strong jawline, which recently sported a Vandyke beard. Ladies of the ton regularly whispered about him, especially when he showed interest in a new woman.

"You haven't answered my question."

Cassie sighed. "It is Christian to forgive, my lord, but difficult to forget."

"You used to call me Andrew." They were dancing close now. Gossiping close. Cassie pushed away, but he held on tight.

She looked away. "That was a very long time ago."

Mercifully, the music ended. She nodded a bow to the man and quickly exited the dance floor. Dashing past several clusters of guests, she glanced behind her. No dark lord in pursuit. She made her way toward the ladies' retiring room, but found a quiet corridor hung with some rather splendid paintings. Snapping out her fan, she took a stroll in the gallery to calm herself.

"I once glimpsed a fairy swimming in the pond at Muirfield." He moved up close behind her. "It was a warm summer's eve, quite late as I recall. I was just riding home from a hunt and caught a glimpse of a naked wood nymph. She was so lovely I watched in breathless awe as she splashed in her pool. Drops of glistening water ran from round, high-pointed breasts down a sweet belly to a hint of curls edging above the water's surface."

Furious, she spun around to face him. "You spied on me?"

"And just days later, is it any wonder I lost all control? Seeing you in your come-out gown? Virginal white, I believe. Knowing what kind of body—"

She slapped him hard across the face and turned away. Catching her by the arm, he yanked. She tried to push back, but he clasped both wrists together behind her back. He held her with one hand as the other moved up the front of her dress. He arched her body against his. She was exposed, vulnerable, her breasts near bursting from the top of her gown.

"I will scream."

The timbre of his voice grew harsh. "I think not, Cassandra. Do you really wish to call attention to such impropriety? The beautiful young widow St. Cloud, just weeks out of mourning, caught with Lord Delamere in a scandalous state of dishabille."

Her eyes glistened with angry unshed tears. "Please, do not do this."

"Just a taste, my dear." He skimmed fingers along the edge of her décolleté, and found a nipple. "Look at me."

Her breath was shallow, rapid. Her heartbeat even more so. She reluctantly complied with his demand and met his gaze. Her mind whirled with the recollection of a few terrifying minutes between them years ago. It was happening all over again, only this time her brothers weren't there to rescue her.

Or Zak. Why hadn't she cried off this party and spent the evening with the one man she truly wanted?

Delamere's voice bit through her thoughts. "You are no longer a virgin, dowager Lady Rosslyn. Do you miss the marriage bed? I would be more than delighted to offer my services."

He tilted his head, positioning his mouth over hers. "You will kiss me now."

She struggled against his caress as his beard scratched her cheek. "I much prefer kissing Zeno Kennedy."

His head snapped back. "This involvement with Detective Kennedy. Is it something serious, Cassie, or are you just being neighborly?"

"Any attachment I may or may not have with Mr. Kennedy is none of your business."

His eyes turned the darkest pigment color in her

palette, terre verte. "The other evening in Stanfield's library—" He pressed closer. She leaned away.

"Cassie, are you all right?" Her brother-in-law pushed the door open wide.

"Ah, there you are, Gerald."

Delamere groaned and released her.

"I've a beastly headache, I'm afraid." Her gaze never left his lordship as she backed away. "Gerald, would you mind terribly if I asked you to see me home early?"

Delamere nodded a bow. "'Til we meet again, Cassandra."

She stepped through the door Gerald held open, but did not speak until they were well away from the portrait gallery. "All that business about wangling an invitation." Cassie whirled around. "Honestly, Gerald, did he put you up to this?"

"I—" His chest deflated. "I believe Andrew is sincerely contrite, Cassie. And so very taken with you." The pink flush up his neck told her everything she needed to know.

Her heart continued to thump wildly inside her chest. "How could you?" She stepped ahead of her brother-in-law and wound her way through clusters of laughter and a blur of vibrant gowns. Her gaze landed on the only gentleman in the room she could trust. A complete stranger. "Awfully forward of me, Mr. Lewis, but might I have the loan of your carriage?"

The princely gentleman raised both brows. "I am at your service, madam." He nodded a bow and exited the ballroom.

"Cassie, do take my town coach—if you must leave," Gerald whined.

Cassie swiveled, eyes cool, narrowed. She could barely

contain her fury at his betrayal. "You have proven yourself untrustworthy for the last time." She collected her evening wrap, made a hurried improbable apology, and fled the party. Standing under the portico, she took in a gulp of cool night air. An unlikely smile tipped the ends of her mouth. She didn't give a flying fig what Margaret Fayette thought of her excuse.

A shiny black brougham pulled into the crescent-shaped drive. Modest, but well appointed. Something vaguely familiar about it. The door swung open. "Your chariot has arrived, Mrs. St. Cloud."

"Please call me Cassandra or Cassie." She nestled into a corner of the carriage and returned Mr. Lewis's gaze.

"I shall call you Cassandra after the goddess you are."

She pulled her evening shawl tighter. "I suppose you're wondering what all that was about?"

The man's eyes flashed to one side and back to her. "Do you wish to talk about it?"

Cassie shook her head, and then raised a brow. "I'd rather learn something about you, Mr. Lewis."

He settled into the leather bench opposite. "Second in line to the St. Aldwyn Earldom. There is an estate in Queensferry and a residence in Edinburgh and London."

"You are staying here in Mayfair, then?"

He shook his head. "A bachelor flat on Sydney Street, Chelsea. I am disowned, Cassandra."

She raised a brow. "So you *do* have a story to tell, Mr. Lewis."

"I will confess all if you will call me Raphael, or Rafe."

"Then I will call you Raphael after the angel you are."

A low smile surfaced. "Mother doesn't think so. She stopped speaking to me several years ago."

Cassie laughed. "I almost envy you, Mr. Lewis. There are times when I'd rather not have to listen to my mother's commentary."

HAVING EATEN A hearty supper of cottage pie and fillets of cod, Zeno moved upstairs to the library and poured himself a brandy. Settling into a comfortable leather chair near the hearth, he stretched his legs across an upholstered ottoman and opened his latest foray into contemporary fiction. Robert Louis Stevenson's *Treasure Island*. A secret pleasure, no doubt, but wonderful escape for the imagination.

The creative mind required regular exercise and plenty of adventure. Brief flights of fantasy, Zeno believed, rested the faculties and allowed the brain to expand its capacity to make intriguing connections.

He spent several hours pleasantly engrossed in the novel, when he became aware of a carriage slowing outside the residence. He checked his watch: quarter to midnight. Cassie must have decided to make it an early evening. He got up to do a bit of neighborly nosing about.

The nearby streetlamp flickered softly, diffused by a drift of fog. Zeno squinted through the atmosphere. His heart pumped extra blood through his veins at the recognition of his brougham and driver. He ticked off a number of irregularities, the most obvious being that the lady had left her flat on the arm of her brother-in-law this evening and returned early with an undercover Yard man. Last minute, he had loaned Raphael Lewis his carriage for the evening and asked him to keep an eye out. Quint jumped down from the top of the coach and opened the door for Cassandra St. Cloud to exit, accompanied by Rafe.

In top hat and tuxedo, Rafe was born for the role he played tonight. He was a brave agent and an excellent undercover operative, but his noble upbringing meant that he could move among the *haut ton* unremarked. Zeno's jaw clenched. Cassie's musical laughter drifted up from the street. Perhaps nothing too dreadful had occurred. The click of her door lock echoed up through his windows. Rafe paused by the coach door and lit a thin cigar, letting the lucifer burn down before shaking it out.

Zeno tossed on a jacket and made his way quietly through his garden to the mews. A trace of glowing red ash helped him locate the detective. "What happened?"

"Couldn't get much out of her without risking my cover." Rafe leaned nonchalantly against the brick wall of the carriage house. "She reluctantly agreed to a waltz with Delamere. Their dance appeared tense. Afterward, she retreated in the direction of the ladies' lounge. When Delamere dropped out of sight, I became concerned. I approached the brother-in-law, told him Mrs. St. Cloud had asked for him." Rafe exhaled a pale gray stream of smoke. "Dutifully, Gerald trots off. A few minutes later both St. Clouds make their way through the ballroom. Cassandra has a few choice words with her brother-in-law, turns to me and asks for the loan of my carriage."

"What do you think went on?"

"I suspect something uncouth happened between her and Delamere."

"Could she have been threatened?" The question escaped between clenched teeth.

"Possibly." His partner studied him. "She's fine now. Whatever transpired between them is done." He dropped the stogie and ground it out.

Zeno exhaled. "Thank you, Rafe."

"Pleasant duty, Zak." Rafe turned up his coat lapels and headed out of the mews. "She's plucky. I like her."

A frown firmly in place, Zeno called after his partner. "Why do you think she asked for your escort?"

Rafe swung around. "Obviously, I'm trustworthy." He shoved his hands in his pockets. "And I'm charming." His chuckle echoed down the alley.

Zeno's gaze followed Rafe out of the mews. Torn between desperately wanting to hold Cassandra in his arms and turning her over his knee, he sucked in a deep breath and exhaled. The woman was having an effect on him. How unbelievably disturbing.

⨳ Chapter Twelve

Zeno emerged from the Underground station at Sloane Square and headed for Lyall Street. Earlier in the day, he had sent an unusual proposal to Cassandra St. Cloud by wire. She had replied an hour later with an invitation to tea.

A young housemaid escorted him to the second-floor studio. At the top of the stairs, he opened the door onto a most provocative world.

"Good afternoon, Zak." Cassie, wearing a paint-splattered apron with her shirtsleeves rolled up, peered over a large easel. Another young woman sat in repose on a chaise placed on a platform that raised the scene to near eye level. Her classically shaped body was nude with the exception of black wool stockings rolled part way up her thighs. Zeno could not help but note her rounded hips, narrow waist and small, plump, high-set breasts.

The simplicity of the tableau enchanted him. A scene of everyday toilet. A young lady dressing in her boudoir. Or was she undressing? Her attention appeared fixed on an adjustment to a garter. From what he could see, Cassie painted a rather erotic aspect of the pose. The girl's torso angled slightly away, her legs parted somewhat, with just a hint of her female triangle.

Aroused, and a bit dazed by the intimacy of the setting, he cleared his throat. "Shall I wait in the sitting room for you?"

"Nonsense, Zeno, please take a seat here beside me. I won't be but a few more minutes." She lifted her gaze above the canvas. "Do you mind, Sally?"

"No, ma'am. Whenever I sit for Mr. Collier he prefers people come and go—likes to keep things out in the open." She snorted a girlish laugh. "He says it puts to rest any ideas people have about artists and their models."

Cassie swished a brush in turpentine and wiped it on a rag stained with daubs of color. The scent of solvents and linseed oil permeated the air. He took in the effect of northern light as it streamed through a bank of tall windows. Flesh tones came alive bathed in soft illumination and rich, dark shadow.

Transfixed by the atmosphere in the studio, he perched himself on the edge of a rustic wooden stool. From his new position to one side of the easel, he discovered a most pleasing view of the model's figure. A perfect S-curved spine pointed the way to a shapely dimpled rump.

"Miss Sally Fincher, I'd like you to meet Mr. Zeno Kennedy."

He stood and nodded to the young woman. "Miss Fincher." Feeling more than a trifle odd, he resumed his seat. Cassie appeared amused yet compassionate.

"Sally poses for both public and private sale works. She

is perfectly comfortable and unapologetic about her chosen profession."

Without so much as a break in the pose, the girl muttered a quiet, "Pleased to meet you, Mr. Kennedy." Eyes a bit wider, her gaze lifted. "The famous Yard man who solved the St. John's Wood murders and brought the Underground bombers to justice? *That* Zeno Kennedy?"

Zeno cleared his throat and tried not to let his eyes wander. "I was one of several agents who worked those cases."

Perspiration broke out on his forehead and temples. He had never in his in life attempted polite conversation with a strange unclothed Englishwoman. Cassie had mentioned this young lady modeled for private sale works, artists' code for erotic art shown by appointment only and kept in a gentleman's study. He placed one foot on a lower rung of the stool and the other on the floor. Eased the burgeoning discomfort.

Cassie dabbed together pigment powders with oil. "Sally models for John Collier's studies of Lady Godiva. Are you familiar with his work?"

What a predicament he found himself in. A trial of some sort, he guessed, and if so, he fervently hoped he would pass the test.

"I have seen his work at the Grosvenor Gallery. The painting *Lilith*, I believe, recently caused quite a controversy."

Cassie's mouth twitched upward and he breathed a sigh of relief. Silently he thanked Mr. Collier, whose stunning female nudes made his artwork nearly impossible to forget.

"Do I make you uncomfortable, Mr. Kennedy?" The young model actually sounded a bit self-conscious.

Zeno ran a finger around his inside shirt collar. Perhaps, he might try a little less formality. "Not at all, I was just admiring your lovely dimples, Miss Fincher."

The remark caused both women to laugh and quite effectively broke the ice. "The light is so perfect right now, I hope you don't mind if I work a little longer?" Cassie rang for help and requested tea to be served in the studio salon.

He racked his brain for a subject that might help pass the time less awkwardly.

"Aha! The exhumation and opening of Abraham Lincoln's casket."

"The what?" Both women spoke at once.

"It was the talk of the office this morning, in all the papers. The press, up to their usual conjecture, disregarded the most straightforward explanation."

"That being?" Cassie's brows knit together as she applied vibrant rosy red strokes to golden skin tones. Swirls of red layered onto yellow tones and pale green hues; all the strokes made up a flesh tone that vibrated with life.

"A security check. They wanted to make sure the dead president remained ensconced in his coffin."

Zeno found the ladies quite taken with the more ghoulish parts of the story, including the fact that they had embalmed Lincoln so many times his body had not decayed. "Indeed, he was perfectly recognizable, even more than twenty-odd years after his death."

So much for delicate feminine constitutions.

The room darkened as afternoon clouds threatened a bit of weather. "We might as well end the session, Sally."

"Yes, ma'am." The model pulled on a wrap and stepped behind a dressing screen.

To gain a better view of the canvas, Zeno sidled closer to study the work in progress. "I believe you are quite an accomplished artist." Almost at once, he recognized his comment to be an abysmal evaluation of her artistry. The look she flashed him confirmed it. And on second thought Zeno found the *accomplished* remark cursory and cowardly.

Straightaway he set about to do it better justice. "Your work has a stylized quality reminiscent of the poster and handbill artists of Paris." Zeno leaned in for a closer look. "Simple, graceful shapes of line and bold color."

He straightened. "I must say, however, I find the emotional context a bit unsettling. There is a sorrow, brought about by her expression and the way you have exaggerated the angle of her body. The loneliness of great beauty, perhaps?"

She nodded. *"La tristesse de grande beauté."* Judging by the gleam in the artist's eyes, he had redeemed himself.

The artist's model emerged from behind the Oriental screen. He marveled at how modest she looked in plain coat and dress, gripping a simple hat. Transfigured from nubile goddess into ordinary London shopgirl.

"Take some tea with us, Sally," Cassie offered.

"Oh no, Mrs. St. Cloud, I'd best be getting home." She turned to pay her respects. "Very nice to meet you, Mr. Kennedy."

Zeno nodded. "Likewise, Miss Fincher." Sally made a quick curtsy and disappeared down the stairs.

Finally, they were alone. "*That* was rather stimulating, Cassandra."

"You might as well get used to naked models about. Men as well as women."

"As long as the men are smallish and not particularly well-formed. Perhaps a homunculus or two?" He brought her hand to his lips and moved to the inside of her wrist. He inhaled French perfume mixed with turpentine. "During my years in military intelligence, I have known palace courtesans in Burma who did not smell this exotic to me." Apparently, he was unable to control his wicked urges and protective affections for the young widow. Strangely exhilarating.

"Burmese courtesans?"

"Mm-mm, lovely women who were most instructive." Zeno reached out and drew her close. "I have a proposal—a compromise of sorts."

He rubbed the curve of her back. "I must ask you again to avoid any further contact with Lord Delamere and his cohorts. This includes your former brother-in-law, Gerald St. Cloud."

He caught the slight flicker and roll of her eyes. "You'll get no argument there."

"That means no soirees, musicales, formal teas, charity balls—unless the event is de rigueur for some unfathomable reason." Zeno continued to focus on her. "You are in danger. Delamere likely believes you heard more of his conversation in Stanfield's library than you actually recall. Your association with me increases your jeopardy."

"You've had me followed." Cassie pulled away. "And you know about last night?" She chewed her lip.

Zeno exhaled quietly. "I do."

A lovely eyebrow arched. "Aren't you the nosy one?"

"I happen to be very good at nosy."

She pressed her lips together. A habit, he observed, often used to hide a myriad of emotions. What was it this time—anger, frustration, amusement? What he appreciated most about the expression was the lovely dimple that appeared. She ventured closer, slightly wary. "Proud of yourself, are you?" She spread her fingers across his waistcoat.

He grinned. "I am." His gaze dropped to her pale rose lips.

She, in turn, focused on his mouth. "You're a man of few words this afternoon."

He had to have her. Or at the very least   . Zeno pulled her against him. He kissed her long and slowly. He did not release her right away but held her in his arms.

"If you agree to cooperate, I have a reward for you. A new assignment."

"What kind of assignment?"

"You are certainly not the delicate, swooning sort." He smoothed a few wisps of hair off her temple. "You are of the bold and beautiful stripe, Cassie. Willful and woefully liberated—independent—whatever you chose to call it. And since trouble follows wherever you go, I will have to arrange my schedule to fit yours. Which is why I thought you might enjoy a bit of adventure with Detective Kennedy."

"I am intrigued. Tell me more."

"There is a surveillance planned for this evening and I am sadly out of contact with two agents. You and I will be taking up the post. We're following up a lead—a possible anarchist's safe house. You will need to borrow some wardrobe from your maid. Tart it up a bit." He kissed the tip of her nose. "What do you say? Accompany me on an evening of detective work. That is, if you are not previously engaged with some boring ton event. I hope not."

"Did you not just declare I no longer have a social life?" She returned a soft, playful kiss. "How long have I to prepare?"

The sparkle in her eyes brought him such happiness that he, oddly, found himself grinning again. "Plenty of time. I'll not fetch you until after dark."

The soft patter of footsteps came from the stairs. One of the house staff adjusted a platter laden with delicacies.

"Well then, may I change the subject while we take tea together?" She cleared a spot on a low table for the scrumptious tray. "I do have a burning question."

"Yes, Cassandra?" He strolled around edges of the room.

The small salon off the studio embodied the quiet ambience of a Parisian apartment. Cassie had left the polished wood floors bare, and the continental furnishings included a wide chaise longue and slip-covered bergère chairs. Several gilt easels in the room displayed framed paintings. All of the works were a riot of color and energetic brushwork. He took more than a few moments to examine several of the paintings.

"How do you take your tea, Zeno?"

"Is this your burning question?" To which he received an arched eyebrow and look of mock irritation. "Cream, no sugar."

He took the cup and saucer from her.

"About the large door, here on the second floor, that

goes to nowhere." She set her cup on her knee and stirred. "I must confess, after wondering about it for weeks now, I seem unable to determine a use for it."

Zeno grinned. "Ah yes, this is it, the burning—?"

"This is it."

"It is quite the architectural oddity, is it not? As you no doubt suspect, we have connecting rooms, Cassie. But do not fear, you are quite safe from me, for it is impossible to open."

Cassie smirked. "How impossible?"

"I'm afraid I've lost the key." He smiled his apology. "Long ago, our two residences were once part of a much greater manse. They were converted just before I purchased them. I did a modest renovation to both homes a few years ago, which mostly involved additional plumbing to the baths and kitchens. I thought about sealing the space off at the time, but I'm afraid it just didn't get done. Is it a bother to you?"

She chuckled softly. "Goodness, no. Doors that go nowhere, but lead somewhere? I quite like such architectural eccentricities. And this is all rather Lewis Carroll, is it not? It seems we have a *Through the Looking-Glass* door between our two worlds."

"HONESTLY, ZAK, MUST I again?" Cassie snuggled against him in the smelly old hired coach. They were parked on a dark street, she surmised, somewhere north of the Docklands.

"Just once more," he urged again. "Humor me."

"Why do you call it a legend?"

"It's your cover, a false biography."

"And what is yours, might I ask?" She raised a brow.

Taken aback, Zeno tipped his cap and scratched his head. "You're quite right. You must know mine as well."

He grinned. "Derek Ferguson. I been meaning to tell ye I work for Mrs. Jeffries, abbess to the finest house o' pleasure in the district. Yer employer, as well, my pretty French lassie."

His marked, working-class accent made her smile. "So, you are from Scotland, Mr. Ferguson?"

"Aye, ye ken the brogue. I canna seem to shake it." Zeno wore a shy smile. "I dinna why."

"Let's see," she teased. "Jekyll and Hyde. Ferguson or Kennedy? What difference, Derek?"

A close-lipped smile appeared. "Aye, I am Derek sure enough, but I wouldna' wish to see ye hurt, should I put ye to work. Ye need practice. Humor me, lass."

She nodded. In actuality, she enjoyed the diversion, thrilled to be a part of what appeared to be a fairly benign surveillance operation. Zeno said they were shooting in the dark tonight, with little hope this particular drop would turn out to be of interest.

Just an hour earlier, she had rendezvoused with Zeno in the mews. A hansom cab took them to Charing Cross Station, where they debarked and paid the driver. He then escorted her several blocks, where they boarded a shabbier rented carriage. Cassie had not realized their driver was an actual member of the undercover team until they arrived at a location Zeno called the dead drop.

"Name?" Zeno asked.

She answered in a voice laced with French inflection. "Émilie Seguret."

"Origin of birth?"

"France, monsieur, un petit village près d'Avignon."

"How long have you been here, in London?"

"Own-lee, uh, how do you say, *deux* monz?"

"Lovely patois, Mademoiselle Seguret. And who am I?"

"Derek Far-goo-son, my procue-rare, *une escort, un pro-tecteur.*"

"How much?"

Cassie delivered the line with plenty of attitude. "I sink, monsieur, more zan *vous* can aff-ford?"

This time Zeno broke out in a grin. "You are a natural born charlatan, Émilie."

She wore a short, ruby red coat, fitted at the waist, which he began to unbutton. "Let's see what kind of costume you and Cécile put together."

The coat covered a skirt of muted plum with a sweep of darker violet folds at her waist. A tight-fitted bodice barely covered a thin chemise. The transparent effect created the most arousing exposure of her breasts.

Zeno swallowed hard. "I believe that will do." He buttoned her up.

"You told me to tart it up, Zak. I have a tattoo, should you wish to display it, but I daresay it requires even more exposure."

He blinked. "A tattoo?"

Good lord, she'd blurted it out before she could stop herself. "Nothing unseemly. Just a little something, almost sweet in a way."

"Which reminds me." He removed a small package tied with string from his coat pocket. "My partner and I found ourselves in Piccadilly trailing a rather nervous gent. We followed him into Fortnum & Mason—had to purchase something." He placed the little box in her hands.

"I am a customer of their tea and coffee. I might have given you my shopping list this morning." She untied the colored twine and opened the small package. Inside she discovered four exquisite Belgian chocolate truffles, wrapped in delicate pastel, translucent paper.

Cassie unwrapped a truffle and bit into the buttery sweet. "Mm-mm, very delectable. Raspberry cream." She held the remaining half in front of his mouth. "Open."

Zeno complied without protest and Cassie popped in the chocolate confection.

"Yes, 'mm-mm' does describe it." Zeno cut his comments short to observe two rough-looking characters on the street. His gaze followed them until they moved well past the drop site. "I believe we were on the subject of a tattoo, and where might it be located?"

Cassie rolled her eyes. "Promise not to scold?"

"The very last thing I feel toward you, my dear, is paternal."

"When I was seventeen, I spent a summer in Paris as a part of an apprentice course of arts study. There were just four of us Brits accepted, of which I was the youngest and the most naive, if you will." Cassie adjusted herself against his chest and the warmth of his body. "This is going to be embarrassing."

"For you or me?" he challenged.

"Me, cheeky spook."

Zeno muffled a laugh against her hair.

"One night," she continued, "I was feeling wickedly and perversely mutinous after receiving a harsh critique. I broke my curfew, went out with some older students and got pissed. Our rooms were close to the Sorbonne. There was an artist in the Latin Quarter who used the human body as his canvas. We all agreed that Etienne's work, especially his color palette, was extraordinary. The pack of us were always poking our noses into his small shop."

"Don't tell me, someone dared you to do it."

Cassie straightened slightly and nodded. "I can't remember whether it was Lydia or Jeremy."

"And?"

"And, there's not much to tell." She shrugged. "It was all over in little more than an hour. The group stayed to cheer me on during the procedure. I hardly remember any of it. I believe I vomited on the way back to my poorly supervised university apartment."

The breath from his laughter played with the wisps of hair at her temples. "And, where is this work of art located on your person?"

"On my left hip. About here." She pointed in the general area.

Zeno pushed her away and sat upright. "I must have a look."

The frown in her voice matched her facial expression. "Remember you are on the clock, sir."

"Yer wearin' a skirt, lass. I willna' get ye naykid, although I wouldna' mind it." Zeno used his most persuasive accent on her.

Cassie groaned. "I can describe it for you."

From a side compartment of the coach, he produced an object that appeared to be some kind of telescopic instrument.

"They're always passing out new spy gadgetry at the office. I suppose they make us out to be a gullible bunch of test subjects."

Zeno twisted the brass-and-nickel-plated cylinder. Nothing. He then banged the instrument in the palm of his hand and instantly a narrow beam of light appeared at one end.

"A little torchlight for my examination."

Cassie played with the new invention, while he unbuttoned her skirt at the waist.

"Keep it low." He spoke in a quiet undertone, easing the fabric down along her left side. He untied her petticoat and drawers just enough to reveal a tangled web of exquisite, colored calligraphy scrawled artfully across a curve of hip. Each word interwoven brilliantly into the next and executed in the most charming manner front to back. Truth be told? She had never regretted getting it.

She handed the impressive gadget over to him. "The power source, is it—?"

"Experimental dry cell batteries, my dear."

The small spotlight illuminated the script. *"La douleur passe, la beauté reste."* Zeno softly chuckled as he read the words.

"Pierre-Auguste Renoir. The very instructor who so upset me earlier in the day." Her voice gentled at the memory.

"The pain passes, but the beauty remains."

∞ Chapter Thirteen

Zeno could not take his eyes off the swirling cursive letters that wandered over the sweet curve of her hip. Mesmerized, he surrendered to the beguiling, bohemian soul of Cassandra St. Cloud.

Without permission, he bowed his head and brushed his lips across artfully drawn words and velvet skin. Her flesh burned hot under his lips. Closing his eyes, he inhaled violet soap and something even more wondrous.

Mysterious female.

He pulled her into his arms and pressed another kiss to her temple. "What a stout little lass you were to trot off to Paris at such an age. I take it your parents had no objections?"

"Oh, Father had plenty, even as Mother pushed me out the door."

"Ah yes, the original liberated woman in your family."

She retied her drawers. "The only eyebrow Olivia Erskine ever raised at me was when I accepted Thomas."

Cassie settled against his chest. "Mother thought him an interloper to my aspirations as a painter."

"I believe your mother is more of a suffragist than you, madam."

He kept an arm around her. "Mrs. St. Cloud has a tattoo on her hip," he gently chided. "Has your mother seen it? I daresay she might have chosen a different maxim. Perhaps, 'Votes for Women Everywhere.' I believe that is the new war cry, is it not?"

He received a wary, lopsided grin. "Be careful, Zak, my mother is dear friends with Emmeline Pankhurst. You would not want the Women's Franchise League circling Scotland Yard in placards."

A hansom cab pulled up alongside their carriage. Zeno peered out the street side window. "It's Rafe."

The coach door opened and banged shut as a new passenger jumped in and sat opposite. Zeno rapped on the roof of the coach. "Let's roll up a bit closer."

Wisps of hazy fog crept along the cobbled lane as the carriage made a slow circle of the block. They stopped in a different section of a narrow cross street. The faint glow from a distant gas lamp made it difficult to see across the short expanse of the coach's interior.

"You're late. I was worried." Zeno laced his whisper with sarcasm.

"Kiss to you, too, mate. Supper got off to a beastly start. Aggie insisted on retelling the bloody details of her birthing story until we were all off our appetites.

"My dear sister just whelped a new pup." Rafe pulled out a thin cigar and held it up. "Do you mind?"

Cassie stared wide-eyed at his partner. "Not at all. Enjoy your cigar." Slowly she raised a brow. "I thought your family hailed from Scotland, Mr. Lewis."

A flick of his wrist shook out the match. "My sister fell in love. Married an MP, one with serious political ambitions. They live here in London most of the year. And I believe you preferred Raphael, did you not? Because I'm an angel." His partner swept a long, appreciative gaze over her. "How delightful to meet again, Cassandra."

"This evening she is Miss Seguret." Until this moment, Zeno had never given much thought to how winsome the younger man was. It rankled him.

Cassie's lopsided grin telegraphed a wary amusement. "Ah well, names aren't really called for in this line of endeavor, at least not real ones."

"Right you are, miss." After a flirtatious smile, he returned to Zeno. "You didn't tell me you were bringing a date, Zak. Anything of interest yet?"

"Deadly dull so far. Not the lady's company, mind you, but the drop." Zeno tucked a coarse woolen blanket around Cassie.

Rafe lifted an eyebrow, thoroughly diverted. "Dear me, it appears I have interrupted a charming tryst of some kind."

Zeno eyeballed him. "Mr. Lewis. This was supposed to be your night, along with Flynn and Kitty." He gave a nod to Cassie. "Miss Seguret was kind enough to volunteer for duty."

Rafe shrugged. "Difficult for Kitty to break away some nights, and I suspect Mr. Rhys has been spending time with the green fairy."

Zeno grunted. "I need Rhys off the absinthe and away from Limehouse if he's going to be any help to us."

"He's not back in opium dens, if that makes—"

Cassie shushed them both and put a finger to her lips. Zeno and Rafe exchanged a grin and hunkered down quietly. A freight lorry, burdened with a heavy load, pulled up suspiciously close to the old boardinghouse.

"Where exactly is this drop located?" Her gaze swept the building across the street.

"A flat, abovestairs." Zeno nodded upward.

She pointed from the wagon on the street to the second floor. They all noted an indistinct shape travel past an upstairs window. "It's a woman," she whispered.

Zeno spoke softly in her ear. "How do you know?"

She answered without taking her eyes off the scene. "Not sure exactly. The window must be open, or I could not have seen a thing."

Zeno dipped his head to have a look at the row of glass frames. "How so?"

She scanned the upper floor. "Note the dark square at the end of the row. There's no glare or reflection from the streetlamp directly opposite. Therefore, the window must be open."

Rafe Lewis grinned. "And would that be based on science or art, miss?"

Cassie thought a moment. "An impressionist's observation, based on the shifting effects of light and color."

Zeno donned a tweed cap. "Ready to go to work, *ma fille de joie?*"

He helped her out of the carriage and they made a

quick run around the corner to come up behind the parked lorry in the alley.

"I take it Mr. Lewis was assigned to Margaret Fayette's soiree to spy on me?" Her eyes flashed silver sparks. Hard to tell if she was just annoyed or truly furious.

"He was assigned to spy on Delamere." Zeno pulled her into a narrow niche at the side of the building. "And protect you."

"From now on you're not to spy on me unless . . ."

"And when would that be, love?" Zeno needled her in character. Nostrils flaring, eyes flashing, she was angry, all right. He opened the buttons to her coat.

"Stop that." She slapped his hands away. "What are you doing?"

"Put your hands around my neck and lift your knee." He could feel her heart pound as he grabbed hold of her waist and lifted her up against the rough brick exterior. Zeno moved his hands under her bottom for support and encouraged her to wrap her legs around him.

"Throw a leg up, love, and let's play smashbox." Zeno spoke loud enough for anyone nearby to hear. Cassie moaned and then giggled uncontrollably. Out of fright—hysteria? Whatever caused her reaction, it was exactly what he wanted. He thrust up against her, and added a few loud grunts before he figured they'd attracted enough attention.

"Use your anger, Cassie," he whispered. "Yell me off."

"Off—you filthy pig, *descendez*! I am . . . *une fille travaillant*—I must work for a living."

Cassie's impromptu threats were delivered with a lot of temper and a trace of French coquetry. A pretty whore

used to dealing with unwanted advances. "Bully—*horrible*."
She pushed him off and gave him an extra shove. *"Merde!"*

Fully aroused from their erotic brawling, Zeno choked
back a laugh and stepped away. She straightened her dress
and coat, but left the buttons undone. Good girl.

"Ye pain me, *ma chère*, but I'll have ye soon enough."
Zeno grabbed her and kissed her mouth. She struggled
and pushed back until he let her go. She walked away
yelling insults. *"Imbécile . . . crétin . . .* do not touch me. *Ne
touchez pas!"*

He glanced ahead. They had captured the undivided
attention of the laborers standing beside the lorry. Zeno
quickly caught up and grabbed her by the arm. Cassie
continued to shrug off his hold.

Two laborers unstrapping the load stopped as Zeno
and Cassie weaved a path through the men.

"Hey now, where dah ye think you two'er goin'? Let's
have an eyeful of this fancy bird, lads—"

Zeno swung around and addressed him. "Sorra mate,
this sweet tart is on her way to a gentleman's bed."

"Crème fraîche, monsieurs." Cassie flashed a smile.

"She's tits-up, awl right; 'ave a look." Zeno moved behind her and threw open her coat. With every eye off the
wagon, Zeno glimpsed a flurry of movement as a shadow
dove under the tarpaulin. Good. Rafe was inside the storage compartment.

Zeno shrugged. "Makin' a house call this evening,
gents, but ye can give her the goods anytime after." He
prayed he wouldn't have to fight them off. Several of the
men looked ready to drop their drawers in the street.

"You got yours, na giv'us a tap."

Zeno forced a grin. "Wha', me? Nah, just coppin' a taste. I'd get the nobbler if the abbess ever caught my wanker in this gorgeous tosser."

"How much for the doxy?"

He tipped his cap and scratched his head. "Well now, that depends on what ye want and how long ye'll take."

A large young tough with a ruddy face rubbed his crotch. "She'll take every inch of me. Aye, lads?"

Zeno caught Cassie by the coattail and backed away. Her beauty worked like a charm, luring the men farther down the lane.

"Catch yez on our way back. Give 'em another look, miss."

Cassie opened her coat. "*Voilà*—you like?"

At the sound of their hollers and groans, Zeno grabbed her hand and pulled. At a half walk, half run they made it around the building. The footsteps of at least one man followed close behind.

"Hold on," he whispered. The moment the docker turned the corner, Zeno landed a stiff punch to the man's jaw. The huge bruiser staggered but didn't fall.

A dark figure leaped out from a wall niche wielding a heavy piece of timber. *Thwack!* The board struck the side of their pursuer's head and the poor bloke crumbled to the ground.

Flynn Rhys, the errant Yard man, emerged from the shadows. "Get her to safety, Zak. I'll make sure this one stays put."

Zeno nodded. "Keep a lookout for Rafe. Come along,

darling." He grabbed her hand and she rucked up her skirts. Neither of them dared to slow their pace until they reached the old carriage parked at the end of the street.

Zeno yanked open the door, tossed Cassie inside, and threw himself upon her.

He whipped an arm around her waist and moved her farther under him. Neither gentle nor undemanding with his kisses, he moved down to her breasts. Try as he might, he could not contain his desire. His tongue lapped over thin fabric, his fingers pulled down her camisole until he uncovered a pale rosy tip for his mouth.

Erect and ready, his body was so charged with lust that if she so much as touched any part of his lower anatomy, he would lose all semblance of control. Reluctantly, he released her and returned the lacy undergarment to its proper place. "I ended our tryst in the garden last night, not to arrange for a spy, Cassie, but to scare up a bit of last-minute security for you."

Her warm sigh brushed over his cheek and ear. "Perhaps I do remember a grumble from you about protection."

The creak and whine of the carriage door abruptly ended the discussion.

Rafe jumped in ahead of Flynn, who rapped on the cabin roof, and with a lurch they were off.

Zeno pulled her coat together and fastened a button before he tugged her upright.

"Libidos fired up?" Rafe cast a roving eye over their newest operative. "I know mine is. I just heard the show you two put on—didn't get to see it."

Zeno ignored both his coworkers and hugged her tight. "You were brilliant. We should put you on the payroll."

"The expense ledger will note a Miss—?" Flynn raised a brow.

She exhaled breathless words. "Émilie Seguret."

His errant operative leaned forward. "Ah yes, Miss Seguret, ravishing French tart."

Even in the dark, Zeno could make out Flynn's wink. He tempered the urge to frown and settled on a grin. For not entirely justifiable reasons, he held Rhys in some regard, even though he considered the man dangerous. Flynn continued to be irksome, eccentric, and very often brilliantly deductive. "Mr. Rhys, how is it your lack of punctuality always manages to work to our advantage?"

"I have an aptitude for timing." Dark eyes glimmered as the agent shifted his attention back to Cassie. "Rather an exciting night out for you . . . Émilie."

She returned Flynn's enigmatic half smile. "I haven't had this much fun since my brothers and I picked the lock of the village chemist shop and raided his candy bins."

Flushed with excitement and disheveled by his kisses, she had never looked more beautiful. "We pinched a single piece from each canister with the idea that no one would be the wiser." She shivered. He knew the reaction well. She trembled from the nervous aftermath of adventure as much as the chill in the air. Zeno kept his arm around her.

"And did you fool the chemist?"

"Hardly. It turns out my youngest brother, Rob, helped himself to a few extra pocketfuls. And old Alastair

Trumble made it a habit to take regular inventory. Word got 'round he was on the lookout for the culprits who broke in and nicked the toffees."

The agents across the aisle exchanged amused looks.

"I decided to deliver us from sin before we were found out. I made my brothers chip in—nineteen pence—two-a-penny. Exactly the number of missing sweets. I folded up the coins in a paper and left the packet on the shop counter. Ran all the way home, heart pounding, sure that someone had seen me and was on their way to Muirfield to have me arrested."

"Have you always been the moral compass for the rest of your siblings?" Zeno mocked.

Cassie huffed. "Nothing moral about it. I just didn't want to get caught. I wanted," she captured them all with an earnest look, "to get away with it."

Zak and Rafe burst into laughter. Flynn grinned. "Enchanted, madam, to have you on our team."

The carriage turned a corner and lamplight filled the cabin. Cassie narrowed a curious gaze at his other cohort. "And was your part in our little spy pageant productive?"

Rafe hesitated, his eyes shifted to Zeno.

"I suppose you couldn't tell me one way or the other." A pretty but rueful grin caused Rafe to raise both brows for help.

"It's for your own protection." Zeno peered out the window. Charing Cross Station lay ahead. "Ah, here we are. Quint will see you safely home."

At the train terminal, Zeno escorted her to his carriage and helped her inside. Before shutting the door, he thanked her again for her assistance. "Take some warm milk tonight. It helps me when I come home late, keyed up."

From well inside the coach, she leaned forward. "If I hadn't been on the job with you this evening, there would have been another woman, an agent or perhaps a prostitute in your employ?"

A stab of doubt rankled his composure. He thought of all the liberties he had taken with her this evening. Would he have done the same with another female operative? Well no, not . . . exactly. A truthful answer could mean the end of their relationship. He nodded his head and waited.

"Get in here and kiss me goodnight, Detective Kennedy." She grabbed him by the lapels and pulled him into the cabin. Her hand swept under his coat and across his chest, bumping into the heavy weight of the revolver stuffed inside his jacket pocket.

Zeno grinned. "My Webley Break-Top. Just in case those blokes at the lorry got a bit too fresh with ye."

"You're going to be busy for the rest of the night, and then perhaps the day after?" She unbuttoned his shirt. Just one button, enough to fit her hand through the worn, checked shirt.

"I'm afraid so." He was tempted to knock on the roof and tell Quint to head for home and take the long route. He would take her here in the carriage. Plunge his aching prick into heaven. His entire body shuddered from the effort it took to hold back.

Her mouth played over his, moist and delectable. Her

fingernails scraped gently along the flesh of his stomach, which caused his pulse to race, and his voice to sound like gravel. "I want ye bad, lassie." He brushed a few strands of hair from her face. "I dinna think ye'd mind if I call the locksmith and have a key made for the door between us?" He kissed her one last time.

He debarked from the carriage, his bollocks a right pretty shade of blue. "Tomorrow night, ten o'clock."

Zeno returned to the old coach and tapped the roof. It was still early enough to sniff around another drop site. From the look on his partner's face, he suspected Rafe coveted excellent news.

Flynn spoke first. "One stunning girl you've got there, Zeno. And what a fast mover you are. Your new neighbor I take it, the lovely widow?"

Rafe nodded. "The lads back at the office will be impressed. A right ravishing beauty and a clever wit. Passionate, too, I suppose, you might as well have all the luck."

Zeno's warning glare shifted from one investigator to the other. "I haven't got her yet, and if I ever do it will be none of your business. Now, you bloody well tell me what I want to hear."

Rafe crossed his arms and rocked along happily with the rumbling coach. "Just a bunch of wooden crates, plain enough, until I found a shipping label, half torn off. Could only make out six grubby words—The Giant Powder Company, San Francisco."

His colleague's eyes crinkled along with a trumpet of laughter. "I figure better than two hundred pounds of dynamite, so there's sure to be another two drops somewhere else in town." Even with more explosives left to discover, Rafe's triumphant smile remained undiminished. "We still have to hook 'em and reel 'em in, but it's confirmed. They've taken the bait."

Zeno failed to answer, due to a sudden and crushing blast of remorse. In his mind's eye, he pictured Cassie standing feet away from a wagonload of explosives. How could he have put her in such danger? Mortified by his own thoughtlessness, he vowed never to put her in harm's way again, no matter how benign or elementary the assignment might seem. How brave and beautiful she'd been all evening! She could bring a man to his knees for just a taste of her.

Zeno grinned. *Ma wee toughie.*

Chapter Fourteen

At the first stroke of the wall clock, a thousand butterflies took flight in Cassie's stomach. Nine strikes later, she held her breath. Any moment now Zeno would walk across their secret threshold and enter her world.

But not yet.

At half past, her heart began to dance an odd beat. He must have been delayed. Certainly in his line of endeavor there were risks and perils aplenty.

But why tonight?

An hour later, she paced a loop from the stairwell through the studio, glaring each time she passed the ridiculous, annoying . . . door.

By eleven thirty she gave up and settled down with a book. After reading the same paragraph twenty times over with little or no comprehension, she set the tome aside, turned out the lights, and climbed the stairs to bed.

She shrugged off her clothes.

Sitting on the edge of the mattress, she ran a hand over the smooth cherry finish of the sleigh bed's curved footboard. A brand-new bed purchased for her brand-new life. The one she planned on initiating this very night with Mr. Zeno Kennedy.

Alarming images of Zeno crowded her thoughts. She pulled on a sleeveless cotton knit undershirt and silk pajama pants—an old pair of her brother's. Slipping under covers, she folded a pillow under her head and inhaled the scents of lilac and lavender. In anticipation of her *nuit d'amour,* Cécile had sprinkled toilet water on the pillows. Sweet girl.

Having worked herself up into a state, she took a deep breath and exhaled. Her body yearned for him—for this night of lovemaking. She closed her eyes, and the disturbing picture returned. Zeno lay unconscious in some back alleyway in the Docklands, injured and alone. She turned over and tried not to think of it.

On the edge of a dream, she awoke to the beautiful strains of a tenor aria. *"Donna non vidi mai, simile a questa!"* Cassie opened an eye. *"A dirle: 'io t'amo' . . ."* She bolted upright. Bedcovers tossed off, she started downstairs and halted midway. Zeno stood at the bottom of the staircase in shirtsleeves and neatly pressed trousers holding a bottle of champagne. His hair looked damp. He must have returned home, taken a quick bath, shaved, and changed. The very sight of him made her smile.

In a simple, pure tenor voice, he intoned, *"A nuova vita l'alma mia si desta."*

Every particle in her body tingled with desire. She wanted to run into his arms but descended one step at a time. As the aria filled the room, she smiled. He was making up the words, some in Italian, some in English, sung softly, beseechingly. *"I have never seen a woman such as this one! My soul awakens to a new life."*

She landed on the last tread and he handed her a dusty bottle of vintage Louis Roederer Cristal. "When a lover is late for a tryst—" She tilted her head to read the card attached to the bottle. *Drink me.*

"He should always prepare a love song and arrive bearing gifts." She leaned across the banister to offer a kiss, which he readily accepted.

A glimpse at him revealed those clear blue orbs dancing with mischief and something more intense. Her lower belly did that clenching, trembling thing again.

"Mrs. Woolsley called the locksmith out." Zeno slipped a brass key tied to a ribbon around her wrist. He kissed her mouth again, with hunger. The sweet breath of his exhale moved across her jaw as he ran a trail of caresses down her throat.

Cassie sighed softy against his temple. "Dear lady."

"Mm-mm, I must add an extra bit to her pay packet." A fire kindled inside her as his tongue licked the hollow at the base of her throat.

THOUGH IT PAINED him to do it, Zeno stepped away. Cassie's hair hung loose in shiny waves to the middle of her back. Instead of a dazzling, sophisticated young woman, a wicked, fresh-faced schoolgirl returned a ravaging gaze of her own. At least he hoped he read that right.

Charming even in sleeping attire, his barefoot goddess

wore silk pajama bottoms in a paisley print. But it was the knit undershirt that raised an erection. With the top buttons provocatively undone, the peaked tips of her curvaceous breasts taunted him from under the thin, transparent material. His prick strained against the buttons of his trousers even as he resisted the urge to tumble her to the floor.

"You . . . I . . ." He stumbled. "You never cease to beguile me, Cassandra."

She leaned close and sighed against his ear. "Your serenade sounded like Puccini."

He turned and her lips brushed over his cheek and mouth. "Indeed, the aria is haunting but I forgot the lyrics and had to toss in a bit of Catullus."

Two champagne flutes sat on a side table near the French chaise. He took her by the hand and led her into the salon, where he poked a few dying coals to life in the fireplace and lit a lamp, turning the wick low.

"You are an admirable tenor, sir."

"Barely tolerable." A copy of Henry James's *The Portrait of a Lady* and another book lay facedown on the sofa. "After my football injury, I joined the choir at St. John's."

He tilted his head to read the spine. "*The Mayor of Casterbridge.*" He flipped through a few pages of the book as he reclined onto the studio couch. "Thomas Hardy. Knotty bedtime reading. Did you enjoy *Far from the Madding Crowd?*"

"Very much so, but I am a snob and a progressive when it comes to my reading list. And what of yours?"

He laughed, just thinking about how indulgent he had become in his reading habits. "I'm afraid I haven't been able to bring myself to read a dark, depressing piece of literature since university. Shakespeare, of course, and always poetry, but I've stayed safely away from modern novels except for adventure."

She raised an eyebrow. "No excuses. You must confess, sir."

"*Treasure Island*." He readily avowed his sins. "I can't help but want to escape of late. Too much thinking on the job. I wish to be spirited away on a sailing ship, or tramping across some vast African savannah."

"Perhaps a tumble down the rabbit hole?" She smiled with her eyes. This evening those silver orbs were the color of a winter sky, wild and stormy. They teased and then dared him to come and play. Another rush of acute lust surged through his body. He resisted the urge to pull those silk pajama bottoms off.

His grip landed on the neck of the champagne bottle. Before Cassie let go, she read the card again. "I shall attempt to unleash this missile without destroying your enchanting boudoir, madam."

While he untwisted wire, she joined him on the chaise, tucking long, slender legs under her. She nestled comfortably against his shoulder and her simple, honest affection gave him a moment's pause.

"I have a question." Bubbles rushed to the surface of the bottle as he nudged the cork. "How long has it been for you, Cassie?"

She pressed her lips together even as the ends turned up. He waited for the dimple on her left cheek to come out. Ah yes, there it was.

With a pop, the blasted cork hit the ceiling. Cassie grabbed both stems as he directed the frothing, golden liquid into the flutes.

She dipped a finger into the sparkling wine and wet her lips. "Over two years. And you?"

He eyed a wet, plump lower lip before slowly lifting his gaze to meet hers. "You are a wicked tease, Cassandra."

"How long, Zeno?"

"Perhaps, not quite as long." He contemplated the open, honest beauty of her. "As a man, I have access to—"

"Relief, as needed?"

He gulped some bubbly. "There was an involvement with a woman some time ago. She was killed. I am not sure what you have heard of the matter."

Was there a dash of irony mixed with sympathy in that roll of her eyes? "Margaret Fayette took great pains at the ball to inform me about a mistress—an actress." She swept the palm of her hand across his cheek.

He took hold of her wrist and kissed the tender pulse point. "And you, Cassie, have suffered a loss as well."

"We both lost our respective partners, within a few months of each other." She tipped her head. "I wonder . . . have you, perhaps, someone new?" He noted how carefully she watched his reaction.

"As a matter of fact," his gaze never shifted, "there is a fascinating young widow—an extraordinary artist, with the most ravishing . . ."

He set down his glass and began undoing her buttons, but gave it up and pushed his hands beneath the soft undershirt. His fingers brushed nipples into harder peaks.

Her eyelids fluttered as he nibbled along her jawline. He listened with delight, in between soft moans, to her sweet attempts at conversation.

He pressed his lips lightly against her mouth. "One thing more." He eased back, reaching for his glass and a gulp. "We will have intercourse at least two times." A wide grin spread slowly across his face. "Because, Cassie . . ."

"Because?" The light in her eyes matched the sparkling bubbles of the wine.

"I don't believe I will last more than thirty seconds the first round."

A glorious flush of golden pink colored her cheeks and chest.

"I insist you give me a second chance to redeem myself." He then splashed, not poured, another glass for each of them, and relaxed onto the soft quilted upholstery of the chaise. "Here's to yer pleasure, lass." He reached out and pulled her across his chest, splashing champagne on them both. He kissed the hair at her temples, the arch of her brow, and the tip of her nose. "I look forward to discovering what pleases you most."

Zeno licked her lower lip, and plunged his tongue deep inside her mouth. A private metaphor that perfectly described the exploration he wished to undertake farther down, past her navel and curls. He moved his hand to her belly, and her womb contracted from desire.

Still holding on to a half-filled flute, she pushed off his chest to finish the champagne with one long swallow.

"Pitiful waste of a grand old vintage—swilling it down

like a drunken sailor." Zeno drained his glass, snatched her empty flute away and set both on the floor.

In one swift move, Cassie pulled the thin cotton undershirt over her head. Blood surged into his penis. She sat up straight for a moment, breasts thrust forward, proudly taunting him.

Near to bursting with arousal, he gazed at tips a dusty shade of rose, erect, and waiting for him.

"Touch me," she urged in a throaty whisper. He cupped the supple weight of each breast in his hands and lifted. Using fingers and thumbs, he rolled nipples and pinched just hard enough to coax a deeper moan from her throat. "Come closer."

She leaned over his torso and offered a breast just above his lips. With his tongue, he circled and teased before he suckled and nipped the delicate pink. His fingertips tantalized a nipple as his tongue laved, trading off one for the other.

Between sighs and moans she managed a whisper. "Your turn."

She righted herself astride his upper thighs and took her time to undress him. Removing his braces, Cassie slowly unbuttoned his pants. The smallest brush of a fingernail caused a deep, husky groan.

Her silver eyes darkened into a smoldering burn. "May I hold you in my hands?"

Amused, aroused, nearly mad for her, he placed both hands behind his head and studied her slightly swollen lips. "You may."

Delicate fingers edged their way past the tails of his

shirt. He was transfixed with lust for this half-naked goddess as she rode his hips and explored the length and circumference of his erection.

He gritted his teeth at the sheer torture of such pleasure. She stroked him from top to bottom, sliding along the hard length with both hands, then drawing his shaft out, where she could examine the beast uncovered. He watched her eyes light up in appreciation and knew his own climax hung by a breath.

"May I kiss it?"

Damn the vixen. He was on the brink and she could well drive him over the edge. He exhaled a breath. "Very carefully."

She trailed soft kisses along his hard shaft as he sucked air through his teeth. Zeno willed himself to think about a jump into an ice-cold firth in his homeland.

"Ah, ah, ah." He took her hands in his and redirected her attention to the last button of his shirt. She pushed the fabric off his shoulders and ran her fingers over the muscles of his torso. She dipped a finger in champagne and circled his nipples before she sucked and nipped. The flat of his abdomen rippled and his speech growled from a place far down in his throat. "Where on earth—?"

"I read it in a naughty French novel." She tugged at his chest hair a bit nervously.

"The lady's reading list expands." Zeno quirked a brow. "I did not hear you ask, 'May I divert myself with the hair on your chest, sir?'"

"Might I, then?" Her eyes flashed with kittenish mischief.

"For every pull, you owe me a kiss, Cassandra Olivia. I suggest you get over here and do your duty." She landed on his chest, and moaned as he turned her under him, pushing her legs open with a knee. He yanked the drawstring of her pajamas, and moved his hands down along her belly and lower to her mound of curls. His fingers delved deep into warm, moist folds.

Lifting her up by the buttocks, he slipped off the pajama bottoms and laid her back, nude against the rise of the chaise. Enraptured by her beauty, Zeno took a moment to admire the languid young goddess reclined across the divan.

"You are exquisite, Cassandra." His fingers dug into the cheeks of her buttocks. He lifted her to meet his stiff, jerking shaft. Scrapping hard, he ached for release. He paused at her entrance.

He would take her like this, first.

Stroking the head of his prick between silken folds, he eased inside her sheath. Good God, they fit perfectly. Unable to stop himself, Zeno thrust into her like an animal. He held her knees apart and pumped harder, deeper. He drove in again and again until he lost all control. He could die inside her.

A surge of pure ecstasy ripped through his being. His heart stopped, momentarily, from the strength of his release. Seed spilled from his body as a second wave of pleasure enveloped him. The accompanying growl came from deep in his chest as he held her tight. He collapsed on top of her and rolled to one side, taking her with him. Holding her close, he remained connected, erection throbbing. His hunger for this woman had only just begun.

"You—" He gasped for breath. Stroking her creamy skin from rump to shoulders, he took a moment to gather his wits. "You did not—?"

"I did not," she interjected, breathless and frustrated.

Zeno propped himself on an elbow and smiled. "You need to catch up, Cassandra."

∽ Chapter Fifteen

"**More.**" Cassie hardly recognized the brazen harlot who urged Zeno onward. He stroked a finger along her moist inner wall. "Close?"

She arched in response to this dark, elemental man who pleasured her, coaxing forth a hussy—a woman she had never experienced. "Yes, Zak."

Licking her from breast to belly, he pushed her legs apart. His face nuzzled the sensitive flesh of her inner thighs as she rotated her hips and pushed upward to answer to his caress. Every part of her hungered for more as he laved her most sensitive spot. He sucked the swollen flesh until she shuddered.

Zeno sat back on his haunches, Prussian blue eyes dilated by desire. His gaze slid slowly over her body. Part man, part wild predatory cat. He might eat her alive and she would give him any access he wanted.

Her skin tingled. The contrast of her nakedness against his tousled dishabille made her feel vulnerable and wicked. With his shirt open and his trousers barely edging his hips, she admired a curve of groin muscle that disappeared beneath the fabric of his pants. From observation she had already surmised he was a handsome specimen of a man. But here, in front of her, he was a marvel of lean, sinewy torso. To think all that had been hidden under stiff shirt collar and frock coat. Until now.

His tongue lapped front to back slowly, patiently, with varying degrees of pressure—just enough to craze her senses with a raw wave of pleasure. She lifted her head, eyes wide open, and stared into dark sapphires. A rush of heat blistered her cheeks—God help her. His gaze explored her most intimate feminine places and his manipulations felt wonderfully depraved. A deeper level of excitement rippled through her body.

"Hold your breasts. Make those pretty tips point for me."

She hesitated, then touched herself. He groaned. "Yes, like that." She grew bolder, rolling nipples into peaks, as she arched from her own wanton self-pleasuring.

Zeno returned to his knees, grabbed his penis and stroked. The stiff rod slapped against his abdomen as he edged her buttocks up onto the tops of his thighs.

He kept his thumb on her clitoris as he thrust back inside her, giving her what she wanted, sensing she was close to release. And he would see her passion, watch her body arch in ecstasy as he began his own crescendo.

Heaven came slowly. Between each thrust, he stroked her with the wide pad of his palm or tapped with a finger. She never knew which caress would come next. Would he cause her to moan or shudder? She lost all focus but one. Pure pleasure.

Her world began to separate around her. Mind from body, flesh from bone, seconds of eternity. She toppled over the crest into oblivion.

CASSIE AWOKE TO the splash of carriage wheels and the wet clop of horse hooves in the street below. During the wee hours of the night, rain had fallen. She predicted a beautiful spring morning and opened one eye. There wasn't a cloud to be seen outside the bedroom window.

A light snore whuffled up from under a nearby pillow. Mr. Kennedy.

Throughout the night he had explored the most secret places in her body. Her cheeks warmed as she remembered his shocking requests. He had stirred passions lying deep inside, curled up in her aching womb, waiting for release.

Cassie stretched and grinned like a Cheshire cat. Such hot-blooded mating.

Pushing back some of the bedcovers, she studied his broad shoulders and lean torso. Farther down, strong thigh and buttock muscles lay exposed for her to admire. He possessed the body of an athlete.

And that brute of a penis, ready twice last night.

Tucked into the crook of his shoulder, she was warmed by the heat of his body. She inhaled the deep spice and lime of his cologne mixed with the intoxicating male scent of him.

After a soft knock, Cécile opened the door a crack. "Breakfast, madame?" Her usual request, croissants filled with blackberry preserve, a pot of good strong coffee, and steamed milk. He stirred under the covers and she turned to find him watching her with a sleepy-eyed, curious gaze.

"Good morning, Zak."

HE KNEW AT that very moment, he would have to have Cassandra St. Cloud again. And again. Last night, she had captured him, body and soul. And what a lass she was. Intelligent, with a crack wit and an enchanting, eccentric way about her. She was also . . . wanton.

She sat upright against a large square pillow, her breasts fully exposed. She smiled at him, all radiance and guileless beauty.

He snaked a hand out from under the covers and found hers. "Good morning, Cassandra."

Her little French maid unfolded a tray table, and set down a platter filled with breakfast items. He pulled the linens up.

"Thank you, Cécile." Cassie turned to him. "Steamed milk?"

"Mm-mm, yes." He pointed at the maid. "Is she . . . going to remain in here?" Cassie proceeded to stir his blood measurably as she poured milk for his café au lait. Morning light streamed through rain-spattered windowpanes, dappling her derriere.

He propped himself on an elbow and displaced the

blanket, exposing more of his thigh. That saucy maid managed an ogle as she set down the silver pitcher.

He stacked a few extra pillows up to the headboard and sat up.

She inhaled. "Coffee has a delicious aroma, does it not?"

"Most stimulating." He traced a finger over the beautiful script that ran across her hip. "I can hardly start the day without it. I have pushed tea back to afternoon."

He lounged beside her, bare-chested, as the maid stoked the fire. It wasn't proper to expose himself to the female servant, though to cover up seemed the height of hypocrisy. And so British. He listened with amusement as the two women conversed in French.

Sipping the steaming, caramel-colored coffee, he fancied himself in Paris. It wasn't difficult in the least.

When Cécile referred to his masculine form and the desirable qualities of his chest hair, he yanked the sheet up farther and swallowed more coffee. When Cassie described him as frightfully large and as hard as a Bengal tiger, he could no longer feign disinterest in the women's commentary.

"*Tu as beaux nénés*, Cassandra." The flirtatious maid winked as she backed out of the room.

Cassie raised a brow.

"If you two can boldly discuss the intimate parts of my anatomy, I believe I might be allowed comment on your pretty breasts."

The rekindled warmth from the hearth began to reach the bed. Placing his cup and saucer on a nightstand, he pressed up against his new paramour and laved the side of a round globe.

"Mine." He felt possessive this morning. "Do ladies often speak in such lurid terms regarding their lovers?"

She fed him a heavenly piece of warm bun and jam. "We all, to some extent, share shockingly intimate stories with one another. Both the large and the small of it, I'm afraid." Cassie lifted a little finger, along with her cup.

Snorting a laugh, he kissed a pink nipple and spread a swath of berry preserve across a swell of breast. "Alas, I have made you all sticky. I shall have to lick it off."

Zeno wet a circle around her areola. Her skin tasted salty and sweet, a honeyed female flavor he could not get enough of. And the mysterious scent of her, a mixture of carnations and light musk, filled the memory of his senses. Last evening, she had arched and thrust under him, a passionate goddess, as she elevated her hips and beckoned him to mount and breed with her. Twice.

Christ, just thinking about their lovemaking made him stiff. Absently, he entertained the idea of a third round as he counted the chimes of the wall clock.

Zeno bolted straight up in bed. "Bollocks. I've got football." He jumped into his trousers. Amused, Cassie sat back against a cloud of pillows while he tucked a half-hard penis into his drawers.

"Oh dear!" She sat upright. "I'm late as well." Springing out of bed, she attempted to dance past him but he caught her in his arms. Running kisses down her beautiful naked spine and rounded bum, he spun her around.

"I'm to meet Lydia for a ride in less than an hour."

"So we're both in a jam." Zeno chuckled. "When can I see you again?"

"I've invited Lydia and Jeremy for Sunday dinner this afternoon, can you make it?"

"What's the fare?"

"Braised lover." Her eyes crinkled. "I suppose there might also be a roast leg of lamb with mint chutney. Spice cake for dessert. But only for those brave enough to attend."

"Cake." He grabbed up his shoes and stockings. "With butter frosting?"

"Luscious, creamy butter frosting."

CASSIE BRAKED HER bicycle and glided to a stop. She reached up under her hat and repinned the boater in place.

"You have such pretty color in your cheeks this morning, Cass." Lydia drew up beside her. "The impact of the bicycle on the health and emancipation of women cannot be underestimated."

"Dear me, you remind me of Mother Erskine."

This made the second time in less than an hour that Lydia had commented on the radiance of her complexion. And what exactly could she say to her female companion? *Oh, Lydia, I have taken a lover who leaves me all aglow from his pleasuring.*

She eased back onto the bicycle seat, adjusting for the deep soreness inside her body. A quiver rolled through all the intimate places Zak had been.

Lydia tilted her head. "There's something you're not telling me. You're holding back, Cass. Don't think you can fool me for long."

Her friend studied her outfit and she could only guess at what was coming next. Lydia could be either overly critical or effusive with her compliments, and often both at once. "Cassie, you have such style, not like all my frippery and flounces. Your clothes are always an exquisite combination of perfect tailoring and simplicity."

Lydia patted down a few unnecessary ruffles. "I'm positively eaten up with jealousy over those navy bloomers and that crisp, white sailor blouse."

Cassie patted the top of her handsome straw boater with its navy grosgrain hatband. "Oh, but it's the hat that is the finishing touch, wouldn't you agree?"

Her friend sighed. "It's just that I feel so—pastel."

"Honestly, Lydia, I have told you a thousand times you wear colors that wash you out."

"Cass, you must go shopping with me again. This time I promise to purchase only what you deem suitable."

Cassie surveyed the park. "Where is the football field?"

The ash blonde, who did look a bit pale, paused for a moment to think. "Past the lake on left, I think. Why on earth . . . ?"

"Men play football, don't they?" Cassie pushed off in the direction Lydia pointed.

"What a wicked idea, Cassie. I do believe you are finally coming out of your black."

As she and Lydia cycled along, they were, at times, greeted by gawkers and a few disapproving stares. There had begun a countrywide backlash against certain advances in women's rights, including the idea of women cycling. The bicycle was fast becoming a symbol of the New Woman. Just this year, male undergraduates at Cambridge chose to show their opposition to the admission of women as full members of the university by hanging a female figure in effigy in the main town square—tellingly, on a bicycle.

It was exasperating! As far as she was concerned, all those opposed to a woman's right to cycle could stare all they like and walk straight into the Serpentine while doing so.

The moment she and Lydia rounded the lake, the footballers caught sight of them. Several players trifled, but more serious jeers began as a break in play. Never one to back away from a fight, Lydia applied the brakes. "Never seen a real lady out for a cycle? Backward, are we?"

Cassie chirped in. "Get used to it, gentlemen. You can't keep us in skirts forever."

Mounting scornful remarks, however, triggered some of the younger men to approach them. And, most unfortunately, the first taunt out of an unruly redheaded chap served to incense Cassie. "Why would a lady wish to show off her bum to the rest of the world?"

She clenched her hands into fists, which landed on her hips. "I daresay Hyde Park is hardly the rest of the world, sir, and would you suggest a woman ride a bicycle sidesaddle? You must not be familiar with the way these vehicles are engineered. Otherwise you would understand that it is near impossible, even dangerous for a lady to wear a skirt while pedaling."

One handsome blond Adonis with rumpled hair and

dirt on his cheek appeared more enchanted than angry. "Perhaps one might suggest the lady not pedal at all?"

"You would fancy that, wouldn't you?" Lydia stuck her nose between them and went off on the handsome lad.

Cassie grinned. She was actually beginning to enjoy this confrontation, for she did not spot Zeno among the athletes. Undoubtedly he played on some other field.

If he were here, he would characterize this raucousness as an unseemly incident in a public park—though she had recently confirmed to herself that Zeno Kennedy was a very different man privately than the reserved, stern gentleman of first acquaintance.

Oh dear.

She spotted him just as her gaze wandered to the far side of the male gathering. He wore a faded blue rugby shirt along with an all too familiar frown. The ice in his stare could freeze the first hardy daffodils of spring.

Their gazes met over the small cluster of players. She backed up instinctively and repositioned her newly purchased vehicle for escape. From the corner of her eye she saw him lob the ball over to one of his teammates.

It took him a few long strides to catch her by the middy blouse and take her boldly in his arms. He kissed her hard, and a thrill shot through her body as he bent her back across his arm.

"Whooo-hooo," came the raucous hoots and shouts. Of course such outrageous deportment would be encouraged, even cheered on by his teammates, who undoubtedly thought his response a shocking but understandable reaction to the ladies' cycling costumes.

"That is what happens to young women who wear bloomers in the park, Cassandra." His grim expression belied his true feelings, for his eyes spoke the truth. He was both amused and bedeviled by her.

When her knees went to jelly he steadied her. Cassie staggered backward with one hand still attached to the back of her hat. She glanced at Lydia, whose mouth, as yet, hadn't closed.

Gathering her wits about her, she thrust out her chin and made a show of straightening her boater. She ignored the boisterous men and proceeded in the most genteel fashion to make introductions. "Mr. Zeno Augustus Kennedy, please meet Miss Lydia Valentine Philbrook."

"Miss Philbrook." His cool gaze slid from one young woman to the other. "When you told me you were riding in the park, I assumed—"

"Yes, I expect you never dreamed your weekend sport would be so rudely interrupted by two women in bloomers. I hope that we haven't put you off your appetite, for you are still expected for dinner at three." Cassie nodded politely and pushed off on her bicycle. "Good day, Mr. Kennedy." She nodded to the footballers. "Gentlemen."

ZENO'S HARDENED GAZE lingered on Cassie's pretty bum as she pedaled away down the path. It appeared his kiss and her reference to his dinner invitation had knocked the wind out of his teammates' sails. The poor confused blokes drifted back onto the playing field.

He gazed at Lydia rather intently. "You've known her a long time?"

Lydia nodded. "Since ballet and art classes." The young lady hurried her bicycle down the pathway.

Zeno accompanied her a few more paces. "Has she always been like this?"

"Why, whatever do you mean, Mr. Kennedy?" Cassie's friend played coy with him.

"Bicycles, bloomers . . . cigars." There were numerous other behaviors he dare not allude to, including tattoos and wanton lovemaking.

"Well, she wasn't nearly this much fun after she married Thom." Lydia climbed astride her bicycle. "You know about the cigars?"

Chapter Sixteen

Between the parlor and dining room Zeno pulled Cassie against him and kissed her. He should have released her on the spot, but his body refused to obey. Instead, he closed his eyes and nuzzled wisps of hair at her temple and breathed in her scent. Her presence electrified him this evening.

She spoke softly against his ear. "I've a bit of awkward news. I'm afraid my parents arrived unexpectedly, moments ago." She fiddled with a button on his waistcoat. "Of course I insisted they stay for dinner."

A cough and *ahem* signaled they were not alone. With the help of a quick shove from Cassie, Zeno stepped away. "Mother. Father. Drs. Olivia and Henry Erskine, I would like you to meet Mr. Zeno Kennedy." Cassie cleared her throat. "My . . . landlord."

This was going to be damned awkward. Zeno stepped forward and reached for Dr. Erskine's hand. "Delighted to meet you both."

He could not help but notice Cassie's parents were a

handsome couple and her mother would be lovely indeed without her current tight-lipped, narrow-eyed, raised-chin expression.

"Where is Lydia?" Cassie glanced about. "Ah, here you are."

"Good afternoon, Mr. and Mrs. Erskine." Lydia tilted her head at Zeno. "Mr. Kennedy."

"We meet again, Miss Philbrook." Zeno nodded politely.

Lydia turned to their hostess. "And wherever is Jeremy? Late again, I take it?"

"Our illustrious chum is hanging a preview and has been delayed." Cassie rolled open the dining room doors. "He hopes to drop by for dessert and coffee." She showed Zeno to his seat at the table and leaned in close. "I advise you to keep your head this evening. You shall need it."

Despite the warning, Zeno sailed through the soup course with small talk, but could not help but feel the eyes of his inquisitors upon him. And he did not have long to wait once the lamb was served.

"So, Mr. Kennedy, from what part of Scotland do you hail?" Erskine stabbed his fork into a slice of roast and a small boiled potato.

"Isle of Skye. Sheep farmers and whiskey makers." Zeno grimaced inwardly. Bad choice of words. Made it sound as if the family were a drunken gang of peat cutters. He cleared his throat. "The Kennedy earls reside at Culzean Castle in South Ayrshire. Lowlanders loyal to the crown."

"The only good drink is a Talisker scotch." Dr. Erskine offered a toast. "Here's to a bottle and an honest friend . . ."

Now, there's a relief. Zeno picked up his whiskey glass and met her father's tumbler with a wink and a grin. "Sin on."

With the barest of smiles, Olivia Erskine gave them the once-over. "Two Scots and each with a full glass. Love at first sight."

Cassie wore a glint in her eye. "Zak does seem to bring out the haggis in Father."

Mrs. Erskine puffed up and studied him. "I take it you served in the military, Mr. Kennedy? Sometime after you completed your education? My daughter mentioned an athletic award or fellowship to Cambridge University?"

"Please call me Zak." He winked at Cassie. "St. John's. My studies were in linguistics, with a postgraduate term spent translating Latin and Greek—minor poets and philosophers." Good lord. Now he sounded like a flighty, unfocused academic.

Zeno removed a succulent piece of meat from a rib before setting his knife down. "After university, my uncle's service made it possible for me to get a placement in the Second Dragoons."

Dr. Erskine leaned forward. "The Royal Scots Greys, a crack cavalry outfit, I must say. 'Second to none,' the motto, what? Well, Rob will be impressed, won't he Cassie?"

"No doubt, Daddy." Cassie shot both her parents a disparaging look, which allowed Zeno to get a forkful of dinner into his mouth. "Goodness, I must apologize for the interrogation, Zak."

He made contact with sparkling silver eyes. She was the picture of loveliness. An effortlessly beautiful woman with a very modern outlook on life and, well, sex, to be honest. And there could be no doubt the two were inarguably linked. As he watched, a shade of pale rose crept from her throat to her cheek. Was she thinking about last night?

He forced his attention back to the Erskines' background check. "The Greys wore bearskins and kilts—breeches for riding. Thankfully, they don't wear kilts on horseback anymore." He relaxed a little, as the remark appeared to amuse everyone at table. "Although I do recall a night when the Highlanders in my squadron got drunk enough to ride around the parade ground in their plaids. Rode past the sergeant major's quarters. Pulled up our kilts—stuck our bare-naked arses out in the air."

Dead silence.

Zeno gulped from his water glass. "Not half so amusing the next morning. Certain parts hurt like hell—"

To the rescue, Cassie cut in. "And was the sergeant amused?"

"We scrubbed latrines for a week. *Nemo me impune lacessit,*" Zeno chuckled.

Cassie's father snorted a roar of laughter. "No one provokes me with impunity." After two tumblers of hard spirits, a lilt had materialized in Henry Erskine's brogue.

Zeno now counted the good doctor, at least provisionally, in his camp.

"Service in the dragoons amounted to daily drills and parade work, barely tolerable, dull duty. I requested reassignment and was consigned to military intelligence. Stationed first to France, then Burma.

"Frankly, I jumped at the chance for a little adventure.

It turns out intelligence work suits me. When my last tour was up I stayed on in London, resigned my commission, and went to work in the Home Office. Later, they moved me over to a new division of Scotland Yard."

Olivia Erskine took an unexpected interest in the conversation. "You seem to have developed quite a reputation surrounding your work, Mr. Kennedy." Her remark was casual, but intoned in the voice of a wary mother.

He studied the woman carefully. "I must advise you to ignore most everything you hear or read that mentions my name. I now work exclusively for Special Irish Branch, and all our operations are secure and unknown to but a few people in government."

"And this work you do for Scotland Yard, it is rather dangerous, is it not?"

He set down his fork. "Yes, ma'am. At times very dangerous."

She leaned forward, grim-faced and unblinking. "A woman was killed in an explosion. Someone of your acquaintance, I believe?"

An icy shiver ran down his spine, as if he walked dangerously close to a cliff edge back home with a cold surf crashing onto the rocks far below. "A great tragedy, but a wholly coincidental one, Mrs. Erskine." He gazed protectively toward Cassie. "I must assure you both, your daughter's safety is my greatest—"

Cassie burst in. "Mother, I must insist you and Daddy give Zak a break from your inquisition. He'll have a sour stomach after all this."

"Whenever Olivia draws my gut, I take tonic water

from a siphon bottle for the cure. Isn't that right, Cassie?" The doctor gave his daughter a wink.

Mother Erskine caught the conspiratorial message between father and daughter and smiled before she returned to Zeno. "One more question. Please, indulge me."

"Fire away, Mrs. Erskine." For the first time all night, Zeno relaxed. He was even amused.

"While it is universally agreed we must put these dynamiters and their horrid reign of terror to an end, I am curious where you stand on devolution for the Irish."

"Ah, the Irish question." Zeno chewed on the last of his asparagus while contemplating a headlong plunge into dangerous political waters. "A tricky and difficult situation, Mrs. Erskine. But nonetheless, I will answer honestly. I believe by not passing Home Rule, we pave the way for a complete break."

Cassie spoke first. "Revolution?"

Zeno shook his head. "I doubt it will come to great conflict. Self-governance will more likely come from a good deal of Irish civil disobedience, and no small amount of constitutional work on our part. The Lords will lose their power to override legislation. It's inevitable."

Olivia picked up her glass of wine and appraised him with a kinder eye. "And high time, too."

CASSIE SMILED AT her lover. Her lover. She wanted more of his body as well as his mind. Her departed husband, rigid in his thinking and strident in his politics, preferred horse-breeding to his seat in Parliament. Tonight

Zeno's speech made her aware of a commendable aspect of his character. He was interested in justice. A man of strong principles who looked at all sides of an issue.

"All right, Cassie, let's have our toast." As her father refilled the wineglasses, she pushed her water goblet into the middle of the table, and held her wine above it. She noted Zeno's smile as he recognized the familiar Scottish salutation to come.

"To the king over the water." Cassie toasted her father.

"I drink to my verra bonnie lass." Father met her glass with a tender look and a quiet clink. "And to my verra bonnie wifey." *Clink*.

Zeno added to the sentiment. "And to the general joy of the whole table." All glasses met in agreement over the water goblet.

"My word," exclaimed Lydia. "Sedition and Shake-speare all in one toast."

As dinner plates were whisked away and dessert was served, Cassie saw her chance to move conversation away from Zeno and his politics. "Lydia, you have been unnaturally quiet this evening. Shall we tell everyone about our stimulating ride in the park today?" To which there quickly developed a lively discussion on the merits of bicycle riding, and a retelling of the incident at the football field.

Lydia, for once in her life, exercised discretion by avoiding the detail of Zeno's very public demonstration of affection, and Cassie jumped in to credit him for taking a moderating role in settling the argument with the unruly footballers.

With a new zeal in her eyes, Olivia catapulted herself

into near ecstatic discourse. "You would be interested to know the American suffrage leader Susan B. Anthony believes the bicycle has done more to emancipate women than anything else in the world. She has said, and I quote: 'It gives women a feeling of freedom and self-reliance. I stand and rejoice every time I see a woman ride by on a wheel—the picture of free, untrammeled womanhood.'"

"You must join us, Mother. You, Lydia, and I will have a cycle together in the park, perhaps next Sunday afternoon if you are in town. We might even appeal to Mr. Kennedy, ask for his continued egalitarian influence so that we might ride unmolested past the rugby fields."

Zeno leaned into his chair and appeared to study the people he dined with. "And what is your opinion, Dr. Erskine, of women out in public in bloomers?"

"Depends on the woman's figure, wouldn't you say, Zak?"

Her father's eyes were merry, and all the women laughed, which forced a smile from Zeno.

Well pleased with himself, Father refolded his serviette and laid it on the table. "I'm afraid, Zak, you'll not get a word of derision out of me on the subject of pantaloons."

"You may have helped me make a point, sir. I have no argument with the fact that the wearing of bloomers is a safe way to pedal a bicycle and I would even go further, riding in breeches no doubt affords better balance and command of a horse. But—"

"But what?" Cassie interjected. "Isn't safety of greater importance than some antiquated idea of women's modesty?" She challenged him with a grin that would surely melt his stern countenance.

Mother squirmed in her seat, a clear sign she could not wait to get a word in edgewise. "I often wonder at the incongruity, Mr. Kennedy: that men believe women sturdy enough to participate in the making and bearing of children, yet find the riding of horses and bicycles astride as indelicate." Olivia dipped her fork into a wedge of cake. "Would you care to elucidate that peculiarity for me?"

Zeno's mouth nearly dropped all the way open before he choked out an answer. "No!"

Father met his emphatic answer with a snort of laughter. "That's the spirit, lad, no sense in arguing with the ladies. They will get their way, I assure you."

"And the vote, as well." Mother grinned.

The pocket door to the dining room slid open and Cécile appeared with a message in hand. She stopped behind Mr. Kennedy and curtsied.

Visibly reluctant to open the envelope, Zeno read and refolded the wire. "I'm afraid I must excuse myself early."

After a brief exchange of polite remarks, Cassie pulled him out the front door to steal a modicum of privacy. A mist of thick fog and a chill in the air greeted them. Zeno opened his coat and she stepped inside. Almost at once they broke into muffled laughter.

"So sorry for the inquisition. I cannot think what got into the two of them." She knew her face flushed with embarrassment.

"I found them exceedingly pleasant, both witty and intelligent. I had a wonderful time." He bent closer.

"Really." His kiss was sweet and sensuous, moving over her mouth in soft caresses. Slipping his tongue between her open lips, he turned his mouth over hers. Shivers coursed through her body and she wrapped her arms around his waist inside his coat.

"Is there a chance you'll return early?"

"Not likely." Zeno checked his watch and grimaced. "I'm afraid Yard men keep irregular hours."

Cassie sighed. "Nothing new there. Mother swears babies never birth until four in the morning." She kissed him and he pulled her back for another. "Wonderful dinner. You didn't by any chance do the cooking?"

"Cook started the roast and prepared the vegetables. Lydia helped. The cake and icing are an old Erskine recipe."

Backing into the fog, he turned up his collar. "You made the cake?"

She laughed at the stunned look on his face. "Be careful, Zak."

Chapter Seventeen

A black fog hung over the East End.

"Ease her over, mate." Zeno's gruff shout traveled through the dense mist. At times, he could barely make out the cobbles a few feet ahead. Fog torches burned on Commercial Road, but not once they turned onto Watney Street.

Rafe bobbed his head and turned the cart. Dressed as a couple of root sellers on their way to Spitalfields Market, Rafe steered while Zeno walked alongside the trolley and pushed a crowbar through the spokes. The wheel made one last lopsided turn and collapsed, tipping the produce wagon on its side. Bushels broke open, scattering parsnips over the ground.

Perfect.

Rafe threw his cap on the ground. "Sod it."

Zeno nodded. "A right shambles, awl right."

They would use the upset wagon as a ruse to gain a better view of the comings and goings around this building on Watney Street. Zeno suspected the run-down boardinghouse functioned as a safe house for the *Clan na Gael* as well as a drop site for dynamite.

Zeno swung a near empty sack over to his junior partner, who appeared a bit green about the gills this evening. "Load this up." He lifted a full bushel and stacked it against a brick building. "You look like hell."

"I swear the bird had one hand on my prick and another in my pocket." Rafe rattled on about his last evening's exploits. "If she had stroked any faster I would have missed the fact she was robbing me blind."

Zeno marveled at the number and color of his abrasions. Red-rimmed eyes, one of them blackened, and sallow around the gills. Not entirely unfamiliar coloring. His partner drank too much and regularly caroused with harlots. Raphael Byron Lewis was going to die young and he didn't seem to care.

"I take it this lovebird's procurer took issue over the attempted theft?" Zeno gave a nod to the scraped and bruised knuckles. "Hope you gave him your best."

"The pub rabble took his side. Flynn and I left a few mugs full of lumps, all right." Rafe tossed him a wink. "But they weren't as pretty as either of us to begin with."

"Ah, Mr. Rhys was there. I might have known." Zeno caught a bit of movement from the corner of his eye and cleared his throat. He dipped his head in the direction of the drop site.

A tall figure dressed in formal attire, including opera hat and cape, stepped out into the alleyway from the rear door of the boardinghouse. Thick atmosphere partially obscured the figure hugging the darker side of the street.

The apparition walked toward a main thoroughfare in a hurry.

"I say, what 'ave we 'ere?" Rafe dropped his h's faster than his sack of parsnips. He pulled his cap forward and took up the broken wheel. "Let's roll this wobbly down the cobbles and 'ave a look for a smithy."

Zeno grunted. "Just don't be gettin' thirsty along the way." He stuffed the remaining parsnips into the last open sack, keeping a watchful eye on Rafe until he turned the corner at Whitechapel.

"Havin' a bit o' trouble this evening?"

He looked up in time to recognize the face with a broken nose. Bollocks. The very man he had punched the night he and Cassie made their run from the dynamiters.

The question was, did this bloke recognize him?

He rose to greet the man when a massive spike of pain shot through the back of his head. For a fleeting moment it registered that he was in deep trouble, then everything went dark.

HE TASTED BLOOD in his mouth. Without cracking open an eye, or in any way disclosing the fact that he had regained consciousness, Zeno gathered his wits about him and slowly assembled a few coherent thoughts. A strong pulse throbbed in his hands. He tried moving his arms and feet, but they were bound and tied to the chair.

A dozen brutal hammers pounded inside his skull. The pain centered near the back of his head, but there was also a dull, persistent throb at his temples. He opened a swollen eye and peered around a sparsely furnished room. A table with an oil lamp turned low and a washbasin. He made out a few crude instruments on top.

A quick inhale sent sharp pains screaming through his torso. The memory of a large fist smashing into his ribs caused him to utter a groan. He tamped down the urge to bellow louder complaints, and took a brief inventory of body parts. Likely his ribs were cracked and there was a sore shoulder that nearly returned him to the black hole of unconsciousness when he rotated his upper arm.

He tried to remember exactly what happened before he went *non compos mentis*, the Latin phrase that would officially describe his insensible state and the reason for his capture. Those three initials would get scribbled into his report of the incident. He reminded himself that his own account of this night would never be written nor would he be put through a long, grueling debrief. Someone else would finish the report. A young clerk, perhaps, would carry his personnel folder to storage, walk down row *K-L*, and perfunctorily file his life away.

From the next room, beyond the door in the corner, there were signs of life. Low mumbles and the shuffling sound of steps crept into his mind and shattered his nerves. Soon the men who beat him would be back. They would torture him until he broke or went insane, then they would kill him. The *Clan na Gael* didn't keep prisoners, especially spies. But they would be very interested in what he knew of their operation and their organization.

Both he and Mr. Lewis. Rafe.

Zeno's pulse increased at the thought of his junior partner. Where was he? Over the last few days, Rafe and Flynn had done a bang-up job confirming the drop sites. The shipment of American dynamite had been split and stored in three locations. With every stick of contraband accounted for, they were on the verge of arresting the dynamiters before any damage could be done. Then Melville purposely delayed the raids, hoping to catch a few bigger fish.

But they had waited too long and now they were discovered.

Zeno's mind wandered. If he died, what had been accomplished? Special Branch could now link the purchased explosives to the Boston anarchists, which established a connection from the American *Clan na Gael* to the Fenian dynamiters. Perhaps he had uncovered the most imperative and potentially thorny part of the ploy.

It seemed as though Scotland Yard had caught a few lucky breaks, but on this night he and Rafe had walked straight into a trap. Was it still evening? Zeno thought about the time. How many hours had passed? Six? Twelve? What day was it? Somehow he sensed that it was early morning, sometime near dawn.

Zeno concentrated. He tried to recall what occurred just before he'd gone senseless. He and Rafe had returned to the first drop site, the largest deposit of explosives.

Images flashed in his head. Rafe sprinting down the alley, tailing a man cloaked in a dark cape and opera hat. Zeno had stayed behind, standing by the broken-down handcart at the rear entrance of the boardinghouse. He had taken a blow to the back of the head.

After that, vague recollections of angry questions and

insults. And a beating. He winced as he recalled the heavy blow of fists smashing into his face and torso. Memory blurred. A second faint.

"Operation Snuffbox" might have been a resounding success, if not for his capture and identification as a Special Irish Branch agent. Their cover was blown to hell and back. The more he attempted to resign himself to his fate, the more he could not accept such a failure.

A muted shuffle of footsteps came from a distant stairway. He heard the sounds of several voices talking at once in low tones in an adjacent room. The door to his torture chamber opened and closed.

Zeno kept his eyes shut and his head down, feigning unconsciousness. He wondered for a moment if he hallucinated, as he heard the unmistakable rustle of a woman's skirts, light steps, and the splash of water in a washbasin.

Whoever stood close lifted his chin. None too gently, a wet cloth was dragged across his face and pressed to his eyes and forehead. Cool relief. Mentally, Zeno prepared himself for the next round of torture and opened his eyes.

A familiar scent brought on a rush of disjointed memories. A face blurred before coming into focus. The female in front of him held a damp washcloth in one hand and a leather baton in the other. He could not be awake, for he dreamed of his dead mistress, Jayne Wells. Dear God, she was alive. His heart sang for the briefest moment, until it skipped a beat.

No. He must be dead.

Mired in terror and grief, he stumbled onto yet another explanation too horrible to think about. As the beautiful, unmistakably familiar face came into focus again, to his horror, he realized he was neither insane nor hallucinating.

"Wake up, Zak. It's time to make your confession." The cold compress further revived him. Or was it the familiar sound of her voice? His gut clenched, which caused his aching ribs to protest, doubling the pain.

"You're dead." He croaked out a response, his throat dry and sore. Her singsong high-pitched laugh once had seemed musical; now her laughter rang coarse and cynical.

"Don't make this difficult. If you do not speak to me soon, they will come back in here and take out your knees with a quarry hammer."

His entire being reeled from the sight of her, but he refused to let her see how much she disturbed him. "Before I tell you everything you want to know, please give me the short version of the events leading up to the explosion near King's Cross. The one that killed you." He reopened a split lip with a smile. "Humor a dead man, my little honeypot."

She slapped him hard across the face. It only served to freshen up older cuts. Numb from their abuse, he righted his head and returned her glare.

"My brother's name is James Carey. Ring a bell, Zak? He resides in Newcastle prison thanks to you, Melville, and Castlemaine."

Zeno clamped his mouth shut and stared at her. Compared to Cassie, her beauty now struck him as hard. Her mouth, particularly, had taken on a cruel twist and her eyes were dark pools of ice. "I suppose that goes to motive, Miss Wells."

"It's missus now."

"You married a terrorist? My congratulations." He nodded and his brain rattled in his skull.

She stood close. Beneath her skirts, he could feel her legs press against his knees. She ran the baton in her hand over his torso and lower, along the insides of his legs. "What will your husband say, Jayne?"

"I promise not to mention it to him, or to that young widow of yours."

A deep breath caused a sharp sting from cracked ribs. He blinked away the burn of sweat in his eyes and tamped down his rage. She reached for the buttons of his trousers. Would Jayne do a job on his lower anatomy? Her other hand held a hard leather baton. He steeled himself for either pleasure or pain.

"Miss me, Zak?" He did not want to think of their past together; just hearing her voice again conjured up an avalanche of old wounds.

"After the blast, I had to identify your ring," he croaked. "It was all that remained of you. But you knew that would happen, you were counting on it."

She stroked him through the rough, torn fabric of his workingman's trousers. "Of course."

He swallowed hard. "Did you attend your own funeral? Hidden under the cover of an umbrella? It rained the whole day, you know."

"Can ya hear me sobbin' for ya, Zak?" Her fingers played down the buttons of his pants.

"Don't."

"I think it's time to take him out. See what kind of courage the stiff little man can muster." She flashed a hard smile that faded with the unmistakable crack of pistol shots.

A loud grunt and thud came from the adjoining room. They both turned toward the battering and pounding—the sound of a door being kicked down. And more gunfire. Jayne crept toward the clash with her baton raised.

Zeno wasted no time with his response to the distraction. Ignoring the ropes that bit into his bruised chest, he rocked his chair forward and lunged for her. They both crashed onto the crude slatted floor. With a violent twist of his body, the full force of his weight against the chair rails smacked her in the face. There was a loud crack to her skull before she grunted and went limp. His female captor lay unconscious beneath him.

He worked feverishly to slip out of the ropes that bound his hands together. The door opened a crack and then swung wider. A wedge of bright light fanned into the room and across his face. He called out for help.

"Christ Almighty, Zak. You look like hell."

Rafe untied his ankle bindings and helped him up from the ground. Zeno untangled the remaining ropes. "So the operation's blown." He rubbed his wrists to help restore circulation to stiff, lifeless hands.

"Not entirely." Rafe removed his ankle bindings and tossed away the cords. "The Criminal Investigations Department is on the way. Melville will soon give the order to raid the other drops. There will be plenty of arrests and hundreds of pounds of explosives confiscated."

"But none of the ringleaders." Zeno cracked a bitter

grin. A feeble groan emanated from the crumpled body on the floor. "Ah, but we have her."

He lifted the chair and his partner turned her over. A nasty gash was above one eye, and her lids fluttered open and closed again. Rafe directed his torchlight onto the face of the unconscious woman. "Jesus, Mother Mary, and Joseph. Am I seeing things?"

He shook his head. "It's Jayne." Zeno caught a glimpse of movement, a sudden shift of light behind the younger Yard man. A looming, shadowed figure appeared in the doorway holding a gun. Zeno shoved Rafe aside.

The bullet ripped through his side like a red-hot poker. Zeno took a table down as he fell to the floor beside Rafe. A broken oil lamp splashed a swath of flame across plank floors and quickly traveled up the window curtains.

Rafe rolled over with his sidearm drawn and unloaded his pistol in the direction of the doorway.

"Get up." Rafe's voice sounded far way.

When Zeno didn't respond, he was lifted onto his feet. He forced a gasp of breath and groaned, willing the pain away. "Jayne."

His partner propped him against a wall. "Stay there."

Rafe slung the dead weight of the crumpled female over his shoulder. "Ready?"

Zeno shook his head. "Go ahead. I'll follow."

Rafe staggered over. "Not likely, mate." Rafe grabbed his shirt and pulled him off the wall. Zeno willed himself to follow his partner's grunted directives.

They stepped past two dead bodies and picked their way down steps black with rising smoke. "Christ, they've set fire to the building." Rafe hacked out the words as Zeno's legs buckled.

"Do not pass out on me, Zak. I can't carry the both of you."

Zeno forced all other thoughts but survival out of his head and concentrated on every movement. One leg. Then the other. One stair step after another. They descended into heavier smoke. This hell was endless. They could easily die here, blown to kingdom come inside a dynamiter's safe house.

"We're almost there," Rafe urged. "Five more steps." But he was lying. There were twenty more. And then, suddenly, they were outside. The cooler air revived. A spasm of coughs raked his chest. He hacked up soot, blindly trailing Rafe out into the street. His lungs strained for air as a throbbing sting shot through his torso.

Zeno couldn't feel his own legs under him.

Consciousness fluttered in and out as he stumbled on. A hand reached out and dragged him across the street. Over his shoulder, he could just make out a torrent of flame licking at the windows of the boardinghouse.

The blast ripped him out of Rafe's grasp and tossed him into the air. He hit the ground hard and rolled over cobbled pavers. Crushed by the concussion of the explosion, his eardrums buzzed and hummed as the roar of the blast faded.

Zeno rolled onto his back. A spectacular, orange-red fireball rose into the night sky. Stars crisscrossed his vision. His eyelids flickered and shut.

Silence.

∽ Chapter Eighteen

Delivered by special messenger:

> To: Cassandra St. Cloud
> 10 Lyall Street
> My darling daughter,
>   Early this morning, Zeno Kennedy was deli-
> vered to the Harley Street surgery. He suffers
> multiple injuries. I have done what I can for
> him. Periodically, he awakes long enough to
> ask for you. Please come immediately.
>   Father

Cassie rapped again and waited on the darkened steps
of her parents' surgery. When a bleary-eyed servant finally
opened the door, she swept past the man and hurried along
the corridor. Heart pounding, she turned into the last room
off the hall and came to an abrupt stop. She wavered for
a moment, holding on to the doorjamb as she stared at an
unrecognizable face hidden beneath bruises and bandages.

A thin, indistinct voice hardly identifiable as her own pleaded, "Tell me he will recover, Father."

Venturing farther into the surgery, she went to remove a glove to feel Zeno's forehead. Only she wore no gloves. In the early gray of morning, she'd sent Cécile out into the cold to hail a hansom while she tossed on a dress and coat. She'd forgotten to put on gloves.

He was warm. Too warm.

"It's early yet. He's fighting an infection, I'm afraid." Her father's words were delivered in the kindest, gentlest fashion, but could not stop the tears from trailing down her cheeks.

"You must tell me everything, Daddy. Is he badly off?"

He sighed. His gaze searched hers, wondering, she supposed, if she could stand the truth. "According to the young detective who brought him in, he was captured and beaten rather brutally. A broken nose, a few bruised ribs, contusions mostly. He has also sustained a gunshot wound. The bullet shattered a bit of rib—no organs are involved, but there is some internal bleeding."

Cassie dug her fingernails into her palms. "Go on."

Her father grasped her upper arms. "There was an explosion. He managed to survive the blast, but we found blood in his ears, which signifies—"

"A possible concussion." Weak-kneed, she fell into her father's comforting embrace. "You must—tell me you will save him, Daddy!"

"Your mother and I will do everything in our power, dear. The rest is up to Zak." Father gave her a gentle pat. "He's a hardy fellow, which gives him a fighting chance. Perhaps he shall pull through."

Father settled her into a bedside chair. Once before she had asked for God's help to save her eldest brother, Hank. But her prayers had come too late. Perhaps this time it would be different. Zeno had a fighting chance, that's what Daddy said.

The dark purple and blue contusions on his face made her shiver.

She hadn't expected to like him quite so much. She had become enamored with the idea of taking a lover. Sophisticated, yes. Naughty, hopefully. Romantic, why not? But she hadn't foreseen this sinking pit in her stomach. Or the unanticipated tears that even now blurred her vision.

She took the offer of her father's handkerchief. "Chin up, Cass. I don't want him waking up to a glum face. I have seen it more times than I care to admit. A person will pull through the most dire of injuries given a bit of hope."

FOR THE FIRST few days, she and Mother and the irrepressible Mrs. Woolsley kept a constant watch. Zeno burned with fever so virulent his bed linens were soaked with sweat. Every few hours, a nurse would change the sheets and bandages and take care of his personal needs. Cassie stood by the side of the bed and bit her lip. His delirium worried her as much as or more than the infection. When he did wake, he was rarely coherent. During the small hours of the night, he would often wake in a heated fury, accusing his captors or calling for her.

She would nestle close and wrap her arms around him. These late vigils afforded her plenty of time to analyze the depth of sentiment and strength of affection she felt for this brave man. The truth of it was, Zeno cared more for her happiness and pleasure than Thomas ever had. For the briefest of moments, that revelation scared her more than the labored, wheezing rise and fall of his chest.

On the fourth day the fever subsided. By the morning of the fifth, her hopes rose with the sun. She had fallen asleep, tucked into a comfortable old armchair Father had placed beside the bed.

"YOU WANT ME to piss in that?"

Behind a screen, Zeno concentrated on the task at hand, urinating into a cup on demand.

To one side of his surgery bed, Nurse Mary Eunice intoned with practiced efficiency, "Mr. Kennedy, imagine you are standing under a waterfall, having a good shower—"

A trickle of urine turned into a torrential stream.

"Bollocks."

Gingerly, he handed off the glass beaker.

Cassie's father held the container up to the window light. "Good clarity, light in color—no more visible blood."

Could the good doctor's medical chatter be any more mortifying? Even though she pretended disinterest, he knew Cassie sat behind the partition and listened to every word. Without a grumble, he would put up with as much medical prying and probing as necessary to convince her he was on the mend. Perhaps then she would not worry quite so much.

"Let's get you to sit all the way up."

With the help of his very capable nurse, he righted himself enough so she could unwind the cloth tape around his ribs. A gentle prod to a bruise forced a sharp intake of air. "Take a slow, deep breath for me." Henry Erskine placed his stethoscope in his ears and listened. "Again." He moved the ice-cold metal cone to the other side of Zeno's chest. With each deep breath he grimaced. "Sorry, Zak."

The doctor stepped away and folded back the screen, beaming. "This is cracking indeed, lungs are clear as well. Your Yard man shall live to defend crown and country another day, Cassie."

"Saints' glory, sir." Ever the chipper one, Zeno's housekeeper entered the room and hugged Dr. Erskine.

"Yes, Mrs. Woolsley, I believe it is time to send him packing." Cassie's father reached for his pocket watch. "In fact, I find him fit enough to return home in your good care. I should think Cassie will want to look in on him as well." He patted the anxious housekeeper on the shoulder and gave his daughter a wink. "I want both of you to watch Nurse as she wraps those ribs. We'll keep him taped up for a few more days."

Mary Eunice unwrapped several rolls of knitted fabric and Cassie rose from her chair to join Mrs. Woolsley at his bedside. Her cool hand stroked his forehead and jawline. "Good morning, Zak." Her smile made everything right in his world.

If it weren't for a mending bullet hole in his side and the damned bruised ribs, he would have pulled her into his arms in front of everyone, including Nurse.

"I must say a healthy body heals itself without much interference from the marvels of modern medicine."

Cassie's father picked up a clipboard. "All the doctor prescribes is a few additional days of rest and he should soon be fit enough for service."

"And what of the matter of a broken nose?" Olivia Erskine stepped through the door carrying a jar of salve. "Which I am now satisfied will heal straight enough."

"Enough?" Zeno frowned.

Olivia Erskine stood back and tilted her head. "I believe he looks rather sweet with his nose bandaged and those green and purple bruises under each eye."

He turned to Cassie. "Enough?"

"No harm done, a bit of a bump along the bridge," she gently prodded. The tease in her smile caused him to grab her hand and kiss the inside of her wrist. His fleeting show of affection was not lost on Mother Erskine.

Olivia handed a jar over to Cassie and sat down on the edge of his bed. "Arnica lotion for his contusions." Carefully, she removed the splint from his nose. "My own personal cure. I discovered it in our travels to Greece. The arnica flower has the most miraculous ability to heal bruised flesh. The Mediterraneans have used it for centuries."

The doctor gently palpated his nose. "I see the swelling is down. My daughter just might have her handsome landlord back by week's end." She replaced the splint and bandage.

Zeno tried not to wince when all four women, including his nurse, helped him back into his bed shirt. "I've decided I dislike being a patient. People hover and conduct conversation around you in a peculiar third-person vernacular."

Settling back into a stack of plumped pillows, Zeno caught a sympathetic grin from Cassie's father, as he scribbled notes onto his medical chart. "We're all taking a holiday this weekend at home. You must come out to Muirfield, Zak. The rest and the country air will fit you up and do your lungs good. I might even authorize a bit of riding. No jumping the neighbor's hedgerows, but a nice slow amble along quiet Surrey roads—just the thing."

Zeno shook his head. "I'm afraid a mountain of paperwork awaits me. Perhaps after I'm back on the job for a week or so—"

"Nonsense, Kennedy. You will spend the weekend with the Erskines." Melville stood in the doorway of the surgery.

Dr. Erskine greeted his boss. "Nice to see you, Bill."

"Henry." Melville smiled. A rarity, indeed.

Undaunted, Zeno continued his protest. "But I must get back and help with the interrogations—all the reports. Rafe tells me he's buried."

"Cheer up, Zak—I should like to have you back in the office." Melville appeared to enjoy his taunts.

Dr. Erskine nodded. "Give him a day or two at home. By Thursday he can put in a few hours."

Melville tossed a morning paper onto the bed blanket. "We've kept the news quiet for over a week now, but—well, have a look."

Zeno opened the paper with a scowl.

"Goodness, a healthy frown." Cassie grinned at his boss. "Another fortuitous sign he is on the mend."

"My daughter, Cassandra St. Cloud." Dr. Erskine made introductions. Melville inclined his head. "Mrs. St. Cloud, your father has mentioned you in glowing terms on numerous occasions."

Cassie perched herself on the edge of the bed and leaned in to read the paper. "We knew something was up, Mr. Melville. Baskets of posies and biscuit tins addressed to Mr. Zeno Kennedy began to arrive early this morning."

THE LONDON TIMES
SCOTLAND YARD CAPTURES DYNAMITERS
500 LBS. OF DYNAMITE SEIZED IN DARING RAIDS

Zeno sneaked an arm around Cassie and stroked her back. Reading farther down, he grimaced when he read his name in the headline of an adjacent article.

YARD MAN KENNEDY TAKES BULLET
FOR RESCUER LEWIS

Melville used his umbrella to press down the top edge of the *Times* and make eye contact. "Just as well we closed in on them early, Zak. We arrested two ringleaders, and a number of henchmen. Mr. Rhys had the jolly good idea to let one of the dynamiters think he'd given us the slip. He trailed them to a nest of outliers."

"Flynn Rhys is a crack agent, despite his irregular behavior." Zeno set the paper down and studied his boss and Cassie's father. "How is it you two know each other?"

"Whist partners. Play together every Thursday night." Dr. Erskine grinned.

Olivia beamed. "Small world, wot?"

*   *   *

CASSIE STEPPED INTO the foyer as someone struck the doorknocker. She set a medium-sized portmanteau on a side chair next to the vestibule table. Since she was the only one downstairs, she opened the door a crack. "Gerald."

"Hello, Cassie."

She had a look down the street. Two men exited the carriage parked along the mews entrance and ran for her front door. They slowed when they saw her wave. "Ten minutes, gentlemen. After that you can beat the door down."

Two police officers dressed in street clothes looked over Gerald. One of them gave a nod. "We'll be waiting close by, Mrs. St. Cloud."

She motioned Gerald inside. "Please note I am under constant guard now."

His eye contact faltered. No surprise there. "Good to see you, Cassie." Her brother-in-law doffed his bowler and followed her into the parlor.

"You're looking grim this afternoon. What is it, Gerald? I hope things are fine at home. Aunt Esmie is well?"

"Yes, yes, Cassie. Fit as fiddle." He checked the room furtively, as if to assure their privacy. "It is you I worry about."

"Me? Whatever for?" She feigned a wider eye. "As you can see I am well protected."

After some fidgeting about, he blurted out his concern. "Cassie, you must promise me you will stop seeing Mr. Kennedy. I have it on good authority the man is dangerous and, well . . ." He stroked the upturned rim of his hat. "Detective Kennedy may well be using you to get to a few gentlemen of my acquaintance."

"I see." Cassie sank onto the edge of a settee. "And what

makes you believe such a thing is true? Who are these authorities of yours?"

Gerald's eyes darted around the room. "For your protection, Cassie, I shall not disclose their names."

"My protection?" His frightful warning made no sense and he appeared nervous in the extreme. She could not remember him ever acting this wary.

Cassie rose from her seat and joined him by the mantel. "Gerald, are you in trouble?"

He looked away and shrugged. "Nothing out of the ordinary. A few too many gambling debts."

Well aware of her brother-in-law's propensity for the gaming hells and racetrack, she was not surprised he had taken up with men of a dubious nature. Unruly types, like Delamere and his cadre. The night of the ball, Zeno had disclosed he suspected Gerald to be a member. She hadn't thought much of it then. Now she wouldn't put it past her brother-in-law to connect, in desperation, with these nefarious characters. "I hardly think your gambling debts could affect me unless you've lost my pension."

He scoffed. "My income is in trust, as is yours. I couldn't get to it if I was hog-tied and kidnapped for ransom."

"Then I don't understand . . ."

"Oh, bloody hell. I do not wish to alarm, but these cohorts of mine might try to get to Zeno Kennedy through you." Obviously bedeviled, he lifted an elbow to the mantel, and rubbed his chin. "I have come to understand that these gentlemen, if one could call them such, are very bad company."

It seemed to Cassie, her brother-in-law's suit against Zeno had just made a rather abrupt turnabout. Things suddenly clicked together. Obviously, this is what Zeno feared most. Some sort of abduction. She would be held and Scotland Yard would be forced to back off.

Gerald shook his head. "It's just that I would never forgive myself if anything happened to—"

Cassie cut him off. "If Zeno Kennedy pursues your acquaintances, I suggest you make new ones." She clamped her mouth shut and straightened her shoulders.

He stepped closer. "I have been trying for weeks to disassociate myself, but they hold on to more than my debts."

"Whatever do you mean, Gerald?"

"No one crosses them, Cassie. I am certain they were behind the Stanfield ball murder. Poor James." He drew a shaky hand through unkempt hair. "Those police guards outside won't protect you. They'll come for you in unexpected ways. Stealthy like—"

A sharp rap at the door caused her to check the mantel clock. "Your ten minutes are up."

She almost felt a bit sorry for him. Almost.

ZENO READ THE pitiful lies in the booking interview.

> 25 May. Miss Jayne Wells aka Mrs. Brian
> O'Shea?? Aka Mrs. Michael Doyle?? Detainee
> has named three dynamiters already in custody.
> Target locations unconfirmed.

The words *taciturn* and *uncooperative* were penciled in on the largely blank sheet of paper. After some deliberation, he suspected, his colleagues had left Jayne for him.

He closed the dossier and stood beside a small table with two chairs. Rafe was bringing her up from the lockup. He drew a breath and did not wince. With each inhale and exhale, day after day, the pangs had lessened to sharp, tingling pricks. His bruised rib cage was truly on the mend— or was he just getting used to the way his body hurt? It felt good to be back to work. Once this interview ended, however, he would race to catch the last afternoon commuter.

Cassie would meet him at the train station in Farnham. He pictured her smile. And longed for her excellent company. In fact, he could hardly wait to leave town. She had rubbed him down with a liniment yesterday afternoon and caused such arousal he would have wrapped her hand around his erection for a private massage, but Mrs. Woolsley entered the room ahead of Rafe. Cassie had laughed at his lusty urges, calling him a hound on the mend.

He had hungered for her ever since and a long morning of paperwork had failed to dull his desire. Dear God, he wanted her—needed her naked and writhing beneath him.

The door to the interrogation room opened. Zeno turned toward the sound of leg chains and the swish of a woman's skirt. "Thank you, Rafe." Zeno excused his partner, who gave him a silent thumbs-up as he shut the door.

He turned to Jayne. She answered his stare for an interminable few moments before the grind and clunk of the door lock caused her to flinch. She edged forward. "Don't we both look a sight?"

His gaze lingered on a crescent-shaped cut and a patch

of green and yellow bruising above her right eye. Another pain, perhaps not wholly physical, shot through him as he recalled details of his capture. How he had lunged at her. The crack of his chair against her skull.

Still, she held her Irish chin up. Pretty, even through layers of jail grime. "Miss Wells, I should say Missus—" He opened her file and searched for a name. "Is it Mrs. Doyle or Mrs. O'Shea?"

"Wouldn't you Scotland Yard boys care to know?"

"Right." He snapped the file closed. "Let's get to it, then." She ignored the chair he pulled out. "I must require you to sit, Jayne." He waited. "You either take a seat, or I will call Detective Lewis in and we will tie you down. Your choice."

She sidled over to the chair and sat down. "Mrs. Brian O'Shea," she sniffed. "Figured you'd soon be wantin' to know about us."

"First, a bit of old history. Let's talk about you and me, Mrs. O'Shea." He noted a wary glance. Her face was laced with fatigue and something else . . . Disappointment, perhaps?

As she appeared reluctant to speak, he tried priming the pump. "Perhaps I can begin," he bit out, "for I have had plenty of time, lying in hospital, to puzzle out a scenario." His voice sounded curt and gruff, and a deep pang of sorrow tore through him. He once cared for her and she had betrayed him. Shoulders back, he met her eyes. She might be able to detect his anger and something of his humiliation, but he would never, ever allow her to see his pain.

"You expected to be able to track me, as well as my associates, as your plot for the bombings drew close."

Matter-of-factly, he cleared his throat. "Due to a shortage of field operatives, I was transferred temporarily to the St. John's Wood case. At that point I was of no further use to the *Clan*."

He shrugged. "It must have been easy enough to plant evidence of your person at one of the explosion sites. In fact, it wasn't even clever."

She smirked a sly, hollow grin. "Yes, if it were clever, you would have spotted the ruse. But since it was not, you missed the obvious."

"Yes, the ring did the trick."

He grilled her on every detail of their operation. She gave up enough small bits of information to keep him interested, but after several hours, his head ached and his unseen wounds began to throb. "I have been authorized to make you an offer. You name your targets, as well as *Clan* safe houses, shipping contacts, ports of entry—"

She snorted a laugh and rolled her eyes even as his speech grew acerbic and clipped. "You will also name your American contacts, as well as Fenian sympathizers in Parliament. If your information proves itself, we are prepared to release prisoners." Zeno paused. "Including James Carey."

Her eyes sparked at the mere mention of her brother's name and her stare faltered. "They never told me much. But . . ." She hesitated.

Feigning apathy, he flipped open her file and held his breath.

Chapter Nineteen

Zeno stepped off the train at Farnham Station at exactly thirty-seven minutes past four o'clock in the afternoon, just seven minutes off schedule. He swayed a bit on his feet.

"Mr. Kennedy?" A tall, athletic young man with sandy-brown hair and clear gray eyes, no doubt a dominant Erskine trait, approached him. "I'm Cassie's brother. Rob Erskine."

He held out his hand. "Call me Zak."

The cooler Surrey air made a refreshing change from the thick, oppressive humidity of the crowded rail coach. A damp shirt clung to his back and he unbuttoned his jacket.

"Splendid, you came dressed to ride." Cassie's youngest brother studied him with an open, honest face and curious eyes. "You look a bit wilted. The commuters bugger us all on warm days."

Zeno nodded, glancing around the emptying platform.

"Cassie waits for us in the woodlot across the lane." Rob pointed to a stand of sycamore trees.

He squinted. "Ah, there she is." She sat astride a striking gray hunter holding the reins of two other first-class mounts. She waved to him.

He raised an arm in return and a bruised rib reminded him he was still on the mend. A cool breeze ruffled his clothes and hair. For a moment, he could not take his eyes off her. Rob politely nudged his bag out of his hand and carried the suitcase to a small luggage cart parked by the side of the station platform.

Zeno followed after, taking long strides to stretch his legs and get the blood flowing. "Cass and I mean to give you a tour. Take the long way round the village and surroundings. By the time we arrive home, you'll have your tosser up again." Rob patted the pockets of his riding breeches. "Sorry, don't have a farthing on me."

Zeno paid the driver and headed off across the road, his eye on the prettier Erskine. Without a doubt. Her hair was tied back with a velvet ribbon and she wore a simple white shirt, open at the collar but neatly tucked into tight-fitting breeches. As he and Rob drew closer, he could see there was no hiding her figure—from anyone. Her shifting seat and repeated glances signaled she expected his disapproval. This modern Erskine woman displayed a rather perverse need to unsettle him.

Zeno determined then and there not to lift an eyebrow over her attire. Two could play this game. He removed his hat and coat. "I find the afternoon air much too sultry for jackets. And the idea of wearing a hat without a coat, well . . ." He shrugged.

"And there isn't much point to this." Zeno unbuttoned his waistcoat.

"I say, grand idea." Rob shrugged out of his jacket and grabbed Zeno's things. "I'll just toss these on top of your bag."

"Hold on." Zeno loosed his tie and unbuttoned his collar, tossing both to Rob. "Might as well finish the job."

"Dog's bollocks." Rob grinned at his sister. "I do believe Zak and I shall get on."

Zeno returned to Cassie and executed a slow, purposeful once-over with his eyes. A faint curl to his lip likely alerted her to his frame of mind. "You look beautiful, as always, Cassie."

Rob's cheerful adviso came a bit late. "That's it, Zak. No use letting Erskine women know when they're shocking. It only encourages them."

She wrinkled her nose at her brother. "It is by mother's request I ride astride. She claims the gates and hedgerows we jump are too wide and high." She handed off reins to her brother. "Besides, Zak has been forewarned."

Rob brought round a handsome bay hunter. "This is Jupiter, he's our brother Jamie's horse. Very athletic, good-hearted character with a bit of a temper. Dad said you were in the dragoons—you're going to love him."

Zeno checked the girth.

"Give you a leg up?" Rob offered.

He nodded. "With these ribs taped, I believe I'll need one." Rob gave him a boost onto the saddle and made small adjustments to his stirrup lengths.

Reining his horse alongside Cassie's, Zeno let his gaze move from her smiling eyes, down the rounded curve of her backside to long legs fitted into tall, black top boots.

She rode astride with beautiful form, shoulders back, toes up, heels down. Exactly where he wanted them later this evening when they were alone together.

"You appear ready for a vigorous romp in the countryside, Cassie."

"Indeed I am." A rush of color to her cheek suggested she took his meaning, but her gaze remained focused on the road ahead. "However, I must tell you I have been instructed to take it slow and easy with you."

"I cannot express how much I look forward to the ride." He waited for a smile. When she tossed back her head and laughed, he collected his reward.

"I find you both clever and charming when you wish to be, Zak."

"Ah." He grinned. "That is because I am inspired, Cassie."

Once they wound their way through the bustling little village, Rob led them off onto rugged back roads where they cantered the horses along a narrow trail that crossed a wide expanse of meadow and jumped a few low hedgerows. Cassie looked back with a smile. "You seem healthy enough for another gate or two."

"Lead on." Zeno's heartbeat drummed in his chest. His leg muscles ached a bit but the exercise felt wonderful.

Wonderful to be alive.

Jupiter sailed over thicket fences, wooden gates, and an ancient stone wall. Zeno followed the two Erskines as they splashed their way through a neighborhood brook, and galloped up a broad expanse of hill.

On the rise of a craggy slope overlooking Muirfield

Park, he reined Jupiter in alongside Cassie's mount. With a shine in her eyes, flushed cheeks, and a few wild wisps of hair about her face, she could not have looked lovelier. He turned to the view of her family home. "So this is where you grew up, Cassie. Enchanting."

She shifted her gaze to him. "It does me good to be home, even for short visits."

Far from a stern gothic fortress, the Erskine manse resembled more of a rambling Tudor manor house comfortably set among an idyllic park filled with formal gardens, wilderness, and a pond large enough for a good swim.

He gave his horse several good strong pats on the neck and received a gentle snort in answer. "What a hardy chap this one is."

"Ripping," Rob enthused. "Jupiter is perhaps the best mount in the stable. Takes an experienced hand though, like you or Jamie. He has sorely tested lesser riders."

Cassie's brows drew together as she chewed a lip. "If we take Piper's Lane through the woods, will that leave us off near to our park entrance?"

"Haven't taken that route in ages." Rob swept a hand through unruly locks and nodded. "Good memory, Cass."

She led the way up a narrow byway just as an open landau approached them. They guided their horses up a berm to one side of the lane to clear the way. The carriage slowed, revealing a merry party of four. A pair of ladies sat opposite two gentlemen, out for an afternoon's drive. Zeno inhaled a sharp, painful breath as he recognized Lord Delamere.

His lordship tipped his hat. "Well, if it isn't the Erskine

clan out with their celebrated weekender." Cold eyes examined his faded cuts and bruises. "In the news again, Mr. Kennedy?"

"Lord Delamere."

Neither Cassie nor Rob greeted his lordship. In fact, Rob's steely-eyed expression appeared murderous, which neatly fit into Zeno's own notions about the man.

Zeno sat back in the saddle, while he and the arrogant lord eyed one another. Delamere had them at a disadvantage. They were, all three of them, in a near scandalous state of dishabille. He and Rob rode without jackets or hats, but Cassie was by far the most provocative of all. His lordship appeared transfixed and made no secret about his admiration, leching over every inch of her.

Zeno glanced across the carriage to the women in Delamere's party, perfectly attired in spring frocks. The young ladies nervously twirled parasols and could not help twittering at the sight of men with a bit of chest hair peeking out of open collarless shirts.

For a moment, Zeno almost laughed. Good God, he was becoming an Erskine.

"Someone must keep me up on the latest rage. Have breeches come into fashion along with pantaloons, Mrs. St. Cloud?" Delamere's expression transmuted from lurid ogler to ruffled peer.

To Cassie's credit, she gave everyone in the open carriage a cool, elegant stare even as her lips curled into a dry, mocking smile.

"A lady may risk such attire when escorted by gentlemen she can trust."

She turned her horse toward the road ahead and with a light tap, her mount moved smoothly away from the carriage into a fast canter. He and Rob delivered a polite nod to the women in the group. "Ladies."

As they galloped up the rise after Cassie, Zeno announced, "I grow to hate that man."

Rob returned the sentiment. "I should have killed him when I had the chance." They crested the hill and found Cassie waiting for them in a field ahead. Zeno cued Jupiter to slow to a walk and Rob followed suit.

"We ran into Delamere at the Stanfield Ball. I have not asked Cassie directly, but there appears to be a story between them too private or distressing to speak of."

Rob glowered. "He tried to rape her when she was seventeen, on the evening of her coming out."

His jaw clenched. "Might I ask what he is doing here in Surrey?" Zeno kept his eyes trained on the fair woman up ahead.

"Part of his estate borders Muirfield. It makes our place look like a tenant cottage by comparison."

"He made a remark to Cassie at the ball. Something about—" Zeno adjusted his seat. "He had asked for her hand and received a bruising refusal?"

"Isn't he the clever fellow?" Rob halted his mount. "He offered for her, and Cassie refused him. On the evening of her first ball, she went missing. Jamie heard a cry and was the first to find them. Delamere had her against a wall with her skirts up. The daft man tried to force the marriage." Rob shook his head. "We beat him within an inch of his life."

A protective and possessive impulse broke in ferocious waves over him. "Ever the practiced gentleman," Zeno bit out. "Would that I had been there with you."

His near primal anger elicited a wry grin from Rob. "Next time you're around him, note the permanent scar above his right eye. I take credit for that."

Zeno glanced ahead as they cleared the wood and approached the meadow. Cassie tugged loose her hair ribbon and unleashed honey-brown waves. "Lead the way, fair Lady Godiva, your chevaliers are here to attend you."

Once inside the park, they cooled off the horses before returning them to a single groom in the stables. The noticeable lack of servants about the grounds and in the house signaled a relaxed, informal weekend. Zeno breathed a sigh of relief.

Cassie led him to the orangery, where he made his greetings to her parents. Dr. Erskine moved to stand as they stepped into the airy conservatory. "So how did it go, Zak? I hope Cassie and Rob heeded my warning and took it easy on you."

"He took a few jumps without complaint." Cassie kissed her father's cheek. "I'm afraid we couldn't talk him out of it."

Dr. Erskine winked. "Legs wobbly?"

"Perhaps a bit," he admitted. "I'll be sore enough in the morning."

"I can see the vigor returned to your cheeks." Olivia gave them both a once-over. "Darling, show Zak upstairs to his room, and do refresh yourselves in a hurry. You are both expected to make an appearance for tea."

Cassie escorted him upstairs and showed him the recently finished water closet. She then opened doors to at least three rooms before they found his luggage. "Ah, Mother has put you in Jamie's old room."

"Your two other brothers, Cole and Jamie—?"

"Off in the Americas. Father has advised them to find their fortune, for he is done financing their adventures."

Zeno grinned. As she turned to leave, he pulled her back into the room and locked the door. "Do you mind?"

"Do I mind what, Zeno?"

"Do you mind stepping out of those breeches and bending over the bed? I'm in great need of you, darling."

"Was that 'darling' an afterthought or an attempt to be charming?" She ran a finger down the buttons on his shirt. "And what shall be left for us to do after supper and requisite Erskine family parlor games? I intend on sneaking into your room after charades and a ripping game of 'Lookabout.'"

They both snorted a quiet laugh.

He approached her gently and nuzzled her neck. "I do promise to be quick about it. And after I am easily sated, I shall pleasure you—just enough to make you aroused for me."

Cassie smiled a delicious, wanton goddess smile.

"FATHER SAYS HE regularly receives alarming reports from neighboring farms about the roadster," Cassie teased her brother. "In fact, Mr. McMurphy claims his cows don't give milk like they used to." She led the way through the garden to a large workshop built under a wing of the house.

"That particular incident was caused by one of my rockets." He turned to Zeno. "Started a small fire in his dairy shed. I ran over and put the damned thing out the moment it happened, but there was plenty of bellyaching over it." Her brother brushed back a lock of hair fallen into his eyes. "No matter. The entire village thinks the Erskine offspring a wild bunch of young bohemians."

"Father correctly calls us *civilized* bohemians." Her gaze slid to Zeno with a wink. He offered a ready grin in return. She found it most satisfying to see him happy and relaxed. Well sated, if you will. In his room, before tea, Zeno had taken his satisfaction, then released her with a playful smack to her derriere. At the touch of his expert hands, she had experienced such a wave of arousal, she couldn't quite stop thinking about the pleasure that would soon be hers. She wanted him desperately, exactly as promised.

"Here we are." Rob rolled back the shed doors. "Presenting Robert's roadster. Powered by one of Daimler's experimental engines. Single carburetor. Uses petrol fuel. Equal to the pull of eight horses."

Zeno's eyes lit up, his hands on his hips. "Blimey, Rob. This is brilliant." Zeno took a walk around the horseless carriage with her brother and even crawled underneath to have a look at the drive shaft and axle.

"Rob, you must take Zak out and teach him how to drive the roadster." Brushing off a bit of grease and dirt, both men emerged from under the vehicle. "It's wonderful fun."

Zeno blinked. "You've operated this?"

His incredulous expression caused a chuckle. "Several times."

"All right then, let's start her up." Rob grabbed a hand crank. "I can teach you the steerage in minutes."

After two failed attempts, the engine roared into service with a couple of heart-stopping backfires. Zeno jumped into the seat beside Rob and off they went.

She returned Zeno's wave as they turned out of the stable yard and through the gates. The roadster easily took the hill grade and disappeared down the lane behind McMurphy's barn.

"Cassie, are you down there?"

"Yes, Mother."

Olivia leaned out the window above. "Come up here and help me pick out a dress for supper. Perhaps you can curl my hair. I feel like a bit of primping and tittle-tattle."

From over the hillside, the roadster backfired. "Coming, Mama."

Chapter Twenty

"**M**umm-ber!" With a number of hairpins pressed between her lips, Cassie rolled her eyes.

"Well, it's hard not to notice the air positively crackles between the two of you." With a gleam in her eye, Olivia sat at the vanity and admired her reflection.

Standing behind her mother, Cassie dipped lower to catch a front view of Olivia's hair in the mirror. Satisfied with the pouf in the topknot, she swept the last lock of hair up and around the high bun and pinned it in place.

Condoms, of all things! And Mother had deposited them in the top dresser drawer of her bedchamber as well as the guestroom of a certain gentleman staying the weekend at Muirfield. "For whichever room you two end up in," Olivia added with a sparkle in her eye.

She removed the remaining pins from her mouth and set them on the vanity. "Dear lord, Mother, have you also discussed this with Father? Please tell me not Rob. Do you plan to have the entire household winking to each other this evening?"

"Oh hush, Cassie. Everyone in the family is thrilled with your Detective Kennedy. In fact, they are most curious as to your feelings for the man." Her mother's eager expression caused a bit of warmth in her cheeks.

Cassie scooted her mother over on the vanity bench. "Well." She brushed a few stray hairs back into her own chignon. "I must admit he is rather dashing to look at, and much more companionable than I once thought."

Toying with the fringe on the dresser scarf, she set an elbow on her knee and rested her chin in her palm. "And even though his work is quite dangerous, I am of the opinion he is a thoughtful and rational man—not reckless or inconstant in the least."

"Yes, I don't see much of Thom in him." Mother powdered her nose and passed the puff.

"And he is quite romantic." She caught her own reflection in the looking glass. Dreamy-eyed. On a deeper level, her feelings for this new man were . . . well, she wasn't sure she could admit them to herself as yet.

Olivia's grin was downright mischievous. "And is he talented—you know, intimately?"

"Do you really care to know, Mother?" Cassie pulled on the puffs of her sleeves. "Oh, never mind. Of course you do." She tilted her head in mock contemplation. "A bit like a ride in an air balloon. Up you go, higher and higher. And then a great sigh as you descend back to earth."

Mother pressed her lips together to hold back a chortle. "I so want you to be happy."

Cassie's chest swelled with love as she took her mother's hands in hers. "I am over the brim with happiness, Mother."

"Yes, I can see you are."

CASSIE SLOWED THEIR trek through a narrow patch of reeds by the water's edge. "A walk by the pond in the moonlight," Zeno had called their exit from the parlor, which effectively ended the after-dinner game of charades. Unable to wipe the smile off her face, it was better she walked ahead of him. For several hours after supper, she and Rob had wickedly trounced her parents and their esteemed guest.

"And how is it Rob was able to get Lewis Carroll when you drew a finger across your throat?"

A breathy chuckle escaped her mouth. "What a suspicious creature you are. Could his guess not be extrapolated, sir, from the most famous line of the Red Queen?" Cassie glanced backward with a smile. "You believe we have developed secret codes? I would think the clue obvious enough. Tell me, Zeno, what came first to mind when I offed my head?"

He reached around her waist and drew her up against his chest. "I should think, Anne Boleyn?" He kissed her earlobe. "Or perhaps, off with the girl's britches?"

Goose bumps crawled up her arms, from the cool night air or from this man? She shivered and he wrapped his coat around her. She had come to very much like standing inside the warmth of his jacket, pressed against his body. The smell of his lime cologne mixed with the light musk of his familiar scent.

"Rob seems happy enough in his workshop." Zeno settled his arms around her waist. "And I certainly heard plenty this evening about the two brothers off adventuring in the Americas."

Cassie nodded. "Cole and Jamie."

"And what kind of a little girl were you, Cassie?"

Her eyes grew dreamy. "I was the baby and the only girl—spoiled, willful. My brothers made sure I could ride like a hellion by the age of six or seven."

"So, they could not help but adore you."

Cassie studied him. She appeared to be conducting a silent evaluation of some kind. "There was a dark period, after Hank died. He was the eldest son and, of course, my favorite. I looked up to him as both father and brother. At the time of his death, mother had already returned to her work in town. We saw our parents on weekends."

"Might I ask how your eldest brother died?"

She sighed deeply. "Hunting accident—he stumbled and his gun went off. Bled to death before they reached the house." Her gaze moved through him and far away.

He pulled her close. "I am very sorry, Cassie."

"I was twelve at the time. I began having morbid thoughts."

Zeno swallowed. "Morbid thoughts?"

"Suicidal urges." Cassie grinned a bit sheepishly. "It's rather hard to describe, but let me try." He experienced the most inexplicable pleasure in her crinkled-up nose and furrowed brow.

"Have you ever been lured by the silver current of a fast running river and thought what it might be like to cast yourself off the bridge into the oblivion of cold, deep water?"

Mouth open and brow furrowed, Zeno appeared flummoxed.

Cassie added a lopsided grin to the flush on her cheeks. "Not even a little trip and fall onto the railroad tracks just before the train arrives?"

His eyes sparked to life. "I remember . . . fleeting urges. A windblown cliff on a patch of coast near my home on Skye. A momentary desire to let go of life—to dive like a seabird off the embankment. I was just a boy . . ."

She nodded. "Yes, exactly like that. Only mine lasted longer, and were worrisome enough that my mother took me to every notable doctor in England. Some of them wanted to throw me into large tubs of ice water—shock the system."

Cassie brushed a few tendrils of hair off her face. "Mother wouldn't allow it, called them quacksalvers. In the end, Father thought it a jolly good idea to keep me so busy I wouldn't have time for morbid thoughts."

He brushed his lips over the small fine hairs of her temple. "So, the art lessons."

"And voice, and dance, piled upon a mountain of difficult schoolwork. They hoped I would take to something, find some sort of spiritually healing avocation."

He stroked her face with the backside of a knuckle. "When I was captured by the *Clan na Gael*, I thought I would never hold you again—never do this again." He kissed her lips softly, tenderly.

Arching away, she took him by the hand. "Come hither, sir."

They made their way back to the house, detouring

through the kitchen larder, where they snagged a plate of biscuits and poured a glass of ale.

"Shh." She led the way up the darkened stairs, detouring around several treads. "Very loud, creaky ones," she hissed. When they reached the upper floor, a beam of moonlight served to guide them the rest of the way.

Safely ensconced in his room, Zeno lit a bedside lamp, but kept the wick low. He blew out the match and replaced the chimney.

"There are condoms in the dresser," she blurted out.

Sliding out the top drawer, he removed a tin of rubber goods. "You do encourage the most lascivious behavior in me." Zeno tilted his head. "Do you find my lovemaking in any way disturbing, Cassie? Because if you do—"

"I don't." She bit her lip. "I suppose that makes me a terrible wanton, doesn't it?"

"It makes you the most desirable young lady I have ever encountered."

She stepped into his arms and gave him a kiss. "Since my naked bottom was exposed this afternoon, it is your turn, Zak, to remove every stitch of clothing." She leaned against a bedpost. "And I shall watch."

He tilted his head and narrowed his gaze. It was a look that could easily strike terror into the stoutest of hearts. But tonight, it was accompanied by a slight upturn at the edges of his mouth. "My pleasure, Cassandra."

He disrobed without much self-consciousness and her attention never left him. When he turned around to place his trousers over a chair rail she thought she might swoon. His broad back narrowed into waist and chiseled derriere.

Those long, sinewy thighs she often admired under his breeches were . . . perfect.

He turned and stood before her, proudly erect.

Her gaze traveled over—well, after his penis, his curved groin muscle, nicely defined arms, and a broad strong chest, dusted with hair. Even the bandages wound round his torso made him the very picture of a gallant, wounded warrior.

"The Greeks could not have chosen a more perfect subject." She lifted her gaze to meet his. "I should like to paint you one day."

Zeno scratched his chin. "I wouldna' mind, lass, as long as ye promise not to display Willy in the Grosvenor Gallery."

Cassie clamped her mouth shut to avoid a burst of laughter that would surely wake the household. Her regard returned to his groin. "He does appear ready for me." She reached out to admire the size and thickness of his erection, which caused his breath to catch.

"For you? Always." Those beautiful sapphire eyes gleamed in the darkness. Starved, was he? For he looked as though he could eat her alive. She hoped so.

She unbuttoned her skirt and let it puddle at her feet. He further helped to pull cords and untie ribbons until bustle, slips, and pantaloons hit the floor. Only a thin camisole remained, and his prick jerked in appreciation.

He pressed her back against the heavy carved bedpost, and raised her arms above her head. Once her camisole was off, his gaze followed the movement of his hands over her body. Like a cool breeze, he caressed nipples, gliding past ribs and torso. Her stomach muscles trembled as his fingers slipped between her legs. Her stark nudity felt perversely mysterious.

He slipped his hand between her legs. His fingers moved through soft curls and slick flesh to lightly stroke and circle. A rush of wetness eased from her as he massaged her most sensitive spot, teasing until the small nub swelled with hot-blooded sensation.

"Have you any idea how difficult it has been this last week? The lurid thoughts and dreams of you." He kissed her temple, brushing his lips down to her ear.

"Mm-mm," she moaned.

His fingers circled gently, increasing speed and pressure until her knees buckled, unable to support her. Zeno caught her in his arms and set her down on the edge of the bed. As she reclined, his hands slipped under her, lifting her buttocks until her triangle met his lips. Her belly quivered as he slipped over the curls of her mound and traced a string of soft kisses to her breasts.

She reached down and took the impressive, rock-hard member into her hands, marveling at the taut velvet skin and the bounce of his enthusiastic arousal. She smiled. "My turn."

Her fingers slid past the bandages of his bound rib cage. She kissed tentatively, then used her tongue, exploring the silken flesh until she took all of him into her mouth. His hands stroked her hair and each breath grew harsh.

She released the broad phallus and made a soft, loving demand, but a demand nonetheless. "I will have all of you, sir." Obediently, he thrust in again—but gently. His groin muscles tightened as she took even more of him.

"Slow, love," he begged. She licked instead.

Only after he growled like a beast and his breathing grew harsh did he pull away and press her onto the bed. He nudged her legs open and slid his fingers inside her body. Two digits gently stroked, causing more slippery wetness to flow.

His lips covered a nipple. He tongued, then nipped. A deluge of pleasure. He suckled one then the other, teasing, caressing as he pressed the tip of his erection along her slippery path—until she arched and held her breath. She marveled at his intuition, for he seemed to know her desire might peak at any moment.

Abruptly, he stopped all his lovely ministrations and rolled onto his back. Blindly, he reached for the condom tin. Squinting in the dark, he read, "Three Knights with Reservoir Ends."

All eyes, she rolled closer. Zeno glanced at her with a close-lipped smile.

"I hope you don't mind? I have never seen this done."

His grin broadened. "Would you care to learn? I would find your hand in the matter pleasurable."

Up on her knees, Cassie straddled him.

He turned the tin around. "Please select one of these fine suits of armor, milady."

She reached in, took out a rubber, and removed a band of paper that encircled it.

"Affixing a condom is simple, but needs to be done correctly."

Her lesson appeared to be hugely arousing, as Zeno had to still the jerking recipient while she placed the rolled up rubber on the head. She encircled his penis with her hand and pressed down. "Grip a bit harder." He sucked air through his teeth and groaned.

Alarmed, Cassie took her hand off. "Don't stop, love." He wrapped her fingers around his girth and rolled the condom down. Lifting her by the hips, he pressed her onto his erection, pushing deep inside. Mesmerized by her gloriously naked form, he groaned and thrust his cock in and out. "Come closer."

He suckled and she murmured musical and mysterious female whimpers and growls that elevated his arousal to dangerous levels. To keep himself on the edge of climax, he held on to the base of the rubber and drew the head of his penis along her cleft. He stroked slick folds until he heard, "Don't stop, please—don't stop. Yes . . . yes."

While Cassie floated in the land of bliss, he moved her under him and reinserted his throbbing shaft. He kept himself ready with easy, shallow thrusts. He kissed her eyelids until they fluttered open and she wrapped her legs around his waist—gathering him into her, deepening his penetration.

His need grew to nearly intolerable excitement as her hips lifted to meet his body, accepting all of him. Slapping hard against her, he growled out his pleasure and she answered him with breathy cries and moans.

"Dear." Thrust. "God." Thrust.

He exploded into her. Or, more accurately, he spilled

into the reservoir of a knight in latex armor. Oblivious and spent, Zeno chuckled softly.

"You are amused?" There was a smile in her question.

"Ah-hh no, love, just amazed."

Cassie rolled onto her side. "What we have is very special, isn't it?"

"Very." He stroked the small of her back and traced his fingers over the cursive letters swirling along her hip.

"SHALL WE GET you dressed before you catch a chill?"

"Must I?" His warm-blooded lover snuggled under the bedcovers beside him.

Of course he would rather she spend the entire night with him. Zeno kissed her nose and reluctantly mumbled words he did not mean. "I insist."

Cassie stepped into pantalets, and he buttoned up her skirt and blouse. They left off her petticoats, bustle, and corset. "There you are, respectable enough for a silent scurry down the corridor."

Cassie patted the loose hairs around her neck. "I suppose my hair is a fright."

He studied her carefully, committing the picture to memory. "You look well pleasured."

He opened the door. An alarmingly loud creak came from the stairs.

Wide-eyed, she hesitated. Zeno put a finger to his lips. Sliding past her, he kept the door open a crack.

The quiet was so complete, he could hear the soft clatter of tools and hammered tin from the workshop below.

"Rob?"

She nodded. "He often works late."

He signaled back toward the hall. "Servants?"

"Possibly." Cassie squeezed in and he let her take a peek. They were chest to chest now. He inhaled the smells of her skin and hair.

She jerked her head back and he edged forward for a better look. Long shadows broke across the expanse of hallway floor as two figures moved into view. The dark intruders turned down the corridor and halted.

"I need to dress, Cassie." Without taking his eyes off the hallway he stepped into the slacks she handed him. "Two men, heading away from us. They just entered the second door on the left."

She frowned. "That's my room."

Abandoning his post, he reached into his luggage and removed a pistol. "Since this is likely no burglary, I must assume this a kidnapping attempt." He tossed on his shirt and she buttoned it. "When they find an empty bed, they will either search other rooms or they will abandon the job." He crossed the room and pushed up the window sash. Sure enough, one of the men had already started down the trellis outside Cassie's window.

Zeno leaned out and fired a shot overhead. "That was a warning. The next bullet won't miss."

Panicked, the prowler jumped to the ground just as Rob ran out of the workshop. Zeno aimed at a limb and fired. The man growled in pain. He called down to Rob. "Two men, kidnappers, watch him close! He may have a weapon."

Rob swung a large wrench at the man's skull and

knocked the writhing man out cold. Zeno grinned. "Good enough." He nodded toward the house. "One more."

Heavy footsteps pounded down the hallway. Zeno backed out the window and in two long strides was at the door.

"Stay here, Cassie." Senses sharpened, Zeno stepped out into the corridor and headed toward the banister. At the top of the stairs he spied a shadow in motion on the landing.

He cocked his pistol, and the intruder froze. "Don't make me shoot you."

But the man chose to flee. Missing a tread as Zeno fired, the trespasser tumbled down the rest of the way. Rob stepped from the shadows to clunk him over the head.

Zeno bent over the bulky frame. "Good man, Rob."

"A couple of crime solvers, I'd say." Cassie stood on the landing, shoulders back with her hands on her hips.

He scowled. "I thought I told you to stay in the room."

She held out her hand. "Give me the gun while you two find something to tie him up with."

"What the devil is going on here?" Dr. Erskine's voice traveled down the stairwell.

"It's all over, Daddy, we've just caught some—" She hesitated. "Zak and Rob have caught a couple of burglars."

Smart girl. No sense in alarming her parents, yet. Zeno climbed a few steps and pressed his pistol into her hands. "Remember to cock first and hold the gun with two hands." He showed her the stance by lifting her arms. "That's it."

He stepped away, admiring the determined expression on her face. "You can put your arms down now."

She nodded, her stare frozen on the fallen man below. "Go on, Zak, I'll be fine."

∞ Chapter Twenty-one

Cassie's heavy-lidded gaze surveyed the chipper crowd at the breakfast table. Stirring her tea, she listened absently to the comfortable undertone of her mother's lively chatter.

"Remind me to never have that pesky creak in the stairs repaired. Forever more that high-pitched squeak will be music to my ears." Mother's gaze stopped on Zeno.

"As for the notch one of your bullets put in my parlor molding, no need to apologize. We'll have a brass plaque made up. 'Here lies the bullet that scared our intruder half to death.'"

"Thickheaded, lucky skunk." Zeno grunted. "After the bullet missed, the tumble downstairs should have killed him."

Rob snorted a laugh and scooped up a forkful of egg.

Cassie stifled a yawn, as her brother and Zeno shoveled platefuls of sausage and ham into their bellies.

Constable Sheffley ladled a dollop of clotted cream onto a warm scone already slathered with blackberry jam. The man's eyes glowed with happiness over prowlers and pistol shots. "You were fortunate to have a Yard man such as Mr. Kennedy here on the premises. We've seen more than our share of riffraff pass through Surrey of late."

"Pass through? I hope so." Father turned over his paper and continued to read.

Their bright-eyed constable shrugged. "Summer holidays coming on, seasonal laborers make their way out to the shore—down Brighton way. Decent folks mainly, but we've run into a few bad characters."

Rob leaned across the table. "I say a bracing plunge sounds about right to me. How about a dip in the pond, Zak?"

With a mouthful of ham and egg, Zeno shook his head. "Knackered, sorry, Rob."

Her brother's raised eyebrows and bright eyes scanned the table. "What about you, Tadpole?"

Cassie scrunched up her nose. "I've ordered a steaming-hot bath and have plans for a long nap."

They had each taken turns recounting a ludicrous cock-and-bull story for her parents, who asked few pointed questions. No "why were you two up and about at such an hour of the morning?" Not even a "from where exactly did you both spot the intruders?" Of course, it helped that both doctors had been too busy bandaging groggy prowlers to inquire too heavily as to her exact whereabouts.

Bone-weary, her eyes drifted shut as she listened to the clink of her mother's teacup in its saucer.

OUTSIDE CASSIE'S BEDCHAMBER, Zeno placed his hands on her shoulders and rubbed her upper arms. "Will you be all right?"

"Happy dreams." Rob staggered off to his own room, leaving Zeno and Cassie alone in the upstairs hall.

She pressed her cheek to his chest with a sigh. "You wouldn't mind a check under my bed for the Dippenhall Troll, would you?"

Zeno chuckled softly and turned the knob to her room.

He tilted his head to see around the door, and made a show of looking about. "Your bath awaits, but I see no sign of the local troll. Perhaps I should have a closer look."

He led her by the hand and closed the door. The light, airy room featured a canopied bed placed in the center. "So, this is Cassie's room."

Zeno stepped around the copper tub to have a look out a large dormered window, which featured an inviting, cushioned window seat. He lifted the sash to let in a warm breeze. One of the intruders had made a hasty exit this way. He noted a torn curtain and a number of displaced pillows.

An old doll stuffed in the corner of a chintz-covered chair lent the room an aura of adolescence. He examined the details of her girlhood, including a bookcase filled with classic childhood tomes.

"As comfortable as an old shoe, yet suddenly it feels a bit foreign to me." Cassie dipped her fingertips into the bathwater.

Anger stirred inside him at the very idea that she would be made to feel unsafe in her own bedroom. He was also in a temper at himself, for this damnable menace, this consortium of danger that had appeared out of nowhere to threaten her. Zeno collapsed onto the window seat. "Take your bath, Cassie. I'll curl up here and have a nap."

He leaned against a stack of pillows as she undressed. She turned her back to him and he loosened the strings of her corset, which dropped off along with her camisole. Small pink lines ran up and down her midriff, pressure marks from the stays of the corset.

"You certainly don't need much help from that contraption." A blush colored her cheeks.

"Mother is forever loosening laces and advising her patients to breathe. 'Let go of your vanity, ladies. Let those dresses out an inch and exercise your lungs.'"

Captivated by her nude form, he still managed a grin at the near perfect mimicry of her suffragette mother. She dipped a hand into the tub and mixed a scented powder into the steaming water. "A bit of Epsom salt, infused with carnation. My favorite."

He settled into a sight most pleasing in the morning light, her lovely figure in profile. A shapely curve ran along the back of her thigh over smooth, rounded buttocks.

"You are staring at my bottom, sir." He caught the prettiest stolen glance, the dart of a narrowed eye, and the dimple of a suppressed smile.

"Yes. I am."

She made no secret she enjoyed his interest, which charged the air in the room with a dangerous level of desire. In his mind, he walked up behind her and cupped each round cheek, running his hands over hips and quivering belly.

"What on earth are you mumbling about, Zeno?"

If he did not control his fantasies now, he would have to toss her onto the bed. "Get in the tub, before I . . ."

She laughed and stepped into her bath.

Zeno leaned into a stack of pillows and closed his eyes. He held on to the picture of her in his head and listened. The drizzle of water drops falling from a sea sponge onto her skin was a kind of music to his senses.

Such fierce natural beauty. Lovely of face and body. Talented, intelligent, and brave. No wonder she captivated him at every turn. Even this bad business with the intruders seemed to have little effect on her until moments ago. He felt buffeted about, upended by this exceptional young woman.

He opened his eye a crack. "Do you need someone to rinse the soap from your hair? I am at your service."

Cassie sat up in the tub and nodded. He found a pitcher on her dresser with warm fresh water. He moved to her bath and she dipped her fingers in to feel the temperature.

"Too cool?"

Cassie murmured her approval, and laid her head back, closing her eyes. Zeno poured the clear liquid over her hair and then worked it through her scalp. He picked up long waves still soaking in soapy tub water and ran fresh water through them. She helped him gather up strands of wet hair and wring them out.

"Might you help me with the bath towel? There, on the chair, please?"

Venus rose from the sea.

He would never grow tired of looking at her. A water droplet traced the slope of her breast before it fell onto the slight curve of her belly. Hesitant to cover her up, he finally held up a cotton sheet and wrapped it around her. She reached for his hand and he helped her step out of the tub.

Cassie drew another towel from a chest and rubbed her long tresses in the rough toweling.

"Dressing gown?" he asked, and she pointed to the dresser. He removed a pale pink gown with little girl ruffles. Plain. Virginal. Cassandra needed rest. He needed rest. A good choice.

He tucked her into bed, kissed her forehead, and returned to the window seat, where he picked up a book lying facedown on the floor. A victim, he supposed, of the intruder's hurried exit.

"Shall I read us both to sleep, then?" As Zeno cracked open the book he heard a deep sigh. It would not be long before she headed off to the land of Nod.

He cleared his throat.

"'Alice was beginning to get very tired of sitting by her sister on the bank, and having nothing to do: once or twice she had peeped into the book her sister was reading but it had no pictures or conversations in it, "and what use is a book without pictures and conversation?". . .'"

ZENO JERKED AWAKE. The novel must have slipped from his hand. Curiously, he caught the rustle of a skirt as the door closed softly. Olivia Erskine?

The young lady lay in bed. A sleepy eye opened and smiled at him. A hand crept out from under the covers and beckoned him to join.

Gladly, he rose from the window seat and collapsed on top of the bedspread. Cassie swept an arm around his chest and hugged him close, spooning against him. He closed his eyes.

SHE FELT HERSELF again.

A long nap and a spot of tea had revived the household. Zeno, ever the Yard man, summoned a late afternoon meeting in Rob's workshop. A re-imparting, he called it.

Brows knitted, she paced the floor. "I wonder how on earth our intruders could have known the exact location of my room?"

"An unsuspecting servant or repairman has one too many pints at the local pub. Tongues loosen." Zeno ran a hand through recently shampooed hair—glossy with a bit of wave to it. "Town servants are schooled to beware of such tactics. Out here in the country . . . ?"

Cassie grimaced softly. "Yes, I suppose so."

Zeno moved on to Rob. "Anything unusual happen recently? Strangers about asking odd questions?"

Cassie's eyes grew wide. "Gerald came to see me. Tried to warn me off you, Mr. Kennedy."

Zeno frowned. "And you are just now telling me this?"

"I thought to mention it earlier this weekend but got distracted." Cassie sniffed. "By you." She trembled as Gerald's words of warning came back to her.

Zeno softened his tone. "Please continue, Cassie."

"As I readied to leave for the station, Gerald showed up at my door making wild claims and the most alarming statements.

"First, he insisted I stop seeing you." Her gaze flew

across the roadster to where Zeno stood. "Minutes later he blamed his own cohorts. He confessed these unnamed friends of his might try to use me to—"

His gaze moved to meet hers. "To get to me?"

She nodded and crossed her hands over her chest to rub her arms. The workshop could be a chilly place in the evening hours. "As much as I distrust him, I do believe he meant well."

Zeno removed his jacket, walked over, and wrapped it around her shoulders. He secured a button. "Generally, I am not at liberty to discuss ongoing investigations or operations, but in this case . . ."

Cassie and her sibling leaned in.

His gaze moved between them. "In this case I will make a rare exception. I placed Lord Delamere under surveillance weeks ago. I suspect it is he who is behind the failure of the Irish Home Rule vote. He may also be the financier of a radical group of Fenians bent on a complete break from English governance."

Rob scratched his head. "Delamere is an Irish as well as a British peer—why would he wish the vote to fail?"

Zeno pressed his lips together in a straight, grim line. "If someone prefers revolution over devolution, might he not work to keep sentiments stirred up against a lawful Irish independence? A man of great ambition wouldn't be interested in the limited autonomy of the Home Rule Act. Not when he might foment a bloody revolt and proclaim himself king. Or, on a lesser scale, president of a new Irish republic."

He leaned back against the tool bench. "Right now my

hands are tied with Delamere. As a peer of the realm, he is nearly immune to prosecution. I cannot have him arrested until I have incontrovertible evidence against him."

"Catch him in the act." Rob's eyes brightened. "Might our prowlers come clean?"

Zeno nodded. "They'll talk, all right, but they won't have a clue who hired them." Using the edge of his shoe, he scraped a bit of dirt about the floor.

He met her gaze. "Your brother-in-law, Gerald St. Cloud, along with George Upton and the late James Hicks-Beach, are members of a small group of unruly peerage led by Lord Delamere."

Cassie nodded. "The Bloody Four."

Zeno's mouth tightened into a flat line. "With the untimely demise of Mr. Hicks-Beach, I'd say bloody, all right."

"As the four are now three," Cassie mused aloud, "Gerald is in grave danger. Why would he get involved with such men?"

"Delamere likely bought his gambling debt for his vote." Zeno shrugged. "I suspect Hicks-Beach saw or heard something he shouldn't have. Then, quite suddenly, it was too late."

Silence.

Cassie stared at the cobbled pavers of the workshop. "Perhaps I should leave for Paris ahead of schedule."

Zeno spun on his heels. "Paris?"

She tilted her chin. "I have several paintings on display this season at the Durand-Ruel gallery. His spring show of neo-impressionists."

"My congratulations, I had no idea." Zeno blinked just

before the spark in his eyes grew darker. "And who is your escort?"

"My maid travels with me—"

"And?"

She returned his glare, eyes wider than his. "And?"

"Incredible." He shook his head.

She straightened her shoulders and tried to ignore his reaction. "Cécile looks forward to a visit with her brother's family."

"It's not safe, Cassie." Even as he stuck out his chin, his voice softened. "Paris is a hotbed of sympathetic anarchists ready and willing to spread revolution. The Fenians have allies there."

She drew up taller and folded her arms over her chest. "I am perfectly capable of taking a brief trip to France without Scotland Yard nosing about."

"I have no desire to clip your wings. But I must insist on a reasonable degree of safety."

Rob stepped into their little contretemps. "I say, Zak, it might not be such a bad idea to sneak Cassie and her maid out of town."

Her smile traveled from her brother to her lover. "You must concede he has a point."

Zeno chewed his bottom lip. "Perhaps."

"Oh, Mr. Kennedy? Zak, are you down there with my two offspring?"

Zeno tilted his chin up toward the voice.

Cassie stuck her head out the door. "He is, Mother."

"Well, tell him to meet me in surgery. I mean to unwrap those tapes and have a look."

Chapter Twenty-two

Zeno perched himself comfortably on the edge of the examination table as Olivia Erskine removed the last of the bandages from around his ribs.

"Lift up your arms, dear."

A warm sensation settled his stomach. Her mother had called him dear.

"I would be interested to know how serious your feelings are for my daughter."

"I am going to marry her one day, Mrs.—Dr. Erskine."

The roll of old bandages fell out of her hand as she took in his words as well as his determined expression. "And when might that be?"

Zeno retrieved the bandages. "Eventually . . ."

"Eventually? I don't like that word *eventually*. Please explain yourself."

Zeno sighed. "Cassie needs time. She is just out from under the mourning of her husband. If I move too fast, she'll resist and refuse me."

Olivia studied him with an elevated brow and the barest hint of a grin. "I will give you this, Zak, you do seem to know how willful and stubborn my daughter can be."

She moved to sit down beside him on the edge of the examination bed. "I never warmed much to Thom. Oh, it was a splendid match by superficial standards. But he was not entirely right for her."

Zeno glanced out the window to the colorful spring flowers that greeted every visitor to the Erskine residence. "Our fates collide in mysterious ways."

"Young man, you read my mind." Olivia shifted to study him carefully. "Compliments are not easy for me, but I will say to you that I have never seen Cassie more contented than I have this weekend."

Taking his face in her hands, she swept a lock of hair off his forehead. It brought back faint memories of his mother, long forgotten. Of being a boy, running wild across the heathered bluffs of Skye.

"Mind you marry her just as soon as she is ready. A small ceremony here at Muirfield by Christmas? Or perhaps a great wedding feast in Scotland next year. The doctor would so enjoy a family excursion north."

There were pleasant echoes of conspiratorial promise in their conversation. Until this moment Zeno had never smiled directly at Olivia Erskine. "I will do my best, ma'am."

The Erskines were taking great pains to welcome him into the fold. Zeno had not felt this kind of familial kinship in a long time. At supper Dr. Erskine invited him to the opera. "We have purchased a box from Lord Sutherland, just for the debut of *Don Carlo*—you must attend with us, Zak."

At the mention of the opera, he dropped his spoon into a parfait glass filled with truffle. "I tried for tickets, but it was sold out in hours. I understand it will be conducted by Sir Charles Villiers Stanford. I wouldn't miss it."

After supper, he met Rob on the front terrace to shoot rockets off across the expanse of Muirfield parkland.

"I've tested and recorded these rockets until I can quite accurately predict their altitude and trajectory." Rob showed him how to sight and fire a rocket.

"And what are your plans for this research, Rob?"

"I present a paper to the Tunbridge Wells Scientific Society this coming week. Sir Kevin Meade-Waldo will be there. Holds great influence with the British Royal Society. I mean to drive the roadster there, as well."

Zeno considered the energetic, bright young man as he busily secured the wooden poles that served as rocket launchers. "I should like to introduce you to our lab men one day. We employ several well-recognized scientists, including Archibald Bruce."

Rob's brows went up. "Archie Bruce is working for Scotland Yard? He and I did a summer tenure at Edinburgh—advanced courses. Well, well, it makes sense, what with the dynamiters and all. He always did like to blow things up."

Zeno's mouth twitched. "I suppose one must first know how to configure bombs before one learns to defuse them."

Cassie's youngest brother resettled his attentions on the rocket at hand. "Not long ago, I shot one straight through both open doors of the stable—ricocheted off the hen house—then exploded. The chickens didn't lay eggs for two days." Rob chuckled. "Cook chased me around the kitchen over it."

Zeno grinned. He could not have found a more eccentric family to join up with. He struck a safety match. "May I?"

Rob stepped back. "Ready, aim, fire."

ZENO CHEERFULLY SAT Cassie on his lap as Rob drove them to the train station in the roadster. He distinctly saw her brother smile listening to them squabble over how much protection he planned to assign to her safety.

"I'll not have more odd characters following me about," Cassie grumbled.

"Was that a harrumph? I distinctly heard a harrumph." Zeno held on to her. "Trust me, you won't know they are there."

"In two days' time, Cécile and I will be off to Paris and I'll not have either one of you worrying over me. Honestly, Zak, I will be quite safe once on the Continent." She narrowed her eyes on Rob. "And what are you laughing about?"

"I was just thinking how much you two sound like our parents bickering."

"We're not bickering." Cassie's frown moved from her brother to Zeno. "We're not bickering!"

"I dunno." His arms hugged her tight. "I like a bit of fight in my woman."

Cassie held on to her hat as the roadster picked up speed on the downhill. "Your woman, is it?"

At Farnham Station Zeno checked both bags with a porter and purchased several papers from boys hawking the news on the station platform.

"I'll make a bargain with you, Cassie. While you remain in town, you will allow me to assign another man or two to your safety." He ignored a roll of eyes. "I will also select a bodyguard to meet you in Calais."

Cassie halted their turn around the platform to fasten a glare on him.

Zeno held up his hands. "Only one man, I promise."

"More of a demand than a barter, if you ask me." Her brows moved together as her lips formed a pout. "Despite what you may believe, Zak, I am not a whimpering, skittish sort of female in need of constant cosseting."

Zeno bit back a grin. "I could never think of you as skittish."

Her brows furrowed. "But you must, Zeno."

"Humor me, Cassie. So that I do not suffer a torment of worry—ah, here's the train." He held out a crooked arm. Cassie hesitated, then slipped an arm through his.

The railcar compartment was crowded with weekenders. He exhaled a deep sigh when she nestled against him. "I am not a wilting lily, Zak."

"No, you are not."

"I mean to show you that."

He passed a section of the morning paper to her. Exactly what he feared most. She was so capable, so brave. It more than worried him. From the very start, odd circumstances had conspired to bring him and Cassie together. At the moment, the darkest demon in this imbroglio preyed upon his mind. The scheming blackguard lurked there, elusive—taunting him to make a move. Zeno checked his watch. They would arrive in London within the hour and Lord Delamere was his first order of business.

ZENO STOOD AT the corner of Upper Brook Street and Grosvenor Square. Delamere's carriage exited the Brooks Mews and headed directly for him. As the carriage slowed for cross traffic, Zeno lifted the silver-handled door latch and jumped in.

Delamere was not alone. A man dressed in a tweed hunting-jacket sat opposite. Pistol drawn, Zeno stuck his gun in the man's ear. He nodded to Delamere. "Who is this?"

His lordship raised a brow. "Detective Kennedy. May I introduce my estate's gamekeeper? We were just on our way to the taxidermist. Can we give you a lift—?"

Zeno kicked open the door. "If you don't mind, I wish to speak to your employer alone." He shoved the man out. The poor bloke hit the ground with a grunt and rolled into the gutter.

Zeno slammed the door. "There's been a change of plans. You've an appointment at Number Four Whitehall Place—please instruct your driver." He settled back into plush velvet upholstery of the town coach. "Must have slipped your mind."

He cocked the revolver and waited. Delamere took

down the brass speaking-cone and gave new instructions. Calmly, without taking his eyes off the pistol, Delamere hooked the cone and tube back in place.

Zeno's gaze narrowed slowly. "Leave her out of this."

"Ah, you refer to the lovely widow. And here I thought you were going to attempt an arrest. But you are no fool, are you, Kennedy? Though one can never be sure. What is this to be? A Scotland Yard shakedown of some sort?"

"Pompous conceit and underestimation will get you killed." Zeno grinned. "All it takes is one shot." He leaned across the cabin and pressed the pistol end to Delamere's forehead. "Right between the eyes."

Steely eyes met their equal. "I'll see you fired for this, Kennedy."

He sniffed the air. The spicy, woodsy scent of cigar smoke, gone a bit stale. "More blackmail? Perhaps, this time you can ask Castlemaine for my head." Zeno slouched back into his seat. He had just given Delamere enough information to provoke a scowl. Inscrutable, beady eyes sparked with awareness. There were times one had to beat the brush, prod the tiger out of the jungle.

"You or one of your henchmen touch Cassandra St. Cloud again and you're dead the moment I get near enough for a clean shot." He caught a glimpse of Scotland Yard's gates from the carriage window. "Agree to leave her alone and I am prepared to negotiate the release of certain detainees." Zeno released the hammer on his pistol.

"Negotiate with Special Branch? I might just as easily see you hang." Delamere loosened his cravat.

Zeno pocketed his Webley and stepped onto the street.

"Shall we have a wager? Who hangs first?" He deliberately held on to the door. "Are you friendly with the Queen? Thought not. What a relief, no pardon."

The moment Zeno closed and latched the door, the carriage rolled off. "Consider my offer."

He had thrown down the gauntlet, but had also advanced the notion of a barter for Cassie's safety. He wanted her out of the line of fire.

Chapter Twenty-three

Cassie froze as she recognized the unnerving, sardonic voice in the foyer of Miss Martin's Academy for Young Ladies.

"My card, madam."

"Lord Delamere! What an honor, sir. And what brings you to my academy?"

"A small favor. As a matter of urgent business, might I have a private word with one of your instructors?"

She heard caution in Miss Martin's voice. God bless her. "And who might that be, Lord Delamere?"

With eyes fixed on the etched, glass panel of the parlor door, Cassie retreated. Her pulse hammered as she placed one foot behind the other and prayed the door remained closed. Only when she reached the adjoining hallway did she turn and run.

Yesterday morning, as their hansom pulled away from Victoria Station, Zeno had barked off a litany of instructions: "Admit no one inside the residence unless they are well known to you. All deliveries are to be left on the step and retrieved later. Should either Lord Delamere or Gerald make an appearance, do not open the door. Go upstairs, through the connecting door to my study. Mrs. Woolsley has left the key in the lock. Turn it." He had taken her hand and rolled back her glove. The feel of his lips on her bare wrist had sent a tingle through her.

"Secondly, should they follow you to either one of your classrooms, do not receive them. Do not bother to collect your hat, coat, or reticule. Just run, Cassie. Get to a busy street and hail a cab. Make your way directly to Number Four Whitehall."

She stepped out the schoolhouse and onto the rough flagstones of the academy's garden terrace. Oh yes, she had heard him well. Now she would give anything to have Zeno by her side.

Cassie picked up her skirt and ran the full length of the garden. She followed the narrow pathway edged by prim, clipped hedges. The crunch of gravel echoed underfoot as she glanced backward, imagining footsteps behind her. She nearly tripped over a flower bed as she made her way along the rear wall.

Finally, she found the gate to the mews and pressed the latch. She cursed silently when the hinges creaked, and quickly turned to press the heavy wooden door shut again.

"Can I help you, ma'am?"

She whirled around, blood pounding in her ears.

The curious groom approached her. "Is something wrong, ma'am?" In between rapid breaths, eyes darting about the mews, she gasped. "Please, might you point the way out? I need to find a cab. Quickly."

The groom lifted a hand toward the south alleyway.

"Men might follow." Cassie launched herself off the gate. "Do what you can to delay them." She left the young lad standing with his mouth hanging open. Sneaking a peek around the corner of the carriage house, she could not see the end of the alley. There was a blind turn in the narrow row before it opened onto the street. If she could make it to Bedford Court, it was a quick dash to the bustle of Shaftesbury Avenue and a cab.

She crept forward.

ZENO HAD MADE a date for an early supper. He looked forward to an authentic Italian dinner at an intimate bistro in Covent Garden. He and Cassie would dine on chicken *piccata* and then he would take her home and feast upon her. Or vice versa.

He enjoyed a brief fantasy. The mesmerizing jiggle of her derriere as she climbed the last steps to her bedroom. He would grab and kiss that beautiful bum as he settled in to listen, enraptured, to the melody of her sighs and moans.

Zeno turned the corner and approached Miss Alice Martin's Academy. Cassie taught drawing and painting to young women of privilege whose parents paid exorbitant fees to have their daughters schooled in the social skills necessary to become accomplished and, more to the point, *married* ladies. As he approached the school he noted a town coach lurch away in a hurry. Instincts pricked, he knew in an instant something was not right.

He quickened his steps and did not bother to ring the bell.

A small, ashen-faced woman met him promptly in the reception parlor. "Oh, Mr. Kennedy, I'm afraid something dreadful may have just happened."

Zeno took hold of the woman's trembling, outstretched hand. "Yes, Mrs. Martin?"

"Cassandra has disappeared." Her hand gestured toward the hallway. "Lord Delamere arrived just minutes ago. The girls said Mrs. St. Cloud left in quite a hurry—"

As Zeno sprinted down the corridor, a young lady standing among a group of shrinking violets pointed the way to the terrace.

He charged down the terrace steps and through the garden. At the mews gate he ran into a stable groom. "Excuse me, sir, but the lady asked me to delay any gentlemen following after—"

Zeno shoved past the burly young man. "Scotland Yard." He passed the carriage house and turned into the alley. No Cassie. The mews was built in a U shape. He dashed around a tight corner and spotted her at the end of the alley. A carriage blocked her exit to the street. The very same vehicle, if he was not mistaken, that had sped away from Miss Martin's door minutes earlier. Nothing to go on—no coat of arms. The coach door opened. Two men leaped from the carriage as it pulled away.

Zeno shouted her name. "Cassie!"

Time stood still. She turned toward the sound of his voice, eyes bright and wide with fear. He drew his pistol. At the sight of his sidearm, both men backed off and turned down the street. Zeno took aim just as an innocent passerby crossed in his gun sight. He reset the hammer.

Cassie ran into his arms. For a moment, she clung to him with the fierceness of a terrified child. "It was Delamere himself this time." Zeno rubbed her back to ease the trembling.

He had thrown down the gauntlet and this was Delamere's answer.

Zeno imagined his revolver pressed to the man's forehead. He squeezed the trigger. The crack of a bullet ripped through flesh and bone. The dead man slumped over, eyes frozen in death. Zeno shook off the image as his jaw clenched and released. All bets, offers, amnesties were off. He would have the murdering, craven traitor behind bars within twenty-four hours if it killed him. Which it might.

Several new men raced toward them from the stables. Zeno glared. "Where have you been?"

"Sorry, sir. We were delayed—a setup."

Impatient, Zeno gestured east. "Two men on foot heading toward Shaftesbury. One in a brown suit, the other a large bloke wearing a seafarer's jacket."

Craning a neck down the street, one of Zeno's men caught sight of them. "There they are." The hired men dashed after the fleeing suspects.

Cassie lifted her chin. "Who were those fellows?"

Zeno frowned. "Hired to protect you."

She stepped away. "Go on, Zeno. You might catch Delamere at this hour—"

He shook his head. "He may have henchmen about. I'll not take any chances leaving you here alone."

A chill breeze whipped through the mews corridor. He didn't complain when Cassie collapsed into his arms again. He held her a few moments longer. "Why don't we skip dinner? I'll see you home."

Cassie straightened her shoulders, eyes vibrant, her face flushed with color. She wore the same determined look he had seen on the Farnham train platform. "You promised me chicken *piccata*."

"Changed my mind. I am now hoping for an evening of leisure at home." He did not think it wise to be out and about with Cassie tonight. Not with Delamere on a rampage. "Lay low—a bit of you upon me, me upon you. Then I sneak you out of the country first thing in the morning. Come." He tugged her hand. "I'll whisk us up something to eat afterward."

Her lips quirked up at the ends. "You would cook for me?"

"I'm not sure I would call an egg scramble and toasted cheese cooking."

Chapter Twenty-four

Cassie picked up a pile of messages. Most were addressed to Z. Kennedy; nearly all of them demanded his immediate attention. Zeno barely had the door behind him when she placed the stack in his hands.

He grimaced. "Between the Yard hunting me down and the intrepid Mrs. Woolsley, I'm afraid I'm going to have to ask you to receive messages for me. I hope you don't mind." He leaned close and stole a fleeting kiss to her neck, just under the earlobe.

Aroused from a stimulating carriage ride home, her body tingled from his brief caress. "It would seem to be the neighborly thing to do."

A grand new flower arrangement had been placed on the round pedestal table in the middle of the reception hall. As Zeno opened one communiqué after another, she gravitated toward the stunning new bouquet. Opening the handwritten envelope, she removed a gilt-edged card.

*For a glorious weekend. And might I further
express my appreciation with a kiss placed just
beneath your ear?*
   All my affection,
   Zak

She glanced up from his note at the same time he finished a message. His frown signaled bad news. "There has been another murder or suicide. Not sure which." Zeno's expression matched his glum tone of voice.

A chill passed through her. "Not Gerald?"

He read on and shook his head. "George Upton. Found him hanging in the mews stable. Down to bloody two. Lord Delamere is losing his minions."

"Poor Mr. Upton." She drew her brows together and wrung her hands. "Poor Gerald."

Sidling closer, he rubbed her upper arm with the back of his hand. "Best not get too worked up over the news. If scandal or blackmail is involved, Upton may have taken his own life."

She put her arms around him and held him for a brief moment. "So you must go?"

He tossed the messages back onto the vestibule table. His gaze roamed her face, earnest and possessive. "I go nowhere until I see you safely onto the train to Dover in the morning."

Twirling a finger around his shirt button, she experienced a rush of desire. Tonight, for some reason, his ferocious defense warmed her insides more than his hands running up and down her back. He kissed her temple. "I insist on a few more hours in your bed."

"How is it—? That is to say, you always seem to know," she tilted her head, "whether or not I have gained my satisfaction."

He brushed his mouth over hers. "I would hope so."

She begged to differ. Most men, she suspected, didn't give a fig. She remembered many a night Thom had dropped off to sleep while she lay discontented beside him.

Unthinkable with a man like Zak Kennedy. She pressed her hand against the inside of his pant leg. "Can you make it up the stairs with such an enormous impediment?"

He grabbed her hips and yanked her against him. "I've grown used to a kind of irrepressible arousal whenever I am around you, Cassandra. Not only can I make it to your bedchamber but I'll have every stitch of your clothing along the way."

By the second-floor landing, he had taken possession of her skirt and petticoats. She helped him unbutton her blouse and untie her corset as he ravaged her against the wall, burying his face in her breasts.

Following her upward climb, Zeno lay a trail of kisses along the curve of her derriere, discarding pantalets as they crested the stair. Stark naked, she arched in his arms as he carried her into the bedchamber.

They both quickly came to an explosive finish. Zeno left a trail of kisses over her shoulder and down her spine. "Give me fifteen minutes." Tossing back the bedcovers, he pulled on trousers and shirt. "Don't go anywhere."

Cassie snorted a laugh into her pillow. "Where would I be going all wobbly legged and naked?"

"Right. No need to dress for supper." Zeno winked and disappeared downstairs.

According to her bedside clock, he was back upstairs with a dinner tray twenty-five minutes later. "An egg scramble, my signature toasted cheese sandwich, and I scrounged a grand bit of pastry. Two slices of apple tart."

Cassie balanced the tray on her lap. "You did this all by yourself?"

"Actually, there is a puckish little kitchen nymph who makes his home in the scullery. The little elf really knows his way around a fry pan."

"I declare you graduated from charm school." Cassie sliced her sandwich in half. "You can be exceedingly winsome when you wish to be, Zak."

"I'm afraid Lord Delamere wouldn't agree." Zeno settled down onto the bed and opened a bottle of ale. "I paid him a visit this morning. Needlessly provoked him, it seems."

Cassie propped up a few pillows behind her. "He may just be getting bolder—or more desperate. Delamere must have some notion you are on to him with all those dynamiters jailed and awaiting trial. He's worried, Zak."

He handed her a glass of ale. "I warned him off you." Zeno scratched his head. "Actually, I threatened him with great bodily harm."

Cassie tilted her head. "What kind of bodily harm?

He looked a bit sheepish. Vulnerable. Like a man

reluctant to share his secrets. "The 'touch her again and I'll put a bullet through your skull' kind."

A smile tugged at the corners of her mouth. "Sweet of you."

"Cheers." He tipped his glass to hers. "Don't go to Paris."

"I can't think of a safer place to be at the moment." She took a sip of beer, and licked the foam off her lips.

He stared at her. An evaluating sort of gaze, one in which she often glimpsed sparks of light—and affection. He broke off a piece of his melted cheese and held it to her mouth. "Eat something. I insist you eat."

Cassie's lips closed around the bread as well as his fingers. She used her tongue to lick off crumbs. "The parents are already making plans for yet another weekend in Surrey. You have a standing invitation to join." Her flirtation caused a grin. "By mid-June it will be warm enough for a bit of skinny-dipping in the pond."

She sampled a bit of egg from his fork. "Oh, my word, this is wonderful. You whisked in a bit of chopped chive and butter—or did the puckish little kitchen nymph? Anyway, I warned Mother you are rather taken up with work at the moment."

"I will move heaven and earth to be there."

Her smile faded. "Perhaps we can travel out to Muirfield together when I return from Paris."

"Speaking of . . ." Zeno sat up. "I have arranged for you to be met in Calais by a French field operative. A detective with *La Sûreté Nationale*, the Parisian version of Scotland Yard. His name is Inspector Tautou. A small, wiry sort of fellow, as I recall, with a large brown moustache. No other facial hair."

She managed a lopsided smirk. "Might there be a secret password or code name, Detective Kennedy?"

He finished off a swallow of stout direct from the bottle. "I shall invent one if you wish."

"Make it eggs and toasted cheese." Cassie grinned.

"Make what?"

She blinked. "Inspector Tautou's password."

"Ah." Zeno picked up a sliver of tart from the dessert plate and devoured it down to the crumb. He studied her for a long moment.

"What?" Her smile was curious.

"You have the reckless soul of an adventurer, Cassie."

"Is that the attraction, Zak?" She plumped up a pillow behind her. "I spent lunch hour with Mother at the bathhouse. We chatted over a massage. Would you care to know the subject?"

He stared, mouth slightly open. "I'm almost afraid to ask."

"Contraception." She rolled bright eyes. "French letters—to be precise—very amusing."

"Do you tell your mother everything?"

"She asked. Pointedly. I can't very well lie to her. What was I to do, play coy? You know her too well. Besides, I believe she is happy for me. I told her you were a brilliant lover."

He coughed up a few breadcrumbs. Cassie held back a chuckle in deference to his obvious need for oxygen. "Mother apologized for the poor quality of the condoms this past weekend. There are new ones, she says, made of a finer quality vulcanized rubber." She sipped the last of her ale. "I did express my opinion that the tricky process seemed to interfere with the spontaneity of the moment."

He swallowed without further obstruction to his windpipe. "Don't tell me, she handed out samples."

Cassie winked. "French. Manufactured with little ridges along the length. I believe the ridges are for my pleasure, whilst you receive increased sensitivity." In a deliberately provocative manner, she leaned forward and spoke in a husky voice. "I was given suggestions on how to unroll them, which you might find enjoyable."

His mind filled with lurid, erotic pictures of her doing . . . wonderful things. Propped on an elbow, he pulled the covers over her leg, exposing a beautiful curve of hip. "Such as?"

"I HAVE ALL your contact addresses and instructions in my reticule." Cassie stood entirely too close to Zeno on the public platform at Victoria Station.

A police officer in plain dress and Cassie's maid, Cécile, had boarded the train and waited in the railcar compartment.

"Officer Farnsworth will see you safely aboard the Dover ferry." Zeno tilted her chin to make eye contact. "You will wire me every twenty-four hours. No exceptions. If I do not hear from you, I will have Melville himself contact the *Sûreté*. They will scour all of Paris to find you even as I cross the channel."

She put up her bravest front, which included a close-lipped smile as she straightened his cravat and patted the lapels of his frock coat. "You have my itinerary?"

Zeno tapped the left side of his chest. "Tucked away in my pocket."

She stood on tiptoes and delivered a brief kiss, which deepened into a long embrace. "I will shout to the conductor to delay my departure for another kiss."

"Damn the railroad schedule. I must insist on another." He kissed her again and held her tight, nuzzling her ear.

"Oh yes, Zak. Yes, yes." Her gaze lingered on the lovely upturned edges of a vulnerable grin. His eyes were the most unsettling clear blue this morning. She could read the strain in them, as he struggled to find words.

"Be watchful. Trust no one but yourself—your own instincts. If something doesn't feel right, it isn't."

"Likewise, Detective Kennedy."

Chapter Twenty-five

A blustery wind whipped through the Devonshire Place Mews. The gust spun the limp body of George Upton ghoulishly from the barn rafter. An engorged tongue, purple in color, hung from the dead man's mouth.

Zeno exhaled. "Cut him down."

He spotted Archie Bruce standing near the entrance to the stable and wound his way past a few inspectors still on scene. "I take it there was good reason to leave this man up all night?"

The Yard's new forensics director used his pipestem to point to the floor under the hanged man. An assortment of clean footprints could be seen in the soft dirt surrounding Upton's body. "A bit irregular, I admit. But the local police on the scene closed off the shed and called us in straightaway."

"What luck, they followed procedure." Zeno pressed his foot into the mix of rich brown earth and wood shavings. A clean imprint.

Arch nodded. "Took us most of the night to scare up

a photographer. We also took a number of molds from the surrounding footprints." He lifted a small cloth evidence bag from his pocket and fished out a broken cigar. The stogie had never been lit, and a wrapper remained on one end.

Zeno examined the tightly wrapped leaves and the break midway down the shaft. "The wrapper is hand stamped. Cuban. *Maduro oscuro* in color. Ring size and the length, *robusto*." He sniffed the cigar. "Spicy. Woody."

Familiar.

Archie got out a small pad and took notes. Zeno sniffed again. "I wager no more than a handful of tobacconists in the city import these."

"Give me another day to two, Zak. There's a good chance we'll be able to prove this wasn't a suicide."

There was a moment in every case when the criminal could feel the sturdy, deliberate net of law enforcement tighten around him. Likewise the detective, by sheer instinct, knew when he was closing in on his suspect. This was one of those times. Zeno's pulse accelerated as he hopped onto the Underground train and traveled back to headquarters.

HAND ON HIP, Zeno leaned against a wall of the interrogation room, keeping a steady eye on his onetime mistress and detainee, the recently resurrected Miss Jayne Wells aka Mrs. Brian O'Shea.

She glared across the barren expanse.

He needed at least one of the dynamiters to identify Lord Delamere so he could bring up charges. "Your brother will be released as soon as we get names, Jayne. Powerful names. House of Lords—members of Parliament."

"You bloody Scot, for Chrissake, you should know better." Jayne paced a half circle around him. "You're a traitor to your people and to the Irish."

Zeno's jaw clenched. "Melville himself is Irish and sympathetic to Home Rule. Have you ever considered the fact, Mrs. O'Shea, that you and your *Clan na Gael* might be unwitting pawns in a more sinister grab for power?"

She turned and screamed like a banshee. "Why should we care if the Brits don't? Which has caused more death, Zeno, our bombs or your good queen's response to the Great Famine?"

A sharp pain shot through him as he sucked in a breath. Lungs expanding against sore ribs, a reminder of the beating. He repeated her words in the safe house as he emerged from unconsciousness. "Now then, lass—can ye not hear me cryin' for ye?"

She flew at him with fists raised. Her knuckles brushed the side of his cheek but he caught both her wrists and held them in a tight grip.

"Feisty today, are we?" Zeno imprisoned her arms behind her. "Calm yourself, Mrs. O'Shea, or you will be returned to your restraints."

She deliberately pushed against him. Her round, firm breasts ground into his chest. He managed to hold any errant arousal at bay. "Enough, Jayne."

She slipped a pink tongue over her bottom lip. "Right

here, love, up against the wall like we used to in my dressing room?"

His gaze lowered to her mouth. The past flooded his mind. He was deep inside her, pumping hard. "Come on, love." Her words came from the present. She tilted her head and leaned in, rose-colored lips inches away.

"All right, Jayne. You give up all your secrets and we'll have a bit of in and out right here." He broke away with a harsh laugh.

"What's the matter?" She stepped toward him, rubbing circulation back into her hands.

"Stay where you are."

She sidled closer, skirts sweeping back and forth across his crotch. Her gaze drifted downward. "Afraid you want me, Zak?"

This time, he shoved her to the wall. His erection pressed into her. "You want to feel this inside you again?" He rocked her backward and her head struck hard brick. He didn't mean to abuse her, but he wasn't about to give any ground, either. "Do you?"

Heavy-lidded, sensuous eyes returned his glare. "Yes."

She was an actress. Apparently a very good one. Humiliated to think he had been so easily seduced by her years ago, a wave of self-loathing washed over him. With a groan, he wrenched her away from the wall and slapped handcuffs onto her wrists.

He turned her around and marched her over to the chair in the middle of the room.

"Sit."

She squirmed under the muscle of his grip. Her wary

eyes blazed with anger. Zeno smiled to himself; he had shaken her a bit. Next, he would remind her of his offer.

He walked around the small table and picked up her folder. Without looking up, he gestured for her to sit again. "If you don't give me the names, I'll gladly make you moan. But not in the way you're wanting."

"I recall more than a bit of groaning on your part, Zak." She offered a hard smile.

His jaw clenched as he directed a pointed glare over the top of her file. "Favors won't purchase your brother's release. Names will."

The jingle of keys and turn of the lock drew his attention to the door. Rafe poked his head in. "Sorry to interrupt. You've been summoned, Zak. M's office, straightaway."

Zeno nodded to Rafe and continued to read a new entry in an already thick dossier. "While I am gone, Mrs. O'Shea, I would like you to consider this. One of your compatriots has just named James Carey as the man in charge of the Praed Street bombing. Which means my offer to free your brother will likely be withdrawn. Much depends on your cooperation, however. You might still be able to keep him from hanging."

ZENO READ THE decoded telegram out loud.

> RECEIVED 29 MAY
> FROM: INSPECTOR OLIVIER TAUTOU
> WILL RENDEVOUS MRS ST CLOUD IN
> CALAIS STOP

BE INFORMED FRENCH RAIL OPERATORS
STRIKE IMMINENT

He checked the desk clock. A strike could affect
Cassie's train. Due to arrive in Paris . . . Zeno pulled her
travel schedule out of his breast pocket. Just past four. He
raised an eyebrow. Melville had not called him into his
office over a rail strike delay.

His boss frowned. "This came in minutes ago."

TO: MELVILLE SCOTLAND YARD HQ
FROM: HM CUSTOMS EXCHANGE DOVER
PRIORY
SCOTLAND YARD PERSON OF INTEREST
ANDREW DARRAGH HINGHAM LORD
DELAMERE EXITED COUNTRY FOUR PM

"British Customs appears to be awake in Dover." Melville grunted. "Delamere is on the run. This tells me we're
close to breaking their network wide open."

Zeno read the message twice. On the run? Very likely.
But could Delamere have known about Cassie? Who
could have leaked the information? Zeno racked his brain.
House staff, perhaps, intercepted messages. Shipping instructions to train porters. Christ. Cassie would be delayed
overnight in Calais, as was Lord Delamere. The waking
nightmare rumbled like thunder through his entire body.

A brief knock and the door opened. Mr. Quincy poked
his head in the office. "The Earl of Rosslyn is in the vestibule asking for Mr. Kennedy. Shall I escort him up?"

Melville caught Zeno's eye. "Well, well, there seems to be a number of scared birds either taking flight or seeking refuge. Please do, Mr. Quincy."

A sullen but apologetic Gerald St. Cloud took an offered seat at the library table. "Cassie is in grave danger."

"Lord Rosslyn, I will need you to tell me in great detail exactly *how* Cassandra St. Cloud is in danger." Zeno leaned in. "And please do so with haste."

Gerald St. Cloud squirmed uncomfortably. "It is not just Cassie who is in danger. I am the last survivor of our—"

Zeno placed both hands on the table and leaned over the earl. "Down to bloody two, are we?"

His face paled. "Did George Upton hang himself or did they murder him?"

Zeno remained stone-faced. His jaw ached from clenching. He decided on a partial truth. "We found evidence of a struggle."

Beads of sweat formed along the young man's hairline. "I will need protection."

"I am prepared to offer you security. Any future charge of collusion or conspiracy on your part might also be dropped—in exchange for testimony." Melville laced his offer with a sincere bit of warmth. "What say you, Lord Rosslyn?"

Gerald exhaled a sigh of relief. "Well then, I might as well spill the beans, tell you what I know."

Zeno met Melville's gaze over the library table. Finally, they would get the names they needed. And this time a peer would inform on another peer. At trial, Gerald's testimony would have the whip hand alongside statements gathered from captured dynamiters, including Jayne Wells O'Shea.

Melville pulled out a chair and sat down beside Gerald. "I'll take this from here, Zak, best be on your way."

Zeno's stare narrowed on the earl. "What do you know of Lord Delamere's immediate plans?"

"Only that he left for Dover by afternoon train, he travels with a French anarchist and several higher placed Fenians seeking refuge in France. You boys do seem to have them on the run."

"Do they know about Cassie—that she left for Paris this morning?"

A bit wild-eyed, Gerald stammered. "I'm not sure . . . exactly."

"Exactly?" Zeno held himself back from choking the young earl.

"I . . . I stopped by Ten Lyall yesterday morning. I was going to apologize, but Cassie wasn't at home. Her maid, the little French tart, was arranging for trunks to be shipped ahead—to Paris. I might have mentioned something to Andrew—Lord Delamere."

Gerald's hand trembled as he raked fingers through tousled, unkempt hair. "Dear God. He did leave town rather suddenly."

Zeno ticked off a hundred scenarios in his mind. "I must go."

Melville nodded. "You'll just make the late train to Dover."

He braked and turned. "I'll need to hire a private ferry."

"Permission granted." Melville's frown softened. "Bring Delamere back if you can. But I'll not lose a good whist partner like Henry Erskine over this. Make sure you bring his daughter safely home."

Zeno jogged down the corridor and tossed the files on his desk. He grabbed a box of shells from his desk drawer and jammed the bullets in a coat pocket. From the telegraph office in the decryption room, he wired Mrs. Woolsley and sent off another telegram to Rob Erskine, in care of Sir Kevin Meade-Waldo, Tunbridge Wells, Kent.

CASSIE IN TROUBLE STOP
WITH ALL HASTE MEET ME DOVER
PRIORY STOP
DO NOT TAKE TRAIN STOP
DRIVE ROADSTER

Delamere would be charged with blackmail, attempted kidnapping, sedition, and murder. The man would surely hang, if he didn't shoot him dead. But first, he must find Cassie.

HIS HOUSEKEEPER MET him on platform five. "Mrs. Woolsley, while I am away I want you to pay close attention to the activity on the street and around the mews—any odd men lurking about and the like—and forward any telegrams from Mrs. St. Cloud on to Number Four Whitehall."

"Yes, sir." Alma handed over his suitcase and a small basket filled with fruit and sandwiches. "Here you go, then, sir."

He grabbed his housekeeper, gave her a kiss on the cheek, and hopped aboard the last train out of Victoria Station.

With any luck, he would arrive in Dover by eight o'clock. Near dark. Rob would head due east from Tunbridge Wells. The journey to Dover could not be more than an hour by fast coach. The roadster would make it in less, but over country roads? Zeno could not be sure.

He was taking no chances. If the French rail system shut down, the public coaches would be full to overflowing and any carriages left for hire long gone for Paris. The more he thought about it, the more sense the roadster made. Should he face a strike in Calais, Rob's automobile might be his only chance of catching Cassie or Delamere.

Zeno exhaled slowly and settled himself in an empty compartment. By his reckoning, he lagged hours behind Delamere and nearly a full day behind Cassie—unless she was still in Calais. He hoped not. Any extended layover meant she could be spotted.

His thoughts turned darker. *Swift, swift, you dragons of the night.* With the words of Shakespeare raging through his head, he fell into a troubled sleep.

TO: ZENO KENNEDY
FROM: CASSANDRA ST CLOUD
DELAYED IN CALAIS STOP
HOPE TO MAKE PARIS BY NOON TOMORROW

Cassie penned her message and handed it over to the hotel clerk. *"Tout de suite, s'il vous plaît."*

The lobby of the Hotel Meurice thronged with displaced travelers and disgruntled, overworked employees. Having overheard snatches of conversation, she surmised the prevailing wisdom centered around the idea that the rail workers had purposely delayed the trains in anticipation of the strike. Only the word to strike had not yet arrived.

Hopefully the morning train would leave on time. She took a turn around the lobby and stopped to read the supper menu posted at the restaurant door. In between a perusal of delectable dishes, she caught sight of a large party being seated for dinner.

Lord Delamere. Frozen for a moment in time, she gulped for air. As if he could sense her watching, he looked out toward the entrance of the restaurant. He appeared to be expecting someone. She shrank behind the large menu placard and peeked through the etched glass of the dining room doors.

She did not recognize any of the other gentlemen with him, if one could call them that. They were not as handsomely dressed as his lordship. Anarchist sympathizers, she supposed.

"May I be of service, madame?"

Cassie whirled around to confront the raised eyebrow of the maître d'. "No. That is . . . I've decided to have dinner brought up."

The eyebrow lowered measurably as he took out a small booklet. "Your room number?" He wished to take her order.

Cassie shrank away from him. "I'll send my maid down

with our selections shortly." She clamped her mouth shut and continued her retreat.

"As you wish, madame."

Wish? She wished for Zeno to be on the next train and boat to Calais and for Mr. Melville to call out the French police. As for her French bodyguard? She squinted a side-glance around the room. Still no sign of Inspector Tautou. He should have met her hours ago.

Making her retreat through the lobby, she stopped at the desk. "I've changed my mind about sending that telegram."

The clerk appeared somewhat strained by her request, but nonetheless answered politely. "So sorry, madame, the boy left several minutes ago."

"Where is the telegraph office?" she demanded.

"Gare de Calais-Ville." The clerk started to give her walking directions to the train station.

"Thank you, I know the way."

Cassie wove a path through the crowded lobby and out the hotel entrance. She must intercept her wire message and send a new, urgent one. Nearly overcome by a sense of foreboding, she now imagined the worst. Delamere could have men following her. Inhaling a breath of brisk ocean air, she fought off her fears and headed north toward the train station. She took a circuitous route and kept to busy streets. Once inside the station, she paused to let her eyes adjust to the dim light.

A draft of steam and a puff of wind whipped through the arched columns of the train platform. Cassie glanced over her shoulder as she hurried in a direction that likely included the telegraph office.

A prickly, spine-tingling sensation coursed through her as she became aware of a figure trailing behind her. Pivoting on her heel, she swung around to confront— nothing. She scanned the station, carefully searching the dark corners and shadows for her pursuer. Imaginary? She thought not. She sensed something, someone.

She whirled around to find a small wiry man, with deep-set dark eyes and a large brown moustache. He tipped his bowler.

"Madame St. Cloud?"

∞ Chapter Twenty-six

Startled, Cassie backed off a pace as she eyed the French man in front of her. Short of stature, handlebar moustache—he did appear to fit Zeno's description to a T. Still, one needed to be cautious.

"Have we been introduced, sir?"

"Forgive me, madame, I am Inspector Tautou."

She waited for the secret code words. More than a few uncomfortable moments passed before she raised an eyebrow. "Password?"

"Pardon, Mrs. St. Cloud?" The man's head tilted ever so slightly. He studied her as if she were a sphinx spouting riddles. "I have no . . . *ne comprends pas,* madame."

Cassie chewed her bottom lip. "No, I suppose not." Her gaze darted about, as she scanned the station. "I'm afraid I have been followed here to Calais by a very bad character. Just moments ago, I spied him in the dining room of my hotel. He and his cohorts mean to use me to stop an investigation by Scotland Yard." Dear lord, she sounded a bit deranged.

Tautou's curious expression disappeared, replaced by drawn brows. "Agent Kennedy has informed me of these facts, Mrs. St. Cloud. Not an hour ago, I received a wire from Scotland Yard."

"You did?" A wave of relief rushed through her. Zeno knew she was in danger, dear man. "And what of Mr. Kennedy?"

"It is my understanding Agent Kennedy makes his way to Calais."

Cassie's stomach settled a bit as she studied this odd inspector, who exuded a watchful, reassuring competence. "Shall we wait here, in Calais, for Zeno to arrive?"

"No, madame. If the trains leave on schedule in the morning, we shall proceed on to Paris; those are my orders."

"I must return to my room at the Meurice. My maid is in need of supper and—"

"I will return with you and help you pack your things. You and your traveling companion will sleep in my room tonight."

Cassie raised an eyebrow along with her chin. "I beg your pardon?"

THE FAINT RUMBLE and bang of the roadster raised Zeno's spirits. He strained to see through a blanket of mist, barely able to make out the glow from the gas lamp at the end of the train platform.

Thick as London fog, but not as black. He paced the broad planks of the Dover Priory station and waited. Finally, two small dots of light, carriage lanterns, danced

a path through the dank gray atmosphere. As the automobile approached, he called out but to no avail. Zeno
squinted. Rob's road goggles were so fogged with condensation, he was about to drive past the station.

Zeno jumped off the platform and waved him to a
grinding, screeching halt. He braced himself as the front
edge of the carriage stopped within inches of his knee-
caps.

Rob wiped a gloved hand over his goggles. "Crikey,
Zak. I nearly ran you down!"

Zeno placed his suitcase behind the carriage seat and
hopped aboard. They were not likely to leave port tonight, but perhaps they might get the roadster rolled onto
a ferry and find a warm berth in the ship's cabin.

The clatter of the engine seemed louder, amplified by
the moisture in the air. Zeno shouted directions. "Let's
have a skulk about dockside."

Rob drove them down a ramp to the ferry launch,
where a number of ghostly, imposing steamships lay
moored to piers. They put-putted past a jumble of harbor
shops and business offices, before they found a promising
dockside public house.

Rob lifted his goggles up over his sporting cap. "Shall
we try the pub first?"

"On a night like tonight?" Zeno turned up the collar on
his overcoat. "I'd say so."

CASSIE HELPED CÉCILE repack her travel bag. "Lord
Delamere and his men are downstairs having a five-course

supper, just as happy as you please. And I am forced to leave my hotel."

Inspector Tautou stood with his hands clasped behind his back. "Madame St. Cloud, your pursuer has taken a room in this hotel. You are not safe. You will take my room across the square. It is not as large nor as well appointed, but it is clean, with no bugs. I checked it myself. *Très bien*, let us hurry now."

As they made their way down the servants' stairs the anxious inspector became pushy and rude. *"Vite."* How very French of him. Her limbs wobbled and the pit of her empty stomach churned, but she could not help but feel somewhat safer in his care. In fact, Cassie would have to admit the small man was a take-charge sort of fellow, and she reminded herself that Zeno had requested him out of many other field agents to be her protector.

Tautou led them at a half walk, half trot around the square to his modest accommodations. Once she and Cécile were settled in the room, he excused himself, only to return minutes later with a young hotel waiter balancing a large tray on his shoulder.

The inspector shook out a white tablecloth and laid it across the foot of the bed.

"Madame, mademoiselle, you are both hungry, no?"

Tautou and the young waiter uncovered a crusty bread, a few cheeses, and a large tureen of chowder filled with local shellfish and mussels. The spicy soup smelled of brine and curry. Cassie's stomach growled in anticipation.

As her new protector turned to leave, she tore her eyes

away from their humble, but most welcome feast. "And where are you off to now?"

"I shall take up my post. There is a dark alcove at the end of the hall where I can observe the goings-on."

"Please, Inspector, you must also be starved. I must insist you join us for a bowl of soup."

He hesitated, his coffee-colored eyes quite inscrutable until they landed on the steaming tureen of seafood chowder. Removing his bowler, he placed it on a hook by the door and used his hand to sweep a few moustache hairs into place. "*Merci.* I am honored, madame, mademoiselle."

WITHOUT COMPLAINT, ZENO poured Captain Mc-Cabe another pint and waited for his answer. The Sea Lion pub, warmed by smoke and a crowd of thirsty customers, seemed inviting enough on a night such as this.

"Well now, I'm always happy to be of service to Scotland Yard, Mr. Kennedy. But it'll cost ye."

Zeno ground his jaw a bit tighter. "How much, Captain?"

"Forty-five quid."

"I'll pay you twenty-five and not a penny more."

"Forty." The grizzled seaman grunted. "And that's bottom."

"Thirty."

McCabe wheezed out a laugh. "Thirty-five, then, but that'll barely cover the coal for the furnace."

Zeno grinned at the wily man. "Deal."

"Ye have a ferry boat, Mr. Kennedy." McCabe, puffed on his pipe. "The fog'll lift well enough by forenoon watch, no later than two bells."

Not having the faintest, Zeno looked from the captain to Rob, who set his glass down. "Ten o'clock in the morning."

Their rusty-haired, red-bearded captain nodded to Zeno's young companion. "Seafaring man, are ye?"

"Not unless you count punting on the Cherwell." Rob grinned a bit sheepishly. "Keep an odd lot of facts and numbers up here." He tapped the side of his temple.

McCabe read Zeno's frown easily enough. "First train out of Calais won't be much before nine o'clock in the morning. Ye'll not be far behind your trouble."

Rob propped his chin on his fist as his eyelids lowered. Zeno grinned. He could barely keep his own eyes open. The heat of the crowded pub and the strong beer worked its inebriating effects on them both.

The captain leaned across the table. "So, laddie, tell me about this here horseless carriage ye want to roll aboard my little Vicky."

CASSIE INHALED A deep breath and sighed. Despite the looming rail strike, the morning train left Calais without delay. At the last possible moment, Inspector Tautou and two other agents she had never seen before hopped aboard the moving train. The two younger men hung their heads out the compartment window on the lookout for any other suspicious last-minute boarders.

Once they cleared the station, the small man directed one of his associates to a post at the end of the railcar. The other man, a rather handsome young agent who winked at her maid, posted himself outside their compartment door in the aisle.

She huffed. "Zeno promised just one man, not an entourage of guards."

Tautou ignored her grumbling and leaned forward. "You have color in your cheeks, Mrs. St. Cloud—you rested well, I hope?"

Cassie blinked, taken aback. "Well yes, now that you mention it. Very well, under the circumstances."

"Très bon."

As the train accelerated onto the main track, her body rocked peacefully along with the sway of the coach. She pressed back into her seat and enjoyed the quiet Normandy countryside. The climate, already pleasant in temperature, would continue to warm if the sunshine held.

"So, we have left Delamere and his gang of thugs behind us."

He returned her gaze directly. *"Tout à fait, madame."*

She frowned. "How can you be so sure, Inspector?"

"Lord Delamere and his party are delayed. At least until their clothing is returned from the hotel laundry." Tautou shrugged in mock innocence. "A reasonable mistake. It seems hotel workers mistakenly removed items of attire from the gentlemen's rooms while they were asleep." The odd man checked his watch. "It should take them several hours to collect their belongings and resume travel plans."

The ends of her mouth tilted upward. "You are a resourceful man, Inspector. I come to understand why Mr. Kennedy thinks so highly of you."

Tautou reached inside his jacket and removed a telegram. "Are these the words you seek?" He passed the rumpled wire across the aisle.

She scanned the telegram from Zeno. Characters had been scratched out and re-penciled at the bottom of the wire, obviously some form of decoding.

TO: OLIVIER TAUTOU SÛRETÉ
IDENTIFICATION CODE WORDS STOP
EGGS AND CHEESE TOAST

She smiled. "So, your name is Olivier?"

ZENO STOOD BY as McCabe's men waved Rob forward. With great care, Cassie's brother drove the roadster along the carriage gangway and onto the boat. Once the automobile landed safely aboard, Zeno helped to secure the roadster to the ferryboat's deck.

Captain McCabe stood on the upper deck and puffed on his pipe. No worse for wear, Zeno observed, after consuming a queen's gallon of stout last night. Frankly, he resented McCabe's fortitude, as he suffered from a throbbing headache and a fierce burning in his gut. First thing this morning, Zeno had made his way to the telegraph office. No messages awaited, and he returned to the ferry in a darker mood.

By the time he and Rob debarked in Calais, Cassie would be far out ahead, with Delamere right behind her. He tried not to think about the danger she might face with or without Inspector Tautou. What exactly did he know about the Frenchman anyway? Tautou had worked in state security for a number of years. Granted, the inspector at one time safeguarded the president of France. The man could surely protect the woman of his heart.

The crew raised anchor and the *Victoria* got underway. Soon the steady chug of the steam engine as well as the undulating churn of the harbor water beneath them helped raise his spirits. They would make the crossing in a bit more than an hour and a half, slow by larger ferry standards, but the passenger ships would not risk setting off for hours yet. The mournful, two-tone warning of the foghorn sounded. Being cut off from either mainland held no appeal but there wasn't much he could do about it.

His teeth scraped across his bottom lip. Zeno consoled himself with the idea that neither Cassie nor Olivier Tautou would depart Calais without leaving him word.

Rob stood at the bow of the ferry, buttoning his coat. He looked back and waved. Zeno forced a grin in an attempt to look chipper. His gaze moved out into the mist drifting above the glassy surface of the harbor, and his thoughts returned to Cassie.

His life no longer felt complete without her. Zeno's stomach churned a bit as their ship met the gentle roll of waves outside the breakwater. He separated a touch of seasickness from the deep ache in his chest.

"Ahead starboard, fog's lifting."

Zeno followed the captain's gaze out over the right side of the ship's bow. A few whistles and cries sounded as the ferry broke through the last of the cloud cover into brilliant, sparkling water and the clear blue sky.

"Ye see that small point of white cliff straight ahead?

Zeno squinted. "Calais?"

Sporting a lopsided grin, McCabe bit down on his pipe. "Thar she be, Mr. Kennedy."

Chapter Twenty-seven

Zeno rubbed his temples. The moment the *Victoria* made port and tied up, things went abominably. The roadster stubbornly refused to start, even after he and Rob pushed the vehicle across the gangway and onto French soil.

"Minor setback. Too much sea air, I'm afraid. A bit of extra condensation in the air valve." Rob spread out a canvas tool kit and picked up a screwdriver. "Shouldn't take me long to get her dried off and running again. You go ahead, Zak. I'll catch up to you in town."

Zeno grunted. "I'll check the train station and the telegraph office. Meet me at Cassie's hotel." He checked her schedule. "The Meurice. I believe it's on the square."

"Right." Rob's head bobbed up from the engine compartment, cheeks aglow and eyes bright. Zeno set off in the direction of town somewhat disgruntled with the young man's obvious enjoyment of their minor setback. He hadn't fully explained to Rob the amount of danger Cassie might face. But neither could he find a good reason to worry him.

At the Gare de Calais-Ville he confirmed the morning train to Paris had, indeed, departed on time. Exactly an hour and a half ahead, Cassie's train traveled at a speed of sixty miles per hour, twenty miles per hour faster than the roadster could make on the downhill. The next train would not depart for hours yet. Zeno contemplated whether or not to ditch his plans to use the roadster.

At the telegraph office, several telegrams waited for him, none of them more recent than yesterday evening. A message from Cassie, forwarded on from Scotland Yard, informed him that she had arrived safely in Calais. There were two from Melville; the most interesting one apprised him of Lord Delamere's status as a fugitive from justice.

Based on Gerald St. Cloud's sworn statement, Melville had secured an international warrant for Delamere's arrest. Now, if they received the cooperation of the French government, things could work out very well indeed. Zeno crossed the square and headed for Cassie's hotel.

The familiar rattle and hum of the roadster greeted his ears. Rob pulled up in front of the Meurice and left the vehicle parked in the street. The stunned doorman gawked at the strange seven-headed hydra on wheels. Caught without a French coin in his pocket, Rob assured the hotel employee a sum of *sous* to keep a watchful eye on the horseless carriage, then vanished inside. Zeno gave the doorman wide berth as the man's snarl turned into a spate of swearing.

He caught up to Cassie's brother inside the lobby. Rob ventured off to exchange a stack of English pound notes while Zeno struck up a polite line of inquiry at the desk. He presented his card, and asked a routine question. "Might you be able to tell me when Mrs. St. Cloud checked out of the hotel this morning?"

The young clerk returned with the most startling answer. "Monsieur, Madame St. Cloud has not checked out." Zeno's heart thrummed inside his chest. Had she received his telegram and decided to wait for him or was this another mix-up?

"Would you, then, kindly deliver my card to Mrs. St. Cloud?"

Zeno dug in his pocket and found a few coins for the clerk and bellhop. A wrinkled nose and muttered shake of the head from the staffers renewed Zeno's frown. Perfectly serviceable British sterling. Bloody French.

"I shall wait here for the lady's answer."

As soon as Rob returned from the bank, Zeno filled him in.

"Rather a stroke of luck, wot?" Ever the optimist, Cassie's brother ran a hand through unruly hair and buttoned his jacket.

Zeno drew his mouth into a thin line and managed a nod. "Let us hope so, Rob."

The wait felt like hours. Finally, a mature gentleman exited from behind the desk and approached them. "*Pardonnez-moi, messieurs*. Mrs. St. Cloud appears to have left the hotel this morning without notifying us."

A rumble began in the pit of his stomach. "This is decidedly out of character for Mrs. St. Cloud. Might I have permission to search her room?"

The elder gentlemen, most likely the morning manager of the hotel, hesitated.

Zeno shoved another of his cards at the man. "As you can see I work for the London police, Scotland Yard. It is our belief Mrs. St. Cloud travels to Paris in great jeopardy to her safety. Again, might you allow me and my associate to examine the empty room? Surely—"

"*Avancez, messieurs,*" the wary manager relented, "but I must accompany you."

He gave the man a perfunctory nod, and followed him up the grand stairway. As they entered her suite, several maids were already preparing the room for its next occupant. Zeno cringed. So much for clues. His heart sank as he scanned the small sitting room. No bags or evidence of occupancy.

A hair-raising cry from the adjoining bedroom interrupted his thoughts. First through the door, Zeno stepped past a wild-eyed, terrified cleaning woman as she shrank from the water closet door. Zeno's blood froze in his veins.

The dead body of a man sat on the commode, propped against the wall. The man's head flung back, exposing a throat cut ear to ear. Blood soaked the clothing of the victim's chest and puddled onto the small white octagonal floor tiles. The acrid, metallic odor caused his stomach to roil. Even the toilet water pooled beneath the body was stained crimson red.

"Call the police." Zeno spoke to the pale-faced manager as he stepped into the closet to get a better view of the man's face. A pair of spectacles fell askew over the man's black, glassy-eyed stare. Thick brown moustache, salt-and-pepper hair. Aged somewhat since Zeno's last meeting with the inspector.

His heart beat a staccato in his chest. Inspector Olivier Tautou had been murdered last night and Cassie was missing.

TRANSLATED FROM FRENCH:

> POST & TELEGRAPHE FRANCAIS
> 30 MAY 1887
> ALL FRENCH RAIL WORKERS STOP
> STRIKE TO COMMENCE NOON TODAY

Was the strike on? Cassie fidgeted in her seat and waited for the train to depart Lille. Inspector Tautou had left the compartment some time ago to inquire about the delay. She glanced at her maid, who stood in the aisle, having a flirtation with the handsome French agent who guarded their compartment. Earlier, the young man had removed his sunglasses and revealed the most striking pale blue eyes. In combination with gleaming dark hair and an engaging smile? Well, no wonder Cécile was entranced.

Zeno crept into Cassie's thoughts. Setting aside the dilemma she currently found herself in, she had not thought she would miss him quite so much. She had every confidence he followed behind, but where? She sighed. He had been right about the danger, of course. But who would have thought Delamere would have pursued her this far? Or was this coincidental? Awfully hard to believe that.

She dabbed at beads of perspiration with a pocket square. Even with all of the windows lowered, the humid air of the compartment stifled. She opened the door and slipped out of the rail coach onto the platform. A plume of white steam greeted her. Squinting, she made her way through the haze to the shaded side of the station. She spotted a street vendor's cart, which featured large glass containers filled with chilled fruit juice.

On such a humid day, a splash of lemonade over shaved ice was the perfect refreshment. Gripping the paper cone, she sipped on the iced treat and wandered farther down the platform. She found a comfortable spot with a pillar to lean against and enjoyed the cooler breeze along the platform.

She spotted Inspector Tautou standing quite close to another man. The two men spoke in low tones and she was unable to overhear any of their conversation. Curious to see the gentleman's face, she curled herself around the post to get a better view. Raising a hand, she nearly called out to the inspector when his acquaintance turned in her direction.

Cassie bit down hard on an ice chip. She swiveled back behind the column, heart pounding. The very same man had sat down to dine with Lord Delamere last evening. Her mind raced in tandem with her heartbeat. What to do? Eyes to the ground, she stepped over some fallen lemon ice and retraced her route along the platform. What an insidious, dastardly little man Tautou had turned out to be.

Fortune smiled in odd ways. The station remained full of bustling travelers. She looked frantically for her coach number, and found it just as the handsome, agitated, young agent flew out the compartment door. His gaze swept the crowd.

Cassie retreated behind a pillar. The man jogged right, then abruptly turned and ran down the platform toward Tautou. The moment he rushed past, she ran to the door and yanked Cécile outside.

"Stay here." She stepped back inside the train and grabbed one of their travel bags. After a hurried glance down the platform, she pushed her maid toward the closest exit under protest. "Hush, Cécile."

Wait a moment. Should they search for her, which they would surely do, they would likely assume she made for the nearest exit. She pulled Cécile up beside her as they advanced on a row of offices and shop fronts that lined the edge of an empty train track. She quickened their pace from a walk to a jog.

A flutter of pigeons in the rafters overhead startled her and she pulled Cécile into the shadows of an office doorway. She inched forward to gain a view of the station and saw three men, led by Tautou, run past the station exit and head straight for them. Dear God, they must have seen her. She pressed farther back into the niche of the entry.

With a groan, the door behind them gave way. Strong arms pulled them inside.

Cassie confronted a very large man with a mop in one hand. He pressed against her, bearing a surly grin with few teeth. He exhaled.

Horrors.

She puffed out her chest. "Monsieur." Fear caused her French to become halted and inadequate. She explained as best she could. He would need to hide her and Cécile posthaste and ask questions later. "There is no time to argue."

With a leering once-over that sent shivers down her spine, he shoved them both into a backroom closet and turned the key.

Through a golden curtain of flying dust motes, she made out the size and contents of the storeroom they were locked in. The walls were covered floor to ceiling by racks loaded down with supplies. A neat row of wooden file cabinets lined up under a high-placed window.

The sound of muffled voices and loud knocks sent her scrambling up to the window ledge using a stack of shelves as a ladder. When she had climbed high enough, she reached across the top of the file cabinets and gave the sash a swift shove. It opened. A breeze flowed into the stifling room. Peering out the frame, she made quick estimate of the distance between the sill and the paved ground below. *Worst case, a turned ankle.*

"The portmanteau, Cécile, quickly."

She pitched the bag out the opening and jumped back down to guide her maid up the shelf and onto the window ledge. "Sit first, and then swing a leg over. That's it."

Demanding muffled voices and the jiggle of keys in the door sent a chill down her spine. Cassie picked up a broken stool and angled it under the doorknob.

Wiping clammy hands on her skirt, she climbed up the

shelves and urged her maid onward. "Cécile, jump, or I'll have to push you."

Could her heart pound its way out of her chest? The click of the key in the lock was her impetus. She shoved. As her maid fell to the ground she released a small scream, alerting the men outside the door.

She had only seconds. Edging onto the file cabinet, she leaped out the window and tumbled on top of Cécile. Grabbing her maid and bag, they ran down the walkway outside the station and headed for a queue of waiting carriages.

The first coach they reached featured impressive equipage including four fast-looking horses. Outriders and footmen, busy chattering among themselves, paid the two women little mind. With no time to think about her actions, Cassie opened the door of the grand carriage and shoved her reluctant servant inside.

Climbing in behind Cécile, she pulled down the curbside window shades and took a seat. A rush of blood swept through her body as her eyes adjusted to the dim light.

A frail, elderly woman sat across the narrow aisle wearing a blank stare in her eyes. The woman appeared unruffled, as yet, from such a rude intrusion. Gasping for breath, Cassie scrutinized the elder passenger. Perhaps the woman suffered from blindness or senility.

She was prepared to beg for their lives.

"S'il vous plaît, excusez-nous, madame—"

"Speak English, girl." The woman held up a quizzing glass and appraised Cassie, then Cécile. "Is this your maid?"

Hands clasped in her lap, Cassie nodded obediently. "Yes, ma'am."

Having seen enough, the matron released the glass and let it dangle from its ribbon. "You both appear to be on the lam. Perhaps you should explain yourself."

ZENO DRUMMED HIS fingers on the constable's desktop as the black-haired gendarme reopened both passports. Leaning back in his chair, the Calais police chief glanced at a few of his most recent stamps. "The moment I receive word from Scotland Yard, Agent Kennedy, I can release you both." The man laced his fingers together across a wide girth. "While we wait, shall I collect your contact information in Paris?"

He shot Rob a glance. The young man's demeanor had sobered noticeably since finding the murdered French agent. Zeno passed Cassie's itinerary across the desk.

"Hotel Pont Royal, *trés gentil, monsieur.*" He picked up a pencil to scratch a few notes.

A vein throbbed in his neck. "Inspector, I cannot stress enough that time is of the essence. Mrs. St. Cloud is in the gravest of danger—"

A knock on the office door interrupted Zeno's plea. As he listened to the intruding officer speak, his jaw clenched. He forced himself to draw in a hot intake of breath.

"It is official." The rotund constable turned to Zeno and Rob. "The rail workers are on strike."

Zeno grimaced. Cassie, as well as her abductors, was

now stranded. Was that good news or bad? He believed they would continue on to Paris. The sprawling metropolitan city was a hotbed of anarchist sympathizers ready and willing to offer refuge.

He still held out a shred of hope that Cassie might have avoided her captors, but he wasted no time on the thought. Inside his shirt, a trickle of sweat crawled down his back. Wasn't it far more likely they had her in their clutches? He wondered if his fearless young widow would attempt to escape. And if she did manage to break away, where might she run to?

A steely kind of calm settled over him as his heart rate slowed. The rail strike gave him a fighting chance to overtake her on the road, perhaps even beat her to Paris.

The inspector held two wires in his hand. "From Scotland Yard and the *Sûreté*." He took one last glance at their papers and pushed them across his desk. "Apologies, monsieur, for the delay."

Zeno swept up the passports. "We'll be on our way."

Outside the police station, he loaded their luggage back onboard the roadster. A few curious onlookers crowded around the vehicle. Waiting, he supposed, for Rob to start the engine.

"*Pardonnez-moi, monsieurs.*" A young man with cap in hand approached them from the crowd of bystanders. "My brother is a gendarme here in Calais. I have been told you are in search of a young lady, perhaps someone traveling alone, with her maid?"

Zeno nodded. "Please, tell us what you know."

"I work at the Hotel le George. Late last night, I

delivered a meal—a tureen of chowder, baguette, and cheese. Two attractive women occupied the room. The gentleman with them seemed to be someone official. When he tipped me, I heard the young woman, a beauty with silver eyes, call him inspector."

Zeno took a deep breath. Yes, they were lovely eyes.

Mulling over the ramifications of the hotel worker's story, he lifted his brows. "Could you describe the gentleman for me?"

As the young man recalled the man's appearance, Zeno exchanged glances with Rob. Close enough for Cassie to have accepted the man as the real Tautou.

"Did the lady seem in any way uncomfortable, let us say, detained against her will?"

The young informant shook his head. *"Non, monsieur."*

Ever the optimist, Rob's eyes sparked to the news. "I suppose it is much less trouble to get two women to Paris if they travel willingly."

"Even if they are unwitting hostages." A chill ran down Zeno's spine. "We may still be in luck. They appear to believe they have abducted a bit of insurance for themselves."

Rob scratched his head. "They mean to use hostages to bargain for their own necks?"

The best Zeno could manage was a grimace.

The roadster's engine coughed and fired up to a round of shouts and applause from onlookers. He hooked the crank onto the side of the engine bonnet and jumped up beside Rob. Nodding to the young man who had stepped forward, Zeno offered a ride. "Would you mind showing us the way out of town and onto the main road?"

A smile as wide as the English Channel itself erupted onto the youth's face and he hopped aboard. They situated him atop the luggage.

Zeno nodded to Rob. "Let's get to Paris."

"I NEED TO get to Paris," Cassie blurted out to the woman. "And, indeed, some very bad men search for me even now. I promise, sincerely, I will explain everything to you, only . . ." She pressed trembling lips together and tried not to appear too wild-eyed.

The matronly woman raised a studied brow.

"Only, might we give the driver a destination, perhaps a circle about the square, just so I can give these characters the—"

"The dodge?"

The coach door opened and shut with a bang as a young man climbed aboard. "I'm afraid we must slog onward by carriage. The rail workers are on strike." Noticing Cassie and Cécile, he tipped his hat, revealing a frightful shock of bright red hair. "I say, Granny, what have we here?"

As he sank openmouthed onto the seat beside her, the elderly woman grinned. She raised an ebony cane topped with an enormous cut-crystal knob, tapped the roof, and the carriage lurched off.

"What we have here is an adventure, Buckley dear." The woman chided. "And don't look so unnerved, young man. It is the very thing this dreadfully dull holiday of ours has been missing." She returned her attention to Cassie.

"Let me introduce myself. I am the dowager Duchess Lady Grafton and this is my grandson, His Grace, Buckminster Fitzroy, the Duke of Grafton."

"Your Grace." Cassie nodded politely. "I am the dowager Lady Rosslyn. Please call me Mrs. St. Cloud, or Cassandra. Cécile is my maid."

The dowager raised an elegant chin as a slow, close-lipped smile curled the edges of her mouth. "Well then, Lady Rosslyn, or Mrs. St. Cloud, as you prefer, we have several hours of dusty ride before us and you have promised me a story."

Cassie spent the better part of the next two hours relating the strange circumstances surrounding her involvement in Zeno's pursuit of Lord Delamere and the Fenian dynamiters. She found the young duke's rapt attention to every detail both curious and telling. At every turn of the story, the adolescent proved himself an inquisitive, avid crime solver. And the dowager duchess shared her own brand of running commentary.

When Cassie finished a particularly grisly description of the events at the Stanfield Ball, the elderly woman sniffed. "I send in a donation every year. Spares me hours of boredom." And she was sparing but incisive with her impressions of Lord Delamere. "Don't really know the man. Flirtatious, is he not? Stylish. Rather full of himself. I believe the late duke thought him unctuous."

Cassie sighed. Leaving out the more intimate side of her involvement with Detective Kennedy proved more challenging as her tale went on. The impression she imparted of their relationship was more than friendship but less than what it really was. A great deal less. The thought made her smile, perhaps for the first time today.

Like an infatuated child, the Duke of Grafton, or Buckley as he insisted on being called, questioned her tirelessly about Zeno Kennedy. "I have a box full of clippings on my desk in Euston Hall, organized in chronological order. Beginning with the bombing of Clerkenwell Prison, the fizzle at the *London Times* building, and both Underground explosions."

"Buckley wishes to become a Yard man after university." The dowager duchess feigned a tight-lipped smile, more unhappy than not.

Cassie tilted her head. "If I'm not mistaken, several peers of the realm are employed by Special Branch."

"I have made a note of them," the redheaded duke enthused. "Detective Raphael Lewis is a St. Aldwyn, and Owen Neville is heir to the Earldom of Warwick. Why, even Mr. Kennedy himself is connected to the Ayrshire earls."

Cassie smiled. "Zeno contends he is a distant relation."

Buckley grinned at the dowager. "There, you see, Granny?"

"Don't encourage him." The duchess raised a brow in mock displeasure. "It is my greatest hope he will grow out of it."

The very idea that Zeno could be following after them caused a certain amount of fidgeting on the part of the young duke, who regularly checked the road behind the carriage as though Detective Kennedy might pull alongside at any moment. "Gadzooks! Another coach, coming up fast behind us."

Cassie craned her neck to look out the window. Pistol shots fired overhead. She returned to the duke and his grandmother. "A warning to slow down or be fired upon."

Buckley removed a pistol from beneath the plush bench seat. "Highwaymen, or Lord Delamere's thugs?"

She shook her head. "I don't believe highwaymen would use a carriage." After a second volley of shots, Cassie sidled over to the coach window in time to witness an injured outrider fall forward. The man caught himself at the last minute and held on. As they rounded a sharp turn, she craned her neck to look ahead. One of the guards riding out in the front slowed his mount and fell back to the rear of the carriage.

As the coach pulled ahead he shouted inside, "I must give the order to return fire, Your Grace." Buckley nodded to the man.

Their driver whipped the teams to a pace much too fast for the curved route they traveled over. The carriage swayed dangerously through a series of turns as they swept past a road sign. Nineteen miles to Paris. Depending on who had the least obstructed view, Cassie and the duke took turns firing his pistol out opposite windows.

The carriage hurtled down a steep slope, pitching onto two wheels as it rounded a blind bend. "Everyone to one side," Cassie yelled and shoved a screaming Cécile to the elevated side of the coach. Cassie threw herself into her maid's lap. Buckley did the same across the aisle. The grand dame clutched her nephew and her crystal-topped walking cane for dear life.

The duke poked his head out the window. "Good God."

Cassie strained to see the road ahead. "Good God."

A wagon laden with hay was slowly making its way uphill. They were going to plunge off the steep side of this road and be smashed into bits of bone and flesh. Slowly, as if in a dream, the teams slowed, the carriage braked and the coach righted itself, narrowly missing the farmer's wagon.

All four wheels returned to the road with a teeth-rattling crack and a thud. The springs bounced them so hard, the wheels literally lifted off the ground for a moment and Buckley hit his head on the roof. Cassie tasted blood. She had bitten her tongue.

The duke's outriders fired a volley of shots, and their pursuers fell back.

The fallen revolver skittered across the floor of the carriage. Cassie took up the gun, braced her arm on the window ledge, and sighted down the barrel. This time she waited to take her shot.

∞ Chapter Twenty-eight

Zeno slid several francs across the counter. The busy inn's cook had filled his travel basket with bread and cheese, several pastries, and two bottles of ale.

"No doubt you've been busy? Many more customers than usual, what with the rail strike." The innkeeper's wife had winked at him earlier. He leaned farther over the bar and lowered his voice. "I have lost touch with some fellow travelers—English—perhaps you could help me?"

The woman wiped off the counter with a damp cloth. "As you say, we have seen many customers today."

"Specifically, two young women traveling together. They may be escorted by . . . well, guards, perhaps. Any similar guests or customers through the inn today?"

She swept back a few loose hairs, noting the stack of bills on the bar. She regarded Zeno with a wary eye. "Perhaps, monsieur." Her gaze returned to the pile of notes on the counter. Zeno added a few more.

"How could I forget *les Anglais?* They claimed to have been attacked on the road by highwaymen. There were guards. *Oh mon Dieu, oui.* Four outriders. One had a wound to the upper arm." She rolled her eyes. "Such a fuss over a scratch."

Zeno swallowed hard and cleared his throat. "Could you describe them for me? In detail, *s'il vous plaît?*"

The innkeeper's wife tilted her head and nodded. "Three English and a French girl—the lady's maid." The handsome middle-aged woman leaned toward him, so he might enjoy a more intimate view of her breasts. Zeno bit back a frown and remained amiable, even as she trifled with him.

"You like, Englishman?" She lowered her voice. "Perhaps you might take a room upstairs to refresh yourself?"

Zeno swept a long, approving glance up and down. "What a shame, madame, but I must make Paris by nightfall." He cleared his throat. "You were saying something about a group of travelers?"

The woman shrugged. "A duke, hardly more than a boy, his *grand-mère*, and two young women. An English lady and her maid."

"A French maid, you say?" He held his breath.

"*Oui.* A beauty, as was her mistress. The English woman was tall. Her hair not blond, not brown. Eyes, *d'argent*, I think." A corner of her mouth curled. "Are these your women, monsieur?"

"The ladies weren't hurt in anyway?"

She seemed surprised at his question. "*Non, monsieur.*"

Zeno wanted to kiss her. At the very least, dance the woman around the dining room. He settled for a brief kiss on each of her cheeks and slapped a few more notes on the counter. "And how long ago, madame, did they pass through here?"

The woman swept up his money and raised her hands in the air. "Perhaps two hours. They . . . *effrayé*—terrify— the travelers in my inn. *Merde!* Several customers took up with them and formed a convoy."

Zeno left the inn whistling. He placed the lunch basket on the seat of the roadster and looked around for Rob, anxious to be on their way. They were hardly out of the woods yet, but there was a glimmer of hope, a chance Cassie had eluded Delamere and his cohorts. He could hardly wait to share the news with her brother.

"Nothing here at the inn, I'm afraid." He spun around at the sound of Rob's voice.

"Our chances improve as we approach Paris. We'll find a bit of industry where we can purchase a few cans of petrol."

"This should get us close enough." Rob retrieved their last container of fuel from the carriage trunk and Zeno grabbed the funnel.

His young recruit wiped the dust and sweat off his brow with his sleeve. Zeno marveled at both Rob's ingenuity and how quickly this odd vehicle had grown on him. Driving was almost routine now. "Shall I take the steerage for a while?"

Zeno jumped behind the driver's seat and Rob cranked.

The engine putted and rumbled into commission as a coach pulled by four horses flew past the inn. Zeno stared after the trail of dust.

Rob followed his gaze. "Every time one of them passes

by, you get that look in your eye." He lifted the basket up off the seat and hopped aboard. "Dare I ask who you are thinking of?"

He offered a dusty grin, but a grin nonetheless. "I have some news to share."

"Good news, I hope." Rob unhinged the stopper on a bottle of ale and took a long swig.

Zeno released the brake and eased back on the hand clutch. "The best all day."

"AT LEAST WE had the good sense to send our trunks ahead." Cassie glanced around the spacious, light-filled hotel room and unpinned her hat.

Her maid moped about the room.

"Dear me, what a sour expression, Cécile." She approached the girl. "I realize you lost a suitcase and some personal items. You know I will give you whatever money you require to replace them. Don't you?"

"*Oui.*" Cécile pushed on paned doors that opened onto a small private terrace. "Oh, madame, come and see. *Très tragique!*"

Cassie stepped out on the balcony and followed her maid's forlorn gaze. There, along the curve of the Seine, stood the much-touted, partially completed ironwork structure that already dominated the cityscape. She tried to imagine the rest of the tall spire.

"What a sight Mr. Eiffel's Tower will be." She bit her lip and moved closer. "Cécile, did you form an attachment to that young French man on the train with us?"

A sideways glance told Cassie she had struck a nerve. "You do realize that even if those men were from the *Sûreté*, they were also in league with Lord Delamere and up to no good? They could have harmed both of us." Cassie twisted her hands together. "In fact, I am at a loss as to who I might safely contact now that we have arrived in Paris."

Cécile cast her eyes downward. "Perhaps I am foolish, Madame St. Cloud."

Cassie put her arm around the girl's slumped shoulders and rubbed. "Cécile . . ."

"*Oui, madame?*"

"You didn't mention anything about where we would be staying in Paris? I mean, to the young man—any personal information they might use to find us?"

"*Non, madame.*"

She exhaled. It was so much safer to be anonymous, swallowed up by this great city. Briefly, Cassie admired the bright red geraniums in flower boxes and inhaled the cooler afternoon air. "There now, let's unpack and get situated, shall we? You must contact your brother. Perhaps you can have a visit this very evening."

Her pretty maid's brows furrowed. "But you should not be alone."

"Nonsense, Cécile, I am due at the gallery before it closes to view my hanging."

Ashen faced, the girl whimpered. "Hanging, madame?"

She reached out and stroked her hair. "Not me, silly girl, my paintings."

*   *   *

CASSIE STOOD IN the front of the gallery and stared in horror. She had no trouble recognizing herself in the painting. *Please tell me it isn't so.* She blinked several times and hoped the blur would resolve into a different face on the naked woman in the artwork.

A girl lay under a tree, *au naturel*, surrounded by several fully dressed men. The gentlemen admired the young lady as they lounged about her. The wood nymph looked as if she had awakened from a dream to discover herself unclothed.

And those breasts. She tilted her head. Well, they seemed a great deal plumper than her own. Dear lord, how on earth had this happened?

Cassie quite emphatically had never posed for this picture. Granted, she had enjoyed a somewhat wild and carefree youth when compared to most young women, but she certainly never removed her clothes for an artist, including . . .

She searched the bottom of the painting for a name. G. Laschate. Gregoire Laschate? She recognized the name from art school. An artist-in-residence, her second term at The Newland School. Was he aware she showed at the Durand-Ruel Gallery, as well?

She bit her lower lip and approached one of the exhibit workers. "Might you show me to the gallery director's office?"

A young fellow led her through a labyrinth of freshly painted walls, all hung with works featuring bold strokes of vivid color. Making their way down a narrow corridor, her escort opened the door to a small, cluttered office. A thin dark-haired man with a pair of pince-nez perched on the bridge of his nose gave her a look up and down before springing to his feet.

"Mademoiselle?"

"My name is Cassandra St. Cloud, monsieur. I believe I have several paintings ready to hang here in the gallery?"

The glasses dropped from his nose. Wide eyes and a lascivious grin told her everything she needed to know and feared most. He recognized her from Laschate's painting.

Heat flushed from her neck to her cheeks as she straightened her shoulders. "There is also the matter of a painting set on an easel near the front of the gallery . . ." She faltered when the impertinent man bit back a grin.

"*Oui, madame.*" His eyes fell from her face to her breasts. "I believe I know the one you refer to."

She lifted her chin. "I wish to have it removed, sir. If I am to show my work in the Durand-Ruel Gallery, I must be taken seriously. Not just by my peers, but by the public as well."

"Madame St. Cloud, certainly you posed for such a beautiful work, why do you care—"

"I certainly did not, Monsieur . . . ?"

"*Excusez-moi.* Paul Durand-Ruel."

Cassie blinked. "You are the owner, monsieur?"

The man nodded a bow.

"Monsieur Durand-Ruel, I did *not* pose for Monsieur Laschat. Several years ago, I was a student of his—"

"*Madame*, no doubt the affair ended badly. But, what can I do?" The man threw up his hands. "I have agreed to show several of Laschate's latest works."

Men. French men to boot. Cassie stood upright, fuming. "You have also contracted to show my work, sir." Her gaze remained steadfast, but she softened her speech. "Don't you see? It is impossible this painting is one of his latest works. I have not set eyes on the man since art school."

The slight, effete Frenchman gathered heavy eyebrows together as he twisted his mouth into a lopsided pout. It seemed he was at a loss to cope with the situation. "I must say your paintings are magnificent, Mrs. St. Cloud. I would hate to—"

"I have not traveled all the way to Paris to have my work cut from the show, sir." Cassie's gaze darted around the office as she tried to think. "If you would be so kind as to give me Mr. Laschate's address? I shall convince him to substitute another. Would that be acceptable to you, Mr. Durand-Ruel?"

"I regret the loss, but . . ." He opened a journal on his desk, pulled out a drawer, and picked out a fountain pen. He wrote the address of Gregoire Laschate's studio on the back of his calling card. "If you convince Laschate to take it down, tell him I want the one of the dancer from the Moulin."

"*Merci.*" Careful to appear respectfully deferential, she slipped the card into her reticule. "Now, before I leave, monsieur, might I have a look at my small space in your impressive gallery?"

ZENO CLAMPED HIS mouth into a thin line. They were in Paris, all right: the hired help was surly. Standing at the desk of the Hotel Pont Royale, he drew himself up to his full six feet. Both he and Rob looked a sight, covered in a layer of road dust, their faces raw from sun- and windburn.

He drew out his passport and calling card. "If there is no Mrs. St. Cloud registered here, might there be a Miss Erskine?"

The elder desk clerk answered with a single cocked eyebrow and another grudging glance through the hotel register. The old man ran a finger over the last names in the register. *"Non, messieurs."*

Zeno racked his brain. Cassie could have easily changed hotels, but this location was their only connection to each other, unless a wire message waited him somewhere—but where?

He turned to Rob. "Did Cassie ever use another name, perhaps for her art?"

Rob shook his head and shoved his hands deeper into his pants pockets.

"Monsieur Kennedy!"

Zeno spun around. Cassie's maid hurried toward them through the quiet lobby.

"Cécile?"

"Oh, monsieur, I have done a very bad thing!" the girl cried.

"Calm down, Cécile. It can't be that bad."

"Oh yes, it is." She moaned. "I an idiot. I told a man— one who posed as *Sûreté*—about madame's art show at the Durand-Ruel Gallery."

"Never mind that, Cécile. Where is Cassie?"

The petite little maid burst into tears. "She has gone to the gallery, monsieur."

He ignored his hammering heart and grabbed his passport and calling card. "Rob, you stay here with Cécile. If Cassie returns, keep her here and don't let her out of your sight."

Zeno queried the clerk, *"La galerie Durand-Ruel . . . l'adresse?"* He turned to Rob. "I'll need you to alert the *Sûreté*, have them meet me at—"

Finally able to be of service, the hotel worker beamed. *"Seize* Rue Laffitte."

∽ Chapter Twenty-nine

Her artist's soul floated ten feet off the ground. Three of her paintings made an excellent showing in an alcove just off the main display room. A tingle of excitement surged through her body as she exited the gallery and climbed into the waiting cab. She unbuttoned her jacket and settled onto the hard leather bench for the long, uphill trip to the Montmartre district. There was still time to find Laschate and convince him to substitute another painting. She glanced at the carriages nearby and reminded herself to use caution. She was in Paris, alone.

And where was Zeno? She had wired Scotland Yard with the request that her message be forwarded immediately. But did the Yard have any idea of his whereabouts? She had certainly experienced her fair share of trouble. He, as well, must have encountered a myriad of delays and difficulties.

A recurring image crossed her mind. Zeno, lying injured and alone in some unknown alleyway. She refused to think of it. Gazing out the window at the towers of

Notre Dame Cathedral, she sighed. She missed him, more than she could ever have imagined.

He was on his way. He had to be.

By the time she arrived at Rue de Montmartre, her initial surge of excitement over the exhibit had dissipated. Passing a corner bistro, she doubled back. Exactly what she needed, a good strong cup of Parisian coffee. At a sidewalk table she sipped the rich, hot café au lait and waited for her body to revive itself.

ZENO STOOD IN front of a painting at the gallery and ached for her. According to the owner, Durand-Ruel, he had missed her by mere minutes.

"Monsieur Kennedy?"

He pivoted toward the voice behind him and confronted a well-dressed young man, who nodded politely. "Metro Police. Inspector Jourdain."

"Zeno Kennedy, Scotland Yard."

"I have a cadre of men with me, sir, at your service."

THE SUN'S LAST rays of light gave way to dusk as she climbed the narrow, steep walkway to Laschate's residence. Oddly, she found the door wide open and the space deserted. "Monsieur Laschate?" Cassie ventured inside the studio. Nothing out of the ordinary. A number of unframed paintings were stacked against a wall in various stages of finish, and more recent works in progress on easels about the room.

She stepped into the center of the studio and onto the platform where his muses posed. The paintings were of dance hall girls, in various stages of dishabille. His influence was Edgar Degas, though his work was not as bold as Degas's vivid pastels of ballerinas and bathers.

Twilight suffused the studio in a cool incandescence, with more shadows cast than illumination. As she pressed farther into the darkened room, her stomach churned in a riot of flutters.

"Monsieur Laschate? Is anyone here?" Somewhere, in a distant room, a loud bang sounded. Cassie jumped and spun around. Instinctively she headed for the door but pulled up short when a figure cloaked in shadow approached her.

"Good evening, Cassandra. Or should I say *bonsoir*?"

A chill shuddered through her body. She strained to make out the tall, dark shape in the doorway entrance. "Lord Delamere. I urge you to give up this foolish idea of using me as a shield." She frankly did not know where the words came from. Even though her knees quaked, her voice sounded strong and deliberate.

"Rather unsporting of me, isn't it, my little English dove?"

Her mind urged her to flee, but her feet remained frozen to the ground. She pressed her arms against her sides and resisted the urge to tremble.

Delamere took a step forward and jolted Cassie into action. Placing one foot behind the other, she backed away from her would-be captor. The moment he lunged, she turned and ran. Spying a crack of light along the wall, she headed for a rear door. Damn this bustle and gown. She picked up her skirts to gain more freedom of movement. With every stride, Delamere's footsteps closed in behind her.

She stopped just short of plowing into a thuggish brute, who opened and closed the exit door. Delamere slipped an arm around her waist and dragged her back into the center of the room. She struggled with each step as figures emerged from the shadows. More of Delamere's men closed in. The heat of his breath scorched her neck. She kicked at his shins and scratched at his face.

"Damn it." He dropped her.

Before she had a chance to back away, he reached out and caught her up again, pushing both wrists behind her back. She continued to struggle against the tall, powerful lord even as he pressed his body against hers.

Her eyes filled with tears she refused to shed. Raising her chin, she met his gaze. "Do not do something you will regret, sir."

His face dipped so close she smelled hints of brandy and tobacco on his breath. "Anything I choose to do with you, Cassandra, I could never regret."

He shoved her onto the platform and released her. "Now, Lady Rosslyn—or do you prefer Mrs. St. Cloud?" Delamere ogled her. "Or is it mistress to Zeno Kennedy?"

She rubbed her wrists and darted a glance about for any avenue of escape.

"I am done chasing after you, madam." With a hand on his hip, Delamere took a leisurely turn around the end of the platform. "You may choose to run, in which case I will instruct Mr. Morel here to shoot you." Cassie squinted at the wiry man in the corner. The man who had posed as the amenable Inspector Tautou emerged from the shadows with his pistol raised.

"Or you can relax and take your clothes off." Delamere's gaze raked over her. "Come, come, Cassie, you have done this kind of thing before, haven't you?"

She bit her lower lip and circled the platform like a caged wildcat. He had seen the picture at the gallery, waited for her, followed her here.

The odious man had the nerve to smile. "Take your time. There will be no one to interrupt our evening together. Laschate is safely tied up in his storage room along with an assistant. We are alone, Cassandra, except for my men, who don't mind watching." A number of shaded eyes moved up and down her torso. "Perhaps you might offer them a sample after you and I are finished." She recognized one or two of the men and dropped her eyes to avoid leering gazes.

She forced down a tremble, lengthened her spine, and straightened her shoulders. She had no option but to defy him. "If you harm me in any way, Zeno will make sure you hang."

Delamere tilted his chin. "Those Yard men do seem to attract the ladies, do they not, Cassandra? I daresay Mr. Kennedy is kept fully satisfied by you and his lovely Miss Wells."

She frowned. "Jayne Wells is dead. Killed by a Fenian bomb, thanks to your support."

"Ah, therein lies the rub, my pretty dove." Delamere's

eyes crinkled even as his lips twitched. "The night Mr. Kennedy so admirably took a bullet for one of his colleagues, he also managed to arrest his mistress." A malevolent grin formed on his face. "Risen from the grave, so to speak."

His gaze took in the paintings surrounding her. "As it turns out, Mistress Jayne is an Irish nationalist sympathizer and her death, a sham. Quite neatly done, I must say. Hard to pull one over on Scotland Yard. Jayne specializes in bedroom favors to British government officials. Detective Kennedy, for example."

Delamere halted. "I understand he has kept her under lock and key for weeks now. Under interrogation, he calls it. Strange he didn't mention it."

Cassie dared not blink, or tears would fall. Why should she believe him? The man might say anything to provoke her. "If what you say is true, Lord Delamere, there is a very good reason for his silence."

"No doubt he is a man of many secrets." His quiet sneer grated. It was meant to.

Cassie backed across the platform and he signaled one of his lackeys. Heavy arms grabbed hold. She struggled to break away from the man behind her. "Bring her closer."

She bit her lip to keep from crying out as callused hands squeezed. Her arms ached under the constraint of the man's grip and she braced herself against the pressure. The brute pushed her forward.

"There now, let's see those pretty breasts we all got to admire in the gallery." Delamere grabbed the front of her dress and ripped, exposing the lace of her camisole and her corset. She tried to twist her way out of the brute's grip.

"Hold her steady." Hook by eye, he unfastened the front of her corset and tore open her camisole.

A lecherous gaze skimmed her face before returning to her chest. "Lady Cassandra in the flesh."

His eyelids lowered over eyes that glistened with hunger. "Exactly as remembered . . . that summer eve long ago. I observed you in the pond. Unawares, you touched yourself . . ."

The cool air of the darkened studio poured over the sensitive tips of her breasts, and she could not help but catch her breath. Several of his men moved closer.

"Twice now I have nearly enjoyed you. When was the last time?" He peeled back her camisole for a better view. "Ah yes, in the gallery at Margaret Fayette's little soirée." He actually chuckled. "Quite a spirited struggle, as I recall."

Blood and fear pounded in her veins, as he reached out a milk white hand with long tapered fingers. She shook her head, but made sure to meet the eyes of the man who would rape her. Her heart drummed an erratic beat in her chest. "Please, I beg of you."

"After I have you, it might amuse me to keep you—for a while."

Cassie jumped as a loud bang echoed through the studio. Something spun Delamere around. The crackling sound of bullets rang through the air—at least she hoped they were bullets. Yes, she could see the bloodstain already forming on the man's coat sleeve.

She pushed away from him as another gun fired. The man holding her collapsed. A red stain spread across his chest. With his good arm, Delamere grabbed Cassie around the waist and held on tight.

"*Ne tirez*. Hold all fire." Zeno's voice. Dear God, she was sure of it. A spark of renewed energy ran through her body. "Let her go, Delamere."

"I shall retain the young lady awhile longer." Cassie felt the cold steel of a pistol pressed to her side. Backing away in the direction of the front door, Delamere's men drew their guns and fired into the black shadows of the studio.

Another volley of shots rang out. The smell of gunpowder and acrid black smoke filled the air. Men were dropping all around. She dug her heels in and dragged her feet. Still, he managed to haul her over the body of a dead man sprawled across the floor.

He opened the door to the studio entrance. The cock of the pistol in her side made her stiffen. She shook off her fear and jabbed him in the ribs. A blow from behind spun them both around, forcing the pistol from her waist. She turned in time to see Zeno wrestle Delamere for the gun.

Zeno slammed Delamere's hand into the stone wall, and the pistol fell. Cassie winced as the fiendish lord landed a punch to Zeno's jaw that snapped his head sideways, enough to make him stagger. Before she could reach the gun, his lordship retrieved his pistol from the floor and flew down the stairs.

Shouts came from below. "*Arrêtez!*" French police ordered Delamere to halt. Shots rang out from the street as she ran into Zeno's arms. He held her for a long moment before he shrugged off his coat and covered her. "Are you all right?" Numbly, she nodded her head. He gave her a sweet kiss. "I must go, Cassie."

In a daze, she watched him disappear down the stairwell.

"Madame St. Cloud?" Cassie turned to face a pleasant-looking young man. He stowed his firearm and retrieved his card: Metro Police. Inspector Jourdain. "Let me escort you to my carriage."

A rush of shivers in the policeman's coach prompted her to pull Zeno's coat tight to her body. She buried her nose in an upturned lapel and inhaled his scent. It came close to making her cry or swoon, she wasn't sure which. The young policeman reached out and handed her a flask. "You are—*en état de choc*—shock, madame. You must drink, please."

CUTTING A TIGHT corner, Zeno felt his foot slip into a treacherous crack between cobblestones. He sailed through the air before tumbling onto a slimy patch of steep road. He rolled to a stop at the end of the lane. "Bollocks." A bloody ankle instantly began to swell. He looked up as Delamere's cab turned the corner.

Ignoring the pain, he raced into a narrow alley, ducking laundry lines and climbing over dustbins. Vaulting a low wall, he emerged back onto a main thoroughfare, where he waylaid a vacant hansom cab. But where was Delamere?

It was nearly dark. He remembered a scarf on the driver and scrutinized the cabs up ahead. After a mile of nothing, Zeno racked his brain. Drawing down the side window, he cautiously peered behind.

Not three vehicles behind, a red scarf blew over the shoulder of a man sitting above a cab. Blimey. In the snarl of traffic he had ended up ahead of Delamere.

Zeno shouted instructions to his driver, who found a spot to pull over. Delamere's cab flew by. He sucked in a few deep breaths and ordered his mind. It was going to take everything in his power not to kill the man tonight.

His driver quickly caught on to the game, deftly following the other cab at a distance. Once they were across the Seine and onto Boulevard Saint-Germain, he slowed his driver's pursuit even more. Delamere must believe he had evaded both the *Sûreté* and Scotland Yard.

Close to a turn in the river, Delamere ditched his cab and continued down the Rive Gauche. After a furtive glance about, he disappeared into a large gardenlike concourse, the Champ de Mars.

Zeno asked his driver to wait and pulled his pistol.

Excellent. The park was near empty. He crept quietly up on Delamere until he had a clear shot through an open pathway. Zeno took aim and fired. Delamere returned a few wild shots before he turned and headed straight for the cover of an enclosed building site. The looming ironwork of the tower thrust upward from the grounds like the metal framework of an erupting volcano.

Zeno slammed up against a construction fence covered in handbills and poster art. Keeping his back against the wood, he peered around the barrier. The grounds were lit by several flickering gas lamps scattered among piles of iron girders and a huge steam-powered crane. A bullet shattered the wood next to his face and he squinted as a splinter cut into his lower cheek.

Zeno dashed forward to take cover behind the imposing steam engine.

He could just make out a wraithlike shape against the inky black of the river and the city sky. His lordship ascended a spiral of metal stairs situated inside one of the tower's four legs. Zeno dashed across an open piece of ground, pausing at a stack of girders. He gazed upward and took half a second to admire the sheer scale of Mr. Eiffel's iron monster.

His lordship had boxed himself in. Delamere was his.

Zeno reminded himself that the *Sûreté* would not be far behind and their gunshots would surely have attracted local gendarmes into the concourse. He made his way up the stairs just as Delamere leaped onto the zigzag pathway of scaffolding above. His lungs burned as he ascended the never-ending steps and reached the first-level platform.

The defiant lord turned and took aim. Zeno likewise approached with gun drawn. "We've reached the end of the chase, Delamere."

"I wouldn't be so sure of it." The man's coat sleeve was soaked in blood.

Zeno halted his approach long enough to deliver one last warning. "You can give yourself up now, or we can holster our guns and wait until you pass out from blood loss. Up to you." Inching closer, Zeno silently cocked his pistol.

Glassy-eyed, Delamere swayed on his feet. "Think you've saved the empire, don't you, Kennedy?"

"As long as men like you are about, I stay busy."

Delamere stood near the edge of the platform, smirking. "God Save the Queen. Arrest Delamere. Case closed, not a stick of dynamite left unaccounted for? Nor a window left open? We shall see, Kennedy."

Zeno estimated they were somewhere around four or five stories high. If the ashen-faced lord fell into unconsciousness, his death was assured. Zeno reasoned it wouldn't be long now. The man was speaking in riddles, a sure sign of delirium.

"Say good-bye to Cassandra—"

"You are not allowed to speak her name." His own voice was foreign to him—otherworldly—as sharp and cold as shaved ice. "Another mention and I will shoot you dead." Although quite suddenly he no longer wished for the man to die, at least not here in Paris. Delamere's trial and subsequent hanging in Newgate gaol appealed to his sense of justice. For the crown as well as himself. Zeno steadily closed in.

Delamere fired his pistol. Only there was no shot. Just the hollow, metallic click of an empty chamber.

Zeno looked up from the barrel of his lordship's pistol and grinned. "You've had your six, time to give up and go to jail."

The man threw the emptied revolver and retreated across the scaffolding. Zeno dodged the heavy metal projectile and grabbed a shoulder. Spinning Delamere around, he tossed off a good blow to the man's right cheek. The injured lord staggered backward.

Shouts and warning shots came from below. No doubt, from such a distance, it was impossible for the men gathering in the construction yard to tell them apart. He and his fugitive were dark shapes silhouetted against an indigo sky.

Delamere got off a swing with his good hand, but missed. Teetering for a moment, suspended in midair, he lost his balance and careened backward.

Zeno lunged forward and caught a slippery, blood-stained hand. Ropes holding the platform together twisted and snapped away. The whirl and hiss of cords whizzing through pulley blocks singed the air with the smell of burning hemp and greased metal. The crack and splinter of wooden planks separated underfoot, slamming them into the tower's girders. One end of the catwalk tilted at a steep angle over the edge the tower.

Caught off balance, the weakened lord fell to his knees and slid off the end of the scaffold. Thrown forward, Zeno struggled to keep hold of the dangling body that dragged him toward the edge of the platform and death. In desperation, he managed to jam a toe into the crook of a girder.

Delamere swayed at the end of his faltering grip. Zeno squinted into velvet blackness. A head fell forward. His lordship had fallen into unconsciousness. The dead weight slipped from his grasp, inch by inch.

"Damn you, Delamere." He gritted his teeth and held on.

Chapter Thirty

"'The daring police chase began in Montmartre and ended high above the city as two men dangled from the iron girders of Eiffel's Tower.'" Cassie sipped her coffee and continued to read. "'British and French police rescued and subsequently arrested one peer of the realm, Andrew Hingham, Lord Delamere, on multiple charges, including high treason against the British Crown.'"

Breakfast started late this morning. She hadn't slept a wink last night, not until the police assured her Detective Kennedy had delivered Lord Delamere safely into custody. She set down the paper. "Zeno will be pleased he avoided the spotlight."

Rob looked up from his own paper. "Ah, but you must read on, Cass. I'm afraid the news writers are already speculating about your Yard man. Listen to this: 'It is now presumed the chase started days earlier, as Scotland Yard agent Zeno Kennedy pursued Lord Delamere from London to Calais to Paris, culminating in fisticuffs atop the tower last night in the Champ de Mars.'"

Rob laughed aloud. "Ha ha, it gets better. 'According to an early wire report, Calais chief of police claimed two gentlemen set out for Paris yesterday morning in a motorized carriage. He identified one of the men as Agent Zeno Kennedy."

Seeing her brother's enjoyment over the mere mention of his roadster, Cassie could not help but smile.

"And there appears to be another related item. Several paragraphs regarding our rescued heroine—that would be you, Cass—something about a dispute with an artist named Laschate. A nude portrait?" Rob layered a bit of egg on his croissant and winked at Cécile. Several times this morning, she had noted Rob's interest in her maid. It seems her little brother was learning a few life lessons in Paris.

A muffled knock sent Cécile scurrying inside to answer the door. She escorted Zeno out onto the garden terrace. Cassie's heart raced, then fluttered as she and Zeno made eye contact. Fresh from the bath, clothes pressed, he looked the perfect semblance of a proper English gentleman, not the daring Yard man who had nearly fallen to his death from the Eiffel Tower. Her chest swelled and her lower body thrummed over the man standing before her.

He came around to her side of the table and leaned over to kiss her. Why not? When in Paris, do as the Parisians do.

"Good morning, Zeno." At the last second she turned a cheek to him and he hesitated at her gentle rebuff. His lips brushed along her cheekbone.

"Good morning, Cassie. After such a harrowing night, you look well."

Rob beamed at Zeno. "Oh yes, she's in top form. We've been reading the papers, all about the chase and the scene at the tower."

Zeno scanned the familiar mansard rooftops of the city. "Sensational view." His perusal stopped at the striking tower. "It was pitch-black. No sense of how high up we were. Had I known, I would have let the man drop." He slid into a chair.

Rob guffawed.

Cécile held a carafe. "*Café*, Monsieur Kennedy?"

"Please." Zeno sat back as Cécile turned over a cup and poured. Grateful for her brother's barrage of happy chatter and Cécile's hovering attendance, Cassie quietly observed Zeno across the garden table. How and where to begin? She wasn't exactly sure what she wanted to say to him.

Well, that wasn't exactly true. A part of her wanted to pound on his chest and scream. His mistress turned up alive. How could he have withheld such information from her? Scotland Yard has her in custody and he makes no mention of it?

She lifted her butter knife and concentrated on adding a bit of preserve to her croissant. To make matters worse she appeared to be caught in a rather awkward place with Zeno. She was a bit at odds—furious at his deceit and in utter awe of his heroism. She slathered more jam over the buttery French pastry and hoped it would help settle her stomach.

With lips pursed and brows furrowed, she glanced across the table. A scrape on his chin and a dark patch under one eye evidenced his struggle with Delamere. Just contemplating his bravery made her swallow hard. His thick, sable hair gleamed from his morning bath, and his cheeks and brow were bronzed with color from hours of travel in the open roadster.

Rob had related something of their adventures from Calais to Paris. A part of her was thrilled at Detective Kennedy's relentless pursuit through channel fog to Calais, dusty roads, and rural French landscape. And the terrible news about the real Inspector Tautou. She shivered at the thought of the poor man's untimely demise.

A gentle breeze ruffled the newspapers at table. She caught the scent of Zeno's lime cologne. Another part of her, the wanton minx, would have him naked in her bed within the hour. Her cheeks flushed at the thought of it. Why did she have to find him so . . . heroic?

Zeno hadn't touched his food. When he caught her eye she recognized the look of distress. His mouth dipped down at the corners and his eyes took on that deadly, liquid, vulnerable expression. The very one she always found so disconcertingly adorable. Chewing a bite of croissant, she swallowed with difficulty.

She turned to her brother. "Rob, did you know Cécile's brother repairs engines of all sorts? Steam engines as I recall, but he has just opened a shop here in Paris. Isn't that so, Cécile?"

Her maid's smile could not have been brighter. *"Oui, madame."*

"The roadster is in need of . . . some sort of repair, perhaps?"

Rob jumped at the chance for a bit of alone time with her maid. Not altogether sure she should be encouraging an affair, the promiscuous trollop in her argued for a bit of romance for her brother.

"And please be back for lunch, as I mean to spend my year's clothing allowance this afternoon . . . on myself as well as Cécile." Cassie's words trailed after the exiting couple.

An invisible shroud of silence fell over the table. Cassie picked up her fork and pushed a few crumbs around her plate. She could feel his gaze across the small wedge of table that separated them. She made small talk. "I'm afraid I lost one of Cécile's bags when we made our break from Delamere's men. I really must replace her lost items—purchase a dress or two."

"I'm sure Rob will appreciate it." His lips pressed together in a grim fashion, even though a corner of his mouth lifted.

She looked up and met stormy blue eyes. "So you noticed."

"Hard to miss the attraction." Zeno picked up the silver coffee server and offered her more, which she declined. "Perhaps you could you fill me in on your adventures thus far, Cassie? I would enjoy putting the pieces together of our separate journeys."

He hadn't touched a bite of breakfast even though she had filled his plate. With little embellishment, she recounted her adventures on the road.

"Jumping out of closet windows. Leaping into strange carriages. Evading Delamere's men. My word, Cassie, you did brilliantly. And bravely."

She related the standing invitation extended to both of them to join the dowager duchess and young duke for dinner one evening. "Young Buckminster Fitzroy aspires to become a Yard man after he completes his education. Collects newspaper articles of your accomplishments, Zeno. He truly would be thrilled beyond words if you would call on him."

He leaned forward in his chair. "I mean to keep my eye on only one person while I am here in Paris. And now that I have found her I shall not allow her out of my sight."

She held his gaze for a moment before shifting her eyes away.

"What's wrong, Cassie?"

She pressed her shoulders back and sighed. "Why did you not tell me your mistress was alive?"

ZENO BLINKED. SO this was the problem. He had listened carefully to Delamere's lurid insinuations to Cassie last night as he crept into position. Zeno's pulse raced as he recalled the rip of her gown while she begged the fiend not to touch her. Enraged, he had taken a shot at the first possible moment.

His jaw clenched as he replayed the event in his mind and squeezed the trigger. Only this time his shot went straight between Delamere's eyes.

Cassie's question made him feel exposed, caught red-handed, his hand up Jayne Well's petticoats, if you will. Unsure of his answer, he stumbled a bit and hesitated too long. "You don't believe for a second I still care for her, do you?"

Her eyes watered a bit, and she turned away. "I'm not sure what I believe at the moment."

"Cassie, she is quartered in the jails at the Yard. I have done two interrogations and nothing more." His face grew flushed with the memory of Jayne rubbing against him. Damn, now he did look guilty.

She crossed her arms and glared.

How to answer? Where to begin? He slowed his speech and chose his words carefully. "I could not mention her capture. No one outside of the Yard and a few Fenians on the run know we have her in custody."

Cassie moistened her lips and looked up at him through sensuous, dark lashes. He loved the way she did that. A surge of arousal shot through his body. He exhaled.

Her pretty pout and furrowed gaze grew darker. "It seems to me you use these odd, veiled Scotland Yard rules of secrecy when it suits you. Is this what life will be like with a Yard man? You are free to lie and I must remain unquestioning about it?"

"I do not lie as a rule—"

"You practice deceit for a living, Detective Kennedy, even if you dissemble for queen and country. You lied every moment you did not inform me your mistress was alive. It's called a lie of omission. The kind of deception you Yard men are so very good at."

Cassie stood up. "From the very beginning you thought to use me to get close to Gerald."

Zeno opened his mouth to protest.

"Don't try to deny it, Zak. You were after this Bloody Four lot, and I ran in exactly the right circles. Perfect cover, as they say at the Yard." She exited the balcony and walked into the parlor of her suite.

A sweat broke out on his forehead. Feeling a bit sullied, he wiped damp palms on the tops of his pants. Apparently she couldn't look him in the face a moment longer.

He grimaced. Were they having a spat? For the life of him, he could not remember a major argument between them. Not like this. This was serious. Well, perhaps they had argued after the ball. But nothing to speak of since then. His stomach lurched. He had little experience arguing with women and he willingly conceded his inadequacies.

Why hadn't he told her about Jayne? And how could he ease her mind if he didn't understand his own reasoning? Folding his napkin on top of his plate, he rose and followed her inside. He wanted to hold her in his arms. Feel her struggle against him, if necessary, until they both fell exhausted into her bed. There, he knew how to make this injury up to her. But when he reached out, she pulled away and walked to the door.

"I think from now on it might be best if you keep an eye on me from afar." She held the door open for him.

Zeno racked his brain for a reason to stay, to argue his case. He recalled more of Delamere's taunts in the artist's loft. Weeks ago, there had apparently been unwanted advances by his lordship at a social gathering. Cassie had dismissed the incident, pushed it aside.

Two could play this game.

He narrowed his eyes and rallied. "Early on, you might have explained your history with Lord Delamere." His mouth settled into a grim line. "I would have killed him straightaway and avoided a great deal of trouble."

She avoided eye contact. "Good day, Zak."

He paused at the door, remembering a few safety instructions. "The French police have a man stationed on this floor and on the servants' stairs. You are still considered at risk from anarchist sympathizers. I shall be in the lobby should you need me."

She dipped her head. "Very kind of you."

Before the door shut, he pivoted. "By the way, what name are you registered under? I couldn't for the life of me—"

Cassie swallowed hard. "Mrs. Kennedy."

ZENO STARED OUT the window of the carriage as he and Rob waited for the ladies to finish at the milliner's boutique. He could see her plainly through the large glass storefront. A young shop worker held the door open for Cassie and Cécile as they said their good-byes to the fashionable chapeau designer.

"Cass will come round. Eventually." Rob had worked heroically all afternoon to put a happier face on Zeno's situation with his sister. "I'd hate to see you two miss out on these few days in Paris."

Zeno tore his eyes off the storefront. "I gather you haven't wasted any time with Cécile."

Color flushed into Rob's cheeks. "I received quite a thorough initiation last night in my bath."

"Initiation?"

He acknowledged Zeno with a sheepish nod and bright eyes.

Zeno's mouth twitched. "My first time was with a French girl."

Rob returned the grin. "We are two lucky men, then."

Eyes always on alert, scanning for potential trouble, his gaze slid outside the carriage to the street side. "I never thought of myself as lucky until I met your sister."

Chapter Thirty-one

A ripple effect of turned heads and raised brows greeted Cassie as she entered the art gallery. It appeared the Parisian beau monde was duly assembled for the opening. Having read the lurid newspaper reports of the capture of Lord Delamere as well as her own unfortunate involvement in the matter, they were out in force for a gala evening of sport. Worst of all, they had come to admire the cause of Gregoire Laschate's unwitting entanglement.

She surveyed the room, drawn to the swarm jostling around the familiar gilt-edged frame that set off the nude sprite in the woods. *Dear me, a crowd*. She took a deep breath. According to the scandal sheets, Laschate's painting enjoyed the title, *Reveuse sur L'herbe*, Dreamer on the Grass. She walked directly up to the notorious artwork, and met every leering eye.

"Madame St. Cloud, *merveilleux*. And after such an experience—*terrifiante!* We were not sure you would attend this evening." The gaunt Monsieur Durand-Ruel approached her with some trepidation.

At least the man's concern seemed genuine. The corners of her lips tugged upward. She supposed a wry, knowing smile would do well enough. "Nonsense, Monsieur Durand-Ruel. I would have to be laid up in hospital to miss this opening."

"*Mais oui.* All of Paris is at your feet, Cassandra St. Cloud. Allow me the honor of introducing you to your new admirers." Cassie lifted her chin. Even though Paul Durand-Ruel himself stood by her side, a chill ran through her.

The man spoke loud enough for most everyone nearby to overhear. "There is mastery and power in your work, Madame St. Cloud." He bowed. "Add a bit of controversy and you have achieved the emerging artist's formula to success."

Her frown lifted somewhat. "If you say so, monsieur."

"Cassandra." A beaming Laschate greeted her with a disconcerting once-over. She did not return the familiarity by calling him Gregoire.

"Monsieur Laschate." She nodded to the artist and the men standing to each side of the painter. "Gentlemen . . ."

Laschate raised his voice. "I believe I have you to thank for such enthusiastic interest in my work."

She tilted her head. "Ironic, isn't it? I was headed to your studio last night to ask you to substitute another work for the one you stand so proudly beside." If circumstances were different, she would be apologizing profusely for his entanglement in last night's affairs; the poor man and his staff tied up and left in a storage closet. Not a pleasant way to spend an evening.

But the entire debacle had resulted in a boom in sales,

as well as a brilliant bit of éclat for Laschate. Hardly unfortunate. Gregoire's grin grew proportionally wider as her lips thinned. "Nevertheless, Monsieur Laschate, it seems our success at this show is assured. Although my name will always be tainted with the controversy, and yours will be elevated to the lofty position of . . . shall we say, artist of record?"

An idea struck and she turned to the gallery owner. "How much, Monsieur Durand-Ruel?"

The horrid man tsked and shook his head.

"I wish to purchase the painting." She would buy the work and have it removed from the show.

The slight, effete owner leaned into their close group. "*Je suis désolé*, so sorry, madame, I am afraid the painting is already sold."

Her eyes widened. "Then I will pay you more, sir."

Durand-Ruel shook his head. "Impossible." He seemed to know exactly what she was up to. Spoil all his fun and disappoint the public's salacious curiosity. To say nothing of the additional sales.

Laschate tilted his chin downward, and batted his eyes. "Now, now, Cassandra, what does it matter?"

"It matters greatly to me." Cassie raised her voice, perhaps louder than necessary. "Since I never posed for you."

A hush fell over many of the artists and patrons, standing near by. She could feel all eyes focus on her.

Gregoire's eyes shifted around the room. He leaned closer. "Recently I discovered an old book of sketches . . . I used to draw you in your bath—in your residence at school." He shrugged. "I am a voyeur."

Air whistled past her shoulder as a blur of fist struck the artist's jaw. Laschate reeled backward, toppling over several attendees in close range. Whoever threw the punch grabbed her by the waist to steady her.

Cassie whirled around to discover Zeno. The instant he released her she stepped away. Wearing a tight, hard-lipped expression, he shook the sting out of the knuckles of his right hand.

She blinked, openmouthed, searching his face. The brief spark in his eyes turned dark and stormy. With anger or sadness?

"Cassandra." He nodded and turned away. His strong form shimmered through misty eyes as he exited the gallery. Clapping her mouth shut, she turned to lend assistance to the fallen artist.

Laschate worked his jaw back and forth as Paul Durand-Ruel primped over him. The gallery owner glared at her. "Someone of your acquaintance, Madame St. Cloud?"

Cassie nodded. "I'm afraid so."

Laschate appeared reasonably recovered from the blow, though she suspected his jaw would swell and darken over the coming hour. Durand-Ruel continued his grumbling as he straightened the infamous painting that listed sadly to one side. "What kind of gentleman would assault such a genius as Laschate?"

A foggy muddle of people and paintings pressed in on her. She stepped back and waited for the scene around her to stop spinning and come into sharper view. Gathering her wits, her gaze narrowed on the disgruntled gallery owner and then shifted to the artist holding his jaw. She suppressed a skeptical grin. If he made a big enough show of the injury, Laschate might sell another painting or two before evening's end.

"What kind of man?" She inhaled a deep, cleansing breath. "Why, I believe a very exceptional one, Monsieur Durand-Ruel." She took a step backward. "A man who has never failed to protect me from those who would do me harm."

Pivoting, she reversed direction and walked out of the gallery and onto the sidewalk. With each step, her stride lengthened and grew quicker. She studied every pedestrian out for an evening stroll along the thoroughfare. *Which way to turn?*

She chose left and ran along the wide, treelined street in search of him. Her eyes darted among the crowd assembled on the concourse. An early summer breeze buffeted off the Seine. The haunting strains of musicians tuning instruments mixed with the rustle of leaves. Her jog slowed along the path as she concentrated. She searched for a tall, dark-haired man. A very handsome man at that.

Please let him be here.

She peered deeper into the looming shadows of trees and shrubbery. She held her breath. There, a man by a stand of poplar. But no, he walked a small dog on a leash.

Zeno had obviously traveled in the opposite direction. It would likely be too late to catch him. She turned around. Dragging her feet, she inspected every new male that exited or entered the park.

She paused at the sight of a lone figure standing to

one side of a fountain, a familiar silhouette. A kind of electrical charge accelerated her heart. The man moved toward her and she quickened her pace. He passed under a gas lamp.

Zak.

The closer they got, the more rapid their pace, until they halted within inches of each other. In the dark, his eyes matched the color of the night sky.

"Cassie . . ." He hesitated. As she lifted her gaze to meet his, the back of his hand stroked her cheek.

The scratch of raw, swollen knuckles caused her to reach out and gently clasp his injured hand. "Are you in pain, Detective Kennedy?"

"I should have told you sooner about Jayne." His voice was thick, husky, as it traveled over a restriction in his throat.

She nodded, numbly.

"I felt humiliated and used by her and the *Clan na Gael*. Apparently it is easy enough to make me a fool."

"You do so take your work to heart." Her eyes met his directly. "And you will never, ever be thought a fool."

"Kind of you to say so." His brows furrowed and the corners of his mouth turned down. The very frown she had come to adore. Passionately.

"I know so."

"Jayne Wells is more dead to me than ever." His gaze scanned the evening sky, as if he might discover what words to speak written in a field of stars. "These past days without you have been an agony. And now I have injured you." His eyes glistened with remorse. "I will do anything to regain your trust as well as your affection. Just tell me what it is you require."

She twisted a lower lip under her teeth. "I suppose candor is too much to ask for. Openness, honesty, and the like?"

"Cassie, there may be times, in the course of duty, when I may not be completely open with you. But I would never betray you. You must believe me." He edged closer. "And I have missed you quite . . . terribly."

"*Missed you quite terribly?* Perhaps I graduated you from charm school too early."

"My feelings could not be more—" Zeno halted mid-speech and rolled his eyes. "Ah, you weren't being serious."

Cassie pivoted on her heel. "You'll have to do better than that, Zak."

He reached out and pulled her back into his arms. The touch of his kiss sent a wave of glorious tingles coursing through her. Her body pressed against him. He blanketed her mouth, slanting his lips over hers.

She broke off their kiss, but left her mouth close to his. "I missed you as well."

His lips brushed over her face, beginning with her forehead and cheeks, and then down to the lobe of her ear, which caused her to moan. Loud enough to draw attention.

"*Embrassez la jolie fille, monsieur!*" A number of elderly gentlemen perched around the fountain couldn't help but encourage their affection.

With the light returned to his eyes, Zeno tipped his

hat to the men even as he rocked her in his arms. "You are going to miss your opening."

"Why don't we skip the opening?"

Zeno shook his head. "You are a most accomplished painter and have earned the right to stand beside your peers and enjoy the reception."

"I'm afraid my chances of being taken seriously have been sorely compromised."

He stroked her back in the most comforting fashion. "The painting will come down, Cassie. I will make sure of it."

THE MOMENT SHE stepped back into the gallery on his arm, Zeno led her directly over to Paul Durand-Ruel and presented his card.

The raised brow and cool facade of the gallery owner shifted to unease when he attached his pince-nez and read the name.

"Monsieur Kennedy, your presence is indeed an honor and a surprise—"

"Remove *Reveuse sur L'herbe* from the gallery, and you will have no further trouble from me, monsieur. If you choose to continue to display the painting, I shall be obliged to remove it myself."

Durand-Ruel sputtered for a moment before nodding his head. "As you wish, monsieur." With a quick snap of his fingers, he quietly gave orders to have the painting removed, accomplished almost without notice.

"Madame St. Cloud?" Both she and Zeno turned toward

a somewhat burly older gentleman, who approached them with a beauty on his arm.

"Your beautiful nude is gone, madame. And oh yes, I do understand," the young woman effused. "As women working in the arts we must guard our reputation carefully. Look at me, ruined by this love affair." She swept an upraised hand toward her escort. The gentleman looked directly at Zeno and shrugged with a crinkle-eyed grin.

Cassie nodded politely to the intriguing couple and introduced Zeno.

"The famous Scotland Yard agent from Eiffel's Tower? Ha ha, I must introduce myself. Auguste Rodin."

Cassie's eyes grew wide. The man offered a calling card held between two fingers. Rough, callused hands that worked the day long in clay and stone, the hands of a brilliant sculptor. "May I present Mademoiselle Camille Claudel?"

Zeno stepped forward to kiss her hand. "Mademoiselle Claudel."

Rodin's gaze roved over Cassie. He had the kind of eyes that evaluated a woman. Lover, model, muse? All for one, one for all. Reverentially, he brushed his lips over her hand. "Madame St. Cloud."

She exhaled a huge sigh of relief. So this is what had swept the prurient interest of the crowd away from the nude painting. The scandalous public appearance of Auguste Rodin and his beautiful mistress, a sculptress in her own right. Cassie bit her lip but couldn't stop a grin. Even in Paris, this couple raised eyebrows.

She turned to Miss Claudel. "I believe we have a mutual friend. Lydia Philbrook, the English sculptress?"

Camille's hands flew to each side of her face. "She is your friend, as well?" She grabbed Cassie's hand and tugged. "How wonderful, I knew at first sight we were sisters! Lydia has two works in the show, a terra-cotta piece and a plaster portrait of me. *Très forte*—so powerful! Come, you must see."

Rodin and Zeno followed closely behind. "What fortunate men we are, Monsieur Kennedy. To bed with beauty as well as talent, yes?" Cassie glanced backward, curious to catch a glimpse of Zeno's expression. A British frown was supplanted by an accommodating grin. After all, they were in Paris. *Mais oui.*

∞ Chapter Thirty-two

"No morbid thoughts, I hope." Zeno's lips brushed softly against the nape of her neck. Cassie leaned far over the stone wall of the bridge and gazed into the icy water of the Seine. Her laughter carried like the breeze wafting just above the river current. Moonlight danced over ripples of sparkling, undulating water. It was one of those special nights, an evening he would lock in his memory and always cherish.

"I don't believe I shall ever have a morbid thought again." She rotated within the circle of his arms. "They've been chased away of late." Her words played softly against his mouth. "By a number of hair-raising adventures with a certain Yard man."

"Mmm, yes. I am about to kiss the very bravest woman in all of France and England." He grazed the tip of her nose with his lips.

"Plucky, perhaps, but hardly courageous. In the face of danger I take to my heels with a care for my neck."

Beguiled by her fiery independence, her astounding,

fresh-faced beauty, he headed for the sensitive spot just below her earlobe. The one that made her sigh. "And such a pretty neck." His trail of carnal delights ended at the base of her throat.

There it was, a little moan of pleasure.

He lifted his head and nibbled soft, sensuous bites over her mouth. "Mmm, you taste of champagne." Her lips opened, inviting him deeper. He needed little encouragement, for he was ravenous for her. "We must get to the hotel, before I ravage you here on the Pont Royale."

On their way into the lobby, Cassie bought a blush-colored carnation from a flower vendor, snapped off the stem, and slipped the fringy bloom into his lapel.

In the corridor not far from her room, she pushed him against the wall and on tiptoe licked the curl of his ear. Christ, she was pure torture. His body burned for her, being in near constant arousal for hours now. She inhaled the fragrance of his boutonniere. "One of my favorite scents in all the world."

The ends of his mouth tugged upward. "Me or the posy?"

Her tongue slipped along the upper edge of his mouth. "Mmm, you are both peppery and spicy."

"And what scent are you?" He grabbed her and turned them both. Now she was pressed to the wall and his body. He leaned in and rucked up her skirt. His fingers slipped between her thighs. "Tell me, Cassie, if I got down on my knees here, and dipped into these moist pink petals, how might you greet an innocent passerby?" The bouquet of their sexual arousal permeated his senses as she answered him with an utterance that was sublimely unintelligible.

"I suppose," he nibbled at her lush mouth as he pressed his length against her, "a gasp and moan is universally understood."

Her breath stirred a delicate tempest in the air around them. The movement of her chest, as it rose and fell—all his sensibilities faded away, mesmerized by the sweep of a pretty pink tongue over her upper lip.

"You do that again and I swear I'll have you here against the wall."

Her slow smile made a dimple, and she challenged him with her eyes. Growling, he took her by the hand and placed the key in the lock.

She raised a brow, "Rather sure of yourself, aren't you?"

"I have . . . a degree of confidence." His grin turned humble.

She slipped between Zeno and the door. With the knob at her back, she opened the door a crack. Peering inside, she found the sitting room empty. No Rob and Cécile. "No doubt you believe you are forgiven?"

Zeno swallowed. "I will never, ever wound you again in such a way. And I avow not a single lascivious thought for Jayne Wells, even when she rubbed up against me."

Cassie blinked. "She rubbed up against you?"

"I . . ."

Her arms crossed, brows furrowed, lips pouted.

"I became hard—but all I could think about was you." He sighed. Christ, he had blurted out this nonsense as if Cassie was a priest in a confessional.

She opened the door just wide enough to back into the room, but did not invite him inside.

"I handcuffed the wretched woman to a chair to keep her off me—" The door slammed in his face. "—Cassie."

The latch turned and clicked.

Zeno paced the floor outside her room. He supposed he looked as guilty as sin itself. Even now, he likely appeared wild-eyed and desperate. How had such a debacle happened? Moments ago he was making love to the woman of his heart and inches away from having her. A dull ache throbbed through his body.

He strode up and down the corridor until his pacing threatened to wear a spot in the carpet runner. Earlier this evening he had waved off her escorts: gendarmes, who were also to have guarded her room tonight. That left no one but him to keep watch.

Zeno exhaled and settled himself against the wall of the corridor. He reviewed his mistakes, including the awful choice of words he used to describe interactions with Jayne during interrogation.

Perhaps the most romantic night of his life, ruined by a faux pas.

What exactly had he fallen into with Cassie? He thought about the word *love*. Certainly, she had tempted him from the moment he turned around that first morning in the mews. Or perhaps even earlier, the moment she stepped out of the carriage to take possession of Number 10. He remembered how patiently she untangled the hounds caught up in leashes and skirt.

Odd bits of their courtship sprang to mind. Zeno recalled every passionate evening and wondered, if he never made love to her again, were there enough memories to cherish for a lifetime? He refused to think about losing her.

Her door opened.

NO MATTER HOW vexed she might be, Cassie's heart skipped a beat when she found him standing in the hallway. A knight in tarnished armor stalwartly guarded her door. Her stomach fluttered as the infuriating siren in her body sang silent love songs.

Zeno raised his head and a shock of hair fell forward. He leaned against the wall in the corridor, his smile slight and sufficiently chastened. "I can explain."

She opened the door wider.

His eyes bulged.

His mouth dropped open.

She wore a new, pale blue French corset and matching camisole edged in black satin ribbon and small bows, the silk fabric sheer enough for him to see all of her. Brief pantalets, black silk stockings, and pale blue garters completed the effect.

A dark fire ignited in his eyes.

Lowering her gaze she discovered the lingerie lived up to the shopkeeper's promise. "Mother once explained to me that a man has little governance over his penis when it comes to arousal, but a commanding mastery over whom he chooses to couple with."

A slow, thin-lipped smile widened on his face. "Dr. Erskine is a very wise woman."

He launched himself off the wall and swept her up

into his arms. Carrying her into the room, he made a half turn, hooked the door with his foot, and slammed it shut.

"Bedroom?"

"Mon Dieu." Cassie moaned. "After days without you I can think of nothing else." She pointed the way.

Zeno placed her on the edge of the plain four-poster and yanked off her pantalets. "Very pretty, but they are in my way."

Cassie uttered sighs of encouragement as he unhooked the exquisite French undergarment. He stood between her raised knees, gently stroking the insides of her thighs. "Let's keep the stockings on for now." A lazy grin enhanced the desire in his eyes.

She lay naked and spread out before him. She wore nothing but black hose and pale blue garters. Her bare upper limbs trembled, waiting, anticipating his kiss.

His sensuous mouth caressed the inside flesh of her thighs. He leaned farther over her torso to suckle nipples that were pointed and ready. Gently at first, and then harder. Her hips arched as a wave of excitement shot through her.

She moaned her own directive. "I will see all of you, Zak."

He did not remove his covetous, hungry gaze as he tore at his necktie. Cassie ripped the buttons off his slacks and his erection sprang to life in front of her. She stroked hard, smooth velvet.

His eyes closed and his head dropped back with a groan. She blew a warm breeze the length of his phallus and he tore at his shirt buttons. Shedding the rest of his clothes, she caught a glimpse of chiseled buttocks, the product of years of horsemanship and rugby. Moisture grew between her legs as she admired the man's lean, hard body and long muscular legs.

Her man.

She lay back on the bed linen propped on her elbows. "Such a handsomely built detective inspector."

He placed himself between her legs. "And he is about to investigate." Grabbing her knees, he yanked her bottom to the edge of the bed.

His mouth pressed past the light brown curls between her legs as she flung her arms overhead and abandoned herself to the long, slow strokes of his tongue. The man had a devilish way of encouraging this commons, wicked side of her. His hands moved over the flat of her belly to cup her breasts and rub over hardened peaks. She shuddered.

"You are the most exquisitely beautiful thing I have ever seen." He voiced the very words she had been thinking—about him.

She arched as his fingers brushed past moist curls. He teased her until she asked for what she wanted. "Inside me. Now."

"It is my pleasure to give you pleasure." He used one, then two fingers to delve deep. She pressed into him as his lips and tongue found the engorged spot between her legs to suckle and stroke and circle.

"Yes." Her body vibrated in arousal.

"I am intoxicated by the taste of you." His mouth glistened with her essence. His every touch became a testament to his affection. He paused, paying careful attention to her every moan and sigh, every arch and shudder. As she neared the edge, he lifted his fingers away. "I shall prolong your climax."

She growled at his deliberate delay and, in challenge, took hold of his shaft and stroked until he forced her hand away. "Cassie," he groaned, "I have no idea how long I will be able to last. I have restrained a substantial passion for you all evening."

He crawled on top of her, a predatory animal after his mate. His rigid, jerking organ ready for penetration. She reached out and he swept her into her arms.

She drew his mouth down over a breast and he suckled and nipped and fondled each nipple while she uttered nonsensical words, in the vernacular of the animal kingdom.

He broke off to come up for air. "Such beautiful, speechless speech."

"And what of yours?" She raised herself up on her elbows to reach his nipples. "What mindless words shall you make?" She tongued and nibbled until he groaned from her caressing.

Reaching under, to the small of her back, he slid his hands lower to cup each buttock. He tilted her pelvis so that she might take all of him. He eased in gently, inch by inch, until he filled her up with the hard, smooth length of his phallus.

And she took all of him. Answered every thrust. Wrapping her legs about his hips, she drew him in. He spoke against her lips. "I will see your finish, Cassie." Commanding, insistent, and completely generous, he coaxed her ever closer, driving in and out until she hovered at the point of orgasm. As if on cue her body shattered into a million pieces of pleasure, shuddered, then bucked beneath him.

He pulled her tight, for he meant to feel every small contraction ripple through her body. "Ahh. God yes," he groaned; his climax came with the next deep thrust. And he answered her sighs with whispers of soft-spoken declarations. Far from the mindless utterances a man used in the throes of passion. These were emotions long stored away in his heart, released into the air, a fleeting gift to her, which made them irrevocable and glorious.

Abruptly, he pulled out. "We didn't use a rubber." He flopped down onto the bed, and gulped for air. His breathing harsh, his groan deep.

She added her moan to his. "We have been rather hit-or-miss at this condom business, haven't we?" She threw a leg over his thigh, tucking herself into the curve his body.

"I'll purchase some first thing in the morning. As soon as I find an open barbershop."

Cassie brushed her hand through the small hairs of his chest. "Tomorrow is Sunday."

"Bollocks." The utterance was all he could manage as her fingernails moved down his chest. She licked a nipple and his lower extremity jerked.

"Cassie, please." If the animal in him got its way, he would have her again and again until they were both raw from it.

Resting her chin on his chest, she ran a hand down his trim stomach and made the muscles contract. Gently, she played with a pearl of semen that emerged from the tip of his penis. "There are other ways, are there not, of pleasing each other?"

He opened a sleepy eye, and propped an arm behind his head. "And what do you know of such things?"

Cassie tilted her head. "I was married. Briefly."

"Did you give your husband pleasure in unorthodox ways?"

"I wanted to." She colored a bit. "But he had a mistress to provide such services."

Zeno's eyes darkened. "He informed you of this?"

"Rather emphatically." Her gaze met his then flicked away. "He informed me a lady did not perform fellatio. That he kept a mistress to perform such services, amongst other duties."

Zeno snorted. "The man didn't realize what he had in his own bed."

She toyed with his chest hair. "It took me months after he died to let go of my resentment."

He tilted her chin to look him in the eye. "Perhaps I understand why this revelation with Jayne so upset you." He grimaced. "Not that your history gives me room for excuse. I was wrong not to have told you. But I honestly feel nothing for her."

Now it was her turn to snort. "Nothing except anger, pain, betrayal, and by your own admittance, arousal."

"But not in my heart." His fingers gently plied through the waves of her hair. "Faithful, loyal, devoted—that's me, Cassandra."

She squinted at him. "Yes, I do believe you are a constant man." It took little more than a delicate caress from her fingers to make him groan.

"Come to think of it, I might have a condom packet in my coat."

Cassie slipped off the bed in search of his overcoat. He smiled at the sight of her naked bottom and nymphlike romp about the room. She pulled a small red leather box tied with a gold cord from the pocket. Heat appeared to travel up her chest and throat, bathing her cheeks in a blush of color.

"I did a bit of shopping on my own yesterday." He studied her expression carefully as she pulled the cord and opened the hinged jewel case. "Oh, Zak, it's beautiful." Her eyes glistened with fear? Joy? There was a nervous tremble in her voice.

He cleared his throat. "Think of it as a token of my esteem. And a promise of partnership should you ever decide to open the doors between our residences . . . permanently. We could even tear down a wall, if you want."

She sat down beside him and slipped the ring onto her finger. She held out her hand for him to admire. Zeno kissed each knuckle, including her ring finger. He squinted. "Lovely. Do you like it?"

She kissed the tip of his nose. "A very large diamond, in the most beautiful setting imaginable."

"Yes, Paris does seem to be the right venue for this sort of thing."

Cassie snorted a laugh. "And what sort of *thing* is this? Exactly?"

Zeno stared at her. Several moments passed like a millennium. "Marry me—in several years, if you wish." He propped himself on an elbow. "Whatever feels comfortable. You don't have to say yes tonight. Perhaps a thrilling 'maybe'? Or a stimulating 'let me think about it.'"

Cassie turned her hand side to side and admired the ring. "I cannot imagine anything more arousing than what we just did in bed."

"As we come to know one another, what we do together intimately will become even better."

"My heart races at the very thought of better." She swept back a wild lock of hair to get a better look at a languid, shriveled penis. "And when will Detective Kennedy be . . . ?"

"Spent, for now." Zeno flopped onto his back. "Do you see what you do to me? I am completely and utterly devoid of utility." He opened his eye a crack. "Give him a moment."

Her smile was light, girlish. "So, you want me for life, then?"

"My dear, you are a wanton *fille de joie*, a nymphet of the highest order, and I consider myself the luckiest man in the entire world."

"I will give you my answer in twenty-two months, then."

"Twenty-two months?" His stare was comically incredulous. "Why that long?"

Cassie shrugged. "A nice bit longer than a year, but not quite two."

"Good God. The gestation period of an elephant, if I'm not mistaken." Without a pause he swept her into his arms. "Ah well, I knew you'd say yes."

"I haven't said yes."

He nuzzled her throat. "Oh, but you will . . . eventually."

$\mathcal{Z}$eno stepped into the familiar morning light of the breakfast room. The aroma of warm bread and eggs reaffirmed they were back in London and safely home.

"Top of the morning, Mr. Kennedy. Set yourself down beside your guest and have a wee bit of breakfast." Mrs. Woolsey piled a mound of egg onto a plate of kippers.

"Good morning, Mrs. Woolsley." He nodded to Cassie's brother, who raised a friendly fork in greeting. "Morning, Zak."

From the platter on the sideboard, he added a ham slice to his plate and poured himself a glass of juice. He picked up the *Times* from the buffet. "Where's Cassie?" He settled into a chair and opened the paper.

Rob stuffed a forkful of mouthwatering smoked fish into his mouth and still managed an answer. "She ate a bit of toast and ran off to Mother's."

"Said she wouldn't be long, sir." Alma turned over a cup and poured his coffee. "Back in time for luncheon."

He frowned. "She left here on her own?"

Rob set down his paper. "I volunteered my escort but she wouldn't have me."

Alma brushed against Zeno's shoulder and set down his toast. "Best that Mrs. St. Cloud resumes her regular goings about, Mr. Kennedy, now that the danger is past."

His housekeeper meant well. And it was most likely excellent advice. Sooner or later he must let go of these nagging fears about her safety and let his brave and beautiful bird soar above the crowd.

"I can hardly believe you're back, sir. And with such lovely company, at that." Alma smiled sweetly at Rob.

Zeno grinned between forkfuls of egg. "I expect you will get used to having this Erskine clan about, Mrs. Woolsley."

Aware his housekeeper hovered nearby, he folded his paper over and continued reading.

"I will say, sir, that it was right quiet around here while you were gone. Although I did get a devilish story out of young Bert Daniels, the other day. Works for Mr. Woolsley, he does. Seems he overheard two shifty types in a pub down south of the Tower."

She fluttered nervously around the table. "What the young man was doing in those dodgy parts, don't ask me."

Zeno set down his paper and stared at the woman. "You are obviously beside yourself to tell me, Mrs. Woolsley."

Alma fidgeted with her apron. "Bert claimed the two blokes, right pissed they were, mentioned Westminster Abbey."

He bit off a bit of buttered toast. "What about the Abbey?"

"Well, sir, I can't quite figure a way to put it all together." She paused, her face twisted up by the riddle. "'If the sticks don't blow her to kingdom come, the shots will find their mark, sure enough.'"

Chewing his toast, Zeno registered a moderate uptick in pulse rate as he considered her story. "What day is today?"

"Why, look at your paper, Mr. Kennedy, it's the twentieth of June, the queen's fiftieth anniversary—Victoria's Golden Jubilee." His housekeeper beamed, glancing at the mantel clock. "The parade starts in little more than an hour, I believe."

His spine straightened. In his mind's eye, he was back in Paris, moments before he and Delamere were rescued from what would have been a fatal fall from the tower. *"Case closed, not a window left open? We shall see, Mr. Kennedy."* An odd message, spoken by a delirious cornered man. Nonetheless, Zeno had pondered Delamere's cryptic words often enough these last few days. Having taken down their headman, as well as key operatives, the *Clan* would be forced to go to ground—regroup. Seemed logical, indeed necessary, but had they? He eyeballed his soon to be brother-in-law, who appeared more absorbed in eggs and kippers than the morning news. "Did the *Telegraph* print a map of the parade route?"

Rob opened up and refolded the front page. "Here it is." He thumped the engraving with his finger and pushed the paper toward Zeno.

He squinted at the engraving. "She crosses over Westminster Bridge, and past a good length of Parliament's impressive facade, to attend services at Westminster Abbey."

Banks of windows came to mind, row upon row of them lined up like soldiers across the stone surface of the palace. His mind shifted to Paris. Once again, Lord Delamere's rambling, delusional last words. *"Case closed, not a stick of dynamite left unaccounted for, nor window left untended? We shall see, Kennedy."* His mind ticked off every possible scenario. He imagined the barrel shaft of a rifle—several of them—all pointed in the direction of the Abbey.

"We haven't got a moment to waste." Zeno shot up from his chair. "Rob, do you still have those rockets at the bottom of the travel trunk?"

Rob wiped a few crumbs off an open mouth. "Crikey, Zak, are we off again?"

Halfway out the room, Zeno pivoted. "Mrs. Woolsley, put Rory on Skye and have him ride hell-for-leather to the Yard. I need every man they can spare. Have them meet me inside the Abbey."

Eyes wide, Alma shook her head. "Oh, sir, you don't think they'd hurt the dear—"

"No time to fret, Mrs. Woolsley, on your way." Zeno made for the door.

CASSIE TOOK A seat on the examination table as Olivia closed up the empty clinic. "Such excitement over Victoria's Golden Jubilee. I understand thousands already line the parade route."

"Yes, I would expect so." Her mother washed up in a

basin of warm water and scrubbed with a harsh, disinfectant bar of soap. It made her fingers red and rough looking

Wiping her hands on a clean towel, Olivia nearly ran the length of the room to give her a hug. "I couldn't be more pleased, Cassie. You've chosen a good man."

"Zak and I are not officially engaged. No wedding plans or announcements, please. You must promise me, Mother."

"No rush, darling. Mr. Christy seems busy enough, what with refurbishing the vicarage residence."

Cassie pressed her lips together and tried not to glower. "Mother, you know the moment our dear village vicar hears a whisper of gossip, he'll begin his pestering."

"I'll deal with that old badger." Her mother sat down beside her. "Now, let me see the ring."

She held her hand up to display the gem. "A solitary marquis diamond."

"A bit over two carats, I wager." Olivia squeezed her hand. "Cartier?"

She nodded. "I knew Zeno inherited from his uncle's estate, but had no idea what a comfortable income he enjoys."

"Your father hadn't a penny to his pocket after medical school. I married for love and potential."

She smiled at the familiar statement. Olivia squinted a bit, placing her wrist against Cassie's cheek, then forehead. "You appear slightly off color, dear."

"I spent the trip from Calais to Dover with my head over the railing. I should have come to see you the moment we arrived in town, but we got in late last evening completely exhausted." Cassie hesitated.

"And?"

"And I'm never seasick." She grimaced. "I believe it was my revulsion over a coddled egg this morning that convinced me to seek you out."

"Well, you've certainly experienced enough excitement of late to cause a bout of fever. We read all about Detective Kennedy's valiant chase through Paris streets as well as your own harrowing involvement in the matter." Olivia swept a few bangs off her forehead. "The excitement of your first continental exhibition, to say nothing of this mysterious betrothal of yours. Dear girl, I was most relieved to read—"

Cassie burst out with it. "Am I pregnant?"

Mother stopped to stare. "A bit early to know yet." The spark of light in her eyes belied a more somber expression. "But then, you do so love coddled egg." Her mother winked, but Dr. Olivia queried, "When was the first possible date of inception?"

Angling her brows together, she chewed her lip. "I believe . . ." She thought back to the Stanfield ball and counted the days forward. "Middle of May or thereabouts."

The doctor retrieved a stethoscope from her medical bag, and attached the earpieces. "My word, you two didn't waste any time."

Her mother gave her chest a listen. "Strong heart. Good wind.

"Are your breasts heavy? Nipples sensitive? More than

normal for this time of month? I do take it your menstrual period is late?"

Cassie nodded silently to all of it.

Olivia placed the stethoscope around her neck, but continued her examination. "Would you be happy to be pregnant?"

Heat flushed her cheeks. She met her eye-to-eye, daughter to mother, woman to woman. "Yes, I believe so."

"Zeno has the makings of a good father, don't you think? Firm but affectionate. Strict, yet fair-minded." Olivia looked as if she might wax poetic.

Cassie could not help a peevish, impatient sigh. "Yes, I believe he will be a doting father."

Her mother's smallish grin took on larger proportions. "Just a guess, mind you, but I would say the chances are very great your father and I will become grandparents eight months from today."

"Is there a test? Just to make sure?"

"None that are reliable." She sighed. "I knew in every instance with you children, early on. What do you feel in your womb, Cassie?"

A slow smile crept over her face.

Mother patted her knee. "Come, I'll make you a cup of tea. And I do advise you purchase plenty of water biscuits to keep at your bedside over the next few months."

JUST INSIDE THE Abbey, Zeno ran straight into Archibald Bruce tugging a red-haired hound at his heels. Alfred and his amazing *canis proboscis* had figured prominently in their dynamite confiscations. The bloodhound had recently been declared the most valuable dog in the kingdom.

"Arch." Zeno breathed a sigh of relief to see the young director of the forensics lab. The canine beat a lazy tail against his pant leg. "Good to see the Yard dog." He reached down to give the hound's ear a scratch.

Archie filled him in. "We received an anonymous tip late yesterday evening. Melville called us up for duty in the middle of the night. Sure enough, Albert sniffed out nearly fifty pounds of dynamite hidden in the back of the Islip Chapel near the high altar."

Arch removed his cap and scratched his head. "Don't know how they managed to smuggle the explosives in. This morning we covered every inch of the college grounds."

Zeno scanned the lengthy facade of Westminster Palace, home to upper and lower houses of Parliament. Hundreds of windows overlooked the Abbey. Hundreds.

He exhaled. "Can we change the route and bring Victoria in through the park and Chapel garden?"

Arch drew his brows together. "Expecting more trouble?"

"Call it a precaution." Zeno looked around. "Who's in charge here?"

Arch shrugged. "I suppose you are."

Arch accompanied him out to the front of the Abbey. He conscripted two Horse Guards to ride out and meet the procession carriage with instructions to bring Victoria in through St. James Park and the west entrance of the Abbey.

"Is the palace closed?"

"Since early this morning, sir."

Conscripting every Metropolitan policeman the Abbey could spare, Zeno directed the men to each floor of Parliament and assigned a guard to every exit door. They had neither the manpower nor time to mount a physical search of Westminster Palace. "Do not be fooled," Zeno admonished the officers. "Let no one inside, detain anyone who tries to exit. The men we seek will likely be well dressed, outfitted as peers of the realm."

The crowd, already ten deep in places, waited outside the Abbey to greet the queen. Guests invited to attend the service were taking their seats for the ceremony. It was a subtle parade route change, but one that bought them time. Everything would appear to go on as planned. The adoring crowd posted around the Abbey would not be disappointed at the unexpected show of pyrotechnics.

"Rob, this way." Zeno waved. Cassie's brother carried a bundle of rockets under each arm. "I believe you two are acquainted."

"Blimey." Arch's eyes bugged out. "If it isn't Rob Erskine, my old lab partner from school." The two men grinned at each other.

"I see you're still working with explosives, Archie."

"And you—rockets, is it?" Arch turned from Rob to Zeno. "What do you have in mind, Kennedy?"

Zeno craned his neck to examine the towers of the Abbey. "How do we get up on roof, above the Lady Chapel?"

Archie's grin was contagious. "This way."

Taking two steps at a time, the men were forced to

slow their pace to assist the lumbering hound. Each man took a turn prodding or pushing Alfred, a healthy fifteen stone, up the narrow cobbled steps. All three men were puffing by the time they reached the first landing of stairs.

"Is the dog always this difficult?" Zeno pushed as Rob pulled.

Arch paused midstep. "Uh, perhaps it might be best if we followed his nose."

Zeno jerked upright and met Archie's gaze. "I see." He signaled a turnabout. "Lead the way, Alfred."

The hound yanked on his lead and promptly led them downstairs, below the Abbey's main floor to a low undercroft, part of the old monk's dormitory.

Zeno never took his eyes off the hound. "What's up, old boy?"

Sniffing along the centuries-old mosaic floor, the canine abruptly sat down beside a vault pillar.

A voice echoed from above. "Where the Christ is everyone—you down there, Kennedy?"

He glanced upward. "Keep coming. We're a bit lower."

Flynn Rhys descended into the vault, eyes adjusting to the dim light of a single lantern. "It took forever to get here. Streets are cordoned off. Rafe is also making his way."

"Mr. Rhys." Zeno breathed a bit easier. Flynn was just deranged enough to be exactly like kind of man you wanted with you on a day like today. He nodded at the hound. "Yard dog is on the scent of something, there may be yet another—"

"Hold on." Arch focused his gaze along the curved roofline of the vault. The lab man removed an experimental torchlight from his coat pocket and banged it against his palm. A narrow beam illuminated a small section of the vault. Every man strained to follow the circle of light as it traced a length of wire along the curved ceiling.

Clusters of rounded cylinders connected by a single fuse lined up along a narrow ledge at the top of every pier in the room.

Flynn exhaled a low whistle.

Arch followed the fuse line all the way round. "Tucked up in the shadows quite neatly. Easily missed." Scotland Yard's young scientist continued to trace the wire down the length of a nearby column. "I'd say enough of these go off in sequence, columns crumble, collapsing the main floor above, which triggers the sides of the nave to cave inward, demolishing most of the Abbey."

"Killing hundreds, as well as the queen." Zeno grimaced. "How long to dismantle this? I've got a number of possible snipers to roust."

Flynn's gaze traced the wire around the room. "Bombs. Assassins. Quite an elaborate plan."

"These bombs are either a distraction or a line of attack." Zeno nodded. "Get on with it, Arch."

The young scientist plucked a pair of wire snippers from inside his jacket. "Give us a leg up and a minute or two."

"Here. Give me those." Flynn grabbed the double-bladed instrument from Arch. "Go with Zeno. Should a Fenian venture down here to set this off—" He patted a coat pocket. "I'll shoot the bastard."

Wide-eyed, Arch stammered. "Cut the lead fuse, here.

Then for good measure, severe all the connecting material all the way round."

Flynn stepped up onto the column base, and traced the wire up the pillar. "Is there any chance I might get blown to kingdom come?"

"With all manner of bullets flying about?" Arch lifted his bowler to scratch his head. "I'd have to say yes."

"Good." He snipped the fuse wire.

Zeno waylaid a cleric on the stairs. "It is of utmost importance that we delay the service." He pressed his card into the young man's hand. "You will meet the queen's procession at the west entrance and bring Her Majesty into—" He looked to Arch. "What might be the safest place to hold her until we remove the explosives?"

"The Great Cloister, perhaps?" Archie did not seem wholly confident with his answer, but it would have to do.

"Explosives, are you sure?" Perspiration beaded the young man's forehead. Zeno pushed the cleric forward. "Tell the queen's guard there has been a security delay. No need to cause a panic. Empty the nave as well. Everyone out on the college grounds."

Zeno sucked in a breath. "Right. On our way, then. No time to waste, gentlemen."

On the rooftop of the Lady Chapel, all three men spread out across the crenellations and assembled Rob's rockets. A roar and cheer from the crowds lining St. George Street came from just across the Thames. There was no time to spare.

Zeno pictured Victoria's entourage traveling slowly across Westminster Bridge. He gritted his teeth and ignored his pulse rate. "We'll need to take our best guess about which windows to aim for, but I mean to keep a lookout for any that open as her carriage arrives. Each of you stand ready to train your rockets as I call them out."

Zeno scanned the upper-level windows of the Houses of Parliament. "Ready as many as you can, quickly. I want a storm of rockets, bashing themselves against the palace. Let the assassins know we're onto them. I don't expect much in the way of accuracy. Pray God one or two actually hit their target."

How on earth would he find the right windows? As he monitored row upon row of glazing, he recalled Cassie's words the night of the surveillance. *Notice the dark square at the end of the row. No glare or reflection from the streetlamp directly opposite. Therefore, the window is open.* She had called it an impressionist's observation, one *based on the shifting effects of light and color.*

A silvered windowpane slid into velvet blackness. "Third floor. Count five over from the left corner." Rob lowered his projectile.

There—another a dark square. Even though the window was close by, he had nearly missed it. "Arch, again third floor. Count . . . eleven over."

"Got it." Arch's focus narrowed. "Rob, get over here and show me how to aim these things."

Rob squinted at his target. "No time to figure terminal velocity and drag coefficient. Sight straight down the shaft, and aim just below the window. At this distance the rockets should have little arc and plenty of thrust. And don't let the stake wiggle about."

Arch adjusted his first two rockets. "How very scientific."

Another roar from the crowd came from the bridge. Both young men lit their rockets.

Zeno's gaze never broke away to check the proximity of the queen's procession, but systematically scanned the massive facade.

There, near the top of Victoria Tower. A flash of movement at the window—an assassin taking up his position. Zeno aimed and lit his rockets.

This was their only chance. The rockets must strike close enough to the palace windows to unnerve the gunmen, or at the very least interrupt their operation.

Two, then four missiles shot off the rooftop with a sharp, high-pitched roar. "Seven, six, five, four . . ." Zeno finished the countdown as his rockets launched in a burst of flame and smoke and sparks. Vaporous trails of pale gray smoke crisscrossed over Abingdon Street. The projectiles crashed and crackled like gunshots against the palace walls.

"Hail, Victoria." After a quick appraisal, he decided one or two rockets may have actually crashed through windows. But would the strikes rattle the gunmen enough to quit the operation?

"Fire everything you've got. I'm going over."

Zeno traversed the street under a second hail of smoke and sparks and cries from the crowd outside the Abbey. He picked up a guard at the palace door and moved upstairs. On the third floor, the wide corridor appeared deserted, as expected. A door slammed open midway and a man fled down the hall.

He removed his pistol from his jacket pocket. "Halt!

Scotland Yard." When the culprit continued his retreat, he brought the man down with a bullet. Another floor guard signaled Zeno from the far end of the corridor.

A haze of dark smoke had begun to pervade the passageway. Zeno walked toward the open entry. He assigned the officer behind him to the downed suspect and signaled the guard ahead to meet him at the door. Inside, a wall of flame licked its way up heavy drapery. The small fire, doubtless caused by one of the rockets, threatened to turn the committee room into a furnace.

"Alert the Fire Brigade. Go." Zeno motioned the guard away. Scanning through heat and flame, he searched for the second shooter still in hiding. A black cloud of haze billowed out of the adjoining room. Christ. A second fire.

Pistol up, back to the wall, Zeno inched along. At the door frame he peered into the next room. Nothing but a thick fog of noxious fumes. Smoke and salty sweat stung his eyes. Zeno wiped his brow as bullets flew past his head.

He ducked and returned fire. In the blackened room, he could barely see past his own hand. "Zak." He pivoted at the sound of a familiar voice. Rafe stood in the doorway. Reinforcements had arrived. He signaled Rafe to go around, flush the man out from the adjoining office.

Keeping his body profile low to the ground, Zeno swept through the door and fired blindly. He pressed on through a curtain of haze and found a desk to take cover behind. His lungs burned as they filled with smoke and ash.

There was a cough, and then another. He rose up to discover the offender backing up to the window. "Throw down your weapon. There's no escape."

Face blackened, the wild-eyed cornered man glanced back out the open window. A shadow of movement through the smoke told him Rafe had crept into the room and was bearing down on their would-be assassin.

Zeno advanced on the shooter at the very moment the suspect raised his pistol. Rafe fired, toppling the culprit backward. The wounded suspect collapsed onto the window ledge and flipped over backward. Zeno lunged, but not in time to catch the man. He watched the body fall silently to the ground.

Zeno leaned farther over the ledge to draw a bit of fresh air. Rafe joined him, gasping for oxygen. He squinted. "You all right?

His partner coughed and gave him a thumbs-up.

"Nice shooting."

Rafe flashed a crooked grin. "Couldn't see a blasted thing in there. Maybe you're just a lucky man."

Zeno stepped away from the window. "I'm beginning to believe so." He signaled Rafe to follow. "One more, down the hall, in Victoria's Tower."

A thick haze of smoke continued to billow into the palace corridors. They met London's Fire Brigade and pointed the way. Jogging down the hall, they found an entrance bridge to the tower. Firemen worked at a feverish pace to seal off the tower and save all the precious records contained therein.

They climbed several stories to reach the assassin's nest. Zeno approached the west-facing storage room and signaled Rafe. On his count they both rushed the door. A man dressed in parliamentary robes swung his hulking frame away from the window. He faced them with his rifle pointed.

"Scotland Yard. Surrender your weapon." Zeno cocked his pistol and stepped away from his partner.

Rafe also raised his gun. "Take your pick. You'll not be fast enough to kill the both of us." The sharp ache in Zeno's ears came from a sudden, ominous buffeting of displaced air. A staccato roar reverberated through the room as a rocket flew through the widow and impaled the gunman.

A swath of crimson sprayed the room.

Stunned, Zeno lowered his weapon.

Rafe blinked. "Egad. Dull's eye."

The front end of a rocket protruded from the assassin's belly. A wisp of pale gray smoke danced an eerie circle around the blackened hole of raw flesh surrounding the missile. The speared man looked down in disbelief. Listing to one side, the marksman dropped the rifle and staggered forward. The man was standing at the edge of death, and his eyes rolled skyward as he crumpled to the floor.

Zeno and Rafe picked around several other floors of the tower, but found no other accomplices.

Rafe slapped him on the back. "God save the queen. You've done it again, Kennedy."

Zeno shook his head. "I left Flynn in the depths of the Abbey defusing bombs. Cassie's brother and Archie Bruce are on the roof of the Lady Chapel setting off rockets. God only knows where they've put Victoria." Zeno jerked at his collar and frowned. "Do you really think we're out of the woods?"

*   *   *

SOMEWHAT PERPLEXED, CASSIE stepped into Zeno's bedchamber. Minutes ago, she could have sworn she heard his voice. Her gaze swept the room and immediately transformed the airy, well-lit space into a nursery. She pictured creamy cadmium yellow walls.

A painting caught her eye. Peering around the draped bedpost, she caught her breath. *Reveuse sur L'herbe*. She squinted at the drowsy, nude nymphet, rising to find three fully clothed gentlemen admiring her flesh. The portrait from the Durand-Ruel gallery. Holding fast to the bedpost, she explored the only possible explanation. Zeno was the mysterious purchaser of the painting. But why had it remained on display at the opening?

"I hope you don't mind, Cassie."

She spun around to find him standing in the doorway. Sweeping aside her immediate angst, she gasped at the sight of him. His eyes red-rimmed. His face and clothes blackened. He reeked of smoke and soot.

She hardly knew where to begin. "Whatever happened to you?"

"Something Delamere mumbled at the tower. Nagged at me for days, actually. This morning Mrs. Woolsley made the connection for me. Something about a plot to assassinate the queen."

Wide eyes looked him up and down. "I trust you didn't ruin a new suit for naught. And Victoria?"

"I am happy to report our good queen seems no worse for the wear. Got her safely tucked away until the danger passed. The Abbey service, after an hour's delay, went on as planned. You know Victoria—show them no fear."

"I expect to read a glorious report about you in the morning papers."

The moment she moved closer, he pulled her against him. "I've made sure the laurels go to Mrs. Woolsley, Rob's rockets, of course, and to you, Cassie."

"Me? Whatever for?"

"For your impressionist's observation of the shifting effects of light." He held her face in his hands and kissed her mouth. "Uh-oh, I've gone and made a smudge."

Zeno pulled out a handkerchief and dabbed. "As for that glorious nude of you, which I shall cherish forever unless you banish the canvas to the basement, the artwork was purchased by wire, through my solicitor. Monsieur Durand-Ruel agreed the painting was to be crated and shipped before the opening."

A familiar frown tugged at the edges of his mouth. "My assumption is, after the grubby press stories, Monsieur Durand-Ruel counted on the now infamous *Reveuse sur L'herbe* to draw a crowd opening night, which it did."

"Ah, so the moment you handed him your card, he realized he was found out and the painting came down."

"Something like that." He managed a conciliatory grin. "Sorry I was unable to spare you any awkwardness."

"You will always be my hero, Zak." Cassie nibbled at edges of his mouth before kissing him. "Eau de singed jacket." She sniffed the tweed of his lapel. "Has a smoky, woodsy, masculine scent." She leaned back in his arms. "At least it doesn't make me nauseous."

Weary eyes blinked as he studied her face. "Are you not feeling well? You were off to see your mother awfully early this morning."

His familiar, gentle stroking of her back brought such a comfort, she blinked back tears. How weepy of her. "Suppose for a moment . . ." She chewed a bottom lip and released it slowly. "Suppose I was expecting a child. What would you think about—"

Zeno swept her up into his arms and laid her on top of his bedcovers. He removed his soot-covered jacket, collar, and necktie. There was something impossibly stimulating about this man. The moment he shed his clothes, she suddenly became wobbly-legged and doe-eyed.

He settled down next to her and pulled her into his arms. "Are you sure, Cassie?"

Her fingers danced over the buttons of his shirt and found entry to the warmth and strength of his body. "Well, the blessed event does seem rather likely, and I am very pleased about it, if you are."

"Over the moon." Zeno took up her hand and kissed each fingertip. "What shall we have? A little Rupert Angus or Fiona Adele?"

She arched away. "I should think a Martin Augustus or a Camille Olivia."

A smile crinkled the corners of his eyes. "Since we cannot come to any lasting satisfaction, I suppose we'll have to make four."

"Well then, Detective Kennedy, I suggest you marry me."